CHASE THE
WIND

CHASE THE WIND

by

Janelle Taylor

KENSINGTON BOOKS

KENSINGTON BOOKS are published by

Kensington Publishing Corp.
475 Park Avenue South
New York, NY 10016

Kensington Books is a trademark of Kensington Publishing Corp.

Library of Congress Catalog Card Number: 94-075128
ISBN 0-8217-4553-0

First Printing: May, 1994

Printed in the United States of America

Dedicated to:

Michael, my husband and best friend for thirty years, who did so much of the on-site research for this book.

The Native Americans of San Carlos Reservation, whose legendary leaders and history evoked a challenging story.

Geronimo III, for his verbal account of olden days and for an interesting insight into his legendary grandfather.

The many people of Arizona and Texas—two of my favorite states for visits and story settings—who aided my research and were so generous with their time, knowledge, materials, and friendship.

Ronn Moss, a talented actor, who was the inspirational image of Navarro Breed in *Follow The Wind* and in *Chase The Wind.* Thanks for the photos and your approval of how I depicted one of my favorite heroes.

"This is my home. Here I stay. Kill me if you wish, for every living thing has to die sometime. How can a man die better than fighting for his own."

—Goyathlay—"Geronimo"

Chapter One

Sunday, April 4, 1886
Tucson, Arizona Territory

Daniel Withers looked his friend and subordinate in the eye and said, "I have to order you to do something that's going to be difficult for both of us. Lord knows I wouldn't do this if I had any other choice. It's about your next assignment." He paused, sipped water, and prayed he wasn't about to make a terrible mistake.

Special Agent Navarro Breed realized his superior was stalling. "What has you so jumpy tonight, old friend? You know I've never refused any order from you or the Agency."

"This might be the first time, after you hear what I have to say."

Navarro chuckled and grinned. "I can't understand what would make you so jittery. I've handled dangerous and trying missions in the past. Heck, almost every case I take on is like running barefoot over hot coals," he jested. "Spit it out; what is it that has you pacing the floor? You're sweating like it's August and you're staked over an ant bed under the noon sun. This isn't like you."

Dan stopped pacing and looked Navarro in the eye again. "If you agree to accept this case, it'll start here tomorrow and land you in Texas soon." He clarified, "On the L/C Ranch with the Cordells."

Navarro's heart pounded as he stared at Dan in disbelief. "The . . . Cordell ranch?" Dan nodded. "What would Matt and . . . Jessie have to do with a case of mine? With any criminal case?"

"That isn't the only crazy angle: you'll have a partner this time, a female; her cover identity will be Beth Breed, your wife."

Navarro straightened in his chair. "Hold your horses, Dan; I'm not—"

"Hear me out before you refuse. It involves Cordell's younger brother: Charles is running guns to the renegades from San Carlos. He's going to cause big trouble for everybody, including your friends in Texas, if he isn't stopped before he can make delivery next month."

"What does that have to do with Jessie and Matt, and with me needing a wife? Tell me where he is and I'll go after him and arrest him."

Dan sat down at the kitchen table in his home where they were meeting in secret under a blanket of darkness. "He's on his way to their ranch for an alleged visit with his kin; that's where you'll catch up with him and start your investigation, because we'll need indisputable evidence before we can move against him and his partners. After what happened between you and Mrs. Cordell years ago, you can't go alone. Or go at all without a credible excuse and impenetrable cover. You have to marry Elizabeth Lawrence; it's the only safe and successful way to carry out this tricky assignment. Geronimo and his braves have never been more determined. If they lay hands on Cordell's weapons and bullets, they'll be on the rampage until this entire region is bathed in blood."

Navarro let out a deep breath. "The old fox thinks he's right, and they've pressed him into a corner. You and I know San Carlos isn't called Hell's Forty Acres without good reason. The Government's crazy for trying to corral different tribes and sometimes different nations on the same reservation. That's asking for trouble. They have to realize all Indians aren't the same, like all whites aren't friends or allies or speak the same language or have the same customs and beliefs. Then, they treat and view 'em as savage animals to be caged, trained, and mastered to suit the white man's purposes. I've warned them over and over that will never work. Trouble is, the ones who can change things won't listen to Navarro Breed because they think I'm only trying to get the Indians a better deal. You know me, Dan, I never let my Apache blood tell me what to do or think. I chose to live in the white man's world where I can do the most good for both sides, so I follow its laws." The gray-haired man nodded in agreement. "They have to realize they can't take great leaders and proud warriors who've lived and ridden free as the wind, bind 'em to a near barren wasteland, and expect 'em to accept such shame and denial, even be grateful for handouts and being allowed to live."

"I concur wholeheartedly, but we've had no luck changing their minds. Now the Mexicans are demanding we do something soon about the problem, and our government wants to keep peace with our neighbor. I can't blame them; it's been only thirty-odd years since a bloody war with them, so we don't want this ruckus to provoke new trouble and conflicts."

"The Apaches and Mexicans have always hated each other, worse than with the whites. You know as well as I do, Dan, that the Mexicans tried to wipe out the Indians, had bounties for their scalps, and sold hundreds of women and children into slavery; and the Apaches did the same to them, so they're all to blame. Geronimo thought he'd made truce with them years ago, but a Mexicano band raided his camp while he and his braves were on a trading visit with others. He lost a mother, wife, children, and friends in that sneak attack. That's when a sacred vision told him he couldn't be killed by guns and bullets. True or not, he and his people believe it, so they follow wherever he leads."

"His many escapes from San Carlos and returns to aggression have made it obvious he thinks he's invincible," Dan concurred. "Everybody has his eye and ear on this new turmoil; they expect—no, *demand*—we clean it up pronto. All of the other nations have been defeated, even the mighty Sioux in the Dakotas. If we can settle this Apache issue, our country will finally be at peace from border to border. It's serious, my friend, so we have to succeed in a hurry. If not, there'll be hell for innocents to pay."

"Peace is what they want, too, Dan, but an honorable peace we've denied them. They yearn to return to the way of life we stole from them."

"I understand. But General Miles is on his way to battle them with orders to 'capture and destroy' if they refuse to surrender. General Crook had them in his pocket below the Mexican border last week, after two scouts entered their Sonora stronghold and persuaded them to surrender. Crook got them to the border but they panicked and bolted again. I can't fault them for being mistrustful when we've broken every promise we made, and I can't blame them for not wanting to live on San Carlos or *any* reservation. At least Nanay, some warriors, and one of Geronimo's wives didn't escape. They were sent back to San Carlos under guard." Dan stroked his thick gray mustache before adding, "Victorio's successor was a powerful warrior and leader so it's good to have Nanay's influence removed from that powder keg. But that canny and fearless Geronimo is another story, the big problem for us."

Navarro set aside his coffee cup. "What's the Army gonna do?"

"Miles is en route to Fort Apache to plan his campaign; they're giving him five thousand soldiers—a fourth of our Army—to go after those Chiricahuas. He'll have thirty heliograph stations at his command for tracking and quick pursuit. Mexico is providing three thousand men, and Indians will add hundreds of scouts and fighters. But I have no doubt

Geronimo will lead our joint forces on a long and bloody chase. He could teach our side plenty about fighting and escaping enemies."

"What were Crook's terms of surrender? What made 'em bolt?"

"Two years imprisonment in the East, then back to San Carlos Reservation if the government didn't change its mind after he was in custody and hang him. There's plenty of talk in that direction, and it makes me nervous. If they dare put a legend like him on the gallows, another uprising will definitely occur. Obviously, Geronimo suspected lies and a trap, probably more from the Mexicans than from us. After he fled last week, he went back to raiding. No doubt that promise of weapons next month keeps his hopes alive."

"How do you know he's the one buying the arms? It's not like him to deal with whites. Take 'em in a raid, yep. Trade for 'em, nope."

"It has to be him; nobody else is famous or strong enough to coax a bargain with those culprits. A big supply is the only way Geronimo can arm enough braves to stay loyal and on the loose. Until the shipment's in his grasp, he'll raid and rob to get money to pay for them. Afterward, Lord help us, it will get worse if we fail. If we can unmask their contact and prevent delivery, he'll have to surrender. But we can't move against Charles Cordell without proof, something we don't have yet. Besides, we need to learn who all's involved and why, or the boss will find another gunrunner. If I live to be a hundred, I'll never understand how some men can be so greedy and cold-hearted. I wouldn't want to face The Maker with the blood of women and children on my hands."

"What happened to General Crook? Why is Miles taking charge?"

"It didn't sit well with Crook's superiors and others that it was taking so long to defeat those renegades, or that he let Geronimo escape. Nor did they care for the terms he offered the Indians. Here's a copy of Crook's report; I'll read part of it to you: 'Though tired of the constant hounding of the campaign, they were in superb physical condition, armed to the teeth, fierce as so many tigers. Knowing what pitiless brutes they are themselves, they mistrust everyone else. We found them in camp, in such a position that a thousand men could not have surrounded them with any possibility of capturing them. They were able upon the approach of any enemy to scatter and escape through dozens of ravines and canyons which would shelter them from pursuit.' After Crook talked with Geronimo, the old chief told him, 'Once I moved about like the wind. Now I surrender to you.' But not for long he didn't! That devious warrior is chasing the wind again."

Dan put aside the report. "As soon as it was filed, Sheridan fired off an insulting telegram to him. Crook decided if he couldn't be in full charge of his military mission, he'd hand it to another officer. He was replaced on Friday but it'll take a spell for the new commander to arrive and get his plans made and in motion. That gives you and Beth an opportunity to work on this matter from another angle. As I said, even if the Army stops Geronimo's current rampage, we need to know who's been supplying them with arms for years and who keeps inciting them to escape and fight."

"Maybe there's more to the ringleader's motive than greed."

"Surely nobody wants the San Carlos land. Not even the Indians want it."

"But the Apaches aren't staying put or being peaceful. Maybe their raids are trampling somebody's plans or business. Or maybe somebody just hates Indians and is using a sly ploy to force the Army to get rid of them."

"You could have something there, Navarro. Needless to say, too many Arizonians would like to have the Apaches removed from this territory, particularly those ranchers, miners, and settlers surrounding San Carlos who are the targets of raids when the Apaches are on the loose. But what kind of white man would provoke and support bloodshed to get the Indians killed or exiled? Whatever his motive, we must expose him and stop him. If Cordell places arms in those Chiricahuas' hands, it might persuade more braves to leave the reservation and join them. As long as we have trouble, Arizona will never be given statehood. 'Course, hostile renegades aren't the only obstacle: outlaws, Mexican bandits, miner feuds, and shoot-outs also give us a lawless reputation to easterners. You and Beth have six weeks maximum to help prevent a crisis."

"I understand, but this is no job for a woman. Watching out for her could be a dangerous distraction. She'll only get in my way, slow me down, and cause me trouble."

Dan Withers shook his head and chuckled. "Beth is almost as skilled as you are, my friend, so you two will make a fine team. She's worked undercover plenty of times; been with us years longer than you have, but you'll be in charge. She comes from a family of excellent agents. Her father and her husband were two of our best men. It's a shame you'll never get to meet them, since both were killed in the line of duty—on this same type of case a year ago when Geronimo and his boys broke from the reservation. We still haven't learned who sent them weapons and supplies. Maybe it was Charles Cordell. I wouldn't assign the two of you to this case if it wasn't imperative, but you have the best skills, knowledge, and contacts for the mission. I was hoping Jake could solve it back East; his loss was bad timing for us."

"You sure his death was an accident? Sure they weren't on to him?"

"Positive. A second agent was shadowing them and saw Jake's horse throw him and break his neck. We had no time or way to get another man in cahoots with Cordell before he headed west, and I doubt he'd hire anyone while en route. It was a stroke of luck Jake got as close to them as he did, but if he gathered any hard evidence, it was lost with his death. He did pass along the date when Cordell would be on the move. We also know Cordell telegraphed his brother in Texas that he'd be arriving at the ranch about the twenty-sixth. He called it a 'visit during a business trip to Mexico.' We figure he's either planning to rendezvous with Geronimo in Sonora or they'll meet up after he reenters the country. If the latter's his plan, he'll probably recross into Arizona or New Mexico after he's used the border to lose any tail we have on him. It's no secret both governments are keeping a sharp eye out for renegades, so he'll be cautious."

"Why not send the arms by rail straight to Mexico for exchange there?"

"Because Mexican coasts are heavily patrolled against smugglers, and overland roads from them are plagued by *bandidos*. Cordell is probably bribing somebody for safe travel through certain areas. Once he reaches his brother's land, his movements and schedule will be cunningly masked from there on, unless you and Beth intercept and trail him. The brothers apparently haven't seen each other in many years."

"That fits what Matt and Jessie told me while I was working at the ranch. If you ask me, there's no way Mathew Cordell could have gone bad. And Jessie certainly wouldn't; I'd stake my life on that being true."

"For Beth's sake and yours, I hope it is. We're searching for any motive your old friend could have for getting involved. I'll keep you informed on our findings by code." He gave Navarro the check-in points and days for contacting him during the mission.

After Navarro nodded, Dan said, "Our timing is perfect; Beth just completed an assignment in the land office, without breaking her cover as usual. She's still working there. You'll pretend to be old friends who start up a romance and get married in a week. Then you'll be on your way."

"A week?" He saw Dan nod. "You're joshing?" He watched Dan shake his head. "Won't that seem suspicious?"

"Not out here where a woman doesn't stay unmarried long. Besides, you're 'old friends.' It'll be understandable, if you're a good enough actor."

Navarro's hazel eyes narrowed and he ran his fingers through his black hair. "How did you convince her to marry and travel with a stranger?"

"She has been fully briefed. She knows this case is crucial, and she agrees a counterfeit marriage is the best cover strategy. It would be natural for newlyweds settling down to ranch in Texas to visit the friends who made it possible by getting you out of prison years ago. Make it look as if you only want to show them you're happy and completely severing your ties to them. Matt should be delighted and relieved to learn any possible threat from you is over. Convince them that's why you came and I'm betting they'll ask you two to visit and rest a spell. Don't you see, you need Beth at your side to prevent past problems from jumping up and exposing your identity and mission?"

"Why not just pretend to be married? Why fake a romance and wedding?"

"If the Cordells mention to Charles you've worked for the Army, he might get suspicious and check on you. We can't afford a flaw in your story. Don't worry about being trapped with an unwanted wife. As soon as you defeat those gunrunners and the Indians are back on the reservation, the marriage will be over and you can go your separate ways, on to new cases in different directions. Satisfied?"

Dan watched Navarro slip into deep thought and knew where the man's worries lay. The unrequited love affair which provided a path to the Cordells—thus, one to Charles—could be a risk to the case and to his friend's emotions. Considering the grim consequences of failure, those challenges had to be met head-on. Besides, Dan mused, maybe the trip would release Navarro from his sad past. Beth, too. "I know this mission won't be easy or painless. I'm sorry, Navarro, and I wish I could give it to another agent, but there isn't time or a credible ploy for someone else to use. And nobody's better qualified to handle it than you are, with Beth's help."

"You don't have to worry about Matt and Jessie or—"

"I won't, if you have a wife along. We've been friends for a long time, Navarro, and maybe I know you better than you know yourself. This will be the first time you've seen her and your son since you lost them years ago. Don't you see, it's reckless to risk temptation and exposure by going alone? I hate to send you into a hornet's nest with or without protection, but you speak Apache and know the Indian ways. You're the best tracker and agent we have, so I can't allow friendship and your personal feelings to influence my decision. This case is too important. You understand?''

Navarro winced. "Yep, but I still think I can do it alone."

"I disagree. You left there five years ago with two gaping holes in your life like bullet wounds you've never let heal. When you return, you can't doctor them. The price would be too great for everyone to pay. That's why you can't go alone, but I believe you'd want to be the agent to keep them safe and out of trouble."

"You really think I'm skilled enough to convince Jessie of such a crazy lie?''

"Absolutely. To protect Jessie and Lane, you'll do what you must. It's possible Charles has or will enmesh Matt in his scheme. I know you don't think Matt would break the law, but people change over time. You're a perfect example of that. I'm not forgetting you promised to stay out of their lives, but you knew the day would come when you'd have to face them and yourself again. That day's here, Navarro. I know that deep inside, you're still hoping you can get Jessie and Lane back. It's time to accept you can't, not as long as her husband's alive. Release yourself from the past or you'll keep hurting until you die. That's no fate for you, my friend."

"How does a man kill yearnings for what could've—should've—been? She was mine, Dan; until she was stolen by the law and Matt."

"The law had good reason to believe you were guilty of those crimes."

"I know, or I wouldn't be working for it now. I admit I'm partly to blame for my troubles. What happened to me cleaned up that prison, but it cost me my woman, my son, and scars on my back."

"She's another man's wife now, Navarro. You must accept that."

"I haven't spoiled her new life. I've left them both in peace as I promised."

"But you've never allowed *yourself* to find peace. As long as you keep looking back, you'll never see what could be ahead for you."

"Only thing ahead is my work. Don't feel sorry for me, Dan; good friends and challenging missions are enough for me. I'll always love Jessie and be grateful to her. Until I met her, I was riding a bad trail in the wrong direction. She turned me around in time to save my neck. She needed me, too, and not just my guns and skills. She loved me and wanted to marry me."

"Ten years ago. Everybody and everything involved in that episode has changed, except you. She has two of his children now. Free yourself and find another trail to ride."

"How can I ever be free of her when we have a bond in our son and in all we shared? And don't say another woman can break it. I haven't met one who can even stand in her shadow. But don't worry; I'll go to Texas and carry out this mission without stirring up trouble and pain for them." He added, "Unless Matt is involved with his brother's crimes. If he is, old friend or not, I'll bring him to justice and do it as easy on Jessie and . . . their children as possible. I won't put blame where it doesn't belong just so I can recover her and my son; you have my word of honor."

"I believe you, but it'll be a hard promise to honor in person. You've kept it so far because you haven't seen or even contacted them in five years. Mark my words, Navarro, it'll be difficult when you're face-to-face with your lost love and son. If you let her, Beth will protect you from temptation."

"Even if I were tempted, Dan, I wouldn't go after Jessie and Lane. As far as everyone knows, he's Matt's son. I admit it cuts soul deep to think I could pass Lane on a street and not even recognize my own child. When I sneaked that look at him five years ago, I realized I had no right to claim him or Jessie. So you see, Dan, I've proven I can resist temptation. Besides, Jessie would never leave her other two children and ranch to ride off with me and Lane; she was never that kind of woman."

"If you truly believe that, get her out of your head and heart. Forget what that old shaman told you, or apply it to another woman." Dan sipped at his whiskey to hide twinges of guilt about two points he planned to conceal. He hoped that his deception would give Navarro time to get to know and accept his new partner. "Jessie still has a tight hold on you, Navarro, so don't fool yourself. You know why she married Cordell and you're of course happy he saved her and Lane from disgrace. Even if she's made a success of marriage, it doesn't mean she's forgotten you. That could lead to trouble and heartache. With a wife along, Mrs. Cordell won't be tempted to act on what-might-have-been. Beth will help you both realize it's over for good."

Navarro thought of the potent feelings he had buried long ago and wondered if they could unearth themselves when he saw Jessie and Lane again. What if she was still in love with him and dreaming of a life together? Would it rip out her heart to see him with a "wife"? Would love and passion rekindle between them? If so, could they resist each other? Yes, they had no choice, as long as she was married . . . "I still say it's trouble to take a woman—a stranger—with me, even as my wife."

"You and Beth will have ample time to get acquainted. You two can keep each other straight; she also has a personal stake in this mission. It may have been one of Cordell's shipments that got her father and husband killed. It won't surprise me if the two cases melt into the same mold."

"If her head's clouded by revenge, why send her with me?"

"Because she's the best choice and she's available. Don't worry about Beth; she won't let personal problems get in the way of doing her job."

"Why are you so sure I can depend on her?"

"She brought in one of her husband's murderers alive. The snake had Steven's possessions when she and another agent caught up with him. Three others went down in a shoot-out. 'Course he never told who supplied the weapons and ammo they'd delivered earlier. It was a tragedy; those villains weren't even Steven and John's assignment; they were on loan to me for another case. They just stumbled onto the scene at the wrong time and spooked that gang into a lethal attack. Those bastards killed our men and rode out fast, probably afraid more agents were hot on their trail. That's what gave us our first real clues to the gunrunning mess. We've had agents working undercover in several areas since that black day. Beth followed their trail until they camped, then went for help because she knew she couldn't take on five men by herself. When she returned with it, one gang member was gone. He's still at large. Before Steven died, he told her that the one who shot and stabbed him had two X's carved near the thumb on his left hand, probably scars from a snakebite. She hopes the last villain will turn up one day, maybe even on this case. She could have killed that culprit on the trail, and the agent with her wouldn't have exposed her if she had. She watched that cold-blooded outlaw hang, then rode out on her next assignment. She's never failed us, Navarro, never. You're lucky to get her as a partner."

"She worked with her husband? Isn't it unusual and risky to have a married couple as a team?"

"They never let it distract them; they were excellent together. Beth doesn't tell me her feelings and secrets, but I sense she hasn't gotten over his sudden death. I hope a good man comes along one day and heals her wounds."

"What kind of man would take his woman—his wife—into all sorts of dangers? What about their family? Who kept them? Where?"

"They had no children; that's how she stayed his partner. But she has family—a sister and brother, both of them married with children. Her sister mostly raised her after her mother died and John became an agent. As for friends, Beth makes them easily and wherever she goes; none of them learn she's an agent when she's on assignment; she's too smart and alert for mistakes."

"Why didn't she resign after her husband was killed? Didn't that prove to her how dangerous this job is? Why would a woman even do this kind of work?"

"A love for justice and country. She also likes travel, adventures, and challenges as much as you do. You'll be surprised how much alike you two are. Beth can defend and support herself, so it'll take a special man to win her heart."

"Like her husband?"

"Steven was a fine man. You'd have liked him and respected him. I guess I should tell you, she feels partly to blame for Steven and John's deaths. She'd stopped to enjoy a field of wildflowers while they rode ahead to make camp. They spooked the resting gang into an ambush. By the time she arrived, the band was fleeing, John was dead, and Steven was dying. She thinks if she'd come faster or not stopped, she could've saved their lives. She's an expert marksman, but I doubt she—or any-one—could have prevented what happened. I've tried to convince her that if she'd arrived with them or soon afterward, she'd be dead, too. She still thinks, with her skills and training, she could have done some-thing to change their fates. 'Course, most of us feel that way when we suffer losses. Who knows, maybe you two will be good medicine for each other . . ."

"You can wipe that grin off your face because that pretty flower won't be plucked by me. Its thorns stick worse than a thousand sharp burrs in your bedroll. Nope, no more chasing wild winds for me."

"Then you and Beth have nothing to worry about on the trail alone because she feels the same way. Will you take this assignment?"

"You sure we have to go as man and wife?"

"Absolutely positive. We can't risk imperiling your lives and this case. You go as her husband or the scheme's off; that's an official order."

Navarro pondered his duty, then eyed his superior. "All right, boss; summon the preacher and my bride before I change my mind."

"Not that fast; you two have a romance to fake first."

Love and romance! Navarro thought cynically. The only time he had experienced them was with the woman he would visit soon under false pretenses. "When the truth comes out after this mission is over, I hope Jessie and Matt forgive me for breaking my promise and don't feel used and betrayed. And I hope Matt understands why I had to expose and arrest his younger brother. Just pray I don't have to kill Charles." He asked, "How will I meet and recognize this Beth?" He pictured a rustic trail woman—large, plain, masculine and bossy—and sighed.

"She's the only female who works in the land office. We had reports of possible frauds and push-outs; she's proven those allegations are false, so her work here is done. Beth . . . Lawrence is twenty-eight, about five feet six, slim, fair skin, green eyes, and . . . black hair. She's a real lady, so treat her as one. She's also beautiful, charming, and well bred. Elizabeth Lawrence will be in Carter's Dry Goods on Congress Street at five tomorrow. She's expecting you to make contact with her there."

"You were certain I'd accept this mission, weren't you?"

Dan sent him a wry grin. "I had only a tiny doubt because of the wife angle." He grew serious. "I'll leave it up to you what to tell her about your past with the Cordells. But it isn't wise or safe to let Beth walk blindly into that old canyon; a slip by her could endanger your lives and the mission."

"I'll tell her only what she has to know, nothing more, and then only when the time suits me. Agreed?"

"Agreed."

"What if this 'lady' you chose objects to working with a half-breed Apache and ex-outlaw? She's used to sending criminals to prison, not teaming up with an ex-desperado who served years in one."

"The mission is all that will matter to her. Besides, Beth's a good woman. She won't give you any problems; I promise."

They went over other details before Navarro sneaked from Dan's home. He stabled his black stallion at a livery and registered at a hotel with the land office in view of his window. As he gazed into the night beyond it, his body was tense, his spirit edgy. His mind whirled in a storm of thoughts and emotions. Jessie hadn't seen him since he left the Box L Ranch years ago, seeming to desert her when she needed him most. But if the law hadn't recaptured him, they would be married today, the ranch theirs. And Jessie and Lane wouldn't be confronting a danger he had to defeat before riding away a third and final time. But he'd only ride away if Mathew Cordell was innocent.

Navarro unbuttoned his shirt and grasped a locket that held a treasure Jessie had given to him on that ill-fated day. He opened it and gazed at her worn and faded photograph. He caught his breath as he admired her long and curly sorrel hair, eyes as large and blue as a summer sky, and the beautiful face he had stroked and kissed so many times. She was a vision of grace and spirit.

Navarro sighed as he closed the locket. There was something else he needed to think about—something Dan had mentioned earlier— Navarro's meeting with the old shaman.

Navarro had told the Apache: "My spirit is heavy about taking you to San Carlos, Sees-Through-Clouds, but whites and soldiers fear the power you have over your people. They fear peace and safety cannot come while great leaders like you are free to keep the Apache heart full of courage and hope."

Calling him by his Indian name, the shaman had replied, "I one man, Tl'ee' K'us. Moccasins walk Earth Mother as turtle. Hair, eyes wear white blankets. Face have many deep paths. Body shakes as leaf in wind. Bones weak. Voice a whisper. Why fear, chain old men to dying land?"

"Your voice is a whisper, Wise One, but your words roar like thunder. Your body is weak, but your spirit is strong. Though your years are many, the young would follow you. These truths, whites and soldiers know and fear."

"It foolish, dangerous, to follow old man this season. Foolish when Tl'ee' K'us's mother follow white outlaw from people; foolish she return, die. Night Cloud not follow Morning Tears' trail; big evil come; Life Giver not have power, way, to protect His people. That season later; when come, *Ysun* send help. No war with white-skins and Bluecoats; they many and strong, not good time. I surrender, not live free as river runs, standing proud as sacred cottonwood, spirit not broken as wild horse's. Last season come one day and bones rest with Father's in sacred mountains."

"That cannot be, Wise One; that glorious day is past. You must walk alone as I do." He had been tempted to let the shaman go to wander free and happy in the hills until death claimed him; he hadn't because he knew someone else might find the old man and be cruel or lethal. And, the revered man had been more than willing to go to the reservation, after giving Navarro some parting advice:

"You not walk alone forever, Tl'ee' K'us. Woman with hair burning as flaming rocks will walk at your side. Much stands between you this moon; it blow away when you chase the wind."

Jessica Cordell had a mane of red hair and he'd never met another flaming-haired woman, so the prophecy had to be about her, as he'd never known Sees-Through-Clouds to be wrong. She was his destiny. Had the "moon" come when the obstacle between them—a husband— would be removed? Was it Matt's fate to suffer in prison, maybe die, for Navarro to reclaim what seemed his by right of first conquest? Yet, that possibility troubled him. An old Apache saying gusted through his mind: "Wherever the Spirit Wind blows, a brave and cunning warrior must chase it and capture it. If he does so, he will have the powers of nature in his grasp, the powers to be and to have all he desires."

Navarro sensed that the days ahead would reveal the many truths he needed for release from his invisible chains, and he wanted peace of mind and heart—something he hadn't realized until tonight. What he couldn't surmise was why he felt so solemn and tense about possibly having his dream within reach. But for now, he ordered himself, the only thing he should concentrate on was courting a black-haired partner named Elizabeth Lawrence. *I'll see you tomorrow, Beth, and don't give me any trouble.*

Outside Tucson, Daniel Withers, who owned a bank as a cover for his secret work, paced, and pondered his earlier decision. Was it fair or right, Dan mused, to withhold three important facts about Beth and their partnership from Navarro? He'd never deceived either of them and it evoked mixed feelings of guilt and a desire to see his two friends healed of their similar wounds. Both deserved happiness, serenity, and new loves; and, in his opinion, they were perfectly matched. With luck, Dan prayed, it would be too late for Navarro to call off the mission or to resist Beth's magic when he learned two of those disturbing facts.

Chapter Two

"**A**nything else, dear?" Kate Carter asked Beth.

"That's all I need today," Beth answered. Mrs. Carter took the money she held out to pay for ribbons she didn't need.

Kate Carter glanced at the handsome stranger who entered her store, approached the counter in a nimble and confident stride, and halted behind the young widow to await service. She exchanged smiles and nods with him.

Beth surmised from a heavy sound of boots on the wood floor and length of the steps that the person behind her was a tall man. She readied herself for the impending ruse. When the man made no attempt to speak to her as Mrs. Carter made change and wrapped her purchase, she assumed it wasn't her new partner. So far, she hadn't noticed any man who fit the description Dan had given to her last Friday when she went to his bank under the guise of discussing a loan to purchase the house she was renting. Perhaps, the worried agent reasoned as she toyed with her wedding band, her contact had refused the assignment. Or perhaps he was only late for their scheduled meeting. It was also possible he hadn't reached Tucson yet, and Daniel Withers had no safe way of informing her of the delay. Whatever the reason for his tardiness, she couldn't stall her departure any longer.

"Here you go, Beth, and thank you. Come back soon, dear."

"Thank you, Mrs. Carter, and I'll see you again next week."

When Beth half turned to face the clerk at the cash register to her right, Navarro had moved to the display case as if to examine its contents of knives and pistols, which placed him to his target's left and in line with her body. As if surprised to hear her name and voice, he lifted his head, looked in her direction, and leaned forward to get a better look at her profile. He feigned an expression of curiosity, then astonishment. "Beth? Elizabeth Lawrence?" As she turned to face him while responding with a "Yes?", he grinned. "It is you. What are you doing way out here? Where's Stephen? Blazes, woman, this is a big surprise."

Beth did not have to fake a startled reaction to the man whose looks were more than enough to make any female's eyes widen. This virile creature was to be her partner, her . . . husband? Dan had described him as tall, with dark hazel eyes, black hair, and a deep tan, but he hadn't told her Navarro was so handsome. She recovered her poise, and hoped he attributed her reaction to good acting. "Navarro! Whatever are you doing here? The last time Stephen and I saw you, you were heading for Dakota. This is indeed a wonderful surprise. It's been so long, too long for friends to be out of contact." She gave him a quick hug and kiss on the cheek as she thought would be natural under the alleged circumstances.

Navarro returned the embrace and smiled as if he were overjoyed to see her. *Quick, smart, and controlled: that's a relief.* He let a tender gaze roam her features as his hands remained clasped to her upper arms. He responded easily to her question. "I'm buying a ranch in San Antonio. I'm heading there as soon as I rest up a few days and resupply. It'll be good to see Stephen again. We've got plenty of catching up to do. Blazes, I've missed you two. Let's go surprise that husband of yours."

Beth lowered thick brown lashes, dipped her head, and took a deep breath for the benefit of onlookers. After a moment, she locked a sad gaze to his inquisitive one. "Stephen's . . . dead, Navarro. That's why I moved here, to make a fresh start. I work in the land office down the street and rent a small house on the edge of town."

He saw the glow in her green eyes fade. He knew he must show a strong and shocked reaction. "Stephen's dead? It can't be true. What happened?"

As fast as possible, Beth wanted to get beyond that part of the story she was telling. To distract herself from painful memories, she concentrated on her partner, their task, and the real Beth Lawrence's sad tale. She hadn't expected Navarro Breed to be . . . so disarming. His wide, full mouth created a sexy smile. He was several inches over six feet tall, muscular, bronzed skin, and . . . Were those, she mused, Spanish or Indian features? No one could doubt, or fault her for a whirlwind romance with an arresting man like him.

As if she'd used those moments of silence to compose herself, Beth nodded and said, "He was killed during a bank robbery soon after you left. At least his death came quickly, so he didn't suffer. I left St. Louis a few months later and finally settled here after trying living back East for a while."

Navarro knew she seemed intrigued by his looks. Since many whites hated Indians and detested half-breeds even more, maybe she did, too. Perhaps Dan hadn't told her about that. If his half-Indian heritage was going to provoke a rift between them, he'd know soon enough. For now, he had a role to play. "You came this far without protection? Why didn't you send for me? This wild territory isn't safe for a woman alone, Elizabeth. You should know better than to take such risks."

"It's no secret to you I don't have any family, and I didn't know how to reach you. My letters were returned unclaimed."

"That was because I ended up in California. I met a man on the trail after I left you two and he offered me a high-paying job protecting gold shipments. I sent word to you; my letter must have gotten lost, or stolen during a holdup. I'm sorry you had to go through that pain alone. I hope they caught and hung his killer. If not, I have a job to do."

"They did. I know it sounds terrible for a lady, but I attended his trial and watched him hang on the gallows. I had to see Stephen avenged, and he was." As if suddenly aware of her distraction and location, Beth murmured, "Oh, my goodness, where are my manners? Mrs. Carter, this is an old and dear friend of mine, Navarro Breed. He and my husband were like brothers. We've been close friends for as long as I can remember."

He shook hands with the store owner's wife. "Pleasure to meet you, ma'am."

Kate sent him a beaming smile. "Same here, son."

Beth told the older woman, "I'm sorry we got so carried away. We're holding up business. Our reunion is . . . just so unexpected."

Kate's mind was spinning with ideas. "I understand, dear, so think nothing of it. Folks don't mind waiting for something special like this."

"Thank you, Mrs. Carter, and we'll get out of the way so you can help the other customers. Navarro, why don't we get something to eat at a nearby restaurant so we can have a long talk? We both have a lot of news to share."

"Sounds good to me, Beth. I haven't had a decent meal in weeks. Just let me buy the ammo I came in here for first." He purchased a box of .44 caliber cartridges. "Before I leave town, ma'am, I'll be back for trail supplies. See you in a few days."

While they were still in earshot of the owner and customers, Navarro said, "I couldn't believe my eyes when I saw you standing there."

With a merry laugh, Beth responded, "And I can't believe you're finally settling down in one place. What inspired this big change?"

They paused to let a woman and child pass in a barrel-crowded aisle. Navarro took advantage of the delay to continue their ruse. "I've roamed around for thirty-seven years riding and ranching for others. I figured it was high time for me to have a ranch and family of my own. Don't you agree?"

Moving toward the entrance again, she asked, "You have a family?"

"Nope, not yet. Haven't found the perfect wife like Stephen did. I hope I get as lucky in that area as he was." As Navarro waited for her to exit, he recalled that Dan had told him Beth was beautiful, well bred, smart, and charming: facts he couldn't argue with so far. Yet, Beth's looks were unusual. Her facial features were a little larger than the average female's, but were very appealing. Her black hair was pulled away from her face on the top and sides and secured behind her head with a blue ribbon that matched a lovely but simple day-dress. Those Texas-size eyes were clear and shiny, and her gaze was often bold and full of self-confidence. She seemed every inch a lady, gentle and delicate as a spring flower. He couldn't imagine this beauty being a trail duster and top agent as Dan swore she was. Surely she couldn't be of assistance in the face of peril or endure the road's hardships. If she were captured and questioned by their suspect, he worried, she'd no doubt spill the truth, faint, cry, or beg for mercy faster than a flash flood struck in the desert. Soon, he'd test her skills. If he found them lacking or detrimental to his success, she'd be off the case in the blink of an eye no matter what his superior said. Nothing was more important to him than protecting Jessie, Lane, and her other children while he carried out his crucial mission. When it came to his loved ones' safety and this assignment, nobody—not even another lawman, or, in this case, lawwoman—should get in his way.

Kate Carter was filled with excitement as she watched the young couple depart arm-in-arm. She liked Beth and was moved by the young widow's tragic past. She hoped this reunion would lead to something special. It could, with a little help . . .

While no one was nearby, Beth whispered, "We don't want to provoke gossip about us too soon, so we shouldn't go straight to my house and you shouldn't come in tonight; that wouldn't be proper even for old friends. We'll eat in town, take a short walk, and part until tomorrow night. Don't say anything private that might be overheard by the wrong person. Okay?"

Navarro was amused by her words; it was as if she thought he was a greenhorn and she was the one in charge of their mission.

As they crossed the street and no one was around, she asked, "What took you so long to arrive and make contact? I was worried."

"You were too much on guard. I decided to wait so you'd have no trouble looking surprised. I wasn't sure how well you could act."

Beth noticed a cool and cocky gleam in his deep-set, hooded eyes; it was an expression of resolve to put her in her place behind him to which she took offense. She was assigned to be his partner, not his underling or ornament. "I've had plenty of practice in role playing, Mr. Breed, so don't concern yourself about me not carrying off my part."

He caught the sudden chill in her tone and the tensing of her body at his reprimand. But he wanted her to know right away who was boss. Dan should have made their ranks clear to her when they spoke last week. She might have been an equal or leader with her husband, but she had to be a follower with him. "Would you be formal and icy with a close friend, *Beth?*"

Vexed, she had to struggle not to frown or glare at him, as someone could witness her odd reaction. According to Dan, this Special Agent was superior to most. He had solved cases no one else could, and alone, and often against larger and stronger numbers. Obviously, Beth concluded, success had made him arrogant. With a safe distance from others for the moment, she murmured, "Pardon the slip, *Navarro*. I was just surprised that a legendary agent like you would walk into a dangerous case without complete trust in his partner. You won't have to coddle me or cover for me. I'm well trained and experienced. I can take care of myself and my assignments, with or without a partner's help. Frankly, I also prefer working alone."

Without hesitation, he replied, "And I'm just as surprised a legendary agent like *you* would make the simple slip of using a wrong name."

She saw his hazel eyes darken and glitter as if tiny sparks were ricocheting off of a stone. She kept quiet while passing local residents and visitors at a busy section, as did he. From the corner of her eye, she examined him in a rush: his full mouth above a squared chin with a tiny dip but not quite a cleft, his straight nose with a slight flare at its base, those remarkable eyes, framed by brows that were thick and far apart. Her gaze shifted to his high and prominent cheekbones and a strong jawline with defined hollows between them and his silky hair that was collar grazing and combed away from his thoroughly handsome face. That midnight mane had a natural part just to the right with a section that swayed to the left and across his forehead. His bronzed skin came from more than countless days under the sun, convincing her he had Indian blood. Perhaps resentment about and problems with that mixed heritage were to blame for his antagonistic personality. She stepped off the planked sidewalk to cross the dusty street.

In dismay, Beth fretted, *a battle for power and control so soon? Don't get off on the wrong foot, woman. Relax him. Cajole him. Do whatever's necessary to keep peace, short of cowering. No doubt he isn't pleased to be tied to a female, or he's afraid I'll outshine him. For now, let him take the lead as most men think they're supposed to do.* She forced out a smile and said in a pleasant tone, "You're right. I'll sharpen my wits and stay at attention so the famous Navarro Breed won't be disappointed or annoyed to have me for a partner."

The sable-haired man heightened his alert because he sensed she was being clever instead of honest and sincere. The way she was twisting her wedding band round and round with the thumb and middle finger of her right hand told him she was agitated. "If you're as good at your job as Dan says, I won't be. The street's getting crowded, so let's leave private talk for later."

She saw him smile, nod, and tip his hat to three ladies they passed along the way. She observed how each of those women eyed her companion with interest and appreciation. *So, you do have manners. How about using them with me, too, because we'll be spending lots of time together?*

"Where we heading?"

"Mrs. Grandy's Place has the best food and prices. It's around the corner, on the right." Beth wondered if he was familiar with the eating establishment and other things about Tucson, as it was policy that undercover agents who reported to Dan did so during a cloak of darkness and with haste to avoid exposing their territorial superior.

"Don't forget," he murmured as she passed him to enter a single door, "we're old friends, *good* friends, so do your best acting." The glance she sent him said he was irritating her again, and rubbing her the wrong way could create unneeded trouble. He warned himself to back off a few steps until their rules were in place. As men eyed his companion with admiration, Navarro concluded she disturbed him so much because she was so memorable. Dan should have realized that anyone—everyone—who'd met Beth on a past case wouldn't forget a rare beauty and spirited creature like her. If she were recognized, their cover and credibility would be destroyed!

After they were seated and had ordered, the flustered woman tried to gain time to study the perplexing male. Dan had filled her ears with ravings about Navarro's daring exploits. She coaxed with a smile and asked in a gay tone, "Tell me where you've been and what you've been doing since Stephen and I last saw you."

"Ladies first, and don't skip anything I should know."

If Dan had omitted relating to him any part of her borrowed identity, as her friend had left out news of Navarro's quicksilver manner, she would correct that mistake pronto. "After you left St. Louis last January, we bought that farm outside of town the very next week. You remember, the one we showed you during your visit?" She paused for him to nod.

"Repairs and additions were going fine and it was looking lovely. Our first crop was planted. The animals were healthy and growing. Everything seemed wonderful. Until Stephen went to town in late March on business and was shot during a bank robbery." She didn't have to fake a sad tone and expression as she related Stephen and Elizabeth Lawrence's tragic tale because she empathized with the young woman who had lost so much to a vicious crime, as she herself had lost a Steven on almost the same date.

"The trial and execution kept me distracted and busy for a while. Afterward, things changed fast as reality settled in. I didn't know many people because we'd been too busy to try to meet them after our move. I felt alone, and the farm was too secluded for a woman by herself. There was so much to do with the crop and animals and property. I knew too little about such things and there wasn't enough time to learn before making costly mistakes. I couldn't finish the work on the house and other structures and I couldn't afford to hire help. Even if I was extremely frugal, without bringing in and selling that crop, I knew our savings would deplete before winter."

She took a deep breath. "As days passed and I worked like a slave, the place reminded me too much of Stephen and I realized I couldn't make a go of it alone. And I couldn't just go into town and find a new husband to rescue me. Two drifters came by on separate days and offered to help me in exchange for food and shelter until I could afford wages, but I couldn't let a stranger live there; it wouldn't look proper and I'd be afraid. You know I'm not stupid or lazy or a coward, Navarro, but neither am I foolish. I faced the truth that I couldn't stay, that our dream was over, and the sooner I acted, the better for me and the property's appearance for a good sale. I sold out to a nice couple with two children, got on a train, and went to Boston. I worked in a ladies' hat shop for a few months, but I didn't like it there. I couldn't seem to make friends or adjust because I didn't fit in with the locals. Then, the shop owner started making . . . crude overtures. I'd read and heard exciting things about

Tucson, so I decided to make another fresh start. With so much progress going on, I figured there must be plenty of jobs available. I packed up, caught another train, and moved here."

Navarro stayed silent when she ceased talking as utensils, napkins, and drinks were put in place. He used the break to study her, and made it obvious he was doing so to test her self-control and to dupe their observers. Her jawline was almost square and her cheekbones were high. Her lashes and brows were thick and dark. Her nose wasn't small or pert but it was sized to perfection to match her other features. Her mouth was an attention grabber with full lips, and a sunny smile that could lighten the darkest room. Her fair skin with its natural rosy shading on her cheeks was soft and clear; neither age nor weather exposure had wrinkled or damaged it.

He recalled that during their stroll, her movements had been as light and graceful as a feather floating to the ground. There was nothing awkward about her demeanor. Whether standing, sitting, or walking her posture was excellent. The dress she wore didn't conceal a small waist, rounded hips, and a chest that gave no doubt she was all woman. Except for when she was vexed with him, she had a warming glow and sparkling vitality. The sound of her laughter was as pleasing to the ear as a running stream. He was certain most people found it difficult not to like and respect her. Oddly, the fact she was so attractive, independent, and refined annoyed him; perhaps, he concluded, it was because those characteristics imitated Jessie's fine qualities.

The only clue Navarro had as to how his bold inspection affected Beth was the way she trapped her wedding band between those same fingers used earlier and rocked it back and forth in place. He decided he wouldn't point out that habit, as he might need it in the days ahead for reading her real mood. As soon as the server left, he coaxed, "Go on."

Beth knew people nearby could hear the well-rehearsed conversation. "I found a nice house to rent, made friends, learned my way around, and convinced the land office I'd be worth my salary to them. I've been here four months. As I told you in Mrs. Carter's store, I tried to reach you about Stephen's death and my two moves. The letters came back, so I left word in St. Louis and Boston where you could find me when you returned. You and Stephen were like brothers; I knew how you'd feel when you heard the bad news."

Impressive control and acting, Mrs. Lawrence. "At least his killer was captured and punished. If not, I'd go after him tomorrow. I promised Stephen I'd take care of you if anything ever happened to him but I never thought that black day would ever come. If I'd gone on to Dakota or you'd gotten my letter while I was in California, you could have reached me."

In an attempt to see if she could disquiet him also, she put a hand atop his larger one and gazed into his eyes as she entreated, "Don't blame yourself, Navarro. I've been fine."

He moved his hand to cover hers and gave a light squeeze as he refuted, "But you shouldn't have been forced to go through something like that alone. I'm sorry you were. Stephen would be hurt and disappointed I wasn't there to give you comfort and protection. That's what best friends are for, and it won't happen a second time, I promise."

"You're here now; we've found each other again. I've missed you, Navarro. At times I felt so alone. I tried to be brave and strong, but it's been so hard."

He shifted his grasp to hold her hand. "You won't be alone or in danger again, Beth, because I'm back in your life. I'll take care of you."

With their gazes locked and hands clasped on the table, she replied, "You always were a good friend and a fine man, Navarro. That's why Stephen and I loved you so much. At least I'm safe and happy here in Tucson; you don't have to worry about me. How long before you have to leave for your ranch in San Antonio?"

"A week. Two at most," he added. "I don't want the ranch I'm considering to sit deserted too long or somebody might tear it apart. I—"

Their meals arrived and cut off his last sentence. He leaned forward and inhaled the steaming scents. "Smells good. Thank you, ma'am."

The server nodded appreciation and said she'd return later to see if they needed anything else.

Navarro took a few bites—as did Beth—then sent her a smile. "You were right about this place; it's the best chow I've had in months. Let's eat before it gets cold and finish our talk later."

Beth was relieved to halt a cozy deception and to break disturbing contact. She needed to clear her head and to master unfamiliar sensations, no doubt because Navarro Breed was too disarming and appealing, especially for a stranger! He made it a struggle to concentrate on business.

Navarro continued a subtle assessment of Beth during their meal. He admitted that Dan's description of her breeding and character was accurate: she was a real lady. He worried about her being able to perform the perilous task looming ahead. He wished he had asked his superior what kind of cases she had worked on and what specific skills qualified her for the impending one. When privacy allowed, he'd question her on those topics. He noticed how well liked she was in town; so many people spoke to her before and during their supper. It was clear to him that some of the men were enchanted by her and were sending him annoyed looks for catching her attention and for spending the evening with the object of their desires.

"What are you thinking about so long and hard, Navarro?" she asked after desserts were placed before them and their coffee cups were re-filled.

He feigned a sad look and lowered his fork to lie. "About the good times Stephen and I shared, we all shared. I can't imagine never seeing and talking to him again. I keep thinking he'll walk through that door and join us. I'm going to miss him. I know it must be worse for you."

Heavens, you think quickly. "It was hard for a long time, but it gets better every day. Sometimes I'm glad we didn't have children who would constantly remind me of him. Other times I wish we had, because a part of him would still be alive and with me." *Darn you, Beth! Why did you say something so personal and true? You had your wits clear until he gazed at you like that. This weakness has to stop, pronto!*

"If you'd had children, Beth, it would've been harder on you after he was gone. You'd be breaking your back on that farm to give them a home and to earn a living. Men would be trying to take advantage of a beautiful widow who owned a good piece of land. You were able to pull up roots and move on to a fresh start away from painful memories. Besides, children need a father most when they're young. While you were struggling and suffering, you could have chosen the wrong man to take his place."

Beth caught a subtle change in his expression and voice during his last two sentences. *A clue to a troubled childhood? Or had he been married in the past?* Dan hadn't mentioned either topic to her. To provoke clues, she agreed. "You're right, Navarro, a child needs and deserves to be loved, guided, and protected by his real father."

Navarro's gaze darkened and stared into hers; he hoped Dan hadn't exposed his secrets. There was no need for Beth to know Lane was his son. That it had nothing to do with solving their case. He'd told only two friends that fact and he would never reveal it to another soul. Those slips had happened by accident, but, in both instances, he was glad now to have those two to talk with during hard times. Mercy, how he wanted to be rearing his only child. If Mathew Cordell wasn't a good man and father and didn't love the boy as his own, he would take Lane away from him. He would—

"If you're finished, sir, Beth, I'll take your payment."

"Beth?" he hinted, and she nodded. "Thank you, ma'am. It was a fine meal." He handed her the right amount of money and added ten cents for good service. Afterward, he assisted his companion with her chair, took her arm, and led her outside. "Which way to escort you home?"

The meeting and pretense with Navarro had been very draining, so Beth was eager for privacy to relax. "Left, about a half a mile. I can go alone if you're tired. I do it every evening after work. It's still light; I'll be safe."

Navarro moved aside for two customers to enter the restaurant as he responded for their ears, "You're in my care now, so I'll see you to your door. Now that I've found you again, Elizabeth Lawrence, I don't want anything bad happening to you. No arguments."

"Yes, sir," she quipped with merry laughter as they passed the sheriff who was speaking with a friend; both men nodded a greeting to her. "You always were bossy. I suppose I can put up with that mischievous trait again."

He raised one eyebrow and teased, "I'm bossy? You were always the one ordering me and Stephen around. Remember that time during my last visit when we wanted to go gambling? You said you'd take a brush broom to us if we did, and you were serious."

Beth knew the lawman was strolling behind them on routine rounds and that was the reason for her partner's behavior. "That place was a den of wickedness and danger. Everybody knew they had fights and at least one shooting a night. I didn't want you two getting hurt, or worse."

"Well, your threats worked because we stayed home."

"And played cards half the night. Stephen lost two dollars to you."

"But I didn't take my winnings because I knew he needed the money for the move you two were planning."

A cool breeze wafted over them, and she grasped her shawl over one arm to ward off the evening chill. He took it from her and placed the covering around her shoulders, then kept his hand on her waist.

"Thanks. You always were kind and thoughtful."

He chuckled and teased, "First, I'm bossy, now, I'm a good man. You're contradictory, Beth Lawrence."

"Naturally. We women can't let you men get the upper hand by learning our mysteries. You and Stephen certainly had plenty of secrets. Both of you were always tricking me so you could get your way."

He placed a hand over his heart. "You accuse me falsely, woman," he joked, and they laughed. "What time for supper tomorrow night?"

"Meet me in front of the land office at five."

"I'll be there."

Beth scolded herself for being too cognizant of his hand on her waist, the way their bodies brushed together, and his stirring voice. It was almost alarming the way his touch awakened desires she never thought to experience again. It troubled her that she could feel this way with a domineering stranger. She had to learn in a hurry how to deal with him. Before they were alone . . . Whether by his intention or an accidental result of the pretense, his unexpected effect on her was rattling, and possibly dangerous to the mission.

"He's gone, Beth. He turned the corner back there."

"I know. His spurs sent out signals coming and going, and his holster needs conditioning; it squeaks too much. Also, he breathes too hard and deep, and he sniffles. *And* he can use a bath and clean clothes when he's downwind. He'd never be able to sneak up on anyone."

Navarro was amazed she'd noticed such clues and was so alert while appearing at ease, or preoccupied. Maybe there was more to her than he realized. She'd done well in town, but it was different and harder on the trail. Yet, he should give her a fair chance. Everybody deserved one. He would be in prison—or maybe dead—if he'd been denied his at the Lane Ranch.

Beth hoped he was giving his low opinion of her a second thought. "We're almost there. Tell me, have you been to Tucson before in the daylight? Do people here know you?" For certain, any female who'd laid eyes on Navarro wouldn't forget him!

"Yep. A few times before I went to work for Dan so I might be recognized. If I am, it won't seem strange because our tale says I went to California and I'm heading for San Antonio. Tucson lies in that path. When I meet with Dan, nobody sees me. His cover has to be guarded, too. Why do you ask?"

"I want to be certain I know all the important facts so I won't make slips while we're carrying out our ruse here."

"What are our plans for this lightning-fast romance?"

As they stepped onto her porch, Beth related a schedule with haste as curious neighbors were watching them. "Does that suit you?"

"Yep. I'll go before those eyes burn holes in my back. We'll play it safe and get down to business Saturday. See you tomorrow evening. 'Night."

"Navarro?"

"Yep?" he answered as he halted his retreat and turned to face her. She was putting her ring on and off rapidly. "Go on."

Beth stopped playing with the wedding band. "Can we have a truce while we're working together? It will be easier and safer than conflicts."

"I didn't realize we were at war."

"It seemed that way earlier. I'm sorry if you're displeased with me as a partner or you don't think I can fend for myself or back you up. I promise I won't let you down and, if need be, I'd die for you during our mission."

Navarro was stunned because she looked as if she meant those words. "I'm not worth dying for, Beth. Nobody is unless it can't be helped. I admit I have doubts about your skills, but I'd feel the same about any female agent, and about some male agents I've worked with."

"What are your main worries?"

"First, you not accepting I'm in charge of this assignment. If Dan didn't tell you that fact, I'm sorry. Maybe you were an equal or even the leader with your husband, and I know you've been working alone and making plans and decisions for a year, but not this time. You'll have to follow my orders because I know this case better than you do and I know most of the people involved, whites and Indians. The other concern is your being recognized from a past case. From what I've seen in one day, people—particularly men—wouldn't forget you. That could create complications and consequences I can't afford, not on this assignment."

She stored his compliment and the emphasis on his last few words because both, she sensed, had special meaning. She knew from Dan that the Cordells were close friends of his, so perhaps Navarro was troubled about them being entangled in or endangered by the mission. "First, I accept you're the boss, but don't treat me as a child or a nuisance or a simpleton. I'm well trained, with seven years of experience and successes to my credit. In the second place, I used disguises, false accents, and other mannerisms in the past. Even if we ran into somebody who thought I favored one of my old identities, they'd soon convince themselves they were wrong. I'll tell you about those tricks later. As for being recognized from Tucson, I'll be using the same identity during our mission. Satisfied?"

"For now. But you don't mind proving yourself to me along the way?"

"No, and you'll have to do the same. That's only fair, since our lives will be in each other's hands. Good night, Navarro. I hope we can become real friends and make a good team."

"So do I. 'Night. Oh, I had a good time even if we were on duty." He sensed her startled gaze on him until he was out of sight.

Beth leaned against a porch post and stared toward the town into which he had vanished. *What an unpredictable and mercurial man you are! Were you being nice and honest or just duping me, too?*

It was undeniable that Navarro Breed exuded self-reliance and confidence. He embodied prowess and excitement. She could learn plenty from him if she kept her wits and control, if she developed a genial rapport. He was a fascinating rogue of sorts, a magnificent male speciman. He reminded her of a powerful, mysterious, and elusive stallion that roamed the wilderness, needing only himself, his freedom, and a leader's task in life. He was a stubborn, independent creature who couldn't be lassoed and tamed unless he was agreeable, or for the love of a special mistress.

Beth had no way of knowing her first impression of him almost matched Jessica Lane's ten years ago. What she did know was that she was looking forward to spending many days and nights with a man for the first time since Steven's death. She mustn't, Beth warned herself, get too close to him and get hurt.

Beth went inside and locked the door, all too aware it was only twenty-one hours until their second meeting. As she prepared for bed, she scolded, "For heaven's sake, Beth, you've only known him for a few hours. You've never let a man do this to you before, so don't start now. You're just impatient to get on to an important and stimulating assignment. You're judging him on all Dan told you about the great legend. You're intrigued, that's all. Flattered to be chosen to work with him. Wait and form your own opinion. See if he's as top notch as Dan thinks he is. Who knows, he might be a big disappointment."

Yes, she reasoned, she was just eager to get back to work, as the assignment here had been too simple. She told herself it might be fun to be part of a team as she had been for six years with her husband. *Oh, Steven, it's been so lonely without you. We worked so well together and had so much in common. How could anyone ever replace you? Certainly not a cocky loner like Navarro Breed who doesn't like me, or trust me, or respect me. Well, my handsome legend, you're in for a surprise because I won't fail in our mission. And I'll make certain you come out of it alive and unharmed. I won't make the mistake of leaving your side for a minute as I did with Steven and Papa. Like it or not, Navarro Breed, I'm sticking to you like a feather to tar.*

Chapter Three

Tuesday, Navarro took Beth to a cantina for supper where she made several discoveries about him. First, she was surprised when he ordered and chatted with ease in fluent Spanish with the owner, a burly Mexican with a jocular personality. During her last two assignments, she had picked up a handful of Spanish words and sentences though not enough to be of assistance to her in future work. But she was proficient in French and had used it in a past case, the only time those lessons had come in handy.

As she observed him, she realized he knew at least three languages: English, Spanish, and Apache. *You're fascinating, enigmatic, and intelligent, partner.* She couldn't help but wonder which was his native tongue, what his parents' nationality was, where and how he'd been reared, and how he'd become a lawman. Would he, she mused, share those facts or bar her from his personal life and stick to their ruse in public and private?

As they ate, Beth glanced around the large room that was lighted by many windows and lamps attached to adobe walls and suspended from a saguaro-beam ceiling. The atmosphere was gay with music, laughter, and conversations. Decorations were numerous and colorful: sombreros, multistriped blankets with white fringes, paper flowers of various colors, and chili *ristras.* On one wall, there was a bull-fighting display: a flowing red cape, *montera, banderillas,* and pike poles. The dishes were excellent, hers not as hot and spicy as those he ordered and appeared to savor. The owner and waiters were friendly. The presence of people she knew or recognized compelled them to play their roles the entire time. In the adjoining social room, men sat at tables—drinking, talking, nibbling, and playing cards.

Things went fine until two dusty and scowling drifters entered the

door, went straight to that room, and soon became rowdy. The newcomers were rude to the owner when he greeted them. It was obvious to
everyone that they didn't like Mexicans, so she wondered why they'd
chosen to eat there. Each time the pretty señorita served them a drink or
snack, as they seemed in no hurry to order meals, the ruffians made lewd
remarks and forced her to evade their groping hands, a vile game they
found amusing.

Beth was aware her companion had come to full alert and was riled
by the goings-on. She couldn't fathom a reason, but there must be a good
one, as men like Navarro—loners or agents—minded their own business. Though she was gifted at reading people's moods, it was a difficult
task with this man before her. Nevertheless, she perceived a stiffening, an
on-guard, simmering reaction in her companion. His eyes darkened with
an emotional turmoil which even his feigned smiles didn't soften. His
prominent jawline was taut, and his brows were lowered slightly. His
elbows were propped on the table with fingers interlocked and thumbs
raised and touching. A few times, she saw those thumbs press together
as if battling to overpower the other. To most, he probably looked un-
moved by the nasty scene; to her, he seemed ready to spring into action
if trouble started, which appeared likely. She didn't want anything to
happen that would call attention to Navarro's alleged talents with guns.
Yet, she experienced a tiny desire to see Navarro in action. Her apprehension mounted as the situation worsened, and Navarro's gaze narrowed. She could almost feel an actual chill exuding from him, and
goosebumps covered her body.

The episode sent Navarro's mind to painful days in the past when his
outlaw father had forced his mother to work under similar or worse
conditions when Carl needed money and had to lay low. If nice people
thought it was difficult for a señorita to deal with such vile talk and
conduct, he raged, they should witness what it was like for a beautiful
and gentle "squaw." Despite insults and fondlings and his mother's pleas
to avoid them, Carl had sent her into such situations over and over until
Navarro had wanted, even as a boy, to kill his own father to halt those
cruelties. His gaze settled on his partner and he saw how alert and
worried she was. He assumed it was because she feared a lethal confrontation was ahead and she didn't want to be caught in the line of fire.
"We'd better go, Beth, before things get rougher and I'm forced to take
care of Manuel's problem in there. If I did, it could cause problems for
us."

"I think you're right," she whispered in return. "I was about to make the same suggestion because I can tell it's bothering you not to help him."

Navarro mentally shook off his tension, and put on a smile to calm her. "I must be slipping today if somebody can read me like tracks on soft ground. Either you're skilled at such things or your good company had me too relaxed."

Before she could respond, he stood and rounded the table to assist with her chair. As he was doing so, Manuel came forward to thank them, to encourage another visit, and to promise a quieter evening.

"Best send for the law, *amigo,* before things get worse. Those *hombres* want to chew on trouble, not *comida.*"

"Maria sneaked out the back to bring the sheriff or a deputy."

"Bueno. Adíos, amigo, hasta la vista."

Help did not arrive soon enough to halt what happened. As they were leaving, Beth was shoved aside by a troublemaker as one of the drifters and another customer made their way outdoors and into the dry street. Navarro grabbed her arm and steadied her, for which she sent him a smile of gratitude. When he looked as if he was about to go after the ruffian, she shook her head and said, "I'm fine; let it pass." He nodded.

Almost everyone left their tables and rushed onto the planked walk as if eager to witness what was about to occur. Beth said for those around them to overhear, "Heavens, they're going to have a shoot-out."

"Don't worry none, Miz Lawrence," a man who knew her from the land office coaxed. "Caleb's better with his guns than an Apache with a skinnin' knife. He'll put a fast end to them saddletramps."

"But it's so uncivilized." She widened her gaze and feigned dismay.

"I know, ma'am, but it's the way out here, law or no law. Maybe you should go back inside till it's over. Won't take long."

She watched the participants walk off the agreed steps and turn to face each other, ready to make their moves when the signal was given and count was complete, a scene she had witnessed too many times and in too many towns. While some men made bets on the winner's identity and shouted encouragement to their choice, Beth frowned and murmured to residents nearby, "Enjoying and gambling on such wickedness should be against the law; it only promotes more violence." It was easy for Beth to look distressed and afraid because she felt a dread anticipation of Navarro's reaction if it wasn't a fair battle or if the wrong man won. She glanced at the second drifter as he lazed against a post and grinned in confidence of the outcome. She could envision the behavior of the two arrogant troublemakers if one of them bested the local challenger in the showdown. But she had no doubt her partner would not allow them to give the cantina owner and customers more problems. She prayed the sheriff would arrive soon and prevent any possible intrusion into the situation by Navarro.

When the gunslingers drew and fired, Beth sent out a squeal and jerked her shoulders as two blasts rent the momentary silence. One man clutched his chest, gaped at his slayer, and sank to his knees in the dirt. He wavered a moment then fell face forward into it. Cheers arose, bets were paid off, and congratulations were given to Caleb.

Beth put on a look of horror and murmured, "Barbaric . . ."

Navarro noted her reactions with concern because he didn't realize they were part of her pretense. *You're as soft as your skin and as gentle as a tamed mare. I can't figure why Dan thought you'd be qualified for the job ahead. I'm sure you can play my wife at the ranch, but there's far more to our assignment than a cozy setting and parlor talk.*

The winner glared at the dead man's pale and quaking friend. "You wanna try me next or git outta town afore I take a few more breaths?"

The scared drifter glanced at his riding partner and shook his head. He swung into his saddle and galloped away, kicking up dust and debris.

Navarro moved in front of Beth with speed and agility to shield her from the thrown rocks that pelted his broad back. With the top of her head about level with his mouth and standing so close, she had to lift her face to look at him to speak words of gratitude. For a moment, her eyes seemed to melt into his. Then they were interrupted by her acquaintance before he could look away.

"You all right, Miz. Lawrence?"

She dragged her gaze from Navarro's. "I'm fine, thank you. I should be accustomed to such evil by now, but I'm not. I wish men would stop thinking they have to fight and kill to prove their courage and manhood."

"Ain't nothing for a fine lady to be forced to watch. Bye, ma'am."

Beth watched the Tucsonian glance at Navarro, nod, and depart. In control once more, she asked, "Still want to stroll to the Presidio?"

As the sheriff and other residents arrived on the scene, Navarro guided Beth away from the crowd where questions surely would be asked. He halted them at the corner. "Let's keep to our scheduled plans. We need to fool as many locals as we can in one week. Do you want to walk? Or would you prefer to ride in a buggy? I can fetch one fast."

"It isn't that far, so let's walk to relax and allow our meals to settle."

"Suits me."

Beth smiled as they began their stroll. So far she was impressed with her partner, perhaps more than was wise. Today, he looked quite handsome in medium-blue pants and shirt and a chamois-colored vest. His boots were brown and the hat on his dark head was tan. His garments were not unusual or flashy, nothing to call special attention to him, except for their perfect fit that showed off an also perfect physique. He was neat, clean, and his manners were impeccable. His hands and nails hadn't been dirty or ragged a single time since meeting him. That had not been what she'd expected from a loner, a trail man. He wore one pistol, a Smith & Wesson single-action Frontier model. The weapon on his right side in a hand-tooled leather holster wasn't swung low on his hip or strapped to a muscled thigh in a gunslinger's style. He didn't wear spurs, perhaps to allow him to move quietly.

At present, he was gazing at their surroundings. He seemed almost distracted. She wished he wouldn't be so silent and withdrawn when they were alone. It prevented her from getting to know the real man, and such familiarity was important during dangerous episodes. Most of the time, *she* was being herself so he could learn what to expect from her, but he wasn't giving her that same opportunity.

Beth tried to concentrate on other things to get her mind off Navarro. They strolled narrow and dusty side streets, unlike the wider ones in the busy section near Congress. Nor did the area have planked walks to cover dirt entries. Some businesses had porches to shade customers from the hot sun; others had two slender poles supporting a small overhang. They passed a barber shop with its red-and-white striped pole where a sign offered: "Shaving 15¢, Hair-cutting 25¢, Shampooing 25¢" He needed none of those services. The majority of structures along their route and in town were one story, light colored, made of adobe, and flat roofed. Those with two or more floors, painted, constructed of imported wood, and with raised roofs, stood out as being different and quite obviously expensive.

The trees they passed were mostly mesquites, in spring bloom and swarming with bees and other insects. Uncleared desert vegetation—cacti, creosote, scrubs, yucca, and others that grew here and there—clung tenaciously to the harsh soil, most with prickly spines to protect them. The landscape encircling the town was open to the foothills and peaks of five mountain ranges that ringed Tucson, with the Santa Catalinas being the tallest and most beautiful. Windmills, giant saguaro, and tall houses or businesses stood out against a clear blue horizon. Near some homes chickens, pigs, and burros roamed in freedom and let a person know when he got too close. Beth decided the region possessed a wild beauty, especially in spring when the engulfing desert came to verdant and colorful life.

They reached Presidio San Augustin del Tucson, built as protection against "hostiles." So many cultures had craved and occupied this area because of its water supply in the Sonoran Desert: Indians—Apache, Pima, and Papago—Conquistadors, Mexican troops and peasants, and American and foreign pioneers. The influence of each was visible inside and outside the magnificent site. The town enclosing it had flourished since the railroad's arrival six years ago. The Spanish structure's walls were three hundred yards long, twelve feet high, and three feet thick. Beth and Navarro paused in the entry to look inside the old fort, which was a small Mexican town with buildings, homes, shops, a plaza, and a walkway with columned arches.

"Can you imagine the work and sweat it required to build a quadrangle this big and high?" Beth asked. "It must have taken years and countless laborers."

"Yep, guess so."

At that point, Navorro took her arm and guided her to the interior. They continued along to the busy plaza. A variety of sights, sounds, and odors greeted their senses. Music, mostly from guitars and fiddles, was being played in the street and in several establishments as accompaniment to eating and for heightening masculine pleasures. Mexican men were cloaked in serapes or ponchos, though the evening wasn't chilly yet. Their women's heads were scarved in *rebozos;* their bodies were clad in peasant garments.

Beth had found the native clothing to be comfortable and colorful, and had purchased several pieces to take with her. She and her companion pretended to check various wares in free-standing booths and in windows of shops built against the outer wall. They looked at pottery, bird and animal figures, cotton clothing, baskets, rugs, flowers, hats, woven blankets and garments, and other assorted goods. They were both careful to remember their roles.

At one lovely spot near a fountain with benches for resting and visiting with friends, they halted. Strolling musicians paused within a few feet of their location as the leader sang words that seemed to make her partner uneasy. As if she didn't notice, she said, "The melody is so lovely, and his voice is wonderful. What's he saying? It sounds as if it must be a romantic love song."

"Nope, it's about lost love."

With a look of curiosity, she persisted, "Is there a story to it?"

"Yep, a man going off to war, leaving his sweetheart behind. She's supposed to wait for him. He returns, but she belongs to another. It's about the pain of losing her. He rides off, never to have her again."

Beth studied his closed expression, then looked away. *Very suspicious, Navarro.*

"Ready to go? It's getting late. Be dark soon."

Obviously too late to do anything about what's bothering you. "Yes."

He stood, cocked his arm for her to take his elbow, and guided her out of the Presidio. They walked through the edge of town, then away from it toward her dwelling. The moment they were a short distance from people, he used a ruse to break their contact and leaned over, picked up a rock, and flung it into the deserty terrain. It went straight into a hole in a towering saguaro, an abandoned home made by a bird, probably an owl or woodpecker from its size.

Beth came to a standstill, looked at him, and asked, "Did you do that on purpose?" He nodded. "Can you do it again?"

Navarro repeated the action several times without a single miss or speaking a word.

"Are you that accurate with bullets?"

"Yep. With knives, lances, and hatchets, too."

Beth studied his profile as he threw the last rock and knew he wasn't boasting. She also realized several of those weapons were Indian ones. He walked onward without taking her arm again.

That heavy silence that disquieted Beth settled around them like an obscuring mist. On the good side, she told herself, no cross words or cocky behavior had surfaced today, so maybe a truce was in force. Perhaps she made him nervous and wary. After all, he wasn't accustomed to working with a female partner, or to marrying one.

At her porch, he halted and said, "I'll be going. You get inside and bolt your door."

"Thank you for another pleasant evening. You're enjoyable company."

"So are you, Beth. 'Night. Same time and place tomorrow."

He departed in such a hurry that she was almost amused. *So, my defensive loner, I make you edgy. That's only fair since you do the same thing to me. At least we aren't battling anymore, now that I've yielded leadership to you. Be as good as Dan says you are or I'll take that rank away before I allow our mission to suffer; it's too important.*

Wednesday, they went to see Shakespeare's *The Tempest.* It was being performed near town by a traveling theatrical company that had set up a stage, props, viewer benches, tents for costume changes, and curtains to hide actors between their scenes. The couple arrived from dinner only a few minutes before the curtain rose. They took places near

the rear of the seating section, as many residents had come to be entertained at fifty cents per head. The play began and everyone fell silent.

Beth was surprised Navarro had agreed to this evening's plans, as a
play of any kind didn't strike her as being his idea of amusement. Yet, he
didn't appear the least bored, tense, or out of place. His hands—large,
and strong—rested on his thighs in a relaxed position. His sable mane
was a little wind-tossed tonight. The red shirt he wore with deep-blue
pants and a tan vest caused his skin to look a darker bronze that made
him more captivating than usual, if that were possible. Each time a
breeze wafted past him, she caught the smell of a light and masculine
cologne, but she didn't recognize the scent. She did notice there was no
odor of horses, leather, sweat, or dust on him. Of course, he had been
in town for days. Even so, his grooming and manners were impeccable.

Within minutes, latecomers compelled her to slide nearer to Navarro
so they could occupy the remainder of the bench. At certain points, the
stranger next to her leaned her way to see around the heads blocking his
view, pressing Beth ever closer and closer to her companion. Soon, she
was almost cuddled against him. Their thighs and hips were meshed
together and her arm rested atop his. She certainly didn't need her shawl
to keep warm. She glanced upward at him and sent him an expression
of apology and helplessness.

Navarro smiled to let her know everything was fine, when in fact, she
was too enticing to his senses. Her soft floral fragrance teased at his nose.
Wavy locks tumbled around her shoulders like a black cape. Their dark
color made her flawless skin look paler than it probably was, but not as
light as the lace at her long neck and slender wrists. She sat with her back
and shoulders straight, like a refined lady. She gazed straight ahead, but
he guessed from clues her thoughts weren't on their entertainment: her
full mouth had a slight part, her chest rose and fell with shallow breathing, and she was working her ring in that nervous habit.

Beth became more and more aware of her enchanting "sweetheart"
than the play in progress, despite a struggle not to do so. In a few days,
she would marry him. She would have to be loving with him to fool
others. Could she, Beth fretted, pull off such a demanding role? When the
last act ended, she stood to relax her taut body and fingered the muscles
at her waist. "Sitting like that for so long is tough on the back," she
murmured as explanation for her hasty move. "Why don't we stop by
Grandy's for some coffee and pie? Hopefully they won't be too crowded
to seat us."

"Suits me. Your ride is rested and waiting."

As they headed toward the buggy, two men started a quarrel and scuffle that soon turned into a vicious fistfight. The commotion and curses drew a crowd that blocked the path to their buggy, imprisoning them at the center of a manmade ring around the battle. One slug across an opponent's mouth sent blood and spittle flying onto Beth's dress and right hand, after which the injured man toppled into her with such force and weight that she would have been sent crashing into those behind her if not for Navarro's quick reaction.

"My goodness!" she panted, lifting her arm to stare at the mess. With haste and a frown, she pulled a perfumed handkerchief from a draw-string bag and wiped off her hand and sleeve. While doing so, she muttered, "Uncivilized brutes, arguing over whether or not the play had a 'fair ending.' Everyone knows Shakespeare mainly writes tragedies, even when there's romance and comedy included. My dress is ruined. This blood will never come out of white lace and cotton. Whyever did I choose a town to settle in where the law can't control such wicked behavior? I shall never grasp why grown men must fight or kill each other over silly things."

As she stuffed the soiled cloth into her bag, folks she knew commiserated with her and tried to calm her. The fight ended with one man left on the ground, moaning over his pains and loss. Beth congratulated herself on the success of her little ruse; she'd acted as well, she thought, as those talented people on stage earlier. "Take me away from here, Navarro, before I'm overcome with vapors."

In the buggy during the short ride, Beth didn't explain that she'd taken advantage of the situation to supply them with another reason for leaving Tucson soon. She decided her partner might think she was bragging.

But Navarro didn't realize it was a pretense. *Spirits help me, woman, because a greenhorn like you will never make it on the trail. What in blazes were you thinking, Dan, when you gave me this pretty tenderfoot as a partner?*

At the restaurant, Navarro ate his pie and drank his coffee without lingering over either. He was trying to come up with a kind and unoffensive way to drop Beth. When the tables around them became unoccupied, he slipped into the chair nearest her and asked, "Are you sure you want to accept this new assignment?"

Beth lowered her cup and gazed at him. "Yes. Why?"

"You seem like a woman who'd feel safer and be more comfortable in a town. It won't be easy out there; there may be shooting, fighting, and certainly hard riding and crazy weather. There'll be days when we can't catch a bath or a breath, hardly time to eat. Once we're trailing them, we can't risk a fire even on a chilly night or have hot food. To keep a close eye on our targets, we'll have to hide in bushes or behind rocks during storms, with only slickers for cover and warmth. Those are sorry conditions for a lady to endure. Why not ask Dan to give you an easier case in another town? I can find a better way to handle this one alone."

She was stunned by the unexpected remarks and suggestion but concealed that reaction. "You don't want *me* as your partner, is that it?"

He ruffled his hair and took a deep breath. "As I said, trail work is dangerous, fast, rough going, sometimes even worse than I described."

And you don't think I'm cut out for it, you underhanded sneak. You're cleverly trying to persuade me to resign because we both know Dan would never concur with your low opinion of me or yank me from this mission. Stay calm, woman, don't behave like a petulant virago.

Navarro assumed from her composure she was favorably considering his suggestion, but he soon learned how mistaken he was.

Beth pushed her half-empty cup and unfinished dessert to the center of the table. Her fingers straightened the wrinkles the actions made in the checked tablecloth, then settled in her lap. She rotated her wedding band as she fused a self-assured gaze to his coaxing one. "I know what trail conditions and demands are like from plenty of experience with them. I don't whine, complain, or slow my partner. I do my share of everything involved."

"I'm sure you'd give it your best efforts, but you're a little . . . dainty, delicate, for what's ahead. Trust me, Beth, it's too much hardship and peril for a lady. Besides, I don't need help this time, not on this case."

The provoked woman used casual glances to check their surroundings for continued privacy. For customers and hired help who could see but not overhear them, the Special Agent kept her expression pleasant and body relaxed, as if they were having a genial—if not romantic— chat. She leaned toward him, feigned a smile, and asked just above a whisper, "How do you know what I can *endure?* You've never seen me in action on the trail. What you've observed here, if that's what's formed your low opinion of me, has been part of my current and future roles. I'm following orders to appear the *dainty* and *delicate* lady so no one will suspect my real identity. I'm supposed to act like a vulnerable female who's swept off her feet by an old friend and carried off to safety and security in a romantic rescue. Or did I misunderstand our superior's orders?"

You can't lead me down a false trail to hide your fragile senses. You may have Dan blinded, but not me, tenderfoot. I'll prove it to both of you.

"All right, Beth, if it's a chance you want, you'll get one, against my better judgment. But I'm warning you, the minute you don't pass the test, you're off the case, and I don't care *what* the orders are. I can't let anything or anybody endanger this assignment for . . . me."

There it is again; I would bet my saddle you have a second motive for wanting to do this case alone, and I aim to find out what it is. "Agreed, if those same rules also apply to you. I'm finished. Let's go. It's late."

Settle her ruffled feathers or she'll never carry off her role for the rest of the week. "They will, but it isn't necessary where I'm concerned."

"Nor where I'm concerned, and that's no brag. I'll wager my entire salary during this assignment if I fail you or it in any way. How about it? Are you confident enough to do the same?"

He took another deep breath, mussed his hair in the back, and said, "Look, Beth, I'm sorry if I burned your feelings or tracked you wrong. You're doing fine here in town."

"But you don't believe I can do fine out there, right?"

He shrugged. "I guess you could say that."

"At least you're honest," *to a degree.* "That counts for something."

What if she and Dan were right about her skills, as Dan had never been wrong before and wouldn't risk a mission's defeat? Navarro mused. "I suppose I haven't gotten used to the idea of working with a woman. Fact is, I don't have many doings with ladies because my kind of missions don't call for it. And I'm not sure I'm playing this romance stuff right. You'll have to be patient and helpful. Okay?"

"Okay." Beth wondered if he was a defensive male running scared on unfamiliar ground and searching for an excuse to get rid of a temptation. Or did he truly doubt her talents? It could be hazardous for them and the mission if he lacked faith in her. If that was the problem, she had to dispel his worries without delay, but not here in Tucson.

The ensuing silence grew heavy and he sought the first thing that came to mind to end it. "Sorry about your dress getting ruined."

"It doesn't matter. All I have to do is shorten the sleeves and change the trim. I was only trying to look . . ." She grinned. "Ladylike and dainty."

"But you *are* a real lady."

"You're going to be surprised at how unladylike I can get at times." She stood before he could respond or rise to assist with her chair, and headed for the door. She smiled and spoke to people before climbing aboard the buggy and settling herself without his help. She didn't look at him when he joined her and guided the horse down the street.

Beth glanced around during the silent ride home. Tucson, she was reminded, was filled with progress and really had little violence. The telegraph, railroad, gas streetlights, and other modern amenities had reached it. There were five thousand residents in it or nearby and businesses flourished. Ranches, mines, missions, and smaller settlements were in the vicinity. Her time there hadn't been difficult or dangerous, but she was more than ready to move on—with Navarro Breed if he allowed it. Despite his annoyance at times, the thought of sharing adventures with him sent waves of excitement through her. Yet, that bold contradiction in him was bothersome: he was an easy talker in public; in private, he was quiet and restless, downright edgy. It was as if he were two men in one body: Navarro the skilled agent and Navarro the loner. For three days she had enjoyed his company, most of the time. When he touched her, smiled at her, spoke to her, she experienced a slow burning heat of desire, and sparks like tiny lightning bolts attacked her core. He was tender, sweet, and flirtatious in public, but in private, he was cool and reserved. Perhaps, she reasoned, he was attempting to make it clear that his interest in her was solely professional.

Considering the way she reacted to him and their ruse, she had best stay on alert or she'd find herself thinking and behaving irrationally. She couldn't let that happen, for the sake of their mission and loyalty to Steven's memory. She must be cautious now that he seemed to be trying to get rid of her. She had never been kicked off an assignment before, nor made a mess of one. This would not become the first time! Her pride and agent status were at stake—as well as the importance of this particular mission, one of the most challenging cases to be offered to her.

"You haven't said a word the whole way home, Beth."

"I didn't see anyone watching us, so I presumed we were off duty."

"Does that mean we talk only at professional times?"

"I thought you preferred it that way. Did I read you wrong?"

"If I gave that impression, blame it on me being a loner. When I'm working, it's easy to play my assigned role. When I'm not, I'm myself."

Feel him out, Beth. "Who is the real Navarro Breed?"

"I'm not sure I know the answer to that question. I'll tell you as much about me as I can later. Until then, put up with my crazy ways and moods."

"You aren't too hard to endure," she said with a grin. "In fact, I was looking forward to working with a man of your caliber. Dan told me many glorious tales about your exploits, so I was hoping to learn plenty from you."

"You can't believe all you hear."

"Maybe not, but it will be a privilege to work with a living legend."

"I hope you won't be disappointed to learn I'm just a man. 'Night."

Just a man? I've met enough to know that isn't true. They alighted from the buggy in front of her home. "Don't forget we're eating with the Carters tomorrow night at six. She wouldn't take no for an answer. I rent from them; they own this entire row of houses." She nodded toward the other five. "They befriended me when I first came here. I hope you don't mind my accepting their invitation. It wasn't our plan."

"I've seen her watching us and smiling like she just got some big present, so I'd say it fits our needs perfectly."

"I thought you would. Pick me up here at five-thirty. Good night."

" 'Night, Beth."

Navarro sat opposite Beth at their host's dinner table, with the Carters occupying each end. He put tender-roasted beef and vegetables his hostess had canned last summer on his plate. He added a catshead biscuit when that platter was held out to him by the grinning older woman. "Thanks, ma'am. It was kind of you to invite us to supper. These smells make my mouth water and stomach growl."

"I like to see a man with a good hunger, son, so eat heartily." As she filled her own plate, Kate said, "I bet you and Beth have been enjoying your reunion. I haven't seen her smile this much since she came here; and that twinkle in those pretty green eyes is new."

"Kate, behave yourself. Don't make the youngsters fidgety."

"It's all right, Mr. Carter. I suppose it's obvious how happy we are to see each other." She fused a glowing gaze to Navarro's and smiled. "We've been friends for so many years and we've been separated too long."

Kate set down a bowl. "I always say, folks need good friends."

Navarro, Beth, and Henry noticed the emphasis Kate placed on her last two words. The young couple exchanged tender looks.

The older man sent his mischievous wife a shake of his head. "Sorry, you two, but Kate just won't mind me at times. I spent forty years tryin' to teach her how, but she's a strong-willed woman."

"Like Beth," Navarro added, then chuckled playfully. "She gave me and Stephen a rough time when we didn't behave right."

"If you men didn't always try to boss us around like children, we wouldn't be like that. Isn't that right, dear?"

"True, Mrs. Carter," Beth concurred with a gay laugh. "Most men think they know more than women, but we're the ones who kept them out of a lot of trouble with our so-called nagging."

As the four ate, they talked about the alleged past the young couple had shared. Navarro was asked all about the ranch he was considering for purchase, and he made up a convincing tale to relate.

When he finished, Kate murmured, "It's a shame you don't have a good wife to help you there. There's a lot to making a home that only a woman's knows. Maybe you can find one here before you leave."

"Not much time for that kind of shopping, ma'am; I leave Monday."

"Maybe you're casting your eye in the wrong direction. Sometimes the best choice is practically under your nose."

"Shush, Kate. Stop being so nosy and in'erferin'."

Beth let her partner handle that overt attempt at matchmaking.

The dark-haired man grinned and his hazel eyes brightened as he gave Beth a quick glance. "Maybe it is, ma'am."

Henry tried to change the subject by going back to ranch talk. "You said you're planning to run cattle and horses?"

"I think so, sir, but I haven't decided for sure. I've learned plenty about both while working other people's ranches and hiring on for drives to railheads. It certainly isn't something you go into without experience."

"Beth's a smart woman, and not a lazy bone in her body. I bet she could learn ranching in no time and be a big help. Besides, you'll need a trusty woman to cook and clean and tend you until you find yourself a wife."

"Kate, am I gonna have to send you away from the table like a bad child?" Henry admonished. "Ain't good manners to poke your nose into other folks' business."

Navarro glanced at Beth and smiled. Both stayed silent, but each wondered what the other was thinking.

For a while, they enjoyed their meal as the conversation turned to Tucson's progress and happenings.

"Least it's safer here now for a woman alone than years ago. 'Course, Beth has many friends who watch out for her. Men take a real shine to a beauty like her. She's probably the most chased female in town. I doubt she'll be allowed to stay unattached long. Some lucky man will snap her up."

"I agree with you, ma'am. Beth's a special woman, always has been. If Stephen hadn't corraled her so fast, maybe I would have."

"It ain't too late, son. Best lasso her while she's in another corral before that gate's opened and she runs loose."

"Kate Carter! Git the apple pie while I fetch coffee or that flappin' mouth's gonna git you in trouble." Henry was losing patience quickly. "Leave the young people alone."

While the couple had their backs to them, Beth looked at her partner, shrugged, and mouthed, "Sorry."

Navarro's grin was meant to relax her, but he noticed she seemed to stare at it too long, then gaze into his eyes when nobody to dupe was looking. As she lowered it to the table, he wondered if he was right in thinking he was getting to her in a way he hadn't expected. Plenty of women had found him appealing and had tried to catch his eye, but he hadn't considered that complication on a job. Nope, it wouldn't do for her to become interested in him romantically, nor for him to allow anything unrelated to the mission to come between them. Yet, he could be mistaken; it might only be a pretense with her, following orders to fake a romance. He hoped so.

As Beth nibbled on the piece of pie set before her, she pondered the unbidden feelings assailing her. *Oh, Steven, what's wrong with me? I'm sorry, but Navarro makes me feel . . . so strange inside. I know it's only a ruse, but I wish . . . Heavens above, he shouldn't be so tempting! I have to remember this is only a job. And Dan, you sneak, if you put us together for more than work reasons, I'll get you good, and so will he. But don't be stupid; Navarro Breed isn't going to be interested in another agent, a widow. He's a loner. He's—*

"Isn't that right, Beth dear?" Kate asked in a louder voice.

Her gaze jerked upward and widened; her cheeks rosed. Whatever was the matter with her? She never blushed or vanished into a dreamy mist! "I'm sorry. I didn't hear you. I was . . ."

"Daydreaming?" Kate smiled as bright as the sun. "That's all right, dear. I understand. Your life's changed in a big way this week."

"Yes, it has. Navarro caught me by surprise." *Get hold of yourself! It should have been, Navarro's* arrival *caught me by surprise.*

"Me, too, Beth. You're the last person I expected to find. It's getting late and you have work tomorrow. I should get you home." Rising, Navarro thanked the older couple for the fine meal and company.

"You're welcome in our home any time, son. I hope you can stay around longer than Monday because Beth's having a good time with you here. She'll miss you something terrible after you've gone. Won't be the same without him, right, dear?"

Beth avoided a reply by asking, "Are you two going to the *baile* at Mr. Harrison's tomorrow night? He invited me and Navarro."

"We'll be there after we close the store and get cleaned up. I want to see you two kick up your heels and make merry. Best watch her good, son, or all the other men will be claiming her for every dance and you won't get a chance."

"I'll be alert, ma'am. See you tomorrow night, and thanks again."

As the couple strolled from the house, Henry scolded, "You shouldna acted that way, Kate. You don't know him good enough."

"But I know Beth and she needs my help capturing that young man."

"What if they don't want to catch each other?"

"Silly man, did you see how they looked at each other? And they been together every night."

"They're just old friends, you nosy creature."

" 'Just friends' don't have twinkles in their eyes bright enough to light up the town and hunger on their faces," Kate refuted. "Are you too old to remember what it was like when them hot feelings nearly burned you up?"

Henry caressed her wrinkled cheek. "No, woman, I ain't forgot. It just takes me longer these days to act on them. Let's get us to bed and I'll prove it to you."

"I'm sorry, Navarro, if the evening made you uneasy. I expected Kate to try to push us together, but not that hard. She wasn't subtle at all, was she?"

"She's a nice woman, a good friend to you. She's playing right into our hands. We'll let her and others think she did the matchmaking for us. Why don't you visit her tomorrow and let her work on you again?" Whether or not Beth went with him to Texas, it was time for her to leave Tucson for her next assignment, so the ruse needed to be carried out as planned.

"I'll go see her at noon after lunch. I hate using her, but I guess I must."

"It isn't a bad trick. With her help, we'll all be getting what we want and need. For most, that's peace and safety."

"You're right, boss, so I'll follow your orders. Good night."

" 'Night, Beth."

As Navarro returned to town, his mind was troubled. He was nervous about the way she looked at him in private, when they were off duty. Her interest seemed more than professional. She also seemed too fragile and squeamish for what lay ahead. He was tempted to sneak a visit to his superior to convince Dan to halt her participation. But at this early stage, that would be embarrassing to his friend and to Beth.

He didn't like the idea of her being attracted to him, especially since she was so appealing. Too damn appealing, his mind added. It was only natural to find a charming beauty desirable and tempting, but he didn't want those urges to go any further than thoughts. The only woman he wanted for more than sexual gratification was already claimed by another man. He couldn't allow anything physical to happen between him and Beth because it would complicate their relationship and create distractions for both. Needing release from tension, he headed to a saloon for a drink and card game, a decision that proved to be anything but relaxing.

Chapter Four

During the third game, two men at the table he chose mentioned the lovely subject he was trying to forget for a while. Without making it obvious, he called himself to full alert.

One remarked as he eyed his cards, "I've seen you 'n' Mrs. Lawrence spendin' time together. You knowed her long?"

As Navarro played his hand, he replied, "Her husband and I were best friends back home. I've known Beth for years."

"She's a real lady. Don't git many of them out here."

Navarro looked over at him. "You know Beth?"

"Just to speak to in passin'. I wish she'd give me a chance for more, but she keeps to herself about men. Guess it's 'cause of that husband she lost. Ain't got over him, appears to me. Still wearin' his ring. If you ask me, she's too pretty 'n' fine to stay a widder."

The second man nodded. "She won't give me no time or eye neither. 'Course she's always nice about it. You're the first man we've seen her with. You're damn lucky."

They stayed quiet as they completed that hand. As the next one was being dealt, the second man asked, "You staying long?"

Navarro picked up his cards, studied and arranged them, then replied, "Leaving Monday. Got a ranch waiting for me in Texas."

A few minutes later, the first one asked, "Got a sweetheart or wife waitin', too?"

"Nope, just settling down for the first time. Been a trail-duster until now. Worked all over out here." Navarro saw the two men exchange glances and shrugs that told him that wasn't the answer they wanted. He fanned out his cards on the table to show a winning hand.

"Yep, one damn lucky devil."

Navarro comprehended he meant more than with the three out of four winning hands. He finished his whiskey, stood, and said, "Thanks for the games and good company, boys. It's late. See you another time maybe."

As he walked away, Navarro caught a few words behind him: "Damn, you know he's gonna git her. I seen the way they look at each other, all moon-eyed. I'm bettin' he won't leave by hizself. I'm bettin' . . ." He couldn't hear any more with the distance between them.

He headed for the hotel. The clerk smiled and asked if he'd had a good time with Mrs. Lawrence. "Does everybody in town know her and try to protect her from harm?" he quipped with a grin.

"Just about all the regulars. Ain't nobody who don't like her. I'm glad to see her getting out and having fun. No woman like that should be alone."

"You're right. See you in the morning."

"Good night, Mr. Breed. Let me know if you need anything."

Navarro thanked him and ascended the stairs, wondering if everyone in town was aware of their alleged relationship and outings. Of course, the land office was in full view of the hotel for the clerk to take note of their comings and goings, so he could be exaggerating. He hadn't thought the news about them would travel around so fast. That should have made him happy, but it didn't; it told him once more how unforgettable she was. That was bad, risky, a possible hazard to Jessie and Lane's safety.

As he removed his boots and clothes, Navarro attempted to visualize Beth riding a fast and hard and perilous trail at his side. He tried to picture her eating and breathing road dust, drenched and unafraid in a violent storm, dodging bullets and returning gunfire, going without food and water if need be, enduring the desert sun, and living in a rough campsite. He sought to call forth images of her shadowing her men's killers, helping to fight and arrest them, and witnessing one's hanging. He failed to imagine her in those situations, most of which would soon be realities. He couldn't envision her sitting under an invisible new moon without a fire for warmth or light for safety; she wouldn't get a wink of sleep and her fatigue would delay his progress and prevent his success. He couldn't bring forth a picture of her staying dirty and sweaty, for days and nights on end. Jessie could and had done all of those things, but Beth . . .

Beth was a soft and fancy city woman who could get them both shot or slow him down or devastate his case. Those opinions, he reasoned, weren't formed because he didn't like or respect his partner. In fact, he hadn't been this drawn to or fascinated by a woman since Jessica Lane! He couldn't grasp why, because the two females were so different in looks and character and skills, as different as an eastern dude to a western pioneer. Despite Beth's beauty and charms, it was unlike him to get snared by a genteel lady's allure. 'Course, he hadn't fallen prey to her and wouldn't! Jessie and Lane had left no room in his heart for another woman, and nobody was going to stampede them out to take over their private property!

There was another questionable mark against his companion: Beth craved revenge and felt to blame for Steven's and John's deaths. Her misplaced guilt and any search for her family's murderer among Cordell's gang could be harmful to the mission. It was best, he decided, to part with her as soon as possible; when she proved she couldn't stand tall with him, Beth and Dan would have to agree she wasn't needed and was a risk.

"Hello, Mrs. Carter, Mr. Carter. I wanted to thank you again for last night. Navarro and I had a wonderful time and the meal was delicious."

Kate halted her task. "Henry, watch the counter while me and Beth talk in the back room. Come with me, dear, so we can chat."

"Wife, behave yourself today!"

"I will, Henry, I will."

Beth followed the silver-haired woman into the adjoining room where extra stock was stored. She moved aside for the door to be closed. "I don't have much time before I must return to work."

"This won't take much, dear. I wanted to point out to you that Navarro is a fine man, and they don't come along often. I urge you, Beth, don't let him leave town without you."

"What do you mean?"

"Grab him and marry him, dear. Go with him to Texas."

"But he's leaving in a few days . . . I'm so confused."

Kate put an arm around the young woman's waist. "What do you mean? He's perfect for you, and you for him. He'll have a ranch and more to offer a wife. No better choice is going to come along."

"We've been friends for ages but I never thought of him like this before. At least, I didn't think so until . . ."

"Until what, dear?"

"I saw him again. He makes me feel . . . so warm and jittery inside."

"That's called love, Beth."

"Love? You think I love him?"

"I surely do, and that he loves you. I bet he's just scared to tell you, afraid you'll take offense or don't feel the same way. Time's shorter than a cactus hair, so you have to let him know your feelings. Don't let him ride away without you, or he might take up with some woman who ain't right for him."

"I can't just blurt out something like that or behave in an unladylike fashion."

"You can act like it slipped out. A man loves it when he makes a woman lose control because she likes him so much she can't think clear."

"But Navarro is smart, too smart to be fooled by feminine wiles."

"Men ain't smart when it comes to love. They're as blind as old Thaddeus down the street. And as stubborn as a mule when it comes to admitting their feelings. It's up to you to open his eyes and give him courage."

"What will people think about me for behaving so recklessly?"

"Don't matter what folks think or say 'cause you won't be living here. But who can go ablaming you two for finding each other again? Since he's gotta leave soon, it'll make good sense to everybody for you to go with him."

"Are you sure?"

"Of course, so stop worrying your pretty head. Act fast, dear, or lose him again. You don't want no other woman taking your man while you're too scared to grab him. Sometimes we womenfolk have to take risks and take charge of things."

Beth pretended to ponder that advice for a few minutes. "I guess you're right; it's be brave and forward or lose this second chance at love."

"That's it, dear; you go after what you want."

"I'll try, Mrs. Carter."

"Don't just *try*—do it, and starting tonight."

"I will." *But not for the reason you think and only for as long as our mission lasts,* Beth thought as a curious sensation nagged at her.

Melvin Harrison welcomed the couple to his home where he was giving a *baile,* a special kind of Mexican entertainment. He smiled and said, "You look lovely, Beth. And I'm glad you could come, Navarro. Beth has talked about you many times this week. It's good to be reunited with old friends."

"I appreciate the invitation and what good care you folks have taken of her. She speaks highly of her friends and job here."

"Elizabeth Lawrence is easy to like and watch over. She's a good worker, perhaps the best I've had since opening my land office. I'd hate to lose her, but I expect I will one day when a lucky gent snaps her up and carries her off."

"I'm sure that will happen. A woman like Beth is valuable."

"And unforgettable," Melvin added with a chuckle and wink.

"That, too," Navarro concurred as he also chuckled, but he hated being reminded of that risky trait. "I want to thank you for giving me the names and locations of those other two ranches. I'll look 'em over soon. Either or both may be better than the one I'm heading out to see."

"If none of them suit you, Navarro, get in touch with me by telegram and I'll see what else I can find through my friends in other towns." Melvin grinned as he said, "When a man gets ready to put down roots, he wants the best he can find and afford in all matters."

"You're right. I appreciate the generous help and kind advice."

"Beth's the one who deserves your gratitude; she asked me to see what else was available around San Antonio for you to inspect. It's wise to have a choice; that gives you bargaining power to get a good price."

"Then I'm obliged to both of you."

"No bother at all. It's a pleasure to be of assistance to friends. You know what these things are like, so enjoy yourselves. Here you go," Melvin said before he left to join other friends, handing them prepared party eggs.

Both Beth and Navarro knew the *baile* customs: the casual mingling, the breaking of carefully drained eggs over the guests' heads upon arrival. First, Beth tapped hers atop Navarro's head, cracking and spilling forth small pieces of gold paper. She watched the slivers make a startling contrast with his sable hair, dark skin, and black garments. The fit and color of his outfit made him look confident, sensual, and tantalizing. When he walked, she was reminded of a black panther she'd seen at a zoological display: agile, lithe, mysterious, predatory, and often dangerous. Around his throat, he'd secured a red bandana in a shade that matched the swirling designs sewn on the front and back yokes of his shirt. He didn't seem to be trying to blend into the crowd on this particular evening, as if he ever could. There was an aura, a commanding presence, about him that caused him to stand out among other men. Steven had emanated one, too, but not as potent as her new partner's. Steven's had become evident with time and continued proximity, but Navarro's was evident at first meeting and strengthened each day. She was almost vexed with him for being so appealing—so disarming—tonight, for daring to outshine her lost husband in any manner.

Navarro pressed his forefinger through the eggshell, split it, and dumped the contents over her midnight hair. Some pieces fell to her green-clad shoulders and to the wooden floor. The color of her dress—one she appeared to favor—caused her leafy eyes to remind him of spring grass with dew on it, unlike Jessie's sky-blue ones. Except for both women having fair skin, the females had no similarities in appearance; and for that, he was grateful. When a slip of paper blew from Beth's hair and landed on a long lash, Navarro brushed it away before she could lift a hand to do so.

She smiled and said, "Thank you, kind sir, for taking care of me."

"That was smart to get ranch sites from Harrison. Guards our cover."

"Thank you again. It seemed a good precaution."

He nodded his head and pulled his gaze from hers. He wished she would stop looking at him like that and giving off a seductive air that made him want to inhale it with every pore of his body. When she turned on her charms and wiles, she was impossible to ignore, which he couldn't do while playing his role. "Shall we eat or dance or visit with others first?"

"Dance. I'm too nervous to eat or chat," she whispered.

Before the people outside could dismount their buggy and reach the entry, he asked, "Why?"

"Because you're proposing to me tomorrow, and everyone's watching us with hawk eyes tonight." *More accurately, eyeing you.*

He knew that wasn't the reason. "I haven't forgotten. Seems as if your friends want us together. Good."

"Is it? Maybe they're just trying to get rid of a nuisance."

He chuckled and shook his head. "Let's give it a try." He held out his hand, which she accepted, and guided her to the dance area. Jessie had taught him how to dance; he rarely put the lessons to use since dancing only reminded him of her.

Beth was relieved they didn't have to stand too close and make too much contact. She hoped he didn't notice her tremblings or, if he did, he blamed them on her alleged tension. Though the windows and doors were open, the room seemed warm to her, and she knew it wasn't the weather's fault. She tried to focus on moving her feet correctly and on listening to the music—a blend of pipes, pans, flutes, harp, fiddle, and guitar. She was amazed to discover Navarro was an excellent dancer. It seemed as if he could fit in anywhere and with anyone, like a talented chameleon. He constantly exposed new traits and facets, and continued to mystify and arouse her. Was there nothing, she mused, he didn't know or couldn't do?

As Navarro rounded her during one sequence, he murmured, "Relax,

Beth, you're as tight as a new bowstring. You're supposed to be in love and lighthearted, remember? Folks will wonder what's wrong."

The following step called for them to stretch out clasped hands and touch first their right shoulders, then their left as their bodies shifted. When the space between them vanished, she whispered, "How do lovers act, partner?"

He glanced into her upturned face and replied, "You should know; you're the one who's been married before, not me."

Beth did the stroll-around sequence, journeying her fingers across his broad back because he was too tall for her clasped hands to travel over his head without straining. As she passed his left arm and retook his hand, she was close enough to ask, "Does that also mean you've never been in love?" She felt his grasp tighten for a moment and saw his body stiffen. His piercing gaze told her she'd asked the wrong question. She laughed and quipped, "Relax, I'm just making small talk, not being nosy."

"That *is* being nosy, at the wrong time and place."

"Yes, sir, no more jests. I only wanted to be prepared with an answer when Mrs. Carter asks me that question, because she surely will."

As he twirled her into his embrace with her back to him to hesitate there a moment as next to the last step, he asked, "Why?"

"To see if I have a rival for your affections."

"Tell her you don't," he said as contact with her was broken.

The music ended and they bowed to each other. As she straightened, she responded, "Fine, just so our answers match if she asks you, too."

The second dance began and more couples came on the floor.

"Let's get something to eat," he said when the music stopped, both having remained silent except for responding to greetings or remarks from others.

Beth accompanied him to tables laden with food and drinks: frijoles, enchiladas, tamales, tortillas, chili con carne, and other *cocido* selections, beer, wine, tequila, coffee, and water. Mexican servants kept the treats and liquids coming and provided any service needed.

While making their choices, they chatted with their hosts and other guests, then sat down to their meals. Though Navarro appeared to be in a relaxed and merry mood, she sensed a change in him, a coolness brought on by her remarks. Without a doubt, Beth concluded, the man had many troubling secrets. It was a stupid—but innocent—mistake to antagonize him, especially since he was eager to drop her as a partner. She found it difficult to force anything down because of the sudden ball of dread in her throat and chest warning that he would find a clever way to convince Dan to agree. She wanted and needed this important assignment. In her distress, it was a struggle to smile, chat, and act happy. The good-natured Carters helped lessen Beth's strain and that between her and Navarro with their arrival. The four talked a while before the older woman began to matchmake again.

"So, you're having a wagonload of fun?" Kate winked at Beth who smiled and nodded. "And you, Navarro? Kicked up those heels yet?"

He answered, "Yes, ma'am. Food's excellent, too. This fruit from Sonora is a treat. Harrison is lucky it got past all the *bandidos* and renegades."

"Sometimes our shipments get stolen by those wicked brutes."

He continued to use the diversionary topic while his partner finished settling down and got into her role once more, as she'd been a mite distant since their earlier conversation. "I thought your store sold dry goods."

"It's called that, but we sell most anything that brings in money. I hope you'll do your trail shopping with us before you leave."

"I will, ma'am, on Monday morning, early."

"So, no changes in your plans to leave?"

Navarro shook his head.

"That's too bad. I'm sure Beth wishes you could visit longer. Don't you, dear? I bet if you work on him good, he might hang around another week or so."

"He . . . I—"

"Come on, Kate, and leave these young folks be," Henry rebuked, and tugged on his wife's arm to take her away from them.

"At last," Navarro murmured, "our best supporter is here. Let's stay close to her so others will overhear her matchmaking."

Beth let him be the leader he claimed he was and tried not to displease him again. She wasn't accustomed to subservience and found it quite uncomfortable. Tomorrow, they were taking a carriage ride. For the first time, they would have privacy to be themselves and get things straight. Maybe then, she could persuade him to keep her on the team. *One more day in Tucson, whether I go with him or not. Tonight, forget your worries; what will be will be. Enjoy your friends and have fun at this last party because there's no telling what surprises he has in store for you tomorrow.*

After Navarro picked up Beth in a rented buggy, he guided it away from town in a southwest direction toward Gates Pass. They journeyed in silence except for the mingled sounds of horse, harness, and wagon.

She let her gaze roam the grandeur of the vast and wild panorama. Soon, a bend in the dirt road and desert landscape would have concealed their presence if not for a continuous dust cloud being kicked up by the horse's hooves and buggy's wheels. The sky was an expanse of clear blue as far as she could see. The air was warm and a breeze wafted over them, the kind that made arid heat deceptive and perilous in the summer. They were surrounded on both sides by a near forest of huge saguaros with floral tips and countless bird holes in their spiny surfaces and cozy nests on branches. The giant cactus stood as guards for the rugged territory with armlike extensions held upward as if ready to fend off any threat by man, beast, or climate. Some saguaros had up to fifty "arms" and weighed several tons. Some were twisted or entangled into numerous picturesque shapes, their contortions a thing of breathtaking and unique beauty.

Intermingled were a profusion of gray-green creosote and verdant mesquites, prickly pear with their beavertailish leaves, yuccas and sotol with creamy blooms and daggerlike spikes, and fat specimens of barrel cactus. She noticed ocotillo with clusters of scarlet flowers on barren and spiny branches, leafless from a lack of recent rain, as foliage grew for only a short time after rainfall. Cholla—tall, short, and in between—with its multiple furry arms thrived in this region. Senna, phlox, paintbrush, verbena, poppy, and other flowers flourished and emblazoned the area with splashes of white, yellow, gold, pink, purple, orange, and red. The countryside was neither desolate nor infertile, but it could be intimidating and hostile, and lethal to a tenderfoot. She was glad she was here at springtime when the setting was so glorious.

The ground was a combination of light-colored sand and mostly brown rocks of various sizes. As the topography changed, undulating land rose up in places to form benches that were studded with cactus towering over other greenery and flora. As desert drifted into mountains, rocks became larger; boulders, foothills, cliffs, and peaks greeted her line of vision. Along flash flood washes and ravines, desert willow, tamarisk, thorny acacia, palo verde, and ironwood grew. Most were an array of loveliness with white, yellow, gold, and purple blossoms that attracted thousands of bees and other insects. Wrens, doves, and other birds feasted on the tiny flying banquet, while several kestrels preyed on those diners who weren't swift enough to escape their claws.

Beth decided the lovely day and tranquil location was the perfect time for eating outside and having a serious conversation. Yet, Navarro was again his silent and reserved self with no one around to dupe. *Don't let him get accustomed to being stone quiet with you. Draw him out; make him talk, if only to answer questions. Get him in the habit of speaking, so he'll feel free to do it more often.* "Have you heard the tale about the stolen gold hidden in Colossal Cave southeast of town?"

I was wondering how long you'd hold your tongue, 'cause silence makes you edgy. "Just a little wild talk in saloons. What'd you hear?" he asked to keep her chatting so he wouldn't have to do so yet.

"Locals say several men robbed a train, fled with the law after them, and hid in the cave. The posse tried for weeks to smoke or starve them out, but nothing worked. The bandits found another hole and escaped. Most of them were located and slain in another town, and the only survivor was captured and sent to prison. He won't tell where the gold is hidden. Locals say it's still in there somewhere. Plenty have searched for it; some have been killed or injured in accidents or just never came out again."

"If you found it, would you keep the gold or return it to the railroad?"

She shifted on the seat to stare at him, but he didn't glance her way. "That's an odd question. Return it, of course. I'm an honest, law-abiding person."

"You'd be rich. You could retire from this hard and dangerous job and live in safety and comfort. Who would know you'd found it?"

"I would. Keeping the gold, when I knew to whom it belonged, would be the same as stealing it in the first place. How can a person live with himself or herself if one intentionally breaks the law?"

"I guess it depends on how and why the law was broken. Sometimes the law is worse than a criminal's actions."

Beth wondered if he was being a little too defensive. Had he committed crimes along the way to catching criminals? Did he believe the end result justified using whatever means necessary to achieve it? Did a lawman have a right to use evil to defeat evil? Steven never had, though there had been times when doing so would have aided a difficult mission. Beth needed the truth from him to avoid any complications, so she asked him those questions. He jerked his head in her direction and gaped at her as if she were loco.

"So far, the answers to your doubts are no, no, and no."

Blast you, woman, you did it again! Repair the damage fast. "I'm sorry if I insulted or offended you, Navarro, but you sounded kind of odd. I have to learn what to expect from you. In the days ahead, errors of judgment on my part can have grim consequences. To pull together best, we need to think and react alike. At least, that's how Steven and I worked as a team. If it's going to be different with you, tell me so I won't make any hazardous mistakes."

You might get to know me better than you can imagine and find me totally offensive. "We'll have plenty of time on the trail to get acquainted. Before we reach the Cordell ranch, you'll have your answers."

There's that odd look and tone again. What are you hiding, Navarro? "I hope so, because this case is too important to be caught off guard. Do me a good turn by teaching me all you can during our partnership."

He watched a bird of prey capture its target. "Like what?"

"Anything and everything Steven didn't have time to teach me. Since I work alone now, I don't have anyone to do that for me. I want to be the best agent possible, while staying alive and bringing criminals to justice. I can shoot and ride like a champion." He glanced at her and grinned. She didn't change her words because they were true. "I can hold my own against most people. But I need to improve my self-defense skills, my tracking, my gathering and reasoning out of clues. According to Dan, you're matchless in those areas. Will you let me be your student for a while? If you say yes, I'll obey without hesitation and I'll work hard."

"You want to be able to protect yourself with more than a gun, is that what you mean?"

"Yes, but I'm competent with knives, too. It's hand-to-hand battles with a man that give any woman problems. Guns and knives can get knocked from my hand, so I need to hone other skills if I'm disarmed. As for tracking and gathering clues, the obvious ones are easy to find or read; it's the subtle or concealed ones I want to be able to sight and glean. Lastly, you've pointed out the reality that I'm a woman, so I think, feel, and react as a female. I've observed men for a long time, all kinds, but I still haven't gotten adept at predicting what they all will do."

"If you understand most of them, don't worry about the few you don't."

"But it's those few who are usually the crux of my cases."

"You want to understand the motives and emotions of criminals?"

"Yes," she said as they reached the spot he had chosen.

Navarro reined in and climbed down. As he was grasping her by the waist to help her to the ground, he responded, "Bad men have as many motives as the desert has sand. Except for a certain weakness and flaw or two, they're not much different than good people. It can be anything that heads one down a wrong trail, something big or little, fate, timing, an impulse, a soured dream. You name it and it's driven some man to crime."

She stood before him and gazed into his hazel eyes. "Will it annoy you if I ask questions and make requests during our trip?"

"I don't know, to be honest. Never had that experience before."

"Can we try it? If it's irritating, you can tell me to slow down or stop. I just don't want you to think I'm doubting your orders when I question them. That's the only way I can learn how you reason out things."

Navarro was touched and flattered that she believed he was so skilled that she could learn from him, and was eager to do so. It was a stirring sensation that she was honored to work with him. The respect and acceptance of others were things long in coming to him, as were love and real friendships. Could it be so troublesome, he mused, to put up with her for a while? He stared into those large and pleading eyes. He'd see . . .

Beth was baffled by the way he pondered a simple request for so long, then grinned and nodded. Maybe he relented because she had gotten to his pride and ego—by which so many western men lived and died—but not by her being guileful. She was serious about him educating her along the way. Too, Steven had told her there were four things a woman shouldn't trample in a man: ego, pride, his name, and his heart. Nothing, her lost love had warned, made a man more dangerous and unpredictable than having those wounded. She had never forgotten those words of caution.

"To finish answering what you asked me earlier, I did my share of wild things—even gunslinging—before I joined the Agency. Since then, I've had to do some stretching of a few crazy laws when I threw in with bad sorts to trap 'em. But commit crimes to trick or catch criminals? No, I don't mount my horse on the wrong side. If I did, I'd be as bad as the men I go after. I'll expect you to do the same while we're partnered up."

"Your answer and sense of honor couldn't please me more; thanks."

Navarro nodded and spread a quilt on the stony ground near a tall saguaro that offered no shade with the sun almost overhead. Beth unpacked the food basket so they could eat as they talked. They put fried chicken and biscuits on their plates, with fruit waiting for a later treat. Beth handed him a tin cup of tea which he secured in the sand until he was ready for it. She did the same with hers, then curled her legs half under her. She set the filled plate on her lap atop a napkin to protect her dress from greasy spots; another one lay beside her and she tossed it to Navarro who caught it in midair and dropped it by his leg.

"Thanks. Looks and smells good. You cook this?"

"No, Grandy's did, by special request and an extra quarter. Time was too short and tight for me to do it. But don't worry, partner, I can cook in and out of doors, and I do it well."

He chuckled. "So can I, so don't think you'll have to wait on me."

Beth glanced at his arms, exposed by his rolled sleeves; they were tanned and muscular. From what she could see of his chest through the unbuttoned section, it was hairless and smooth. She didn't want him getting hurt, but couldn't wait to see him in action, physical action, as he was agile in mind and body. She focused on her meal to distract herself from him.

Navarro looked at her biting into her chicken while her gaze was lowered. Black hair peeked from under a pretty sunbonnet, its dark shade odd with her coloring. As fair as she was, she could make use of the same flour paste with which Mexican women protected their skin from the sun's power and damage. As he studied her, she ate and moved—to him—in a dainty fashion. Her yellow dress was simple, but its brightness called attention to her.

Use this time and location wisely, woman. "Dan told me you're old friends of the Cordells. I'm sure it will be difficult to seemingly betray their trust. He said you'd fill me in. How did you meet them? When?"

"In March of '76." He put aside his plate and wiped his fingers and mouth. "My mother died when I was young. I was left on my own, so I became a drifter. I've been all over these parts. Done about every job there is. I ran into a Lane in San Angelo who was hunting for a certain kind of man for a dangerous job, and I was picked. A villain named Fletcher was trying to grab Jed Lane's property near Fort Davis in south-west Texas and the snake was willing to break any and every law to get it. The ranch was called the Box L back then, a big spread with lots of stock. No matter if anybody believed Jed's charges against a rich and powerful man like Fletcher, it didn't make any difference because the law couldn't pin any of the doings on him. Jed hired me to teach his boys how to fight Fletcher and his hirelings. He also needed me to protect his family: two daughters, a half-crippled son, and his mother."

Navarro drank some tea to wet his throat; he was surprised she didn't jump in with questions or comments. "I couldn't have done my job better. But I had a run-in with his youngest girl; she was twenty at the time." *Better mention that incident because others at the ranch will be sure to do so.* "She took a fancy to me and I turned my back, which didn't sit with her. She accused me of trying to attack her; she tore her dress and scratched herself up to make me look guilty. I was fired and sent riding."

Beth was intrigued by how calm he sounded *and looked* while relating an experience that must have been humiliating and riling. "They believed her? Didn't they know what she was like?"

"Best I could tell, nobody took her word against mine, but nobody would call her a liar. The old man just wanted me gone to prevent worse trouble with her, and maybe he didn't want to accept the dirty truth about his own child. I was told she'd been a problem for a long time, so I guess he didn't want to dig a wider canyon between them by taking my side. And how would the boys treat and view his girl if her own father doubted her? I suppose it's hard to raise girls without a mother."

"She had a grandmother and older sister to help rear her right." When that remark seemed to annoy him, Beth added, "Of course, family isn't always to blame when a child sours. So, what happened afterward?"

"I didn't get far before I realized I couldn't just ride away because I'd made friends there who needed my help. Besides, I'd given my word, and I never go back on that, unless I'm forced to for a good reason. Trust me, they were my friends, even if they couldn't side with me. Don't you see, they couldn't go against the boss's daughter for somebody who'd be gone soon? We all knew it was best for them to stay out of that fire. But the oldest girl, Gran, and Tom wouldn't keep quiet; they argued in my defense." Navarro smiled in recall. "The boy had become my shadow, like I was his older brother. The grandmother liked me, too, and the older girl knew I was needed there. We learned a lot from each other."

Navarro's smile faded. "By the time I got back, the old man was dead and Fletcher's threat was darker and bigger. The law still couldn't prove anything against him, but we knew he'd had Jed murdered. I won't go into the terrible things Fletcher did to the Lanes, not at the eating table. In all of my past cases, Beth, I've never come across more cruelty, violence, and coldness. The Lanes could have used a skilled Special Agent to help them."

"Because the local law couldn't or wouldn't?"

"Couldn't. Fletcher was too cunning and evil to make mistakes. After we finally defeated the bastard, my job was over, so I left in June."

Three months, her mind tallied, a long time for a loner and drifter to stay put; he must have developed deep affection and respect for the Lanes and others on the ranch. "Have you seen them since you left?"

"The oldest girl married the foreman; he's our target's older brother. Matt Cordell is a fine man, Beth; I can't think of anything making him go bad. It's been five years since I saw him, but few men change that much."

"What happened to your troublemaker, Tom, and the other hands?"

"After Jed was killed and before I returned to help, Mary Louise married Fletcher." When Beth looked astonished by that information, Navarro said, "Yep, your ears are working fine."

"She turned against her own family and married the villain threatening them? How could she do such a terrible thing?"

"Fletcher was rich, well known, handsome, as you women would say, and a bachelor. He started romancing her; I think his motive was to try to get the ranch through her after he did away with the others. She said she didn't believe he was to blame, and maybe it was true. Who knows what others really think and feel?"

"That's very generous and kind, but I don't believe it for a minute. A female who's cunning and greedy enough to frame a smart man like you, or any man, in such a despicable manner isn't stupid. Saddling up with the enemy is about as low as anybody can get. But I'm sorry I interrupted. Go on."

"After we arranged a trap and Fletcher met with justice, Mary Louise sold her widow's inheritance to her older sister. She moved back East where she'd been wanting to live since attending school there. Matt told me she fell on hard times but finally straightened out. Married a doctor who helped Tom with his eye and foot problems. Tom's married and doing fine, last I heard. The grandmother is quite a woman, real pioneer stock; you'll like her." He drank more tea, and she remained quiet and alert.

"Not long after I left that second time, there was a fire; lightning caused it. Burned the Lane house, so the Cordells moved to Fletcher's home. It was bigger and nicer and they owned it, so they didn't rebuild the original house. The L/C Ranch is large and prosperous; money couldn't be a motive. There *isn't* a motive, 'cause they wouldn't turn evil, not those two."

"Does L/C stand for Lane/Cordell?" she asked to prompt more disclosures after he went silent and pensive, a clue he was withholding something.

"Yep. They're good people, Beth, including the hands who work for them. Most have been there for years. You'll like all of 'em, I promise." He told her they had three children, spoke some about the hands, and related many things he'd done there. "After we arrive and you get a look-see, you tell me if they aren't one of the happiest and best matched couples you'll ever meet. I'd bet my life, Jessie and Matt aren't involved in his brother's gunrunning."

"Being a part of a family and ranch life didn't make you want that for yourself?"

"Never found the right time or woman to make it possible."

Beth was surprised by that admission, and *he* looked as if he were, too. Yet, she sensed gaps in his revelations and detected a change in him when he reached certain points in the story, and when he finally mentioned the oldest daughter—Cordell's wife—by name. Had he, she mused, avoided saying it on purpose? Why, when he knew her well enough to call her "Jessie"? Was she a possible complication at the ranch? The real reason Dan was sending along a "wife" as his partner? She let Navarro finish his meal before she asked about Geronimo.

He related facts given to him by Dan and their superior's conclusions. He brushed over the Apaches' history and their battles with the whites. "You can't blame Geronimo and his people for hating San Carlos and captivity. No man leans to losing his freedom, being locked away, *abused.* There'd be no trouble, or less of it, if the Apaches had been left at Warm Springs as promised. That was a good location and they liked it enough to accept reservation life there. They were put in chains and carted or marched to the barren prison that was their new home."

Beth perceived his bitterness and resentment. Were those his people? Had he lived on a reservation? Had he hired out as a scout, as many conquered braves did? Had Dan rescued him from that dark existence? "That's horrible, Navarro; no one should be forced to live that way."

"But they're only Indians, savages, animals, people say."

"They're humans, God's creatures, too. It's wrong and cruel."

"Most out here don't see it that way." *But I'm glad you do.*

"If they did, and they'd be wise to do so, peace could come."

"It isn't peace whites want; they want the Indians defeated and removed. Geronimo claims the newspapers lie about him and provoke people against him. I know for myself some of those reports and charges aren't true or are exaggerated. After Mexican raiders killed his family, he burned his dwelling, his family's possessions, and his children's playthings: that's their custom—and revenge, too. He's wreaked plenty of that on his worst enemies below the border." He explained the fierce hatred and bloody conflicts between the Mexicans and Apaches. "Geronimo—Old Goyahkla, that's his real name—surely loves his *tiswin.* It's gotten him into barrels of trouble." At her look of confusion, he clarified, "Corn beer, Apache-made."

Again, he ceased talking and drifted into deep thought. Beth waited a while before remarking, "If he's involved with Charles Cordell and illegal arms, he's in bigger trouble now."

"I know."

"And you'd hate to be the one to bring him in or have to kill him?"

"Yep."

It was apparent he didn't intend to elaborate so she changed the subject. "How did you meet Dan and go to work for him?"

"Trickery," he said with a grin and chuckle to mask his torn feelings about his mother's people and his past with Jessie. "He said if I refused his offer, he'd make sure I couldn't find another job in the territory and, when I was hungry and broke, I'd come back to him for work."

Beth's eyes widened and her lips parted. "Daniel Withers black-mailed you? He coerced you into becoming an agent?"

"Just joking," he said.

"A sense of humor, I like that quality in a . . . person. Please continue."

"I did a lot of troubleshooting jobs for people and the Army, some of them concerning Indians. Somehow I caught Dan's attention, so he looked me up and convinced me to hire on with the government. The pay was better, my results more important and appreciated, and I was my own boss in most ways. I've handled all kinds of missions for him. The last one was investigating allegations against the railroads. I finished that case in January and my findings are in the hands of a Senate committee. Between then and now, I've been hunting down outlaws and renegades while waiting for a new assignment. I certainly didn't expect it to be this one."

You're well spoken and educated. How did an orphan get that way? Why no mention of a father? "You've been an agent for three years, right?"

"And you've been one for seven. Any problem with who outranks who and should be the leader of our team?" She shook her head and smiled. "Good. So, what's *your* story, Beth?"

She watched him recline on his left side, prop his head with a hand, and focus his hazel gaze on her face. *Trying to relax me or unsettle me?* "I just completed that alleged fraud case which Dan mentioned to you. There was no evidence to substantiate the accusations made by several men from back East; either they were mistaken or were trying to ruin Harrison because they used bad judgment in land buys. They said he lied about the properties, then offered to repurchase them at a lower price when they arrived and found the parcels worthless. I saw copies of the correspondence, reports, and sales agreements; and I saw the parcels. I'm glad they were wrong, because Melvin Harrison is a fine man. Men who buy land without seeing it are asking for trouble, and they can't expect the seller to cancel a deal and return their money because they aren't satisfied. The files clearly prove he didn't deceive them, and he had no obligation to negate the deals and take a loss on the business expenses he had incurred. As far as I could discover, the properties are worth what he charged. He's offered to act as agent for their resales, but the men are balking against his fees. I don't see how he could be any fairer to them."

Beth brushed aside an insect that landed on her dress. "One of my first assignments was investigating to see if President Garfield was killed by a lone assassin or if a conspiracy and other people were involved.

That was in '81. It didn't take long for our group of agents to discover he'd acted by himself. I've had all sorts of cases, but that was one of the most fascinating. Believe it or not, Navarro, the Agency needs women because there are some cases only a female can handle."

"Such as?"

At least you don't look as skeptical as you sound. "I helped destroy a white-slavery ring. Only a female could get inside something like that."

"What happened?"

"The Agency received reports about young women—unattached, widowed, and married—disappearing from towns within a hundred-mile circle of New Orleans, then St. Louis, then Dallas. Lawmen, and even private detectives hired by some families, couldn't find any of them. It was as if they'd vanished from the earth. But there was a suspicious pattern."

"What kind of pattern? Who made the connections?"

"I did; that's partly why I was assigned to the case." He sat up. "I was in the territorial office when the events were being discussed. It turned out that one of the missing females was the daughter of an agent's friend. He mentioned there had been similar crimes in the area. I asked if anything like that had occurred anywhere else and if the women had anything in common. Telegrams were sent to other offices to collect facts on all unsolved abductions. I was still there when the replies came back, so I suggested we pin disappearance sites on a map. When we did, it was as clear as water that somebody was working a specific area, then changed locations to do it again. They told me to take charge of the preliminary investigation. I went over the reports and requested more facts. I learned that all of the victims were young and very pretty, so there could be only one motive for stealing so many. We knew what was happening, but not how. We were stumped because no one had seen or heard anything, or wasn't telling. All we could do was alert our agents to be on the lookout for similar reports, wait for the culprits to reveal their current target area, then move in and try to capture them redhanded."

Beth realized he was paying close attention. "We got our first break when one of the victims escaped a brothel and confirmed the sinister motive behind the crimes. She'd been beaten and drugged numerous times, and subjected to unmentionable evils for money. She died before supplying the names and facts needed for arrests and convictions, but she'd given us a place to start: the Red Palace in Sante Fe. That's where I worked before I came to Tucson. To conceal his crimes, the ringleader hired women to perform, serve drinks, and entertain men in his business front: a very expensive and respectable house of diversions for men.

When a customer wanted . . . other things, he was taken to a fancy brothel outside of town where he could have his choice of women and the pleasures they offered. For the right price, he could do anything he wanted to her. If one woman died from abuse, she was buried secretly and another was stolen to replace her. I hired on at the Red Palace and obtained the evidence against him. He was so cocky and confident, he kept a record of his *properties* and their fates and how much each earned for him. He got rich off women's torments. If I'd had my way, every customer would've been charged and punished, too! They had to know those women were there against their will."

"You could have vanished, too; that was dangerous and risky."

"Dan had me watched closely. If I failed to report in every two days, he was to mount a rescue. It never came to that."

"In two days a lot could have happened to you, Beth."

"I know, but I had to stop those villains from harming more innocent women. Can't you imagine the sufferings of families and friends who didn't know what had happened to their loved ones? We rescued most of them and returned them to their homes."

"Why do you look so angry? You succeeded."

"Not all of them were welcomed back after what they'd been forced to do. Some were considered dirty, worthless, at fault. Even husbands turned their backs on women who had been good wives and mothers. If you ask me, those snakes didn't deserve good women in the first place."

"I agree. Victims shouldn't be held to blame for criminals' actions; they were powerless to help themselves."

She caught an odd hint of bitterness in him. "That's why I want you to teach me how to defend myself when I don't have a weapon handy; I don't ever want to be helpless in any situation. As soon as we're on the trail, you can begin my lessons, if you haven't changed your mind."

He shook his head and she sighed in relief. "We'll have to get you a horse before the livery closes today," he said.

"That isn't necessary; I have Sunshine, a golden palomino with a blond tail and mane. I've had her for years, so we know each other well. She's wonderful and well trained. Dan's keeping her. He's going to pretend to give her to us Sunday as a wedding gift. Let's go over the remainder of our schedule for today and tomorrow. Time's short."

After they'd gone over everything, Navarro said casually, "You didn't tell me much about yourself, partner. Will you?"

She nodded. "You want my professional or personal story?"

"Both; everything," he replied with a chuckle, unaware he was in for a startling surprise, one of three which Dan had concealed from him.

Chapter Five

Beth wanted Navarro to know her well enough to like her and trust her. Then, maybe he would open up more. "I was born in Atlanta twenty-eight years ago," she began. "When the war with the North approached, Papa didn't want to take sides. He thought we'd be happier and safer in the West, so he moved us to Denver where his two brothers and their families live and work in the mining business. Before he became an agent, my father was a lawyer, the best. Everybody liked and trusted him. I wish you could have met him, Navarro; he was a special and unique man; they don't come any better than John Wesley Trask."

Her eyes glowed with love and respect, then dulled with sadness, feelings he'd never experienced where his own father was concerned. He saw her shake off painful memories; he did the same.

"Mama took ill one winter with a chest ailment and died when I was sixteen. So we both know what it's like to lose a mother," she added to stress the common bond. "Papa took her death hard; no two people could be closer or love each other more than they did. They set a good example for us as to what a marriage should be. Everything in our home had Mama's touch; it was as if her spirit lingered in every room. He didn't want to stay where they'd been so happy; that's where I got the idea for that part of my cover story. He seemed lost without Mama. Of course he loved us and was a good father, but a vital part of him was gone forever. After I lost Steven, I understood what Papa had endured.

"Losing someone you love and who was a big part of your daily life changes you. When Papa was offered an agent's job, he took it with our blessing. The challenging missions rekindled his old spark as much as possible, but staying on the move prevented him from meeting another woman and remarrying. He had a loving family, exciting work, and good friends, so he was happy and fulfilled to a point, but he never allowed himself to get over Mama. No one could replace her, but I sometimes wished that wasn't the case when I saw how his grief ate at him. Papa had so much love and joy to give. Before he lost her, he had an infectious zest for life that made everyone near him feel wonderful. People sensed they could trust him and depend on him, and he did his best to prove them right."

Beth didn't realize her green eyes were misty and her voice husky with emotion. "Sometimes I would watch him presenting cases in court or working on papers at his desk or interacting with people, and I'd be awed by his intelligence, charm, and self-confidence. Then, Mama was taken away. Even though Agency work rescued him, he never revived fully to the great man he had been. Until the day he died, I sensed his loneliness. Fate can be cruel; he didn't deserve to be left alone at a young age or to have half of his heart cut out."

Navarro empathized with John's similar tragedy, and with Beth's. Although her poignant words rode too close to where he lived, he didn't stop her because he was learning so much about her.

Feeling uncomfortable, she rushed on. "My older sister, Caroline, took over the house and my mother's role with me and Robert."

When she paused, he coaxed, "Tell me about your brother, sister, and kin in Denver." A family, something he'd missed during childhood and would go on missing until death.

"Robert's married, with five little ones. He's a doctor and has a practice there. Caroline and her husband have three kids, and they own a hotel and restaurant. After they settled down, I kept house for Papa. When he was away on missions, I had plenty of free time, so I helped my brother and sister with their children and work. That allowed me to meet all kinds of people from countless places. But something was missing. I felt as if my destiny was elsewhere. It was as if somebody was calling out to me."

"What did that voice say to you?"

"I suppose it sounds silly. 'Come, Beth, ride with the wind and you'll find what you're seeking.' Those were the words. I wanted to obey, but I didn't know where or how to look for the caller. Weird and foolish, yes?"

"Nope. I talk to myself, too. So you married instead of leaving Denver?"

"Papa brought Steven home after a joint assignment. At nineteen, I was considered a spinster by most people's rules, so everyone was delighted to see me with a young man. Steven and I became friends quickly and easily. During visits between cases, he'd relate inspiring tales about his missions. He taught me all types of skills and tricks. His love for his job, going to so many places, meeting new challenges, doing important things—it was all contagious. Papa had already whet my appetite, so Steven increased my hunger. I wanted to experience that same magic, that surge of excitement, that thrill of victory. I'm sure you know what I mean. Every time he and Papa returned, they'd give me details about how they'd planned and carried out their last assignment and what was in store during the next one. By then, they were working and traveling together most of the time," she explained.

"How did you convince them to let you tag along?"

"A case came up where Steven needed a female cover and none was available; back then, the Agency employed few women. I asked him to hire me, and he thought it was a good idea because the case was supposed to be simple, fast, and peril-free. But Steven and Papa were old-fashioned; neither believed we should travel as a couple without the respectable bonds of wedlock, and I agreed. We were married the next day and took off as a team. I was twenty-one and no longer a spinster, so Caroline was relieved on that point but worried about me hitting the trail to hunt down criminals."

So, your marriage began as a work partnership, a way to get what you wanted . . . Did you stay only friends since you didn't have children in six years together? "I take it that first case was neither quick nor easy nor safe?"

Beth wondered why he looked and sounded odd after her last few sentences. No doubt—as with most males—he assumed a woman's, a wife's, place was at home, definitely not on the road. "You're right, but we did fine; I did well enough to get myself officially hired," she finally responded. "From day one, Steven and I had a special rapport. We'd known each other and been close long enough that we were like hands on the same person, if that makes sense. Some people think it's monotonous when two people are so alike, but we were too busy and happy to get bored with each other or our unusual existence. We saved each other's lives several times. When danger struck or an assignment got tricky, Steven usually knew what to do, so I learned plenty from him. You're the first agent I've met who has skills greater than his, according to Dan; that's why I'm so eager to work with you."

Navarro wanted attention to stay focused on her, so he smiled his gratitude and asked, "I suppose you made plans about what to do and where to live if a baby came along? A child can change everything."

"It would have, but fortunately it didn't." She dropped that heart-searing topic in a hurry. "After Papa and Steven were killed, I wanted to stay on the move. I loved my work and having new adventures; it was in my blood. I also needed to continue for the same reason Papa had to leave home after Mama's death. I didn't want the time to grieve and suffer; that changes nothing; only makes one bitter and self-defeating. Steven was gone and I couldn't get him back, so I had to accept it and get on with my life." Except for one remaining link to be broken . . . She hated the thought that her husband's and father's murderer was still free while she and her family endured their losses. Somehow and some way, she had to find and punish that villain. She had a gut feeling she'd locate him during this assignment. No matter if she had to grovel to Navarro to stay on this case, she would. If he tried to push her off it, he'd have a battle on his hands!

Navarro didn't believe her last claim was accurate, though he didn't think she was lying, just misleading herself. Her voice had danced with joy when she'd spoken of her husband and good memories. Then, anguish and bitterness and anger had taken control of her. He concluded Dan was right: she still loved Steven and wasn't over his loss. He understood her feelings and loyalty, but she was too young and beautiful to spend her life alone and in torment and danger. "What about a second marriage?"

Afraid I'll cast my eye on you? This should halt your fears. "I haven't looked for another husband and doubt I will. That kind of loss isn't an experience one wants to repeat. Besides, I think I'd be bored and restless if I settled down to family life after being on the road so long. Surely that's something you—as a loner and agent—understand, right?"

Navarro wasn't about to lift that hot poker and handle it. "Didn't your family try to change your mind about not retiring?" He watched her smile.

"Too many times to count. I'm the baby of the family, so they worry about me. I was always active, getting into any and every thing. While I was growing up, I could hardly sit still for more than ten minutes at a stretch. That made teaching me hard for my parents and tutors. You're lucky I've calmed down and learned self-discipline. Mama and Papa insisted I take piano, dance, etiquette, French, and other school lessons to help me be 'a well-rounded lady.' We were a close, tight, loving family. But I was a handful. Sometimes they didn't know what to do with me."

Beth laughed. "Robert and his friends used to tease me. He'd yell, 'Come on, boys, let's chase the wild wind,' and I'd be on the run. I always escaped them because they were too scared to climb trees as high as I would and they didn't know the best places to hide. It was strange that I grew up to marry a wild Wind."

Navarro was amused when she compared her husband to that force of nature. Sometimes she looked and sounded as bubbly and free as a mountain stream. She had a depth he hadn't noticed or explored, and shouldn't. She'd played with her ring only twice today, when first mentioning Steven and while she talked about that slavery case, so she'd been mostly honest, too.

"I'm ready and eager to move on," Beth added. "The case here was too simple and quick to resolve, and my Elizabeth Lawrence identity is too settled and homey, too sedate. I'll be glad to be myself again, until we reach your friends' ranch."

"I figured Beth's your real name. Dan called you that in private."

"Beth *is* my name, so it was convenient. She's a real person and most of that story I used about her is true. But her husband spelled his name S-T-E-P-H-E-N, my husband spelled his S-T-E-V-E-N."

"Those are odd coincidences; two Beths marrying two Stevens."

"Not really; they're common names." *Unlike yours that sounds so romantic and mysterious.* "One of our agents in St. Louis who worked on that robbery/murder case knew she moved to Boston, did what I said, moved again, and dropped out of sight. Since we couldn't track her down, we knew no one else could if they tried. Dan had the other agent set up that added part in St. Louis and Boston about Elizabeth's move to Tucson, those alleged letters to you, and your friendship with her and her husband. If anybody at the ranch or in Tucson checks on me or you or us, his work will corroborate our story. Tomorrow, I'll be Beth Breed."

"I was getting used to your fake name; that isn't good."

"Why?"

"I could slip up and use it at the wrong time."

"But I'm going to the ranch as Elizabeth Lawrence, so it won't matter if you call me by her name. Remember, you'll be calling me Beth Breed after tomorrow?" Why, she mused, was he so disturbed and not thinking clearly? After all, their marriage wouldn't be legal and binding.

Navarro realized he'd exposed his distraction. It was the result of an unbidden thought darting across his mind: The only woman he had believed he'd share his name with had accepted the one of Cordell before he could give it to her. *Get off that lame horse and get a fresh mount or you'll ride into trouble!* "What is your real name?"

"Bethany Trask Wind. Didn't Dan tell you who I was?" She laughed.

Wind . . . Beth Wind . . . Chase the wind . . . Beth Breed . . . "Your last name was never mentioned; neither was your husband's."

She couldn't understand why he looked and sounded so strange again. "At least not being familiar with it will prevent slips. Don't worry, Navarro, I'm sure you never make mistakes. I've used lots of names and disguises. One of my best was during that slavery assignment. I had to paint my face with that garish color those dancehall girls use. No one saw me without it because I put it on first thing in the morning and took it off last thing at night. I lived alone, so my privacy was protected. I was called Sunshine Nellie because of my hair. I was hired to dance with customers to keep them thirsty for countless drinks." *And get them aroused to the point of needing to visit that bastard's brothel of bondage.* "I even did a little singing and dancing on stage; that was kind of interesting and amusing. Heavens, my feet ached every night when I went to bed. Too bad all those customers couldn't dance like you; they were all over my toes, and trying to hold me too tight and close, and breathing their stench in my face. It's nice to be around a gentleman who practices cleanliness and manners."

"Thanks. Why did they— Somebody's coming. I'll check it out," he said as he stood, and forgot to ask about her Red Palace nickname.

Beth watched as, with fingers grazing the butt of his pistol and body ready to spring into action, Navarro moved forward to peer beyond the thick vegetation sheltering them from view. She followed and observed. He eyed the approach of visitors, then visibly untensed his muscles and jawline. Though trained and experienced in being watchful and perceptive she had not heard the carriage coming before he did. Perhaps she'd been too disarmed by him and had felt safe enough in his care to suspend her constant guard.

"It looks as if the sweethearts want to use this beautiful location for romancing. You ready to leave, Navarro, and give them privacy? We have to speak with the preacher, see Mr. Harrison about quitting my job, and tell the Carters they need to find another tenant to rent their house. We talked so long that we don't have much time to finalize our plans; we should hurry. We must be ready to leave Monday, if I'm still your partner."

"You are, so stop worrying."

As they headed back to prepare for departure, she remarked, "For a time there, I wasn't sure you'd accept me."

"I had doubts, but you've convinced me to give you a chance."

Despite his words, she sensed continued reluctance. Once they were away from Tucson and the role she had to play there, she'd remove his uncertainties.

"After we make those visits, you pack while I buy our supplies."

"I'm not taking much. I'll ask the Carters to store most of my things until I send for them later. I won't need my town wardrobe on the trail."

"I'm glad you know how to travel light." *Leastwise, I hope you do.*

"Any quick last questions, suggestions, or orders, boss?"

The carriage was almost within sight, so time was limited. Navarro knew that suspicions at the ranch about their claims could endanger his loved ones, something he had to prevent. "Maybe asking the real question will help you be more convincing later when you talk woman to woman with Jessie. Will you marry me, Beth?"

She was enflamed by his sexy grin and husky tone. "Yes, Navarro, I will; and thank you for proposing."

He made a playful bow and joked, "Thanks for accepting. I would have felt kicked in the teeth if my request was rejected."

Beth looked up from her kneeling position where she was loading the basket in a rush. As she replaced the last item, she laughed and quipped, "I can't imagine any woman doing that to you in a real situation."

Navarro folded the quilt after she stepped off it. "Kick me in the teeth or refuse my offer?" he queried.

"Either, but I was referring to a proposal. A man as smart as you are wouldn't make one unless he was sure it would be accepted. That's the only reason you're still unmarried."

You're wrong, Beth. "You're a keen-witted woman, partner. Let me put this in the back and we'll be ready to be generous to those two."

The driver of the buggy reined in when he saw them. Navarro waved him forward as he yelled, "You can take over here; we're leaving."

The young man grinned. "Thanks, Mister, Mrs. Lawrence. This is the prettiest spot near town. It's quiet, so we can talk."

Navarro smiled and said, "I hope you enjoy it as much as we did."

Both young people blushed and stayed quiet.

Enroute, Navarro remarked, "You must know everybody in town."

"Hardly. That was Mr. Harrison's oldest son and his treasure."

Navarro cocked his head to look at her. "Is that what a woman's supposed to be to a man?" He realized she had made an embarrassing slip.

Beth wished she hadn't used that endearment of Steven's for her. "I'll let you answer that question for yourself when you fall in love one day."

He faked skepticism and amusement. "That means it will go unanswered."

"Even loners get tired of being alone forever, don't they?"

"Do you?"

"Sometimes, but not enough to act on it."

"Same here. Men like me don't stay put in the same place long enough to find the kind of woman we can love and marry. In the other pocket, a man with dust in his boots and blood shouldn't have a family he's always leaving behind to fend for themselves. When he's gone, another man usually takes his place, somebody who's dependable and always pouring love and attention on them. Can't blame a woman and little ones for wanting more than our kind can give them." To dupe her, he alleged, "Seen it happen too many times. The men stayed gone too much or too long, so when they returned, everything was lost."

You don't fool me, Navarro Breed. Somewhere and somehow in the past, a woman you loved broke your heart. Maybe you're still haunted by her. Maybe I can help free you. Maybe I can teach you to trust women again. In exchange, you can teach me things you know so I'll be better at my job. If I get good enough, I can track down Steven's killer. I owe him justice.

Navarro nudged Beth's arm. "Did you fall asleep with your eyes open? Did I tire you out or bore you too much?"

She collected her lost poise. "No, I was just thinking."

"About what?"

"About what you said. I believe, if you met the right woman, she'd never betray you or desert you, even if you stayed gone too much to suit her. She'd understand you have to do what you have to do. What you can do when the right one comes along is either shake that dust from your boots or fill hers up with the same kind."

Like I couldn't do with Jessie? "Like Steven did with you?"

"Yes. If the timing and person are right, that strategy works."

Navarro wondered if she was always so bold and outspoken; or if she was playing a questing game with him. Surely he wasn't the reason for that tormented look. "Putting dust in her boots wouldn't matter if there's a family at home to keep her there. Face the truth, partner, not many females want to eat and breathe dust and suffer all kinds of hardships and punishing weather."

Beth laughed merrily to cover her tension. "You mean, it takes his perfect match to love and endure the same things he does; but few sane men want to marry a flighty, independent vixen?"

"From what I've seen and you've told me, you're as much of a loner as I am."

"But I haven't been one for life, as you have. Besides, it's not as if I'm a drifter or saddletramp. I travel doing important work. I'm rarely by myself. I've never avoided people or friendships with them. I trust and like most folks I meet. I'm not hiding from life or myself. The only relationships I avoid are with men; that's the best self-protection I've found."

"Protection from what?"

"The obvious: being hurt again. I lost my mother, father, my husband; those are hard things to get over, if one ever does. Time is supposed to heal such injuries and dull painful memories; it doesn't, or it works too slowly. If you'd ever lost someone you loved and needed, you'd understand."

The conversation was getting too close for comfort, too excruciating for him. He cut it off fast. "Let's drop the sad talk before we reach town so people won't wonder what's wrong between us."

"Sorry, partner. I haven't had anyone I could speak openly with in a long time. In our line of work, we have to stay on guard and keep our thoughts and feelings to ourselves. Letters back and forth with my sister just aren't the same as talking with somebody special who'll honor my confidence and not endanger my cover. Besides, I don't like to worry and burden my family, and there are things about my job I can't tell them or anyone. But I know how you men hate discussing feelings and such, so I won't mention personal things again." *Struck a raw nerve, didn't I? I am sorry, because you've been hurt enough, too.*

Her words touched Navarro, but he tried to quell his own strange yearning to confide in her. He couldn't purge himself at her expense. The only woman he'd gotten that intimate with had stolen his heart and soul, and hadn't returned them. He mustn't allow his emotions to run wild and free again and get himself trampled a second time. "I don't mind listening, Beth, but talk doesn't help. I don't want you keeping those wounds open by dwelling on them."

She struggled to sound calm when she said, "You're right, boss." *But you aren't the one to give advice you haven't taken. You've been hurt badly and perhaps it evoked mistrust and dislike for all females, and that's really why you don't want me in tow. You exude such bitterness, resentment, and anguish at times that I can feel them.*

During the rest of their silent journey, she fretted that he was just pretending to like and accept her so she'd do a superior job as his partner. Navarro Breed, she decided, was a true lone wolf and preferred his existence that way, no doubt with good reason. She mustn't allow him to work his many charms on her then vanish. A false lover was worse than a robber who took one's horse and water in the desert, because he stole heart, spirit, and soul: things as vital to one's survival as life itself. She scolded herself for indulging in such reverie, as she and the man beside her were professionals working together for a short time, nothing more.

The buggy halted before a local preacher's home, and the next step of their subterfuge was put into motion.

The Sunday service ended at the church Beth had chosen to attend after her arrival in Tucson. Attendance was not part of her ruse, but something she was accustomed to and needed in her life. She was wearing a cornflower-blue dress that was pretty but not the usual attire for a bride.

The pastor told the couple, "I'm sorry this ceremony has to be rushed but, as I told you yesterday, I have to hurry home to eat before I leave to say words over our departed brother's grave. We're burying him at two, so time is short."

"Just so we're hitched proper and legal before this fine lady leaves town with me. I can't sully her good name, even if I am replacing it."

As the two men spoke, Beth glanced at the people who had stayed behind to attend the ceremony: the Carters, the Harrisons—among other friends—employees at the land office, and Daniel Withers. She knew Dan's presence would seem quite natural as the banker and longtime resident of Tucson was acquainted with and liked by almost everyone in and around the city.

The pastor positioned them before him and opened his Bible. "We're here to bear witness of our friend Beth's marriage to Navarro. This is a happy and proud moment for us to share. If you two will join right hands while I read from the Lord's Holy Scriptures."

Navarro grasped Beth's and noticed it was almost cold and stiff. Nerves, he decided. At first, he listened as the pastor began to read passages about marriage, husbands, wives, and love. But his thoughts drifted as he wondered what Jessie had thought and felt as she stood before a minister to marry her foreman and friend. Yet, it hadn't been just Jessie and Matt standing there: his unborn son had been there, too. Had Jessie been bitter and angry with him for deserting her in need? Had she been worried about what he—gunslinger and desperado—would do when he returned and found her out of his reach? Did her heart break as she severed their entwined destinies? *Leave that heartache behind and pay attention!*

Beth's thoughts wandered for a brief time, too. Her wedding with Steven had been so different, so joyful, so lovely. The only thing missing had been her mother's presence. It was almost depressing that even a fake marriage didn't have at least a few special touches.

"Do you, Navarro Breed, take . . . this woman as your true and lawful wife? Will you love, honor, and protect her in sickness and health and in all manner of life's demands? Will you forsake all others for her?"

"I do; I will."

"Do you, Beth, take Navarro as your true and lawful husband, to love, honor, and obey in all manner of life's demands and problems, forsaking all others for him?"

"I do," she replied to the clipped, unromantic, hasty vows.

"You have a ring, son?"

Navarro placed a gold circle in the minister's open hand. It was blessed in a quick prayer and given back to him to slide on her finger. He repeated after the reverend, "With this ring, I wed you."

Beth was relieved to have the borrowed treasure back where it belonged, and a little dismayed at having to make it a part of the duplicity. The preacher didn't ask her to say anything about accepting it, and his rush was slightly and inexplicably annoying.

"If there's anybody or any reason to object, speak up now or hold your peace forever." Without hesitating, he continued, "I pronounce you man and wife until death parts you. What the Good Lord has joined together for His own purpose, let nary a man nor deed cast asunder. You can kiss your bride, son. You're married now."

Beth hadn't considered that part of a ceremony. *Oh, no . . .*

Navarro decided to test his suspicion about Beth's attraction to him by giving her a real and thorough kiss. He also wanted to take his troubled thoughts from the preacher's words: "Until death parts you." At Jessie's enforced marriage, those words had sealed his fate and hers, bonded her to Matt; they had sentenced him to a different kind of prison than he was in on that terrible day. At least, those words were true and binding until Matt's death.

Navarro cupped Beth's face between his strong hands, glued his gaze to hers as he lowered his head, and touched his lips to hers. For an instant, he closed his eyes and pretended she was Jessie. That illusion faded rapidly as Beth's taste, smell, and response were totally unlike Jessie's. This kiss was more than pleasant and stimulating; it reached to the core of him and sparked to life yearnings long buried and denied. He told himself it was only a physical reaction to Beth; his body wanted and needed carnal release with a special woman. If it weren't so reckless, he could share that part—that much—of himself with his "wife," but his heart would forevermore belong to Jessie and Lane. Wouldn't it?

Before Navarro had captured her lips with his, Beth had steeled herself against showing her true feelings. It was difficult—almost impossible—to feign love and a response for the witnesses while keeping the truth of her dilemma from her partner. She knew the heady kiss lasted longer than was proper or necessary. She was relieved when the pastor cleared his throat to bring them back to reality. She lowered her head as if she were embarrassed.

With effort, Navarro managed to grin and say, "Sorry, sir, but it's taken a long time to find the right woman to become my wife."

"That's all right, son, I understand. You two will have a lifetime to enjoy the happiness you've found together. May the Good Lord bless you and keep you safe from all harm and temptations. May your love grow stronger and never end. Congratulations, Beth, you deserve this new start. I'm sorry to lose you in my congregation and sorry I must rush off. Goodbye, and never let anything or anybody come between you two."

Those words worried Navarro but he dismissed them from his mind as he responded, "Thank you, sir, for everything." He took the marriage certificate the preacher handed to him, one the man had filled out earlier. As friends surrounded them, he cuddled Beth close as was expected of him. He saw Dan walk the pastor to the door and speak for a moment; then, both glanced back at the bride and groom. Navarro focused on Kate.

"We won't keep you two long; I'm sure you've got plenty of talking to do and plans to make. Henry and me want you to have these to remember us by. I chose something that wouldn't be heavy or hard to carry. Just tie them to your saddles and they shouldn't be any trouble. You can use them on the road and in your home. God go with you, Beth; I'm going to miss you. Don't worry about your trunks; they'll be safe with us."

The two women embraced as Beth said, "Thank you, Mrs. Carter, you've been wonderful to me. I'll miss you, too. Goodbye, Mr. Carter, and take care of my dear friend."

"If the old girl will let me," Henry joked. "If you two pass this way again, our door's always open."

"That's kind of you, sir. I want to thank you two again for befriending Beth when she was alone and for being so nice to me during my visit."

"It was as easy as smiling, son. I hope you two will be as happy as me and Kate and have yourselves a passel of children. You got a fine woman."

Melvin Harrison spoke up before the groom could. "I agree, Henry, but it cost me one of the best workers I've had. Goodbye, Beth. Our prayers and thoughts go with you. Take good care of this fine lady, Navarro."

Beth used a handshake with her ex-boss to break away from Navarro. "I appreciate your friendship and everything you did for me here." She spoke with his wife and children for a few minutes before telling Melvin, "Goodbye, sir. We'll let you know about the ranches."

"This is for you two, a gift from me and my family. As Kate said, it's the perfect size and weight for easy travel. Use it to help pay for stock and any needed repairs at whichever ranch you select."

"Thank you, sir." She handed the money to her "husband."

Navarro accepted it, then shook Melvin's hand and thanked him. The two blankets the Carters had given to them were on a pew. He watched others congratulate them and present gifts, mostly money to help on the alleged ranch. He was touched by their warmth and generosity, and impressed by the effect Beth had on people. Daniel Withers was last to shake his hand, hug Beth, and say a few words.

"I hope you won't mind if I give you two a horse for Beth to ride. She's gentle and saddlebroken and she'll be easy to take along to that ranch. I got the idea when I overheard you telling Henry yesterday that you'd be looking for one at the livery today."

"That's much too generous, Mr. Withers," Beth gave a weak protest.

"Considering all the business you've sent my way from new land buyers, it's more of a thank-you present. You must accept her; my Billy Boy doesn't like her, so I need to get her out of my corral. Say yes. You need a mount."

The others coaxed Beth to agree. "If you insist. Thank you."

"Her name's Sunshine and she's a well-mannered and intelligent lady like you, so you two will get on fine. Here's the ownership papers for her."

"Let's get moving, folks, so these young people can go home," Kate coaxed, then took charge of ushering everyone out the door.

Navarro and Beth stood by the buggy he had rented for the day and waved to departing friends. He placed the gifts inside and helped Beth onto the seat. He hopped aboard, lifted the reins, and off they went to her house, in silence.

Navarro halted before the adobe dwelling, helped Beth down, and carried the armload of presents inside. He left her standing on the porch after he secured the mare's reins to a hitching post. He returned the buggy and retrieved his black stallion, then stopped at the hotel to gather his things and check out with a grinning clerk. As he went about those tasks, he hoped he wasn't in for a long and arduous stay in the cozy house with Beth tonight.

Beth went inside after his hasty departure. She glanced around the small and sparsely furnished house she had occupied for months. It was so unlike the one she had grown up in Denver. The Trask home had been a cheerful, loving, nurturing, and beautiful place—one in which she'd been allowed to be herself, a haven she and Steven had enjoyed when not on assignment. She had let Caroline sell it after her father and husband's deaths, knowing she never wanted to enter it again. Sometimes, Beth admitted in her current solitude, she missed that peaceful and cozy residence and her old life, but she'd always controlled or quelled those longings. For some strange reason, she was feeling them again today.

Beth ordered those wild thoughts to leave her alone, and focused on the present. She hadn't bothered to fix up the house during her stay. Now she wished she had made this place prettier because she hated for Navarro to see how she'd lived in such a dull setting.

She looked in one corner where most of her possessions were packed in trunks, to which she added the wedding gifts. Henry Carter and a friend would collect her things tomorrow morning and take them to his storeroom. If anyone nosed through her belongings before Dan arranged a pickup, there was nothing to expose her identity. Her keepsakes were in crates in Denver in her sister's attic. This would be the first time she had to travel so light, but she didn't mind. She looked forward to the freedom of trail clothes and liked her traveling companion. Such a glorious adventure was before her. They would—

Get dinner ready! Your husband will be home soon. Beth Breed . . . That name has a nice sound. Just don't get too used to it because it will be gone soon. Remember, that marriage certificate isn't even in your name.

As she set the table and put out food Mrs. Carter and other friends had provided for the occasion, she wondered what kind of parents and home Navarro had before he lost them. Where and how had he existed afterward? What about a father? No doubt, a series of harsh experiences had helped harden and embitter him. Could a man like that be changed, softened by the love of a good woman?

Beth entered the living area where Navarro was going to bed down for the night. "We head out early, so I'm turning in, boss. Anything you need?"

"Nope, but thanks. 'Night."

Back to your old quiet self, my handsome groom? You've hardly spoken a word since our wedding. "What are you doing?" she asked and came forward to stare at the numerous items scattered about. "Heavens, Navarro, you have so many weapons."

"Different problems call for different solutions. Lesson time. Just give me a minute to finish what I'm doing."

Beth took the hint and moved close to where he had been cleaning, sharpening, checking, and loading a variety of weapons. She noticed two pistols this time, both in holsters on the same leather belt: the Smith & Wesson Frontier .44 and a Colt double-action .44 with personal modifications. She also noticed that the thongs for securing the holsters to his thighs had been run through loops on their bottoms. Nearby lay a Spencer lever-action repeating rifle that had two ready-loaded tubes for quick insertion in its butt. There were fieldglasses, a rope, two knives, a hatchet, and . . . a whip! She realized his rifle sheath had been specially made because it featured a long and narrow holder for arrows. She didn't miss the clue that several of his weapons were Indian.

"The revolvers and rifle need no explanation because Dan said you're an expert marksman. Should that be, markswoman?"

"Doesn't matter to me; it's only a word. No offense taken."

"Good. This six-inch blade fits inside my left boot in case I'm ever disarmed by a target. This big fellow is a James Black special, like the one he made for Jim Bowie. Not many of these around. Glad I happened on to one. Knives are for silent or close work, if you catch my meaning."

Beth nodded. She observed and listened as he held up each weapon as he talked.

"Never use your knife for anything except protection or attack. If you dull or nick the blade with cooking chores, it'll fail you at the wrong time. This hatchet is also effective for quiet tasks. Good for distances, too, better than a knife for throwing. The handle is heavy and thick to give the right counterbalance to the head, and it's short to fit into a saddlebag for concealment. The whip is for disarming two-legged snakes; I'll show you on the trail. Bow and arrows make the best silent weapon because of their speed, accuracy, and distance capability."

She glanced at the array on the floor. "I don't see a bow."

"They have a tendency to make folks nervous and insulting, so I make one after I leave a town when it seems likely I'll be needing one. I can cut a sapling and ready her fast. I carry two strings at all times. I've got tips, feathers, and ties in one of my bags. When I'm sitting around a campfire, I relax by making arrows or practicing with them. Indians taught me how. I'll give you lessons when we have plenty of privacy."

"I can use one already; Steven taught me. A Cheyenne taught him."

He stared at her in surprise. "You can handle a bow and arrows?"

Don't brag, woman, just give a simple answer. "Yes, I'm adequate."

"Knives, too, you said?"

"Yes." She saw how he gazed at her as if pondering whether or not to believe her. He'd discover the truth as soon as he tested her, which he was certain to do. "No spurs to give away your presence to enemies?"

"Night Cloud doesn't need them; he obeys without force."

"That's his name?"

"Yep." *Named after me. Tl'ee' K'us, half-breed Apache. I wonder how that news will strike you when you learn the truth.* "You best turn in now."

"Good night, Navarro, see you at dawn. By the way, I checked my almanac and the weather should be fine for our journey."

He nodded, impressed by her attention to detail, but didn't look up from his return to work. She was too appealing in that gown and robe. Her dark hair had been brushed and braided. With her hair pulled back, her beautiful face was all too apparent. The only way to get rid of this temptation was to ignore her. *Spirits, help me, because I'm not as dead inside as I thought I was. If you know what's good for you, Bethany Wind, you won't come near me and get hurt. Don't be loco, hombre, she wouldn't want a half-breed bastard like you in her arms or bed in a hundred years.* If being with her in a separate room was strenuous, Navarro didn't want to imagine what it would be like on the trail. Yet, he'd make that discovery beginning at first light tomorrow.

Chapter Six

After a breakfast of eggs, bacon, biscuits, and coffee Navarro and Beth saddled their horses and left at daybreak. They took the dirt road toward Benson, traveling in silence at a steady pace.

Soon, it was apparent to Navarro that Beth had not misled him about her riding ability, as she seemed born and bred to the saddle. She looked fresh and lovely this morning. She wore a blue cotton blouse, a brown vest, a split-tail riding skirt that ended just below the tops of her brown boots, and a tan western hat. Her dark hair was secured by a blue ribbon at the nape of her long neck. A Winchester lever-action rifle, a fifteen-shot repeater, was in a saddle holster. A rope was hanging in place. On her right side, a Colt double-action was strapped around her small waist. On her left was a Spanish blade in a hand-tooled sheath, and suspended beside it in a leather drawstring pouch were extra cartridges. She also carried a concealed derringer, a Remington double repeating model. She seemed to know weapons. Question was, did she know how and when to use them?

Beth noted Navarro rode either a little ahead of her or created a wide space between them, as if to make talk impossible. He appeared determined to behave as if he were alone. Perhaps, she reasoned, he was mentally adjusting to her company. It was as if he feared revealing himself, or of her getting too close. Surely he wouldn't stay tied in knots during the entire case.

Beth couldn't get something out of her mind she had seen by accident. While Navarro was shaving this morning with his shirt unbuttoned, he had turned to answer her query about how much time he needed before she cooked the eggs and how he liked them. That was when she noticed two things suspended around his neck on thin leather thongs: an

Indian amulet, and a locket resting near his heart. The piece of feminine jewelry looked old. She surmised it might have belonged to his mother, but maybe not. She was intrigued by whose picture was inside and why he wore it. But how could she sneak a peek when he didn't remove it? *Who and what are you, Navarro Breed? What happened in your past? How will I ever get to know you if you keep to yourself so much in private? I must think of ways to draw you out of that shell.*

Beth watched the scenery alternate between scrub-covered areas on flat terrain, to an occasional hill, to sites with countless boulders and brown mountains. Grass, where it grew, was green to greenish yellow. At times, thousands of yuccas flaunted their dagger leaves and numerous creamy blossoms. A variety of cacti, some crouching low to the stony ground and some standing tall against a blue horizon, greeted her line of vision no matter which way she looked. The arid countryside possessed an untamed beauty with its abundance of bloom- and insect-covered trees and flowers, sturdy varieties that could survive the harsh territory and climate.

During a walk to rest the horses, Beth was surprised when Navarro closed the gap between them. His black stallion followed on its own. Still, her partner didn't begin a conversation. The silence a strain she didn't need, she asked, "Do you like to fish or hunt?"

"Just for food or protection. Creatures aren't here for sport and waste."

To her, that sounded like an Indian belief. "What kind of protection?" she queried to continue the brief chat while he was willing to talk.

"Attack by a hungry or injury-crazed animal."

"Does that happen often?"

"Nope."

"Have you had personal experience with rogues?"

"Yep."

Don't go mute again. "Mighty stingy with your words today, partner."

"Hadn't noticed. I stay alert on the trail. Danger can jump you fast."

"Is it too distracting to tell me one or two of those episodes?"

"Guess not."

Beth watched him remove his hat, hang it over his pommel, and give his mount a few affectionate strokes, to which the animal responded with matching love.

"I took a job years ago tracking a mountain lion who was preying on people and stock on the Mexican border. He was strong and fast, took me on a wild chase on horseback and afoot. That *'idui* was more cunning than most outlaws I've pursued. Almost ambushed me a few times. I hated to kill him after I got to know him. He was only protecting his territory and getting food. Most men, even women, hunt mountain lions for pleasure; they like to display their heads and hides to show others what great prowess they have."

"But you killed him?"

"Yep, had to, after a child got in his path. Some stupid hunters had brought their families along and let a kid wander from camp. Strange, but that *'idui* only scratched him up and scared him a little, like a warning to the others to get out of his territory. I knew what would happen; they wouldn't yield to his threat and he'd give them a bigger one."

"It's a shame you had to go against your wishes."

"Earned a reward for his hide. It was demanded as proof I'd done the job. But I didn't want it as a trophy, even if I'd had a wall to hang it on."

"How did your employer know you gave him the right hide?"

"Markings. Had an unusual patch of white hair on his left jaw. Reminded me of a warrior's symbol. You know Indians paint their faces for raids and ceremonies?" She nodded. "Each man has his own pattern. Some believe, when a warrior dies in a bad way, Ysun—Giver of Life—allows him to return to Earth Mother in animal form to . . . redeem himself."

"What do you mean?"

"If he's murdered in an ambush, massacred while asleep, tortured and killed by enemies while he's bound and helpless. If he died without a weapon in his hands, if he couldn't defend himself, he gets to return to at least die while using his courage and wits and new body's weapons; he gets to die in pride and freedom."

"Like your valiant mountain lion?"

"Yep."

"That's partly why Indians hate reservations so much, isn't it? Because if they die in dishonor and captivity, their souls wander in misery."

"Yep, and how they're treated there."

She watched him disappear into himself again. *Move to an easier topic; you're stirring up painful memories.* "I was told this region has a wealth of gold, silver, and copper. You had any jobs connected with them?"

"Yep, and such . . ." he began, and paused to glance at her and grin, *"treasures* cause big and greedy appetites that lead to plenty of trouble. I've settled feuds over claims, investigated frauds, solved robberies and killings. Some people will do about anything to have those shiny rocks."

Beth laughed as she replied, "Because those 'shiny rocks' are valuable and useful. My uncles in Denver have become wealthy and power-ful from mining, but they haven't had many serious problems. They've also been generous with their good fortune; they built an orphanage near town and support it from their earnings and from donations from kind people like them. Bustling areas like that have so many children whose parents have died, babies born to soiled doves who abandon them for one reason or another, or widowed fathers who just take off when gold fever strikes. I can't imagine a parent deserting a child for any reason. No matter what happened, my father, mother, and Steven would never have done such a horrible and selfish thing. Neither would I."

You could if your motive was right, if you had no choice, if you wanted what's best for the child. But it's the hardest and most unselfish thing you'd ever have to do. "Did you help at the orphanage?"

"Yes, by cooking, cleaning, and teaching lessons when other workers were sick. Some of the stories the older children told me almost broke my heart. I'm glad they were kept off the street where they'd have grown up too fast and hard; many of them would have gotten into trouble and been killed or sent to prison or wound up in saloons. It must be terrible for a child who has no one for guidance, love, and protection." Recalling what Navarro had halfway exposed about his childhood losses, she scolded herself and dropped the sure-to-be touchy subject. "I've watched the gold and silver mining processes from beginning to end, and they're fascinating. I haven't seen the copper districts or work in-volved in its mining, but I bet it's interesting, too."

"Destroys too much land, scars her for a long time or for life."

"Copper mining does?" she asked.

"Yep."

"How?"

"You'll see for yourself if our mission takes us through any of those locations."

Beth knew that mining and related businesses created many jobs. Towns sprang up nearby for bringing safety, supplies, and civilization to the settlers who'd been there first. Railroads arrived and did the same. Progress and fulfilling dreams always had prices and sacrifices, she concluded, but didn't vex her companion with speaking aloud those excuses and reasons for what they did to . . . perhaps his homeland and people.

"Why did you become a lawman, Navarro, a Special Agent?" she asked as he gave the signal to mount up by doing so himself.

He realized she had caught her innocent mistake and rushed to correct it. She was a good person with a kind, tender, and compassionate heart. He shouldn't be angry with her for what happened to him as a boy. While she was mounting, he replied, "Probably for the same reasons you did and why you stay in this job: to make sure the right people are captured and punished for crimes; to protect people too weak, helpless, or unskilled to defend themselves. To be able to have the exciting existence I do without breaking laws myself," he added and chuckled to let her know he had relaxed. "Let's get riding, woman, if we want to make Benson by late afternoon."

Beth didn't allow his humor to dupe her about his mood. Yet, his other statements surprised and pleased her.

The road to Benson was an easy ride. She wondered about their leisurely pace as she didn't quite believe his explanation about protecting their ruse in case they were checked on later or followed today. For their partnership to work smoothly and for them to succeed with their assignment, he had to learn to trust her, to have faith in her capabilities, and to let her discover how to function with him as one person in the face of peril. The only way she could accomplish those goals was to do the same with him. As she thought of their impending destination and how they'd pass the long night, it seemed odd that he'd made it necessary for them to share a snug and suggestive space in a hotel. If they camped in the open, they wouldn't have to try to fool anyone. They could use the excuse, if questioned later, of saving money for ranch expenses. Why subject himself to being confined with her and having to use the newlywed ruse in public?

In Benson, Navarro checked them into a nice hotel without telling Beth why they didn't camp on open terrain. He wanted to make the trip as easy on her for as long as possible. He wanted to give her sufficient time to adjust to trail life, to get used to being in the saddle all day. It also gave them a chance to practice their deceit, which they needed, because soon they would be heading across country and they couldn't continue to behave as strangers.

At the restaurant, she queried him about ranching. She knew the conversation would not be suspicious to any eavesdroppers, and it would reveal what he had done on the Lane and other ranches. She'd never stayed on one, so she didn't want to reach their destination in total ignorance.

While awaiting service and between bites, Navarro related facts about roundups—in spring for branding and in fall for cattle drives and sales. He talked about the breaking in of wild horses, chores on the range in all kinds of weather, life in a bunkhouse, routine repairs, and other

daily or seasonal tasks. As Beth listened, she looked almost too enthralled and stimulated to eat. Her large eyes stayed on him, as did her
full attention. Her cheeks pinkened and her body seemed on alert. He
went on to tell her about rustlers, fence cuttings, renegades, droughts,
floods, fires, and diseases: what made failures and successes on a ranch.
"I've seen and handled them all, my love, but don't worry that pretty
head about us having bad luck."

"My love"? Really getting into this act, eh? "It sounds so exciting. I can
hardly wait to do all those things on our ranch. I have so much to learn,
but I have a smart and patient husband to teach me. I want to be a part
of everything."

"You will, my love. It's a good life, but it can be hard and demanding
when nature or outlaws give you problems. It's said that ranching either
makes or breaks a man."

"Nothing could make you any stronger or braver or defeat you."

"You're biased, my pretty wife."

"Naturally. Aren't you?"

"Naturally."

"It sounds like the best place to bring up our children after we have
them. Just think, my husband, sons working beside you and daughters
with me, or all of us together. What a beautiful and perfect dream. I'm
going to love ranching and be the best rancher's wife possible."

Navarro didn't doubt that last sentence was true, if she were given the
real opportunity. He was glad when the server left their table so Beth
could stop creating such disturbing images of something he would never
have with Jessie and Lane, the place in their lives Matt had taken. He
went to work on his cobbler and steaming coffee with hopes she'd take
his clue and keep silent for a while.

Beth had learned to recognize when he gave the unspoken order to
be quiet or change the subject, as he was doing now. Did his anguish and
resentment come from a bad childhood or an ill-fated romantic experience, or both? She wished she knew, but dared not ask—not yet. One
point was undeniable, he loved ranching.

Navarro sensed she'd picked up on his mute command. His tales
about ranch life had clearly caught her interest, no doubt in the same
manner Steven's agent stories had done long ago. Her shiny eyes must
have sparkled as they were doing now. Her heart must have raced with
stirring emotions, as the pulse point in her throat indicated. Her keen
mind must have filled with ideas and goals. From what he had observed
and been told about her, she would make a fine rancher's wife. Though
she and Jessie possessed some similar traits and qualities, the two

women looked and behaved nothing alike. That suited him, because it wouldn't allow him to confuse his love and his "wife."

After his cup was refilled, he asked, "What's that dreamy look about?"

Beth wasn't totally rousted from her reverie when she answered, "Ranch life. I've never thought about it or about settling on one until we were reunited and you swept me off my feet and married me. With so much to do and so many stimulating tasks involved, it sounds like the perfect setting for me one day."

"That day isn't far off, my lovely wife," he covered her minor slip.

She cleared her wits, smiled, and nodded. "Even a week can seem like forever when you're waiting to capture your dream."

"After we reach home, woman, you'll be too busy to dream."

"It won't be necessary anymore because the best one came true the day I met you. We'll make good friends there and do good work together. We have such a wonderful adventure ahead, my husband."

"I'll make certain we do those things. Our destination is important to me. We can't fail, my beautiful partner—too much of the future is at stake."

"Yes, it is, my love. Why don't we stroll to settle our meal?"

He stood without delay. "Let's go, wife. Fresh air and movement are just what we need before bedtime."

You're right, Navarro, they'll give me release from your many charms.

Once they were in their room, Beth hoped to ease the slight strain between them by chatting. "Next time you marry, Navarro, it will be a beautiful and special occasion. The pastor condensed our vows into near nonexistence and he handled the ceremony as if it were a business meeting that had to be over in three minutes. I know he said he'd be rushed, but I expected to receive more time and effort than he gave us. Something a tiny bit nicer for our friends and witnesses to share."

"More romantic? Pretty trappings? Don't worry, it was convincing."

"Trappings," she echoed with mirth. "That's an appropriate word choice for a loner set against the bond of wedlock to use."

"I'm not against marriage."

She glanced at him with open skepticism. "For other people."

"For anybody, everybody, if the right mate rides along."

"So, there is hope for Navarro Breed after all."

He warmed to the sound of her musical laughter and sunny smile. "About as much as there is for Beth . . . Wind."

"We're a fine pair to be playing a husband and wife: two loners so down on marriage we're scared stiff faking one. We're going to require barrels of practice to relax enough to fool friends who know you well."

"You're right, partner, but not now. We need to turn in. We have another long ride tomorrow, so you need your rest more than lessons."

"First, I'm taking a bath to remove this trail dust, if the water closet is unoccupied at this hour." When he grinned, she shrugged and said, "One should never waste a chance to indulge oneself, right? Be glad, partner, because pretty soon, I may be a dirty, smelly mess you'll have to endure."

As Beth left the location, a young cowboy accosted her. He blocked her departure and looked her over with an insulting gleam in his eyes.

"Whatda we have here? If yo're done in there, you kin clean my room and clean me out, too."

Beth shoved away the hand about to touch her breast. "I don't work here, mister. I'm a guest. If you'll step aside, I'll—"

"Guest?" He laughed. "If you sally to my room to have a drink and some words, I won't tell yore boss you wuz bad to me. Old man Johnson don't take to losin' money 'cause his workers don't give customers what they wants and needs. You don't wanna go alosin' yore job when he gits mad."

"You've made a mistake; I don't work here. Even if I did, your words and behavior are rude and offensive." Beth saw how he looked at the colorful peasant garb she had donned for the short walk.

"Guests don't look like you, so don't play no game with me, *señorita."*

"I'm married; my husband is waiting for me. Out of my way, cur."

"Whew, look at them little fires jumpin' outta them green eyes and flamin' on them cheeks. Good, 'cause I likes my women hot."

"This won't be hot or ever work again if you don't back off," Beth warned as she pressed a sharp dagger against his aroused groin.

The cowpoke glanced downward, grinned, and refuted, "You ain't gonna use that little pick on my big one. Behave or I might git real mad."

"Is there a problem, love?"

She glanced past the cocky stranger to see Navarro approaching the scene. Her chilled and narrowed gaze returned to the troublemaker. "Is there?" she asked him in visible contempt.

"Me and this pretty *señorita* wuz about to take a ride in my room."

"Only in your dreams, you foul beast."

"You chose the wrong woman to ask; she's my wife."

The stranger looked Beth over, fooled by her Mexican garments. He knew that maids at the hotel gave extra services when requested, and now some man was trying to steal his choice. "Don't say?"

"I do say," Navarro replied, anger kindling within him. "Beth, go back to our room. I'll be there in a minute."

The stranger half-turned to study his rival, still blocking any escape path for the girl he wanted. "What if I don't take yore word on it, mister? What if you jest want 'er for yoreself?"

As he talked, Navarro studied the intruder. The ex-gunslinger knew what the man's dilemma was: backing down could make him look and feel like a coward. The only way to prevent a lethal showdown was to let the snake save face. "Nobody's witnessed our disagreement, so your reputation won't suffer if you leave and let it pass. *Now.* Look at her left hand," he suggested, and Beth lifted and held it before the stranger's wide gaze. "See, she's married. To me. No harm's been done *yet,* so let it go, stranger. If that doesn't suit you, let's find privacy away from my wife to discuss it any way you choose."

Beth and the stranger noticed Navarro's stance was that of a skilled gunman. Neither missed the icy tone of his voice nor the words he stressed, nor doubted he would defend her to the death.

In a mellower tone, the Special Agent said, "I'm sure a fine-looking gent like you can find a woman who doesn't already have a man. Why don't you try Peggy's Parlor down the street? She has some lovely gals who'll be happy to spend time with you, but this one belongs to me."

"Sure, mister. See you around."

"We'll be gone tomorrow. This incident didn't happen, remember?"

"Sure."

Beth watched her accoster leave as fast as possible without breaking into a run. "He didn't take my warning seriously," she muttered as she concealed her blade and followed the well-armed Navarro to their room. She saw him lock the door and prop a chair under the knob.

"He was too captured by your beauty to see the deadly gleam in your eye."

"Thanks for the compliment and rescue, but I'm still angry. I'm sorry you thought it was necessary to come to my aid. I just wish men like that wouldn't force a woman to get riled or to harm them before they'll back off. He didn't have a problem taking your threat to heart. He ran like a scared rabbit with a hawk circling overhead."

"I'm bigger and meaner looking, and he wasn't really in the mood to challenge me when there are available women down the street."

Beth laid her possessions on the bed to fold and put away. "I pity them having to oblige customers like that. I don't know why so many men refuse to take no for an answer. Too many think they can cajole or frighten a female into changing her mind. If a woman is polite, nice, or helpful, too many men misunderstand. I can tell when a male isn't interested in me, when he's only being kind and friendly and courteous. Why is that so difficult for a man to do?"

"Can't answer, 'cause I don't know. 'Course, reading some people is about as impossible as trying to read a foreign tongue you haven't learned."

Her questions had been more like statements, but he had answered. Intrigued, she asked, "Do you have trouble picking up on a woman's clues?"

You wanna make sure I catch yours and leave you alone? Don't want a low-bred man like me touching you? Afraid I'll have to do it in the line of duty so you'll just have to suffer through those times or get off this case. "I understand what no means and I honor it. If a woman speaks it and doesn't mean it, she's defeated herself 'cause I accept what she says."

"Even if her actions and mood say yes? Or you think they do?"

"I go by what a person says, truth or not."

"But—"

"I'm not in those situations, so I'm not the one to question and study."

He's telling you to shut up Beth. "Sorry, partner, I got carried away again. You have a way of doing that to me. I suppose it's because you're so fascinating and intelligent. You've been so many places and done so many exciting and dangerous things. I'm going to learn a lot from you, partner, and become a far better agent than before we met."

"Thanks for the kind words and faith in me. The same may be true of you; I just might learn some stuff I don't know. We'll see."

"I hope you profit from teaming up with me, Navarro."

He took a position near the front window to make certain the young stranger didn't return to the hotel. His left side was propped against the wall, with arms folded over his chest. One booted ankle crossed the other. His head was cocked downward so he could steal quick and furtive looks outside without worrying her. He hoped the man wouldn't return because it was possible he had friends or brothers who wouldn't take kindly to his death, even in a fair gunfight. That was how he'd met Jessie ten years ago in that San Angelo saloon. One of the Adams brothers had attacked her when she was seeking a gunslinger to help thwart Wilbur Fletcher. He had rescued her, then had to battle vengeful kin to escape. He couldn't afford to attract attention to himself today.

Navarro dragged his mind from the past. "If you don't settle down and forget that bastard, you'll never get to sleep. I would've licked him for insulting and scaring you, but I figured we shouldn't call that much attention to us, unless he gave me no choice. If you feel different, tell me and I'll go find him and punish him like he deserves." *He's in the saloon, maybe summoning courage from a bottle to return and challenge me.*

Beth struggled not to look—or even glance—at her companion. He was far too seductive in their seclusion. "That's a generous and touching offer, but no thanks. It took more courage for you to walk around that trouble rather than storming headlong into it. No one should take another's life lightly, even a suspected criminal's; that's for the law to do. I'm not disappointed or hurt because you handled it peacefully. Besides, you forced him to back down and suffer humiliation, gave him a sour taste of what he puts women through; that's sufficient for me. You're a very clever talker, my friend. Without you having to back up your words with actions, I know you could have done so with ease and speed and victory."

"Thanks for the praise and confidence in me."

"You earned them; no flattery intended. I just dislike bullies. But he wouldn't have gotten any further with me, even if you hadn't been around to help. I would have used that knife on him before he had time to harm me. It just riles me to let him stroll away because he'll do it again, probably to a female who can't protect herself or who isn't allowed to say no to any kind of beast, like those unfortunate souls in that slavery brothel."

"If it's still eating at you this much, I'll go find him and teach him a lesson about how to treat ladies."

"No, really. I'm fine, and we can't afford any undue focus on us. We should turn in. Why don't you take the bed? I had one last night."

"I'm more used to bedrolls, so one fits me better than it does you."

"Fine with me, boss. Would you please turn around so I can change? Pull down the shade, too, unless you need to continue your lookout."

Navarro chuckled and complied. But the rustling sounds she made as she undressed were disturbingly erotic. Beth Wind was the first female he'd wanted like this since Jessie, and that rankled. It wasn't good for him to desire her this much so early in their relationship, or at all. If she—

"Finished. I'll slip into bed and turn the other way to give you privacy."

After he faced forward, he watched her fold the Mexican garments and unmentionables and put them away. She was clad in a green nightgown, without a robe. He thanked the spirits it was too thick and dark to see through, or his hunger and discomfort might heighten. She tossed aside the coverlet and top sheet, eased onto the feather mattress, and pulled the covers to her shoulders. "Ready," he heard her say after placing her back to him. He gazed at her shapely curves. His wayward attention lingered on her black hair for a moment; he was grateful it wasn't red. That plus her name might send him running from evil spirits who'd be playing tricks on him!

He yanked off his boots and garments. He wriggled into his bedroll and settled himself into a relaxing position, his weapons within easy reach. Wed two days and sleeping alone, his troubled mind taunted. Not what he'd expected marriage would be like, but this wasn't a real marriage. Even if he'd wed the woman nearby as Bethany Wind instead of Elizabeth Lawrence, the situation would be the same. He resolved that was how it was, how it should be, and how it would stay.

Beth received a shock the next morning while Navarro was saddling and loading their horses. She was bringing down the last of her things when the stranger who had waylaid her last night met her in the hallway. She came to instant alert, ready to drop her possessions to draw a weapon. She saw him look her over in a polite manner and, from the way she was dressed and his penitent expression, convince himself she was a lady.

"I'm glad you ain't gone, ma'am. I wanted to say I'm sorry for treatin' you so bad. My girl just sent me ridin' and I wuz hurtin' bad. It festered in me all day till I wuz about loco. I figgered another woman and some heavy drinkin' would make me forget her. I wuz spoilin' for a fight, but I ain't like that most days. I'm mighty glad yore huzbend talked me outta one and didn't kill me over a stupid mistake. Jest wanted you to hear I'm mighty sorry and ashamed and I won't be doin' nothin' like that agin."

"That sounds good and I hope you mean it, because if you ever do, the man you offend might not be as nice and slow-tempered as my husband. A word of advice: If you treated your sweetheart as you did me, maybe that's why she left you. A man has to be kind and respectful to his woman." The way he hung his head in remorse told her he was being sincere and honest; she was glad.

"I understand, ma'am, and I'll be good."

"If you want a wife one day and want to stay alive and well, I hope so."

"Thank you, ma'am. I'll be takin' them smart words to heart."

Beth descended the stairs and met Navarro outside. After her things were in place and she mounted, she saw the young man on the hotel porch. He was smiling; he appeared relieved, and looked his young age of eighteen.

"So long, ma'am, and thanks. You, too, mister."

As the youthful stranger headed down the planked walk and paused once to wave at her, Navarro asked, "What was that about, woman?"

"Gratitude and contrition." She related the episode to him and watched his quizzical expression change to one of amazement and respect.

"I'll be damned. Life's loco sometimes." He wondered if she won over everybody she met.

"Goes to show unrequited love can make a normally level-headed man unpredictable and dangerous. Aren't you glad you won't ever suffer from that condition?" She rode off before he could respond.

They journeyed northeast at a steady pace, crossed the San Pedro River, and headed toward pointed peaks called the Narrows. For a time, they would travel between the Sonoran and Chihuahuan deserts. The terrain was a mixture of open spaces, distant mountains, rolling hills, and a bushy landscape that displayed a supply of yuccas and cacti, particularly prickly pear that often spread out to cover spaces of three to five feet. Mesquites became fewer and fewer and other trees replaced them in most areas. Outcroppings of reddish boulders appeared on both sides of the road, part of the Little Dragoon Mountains. Between piles of various-size ones and huge solitary ones were mini-canyons, washes, and ravines with grass and an occasional seep. Other mountains appeared close enough to reach in a few minutes but they were over twenty miles away.

Both agents stayed on alert while traversing the rock-enclosed location that was perfect for enemy concealment and ambushes. Soon, they heard gunfire, pounding horses' hooves, and the rumbling of a fast-moving stage; and they knew what was taking place out of sight.

Navarro reined in and shouted to her, "Take cover while I help!"

"Don't be silly; I'm a trained agent, a good shooter. Let's go!"

"Listen to me, woman, it's too dan— Beth Breed, halt!"

Hearing that name and recalling he was in charge of their team, she stopped and waited for him. "Sorry, boss, I forgot myself again. I'm used to responding fast and without thinking twice. It sounds like enough villains for two lawmen to handle. You might need my help; they might need it."

"All right, let's take cover, let 'em go by, then attack from the rear. That'll give us the advantage of facing forward and sun to our backs. Get ready. They'll be coming around that bend and over that rise any minute."

The agents weaved their way between and behind boulders to prevent being seen. The sound of numerous gunshots rent the air. As the stage thundered past them, they saw the driver urging wild-eyed horses to a breakneck speed to outrun the gang in pursuit. A whip sang over the animals' heads to encourage them to do their best but it never touched their hides. The coach groaned and creaked as it bounced up and down on its wheel base. If the trunks and cases had not been properly secured, they would have been flung in all directions. They heard the driver yelling to his team before the stage rounded another bend. So far, both driver and guard were still alive and unharmed. As soon as the five men galloped past their hiding place, Navarro signaled for Beth to ride.

On a straightaway, the agents saw the gang closing in on its target. With revolvers blazing, they caught the criminals' attention, as well as that of the stage occupants. The "shotgun" and a passenger ceased firing to avoid hitting their help with stray bullets. The outlaws dropped their original focus to respond to this new threat; they twisted sideways to return the gunfire thwarting their intention. One was struck in the shoulder and another in the back; both toppled to the hard ground, wind knocked from their lungs. As a third robber shifted in his saddle to defend his vulnerable flank, he took a bullet in the arm but managed to stay seated. A fourth man broke off his attack and tried to vanish into the boulders, but Beth grazed his head and sent him falling onto a large rock. Navarro shot the third man again in his other arm before he could get his pistol aimed, evoking a yelp of pain and thud on the road. The fifth bandit had nowhere to escape with the rifle-pointing guard in front of and the two skilled intruders behind him. He lifted his pistol to signal surrender, then halted his horse.

The driver reined in his lathered and wheezing team and the coach stopped. The first outlaw to get hit fired two shots from his position on the road behind the rescuers; Navarro whirled in his saddle and handled the peril in a fluid motion. While the "shotgun" stood guard and Beth remained where she was, Navarro and the passenger gathered the defeated gang. Three were injured; their wounds were bound with their bandanas. The unharmed bandit was tied up with his own rope. The dead man was secured to his saddle. The reins of five horses were knotted to the stage's rear. After thanking the couple over and over, the driver flicked his whip in the air and continued toward Benson with his unexpected load.

Navarro trotted to where Beth had been hanging back from the noisy and bloody scene. She looked calm, he observed, but the event had chilled her because she'd put on her jacket. He smiled and said, "Dan was right about your skills and courage. You haven't complained, slowed us down, or given me any trouble. Seems I underestimated you, Bethany Wind."

She smiled in pleasure. "Maybe that's because you haven't given me anything to whine about, and a child could keep up with the gentle pace you've set for my benefit. It may not be wise to tell me I'm wonderful or it might go to my head," she jested. "I figured I should get back into my 'lady role' and let it appear you did all the work."

As he reloaded his weapons to be prepared for any new trouble, he said, "Anyone with eyes could see that wasn't true. Speaking of work, when we halt at noon to eat, it's your turn to do the chores. I don't want you to think I'm being too easy because you're a woman. We'll need to hurry because we're covering more miles today and we've been delayed. The reason we'll be a little slow is because we don't want to reach the ranch too far ahead of Charles and have no excuse to hang around until he does. Dan'll keep me alerted at check-in locations about that snake's movements and schedule. I'm also traveling this pace to give us time to get better acquainted and become more at ease with each other. We need to have our story straight and familiar so we won't make any slips."

Having reloaded her pistol, she said, "Thanks for enlightening me. But why was there such a rush with our romance and wedding?"

"Having lots of time in private was Dan's idea. Knowing what loners we both are, I guess he figured we needed it to be convincing later."

They exchanged matching looks of skepticism at their superior's alleged motive, yet, neither spoke their suspicion aloud.

"Let's get moving; we have lost time to make up."

Beth knew the rapid moving stage was a good distance away. "If you don't mind, I'll . . . excuse myself before we ride out again." She didn't wait for him to respond before guiding her mare into a sheltered ravine, because she had a big problem to tend fast and in secret.

Chapter Seven

Beth dismounted, yanked off her jacket, and removed her torn shirt. She checked a laceration in her upper arm; soon, blood would be dripping off her fingers. The reasons the scarlet liquid hadn't saturated her jacket and exposed her wound were because of a loose sleeve, the intervention of her shirt, and the fact that she'd held her arm downward. Her jacket had hidden the problem, but not for long. She had to bind the wound and rejoin her partner before he realized something was amiss and his opinion of her lowered again.

In a rush, she grabbed a clean cloth from her saddlebag and removed the top of her canteen. She soaked the rag to begin ministrations but was interrupted.

"Blazes, woman, you're shot! I knew something was wrong by the way you looked and acted. Why didn't you tell me?"

"Because I knew what you'd think and say: that I'm careless and unskilled, and you'd praised me too fast. I wanted to at least hide it long enough for you think about how well I'd done, allow the positive to settle in before you discovered the negative. Besides, it's only a scratch, a flesh wound, nothing to get excited about. It's not my first and probably not my last in our kind of work."

"Let me see it." He took her arm in a gentle grasp and eyed the injury, which she had assessed with accuracy. He had expected to find her crying in a hanky or sick to her stomach and in need of soothing herbs, not wounded.

"It was that first man to go down, the last one you shot in the road behind us. He was lying so still when we rode past, I thought he was out cold. I shouldn't have turned my back on him without checking. He wasn't that good of an aim, just a lucky shot. It hurts, but it's not a bad injury."

He couldn't fault her for being careless about the downed man when he'd done the same thing. "It needs tending. Let me fetch my things."

Beth started to reach for the shirt she had discarded to hold before her chemise-clad chest but realized she was as covered as she had been while working in the Red Palace. She watched him return to squat beside where she'd taken a seat on a low rock. "What's that?"

"An Indian medicine pouch and a bandage." He didn't tell her to sit still because he somehow knew she would. He used water from her canteen to wash away the blood, then tended the narrow gash with herbs.

As he worked, Beth was aware he was being gentle and thorough. She also noticed how he refused to look at her face. He seemed nervous about touching her, so she should have covered her torso; to do so now seemed silly. As he doctored the injury and dressed it with a clean cloth, she observed him with keen intensity. He wasn't the only one aroused by this closeness between them. Just imagining playing his wife heightened her desire for him. She wanted to run her fingers through that midnight mane, across his bronzed chest. She longed to gaze into his deep-set eyes without hesitation, or fear of any repercussions. He was a potent force and she was being drawn to him.

Navarro was impressed she didn't so much as flinch as he tended her. When he risked a glance, he expected to find her brow furrowed and her teeth clenched; instead, she was watching him in a strange manner. With haste, he yanked his eyes from hers before he lost himself in those swirling depths. To distract them, he asked, "Did Steven ever get you wounded like I did today?"

"This wasn't your fault."

"As much mine as yours, so don't argue. Did he?"

"No. But he took a bullet a few times because my overly protective husband gave those same orders you did about taking cover and letting him handle the trouble. I tried to convince him it was foolish to take those risks when I was a trained and capable partner." As he leaned back on his haunches, she urged, "Please don't do the same thing, Navarro; a team should stick together in all situations. Besides, accidents will happen on occasion because we're in dangerous work."

"You're not over him, are you?"

That question caught her off guard. She stared at him as he held on to her captive gaze. "I still think about him, miss him, and love him; that's only natural. He was my husband and partner for six years. He was also my best friend. I was struck with three losses at once, four counting my father. We did everything together. It was like losing half of myself. At first, I was angry, bitter, sad, even depressed. I felt as if my future had been stolen, my dreams destroyed." *Does that sound and feel familiar to you? Do we have something in common?*

"It's easier now. My job helped me get through the worst period afterward, kept my mind and energies focused elsewhere. After he and Papa were murdered, I felt challenged to get rid of as many criminals as possible so other innocent people wouldn't have to go through what I had. The man responsible for their deaths is still alive, though, free and happy somewhere. Maybe he's killed others before or since my family and ruined their lives, too. It riles me to be unable to do anything about him."

"Maybe he'll be caught and punished one day. Maybe he's dead now. Men who live and work as he does don't last long."

"I hope he meets with justice soon. Those beasts didn't even try to bluff their way out of the situation. For all they knew, the two men riding into their campsite were drifters. They just gunned them down without waiting to see who they were or if they'd been exposed."

"So you had a good marriage but don't want to repeat the experience?"

It was another startling query. Why did he want such private information? Was he aiming for a clearer image of her or was there more to his curiosity? *If you want to know if I'm man-hunting or Navarro-hunting, ask me straight out.* "As you said, I don't remain in a place long enough to find a man who suits me."

"Maybe you will some day when you get tired of this kind of life."

"Maybe, but I doubt it. By the time a woman is my age, the best men are either attached to someone or not interested in marriage. The rest either have unbroken ties to their pasts or dark reasons why no woman wants them." She looked away before adding, "If you're done, we'd better get riding."

"You should rest a while."

"I'm fine, honestly. In case you haven't noticed, I usually speak my mind, so trust what I say."

"If you have trouble along the way, tell me. I want that gun arm healed in case it's needed again." He stood, as did she. "You've proven yourself to me, Beth, so relax and stop trying so hard. No more secrets like this one, all right?"

"Agreed. Sorry. I just doubted you'd be so understanding. I was afraid this would convince you to dump me in the next town."

"Stop worrying. This job is yours; you have my word."

She laughed and quipped, "If memory serves me today, you once said you never go back on your word unless you have a good reason."

"So far, you haven't given me any reason to break up our partnership. Fact is, you've proven to me Dan made a good choice."

"Thank you. I'm glad to hear that. Tell me, why did you strap your pistol and holster on the right side in Tucson and Benson, and why do you wear only one in towns? I've noticed you use two on the trail, and tie them to your legs, and you're definitely left-handed."

He stared at her for a moment, then grinned. "You have keen eyes. I wear only one and don't secure it to keep from looking like a gunslinger eager for a showdown. I'm also good with my right hand, but I do it so any challenger who follows me for an attack or call-out will be fooled into watching the wrong hand. On the trail, I stay ready for trouble."

"That's a cunning trick, partner, one I'll remember and use."

"Thanks."

"I'm fine, so let's ride."

Soon, they left the well-traveled road and headed overland in an eastward direction. They traveled past Dragoon and the trail to the old stronghold used by Cochise when he ruled and terrorized this area. It wasn't long before Navarro halted them so they could eat and rest and he could check her arm.

She was appreciative of his concern. "See, I told you it's nothing much."

He placed more herbs on it as he replied, "I want to keep it that way."

They crossed the southern tip of a playa below Willcox. The vast, dry alkali sink was windswept and lacked any greenery to soften its harsh barrenness. Even without shallow liquid after heavy rains, the lake bed created shimmering mirages, illusions of deep and refreshing water. Both agents were glad to traverse only a narrow section and to get beyond it.

As they rode south of Dos Cabezas, Navarro pointed out bald knolls in a mountain range that gave the town its name that meant two heads. He told her it was a region rich in gold and silver and a precious watering hole for cattle.

Upon reaching Apache Pass, a six mile twisting and winding passage between two valleys, Navarro related that local Indians had allowed a twice-weekly stage to go through years ago until conflicts escalated into war. Since then, railroads had built lines northward and coaxed most of the traffic to that location. He said their destination was fourteen miles from the other end of the pass: Bowie Station, a town north of the fort where missions against renegades were initiated.

Beth guided Sunshine up the steep and narrow trail behind Navarro and Night Cloud. Grasslands and vegetation intermingled with agave, piñon, juniper, sagebrush, ironwood, mesquite, and varieties of cacti and flowers. Oak, hackberry, willow, black walnut, cottonwood, and other trees appeared and seemed to decorate the Chiricahua range. The rugged mountains were snaked with sandy washes, arroyos, and canyons; they displayed rocky slopes and picturesque spires and peaks.

Near the trail's summit, they halted to rest themselves and the animals before heading downward toward the scrubland around the fort. Navarro let his black stallion drink water poured from a canteen into his hand, so Beth did the same. Afterward, she strolled to loosen tired and sore muscles. She peered at the untamed panorama before her. When Navarro joined her and did the same, she began a conversation.

"You've told me just bits and pieces about yourself; so, who is Navarro Breed? What do you want in life? What's important to you?"

He glanced at her in surprise. "Doing my job the best I can."

Beth waited for him to continue, but it didn't seem as if he intended to say more. Those deep-set hazel eyes had a haunted look that tugged at her heart. He was so tough, hard, and driven, so private. Yet, he could be gentle and tender when it suited him or his emotions were touched. Beth sat on a rock a few feet high. She placed her palms on it behind her and leaned her head back to feel warm sun on her face.

Navarro reasoned that if she was becoming too attracted to him, what he had to tell should halt any unbidden feelings. "There's something you should know about me. It might change your mind about wanting to travel and work with me."

Beth eyed him. He looked and sounded serious and uneasy. When he remained silent and gazed over the terrain, she prompted, "What is it?"

Navarro looked her in the eyes and said, "I'm what people call a half-breed bastard. My mother was Apache and my father was white; they were never married."

"I see," she murmured, feeling an ache in her heart at his tone of anguish and bitterness. She waited for him to continue.

He went to stand behind her and lean his right hip against the boulder where a section rose higher than the part upon which she sat. He tucked his left thumb into his pants' pocket and curled his fingers into his palm. He searched for the right words. Now that he had begun, he hated to stain his "legendary" image in her eyes. But he had no choice except to get it into the open because he didn't want her repelled later if someone else told her. He also wanted to build an obstacle between them to keep her at a safe distance.

Beth felt his body make light contact with hers. It was as if he'd taken a position where she couldn't look at him while he finished his confession, as if he couldn't gaze at her while making it. "Is that all you're going to say?"

"Nope, you should hear the dirty story from me so you won't be shocked if someone drops words about it later. Until I was certain you'd be riding, living, and working with me for a long time, I didn't see a need to tell you anything about me. Now that you've proved yourself, I have to give you a chance to see if the truth makes any difference to you. If it does, speak up today and we'll part at Bowie Station."

Is that really why you've been secretive and evasive? At least I'm off the firing hook. "Break up our team before a crucial mission? Never. That you are illegitimate and half Indian doesn't matter to me."

"Most women—particularly ladies—don't want to get near either one, and I'm both. We'll have to kiss, hug, and touch during our act at the ranch; think you'll be able to abide it?"

"There's nothing to endure, Navarro. And there's nothing for you to be ashamed of; no one has control over his birth, only over his actions afterward. People who treat you as if you're dirt aren't worth knowing. Don't let anyone rip at your pride or hurt your feelings or embarrass you. Don't let their prejudices and cruelties put a chip on your shoulder or hardness in your heart; if you do, you'll be harmed, not them. I realize that advice is easier for me to give than for you to accept, but I hope you will take it."

"You don't seem surprised by this news. Why is that?"

"I'm not; I've picked up your clues along the way, whether you meant to send them out or not. To me, you're a man, my partner, my friend, my leader. What you said about your birth changes nothing between us."

"Does that mean you will carry out your part of the ruse?"

Do you need clarity and reassurance? "Yes, without any hesitation, honest. Half-breed and bastard are only words, vicious and evil words; they don't alter my opinion of you, which is a good one. Didn't I tell you what an honor and privilege it is to work with you? It's true."

He reasoned, either she was dedicated and determined to carry out her orders no matter what, or she was being honest and compassionate. He decided she was all four. "I'm far from perfect like your Steven was."

"My husband wasn't perfect, and I didn't mean to imply that he was. Steven was a good man and a skilled agent, but so are you. He was the best I've known, but he wasn't without human flaws and weaknesses. Please don't think I compare you unfavorably to him in words or thoughts, as a man and a partner. In fact, if any man or agent can outshine Steven, it's Navarro Breed." *Whoa, Beth, bridle that tongue and don't give away your secrets!*

Pride and elation made Navarro's heart run fast. "I love my work and do it better than most. That's no brag; the records prove my claim. But I wasn't always a good man, Beth, and I may not be one now."

Beth felt him shift his weight and lean closer to her, his chest touching her back and left arm. She did not move away, in case he was testing to see if she had an aversion to him. "Confidence and honesty aren't the same as arrogance and boasting, partner. I know you have the first two traits, not the last two; and those are the ones needed in our work. But don't live under the impression you aren't a good man, because you are. Does it bother you that much you don't have your father's name?"

"I do use my father's name."

She leaned against him as she said, "Well, you have a right to it. That's what I'd do, unless there's a reason you wouldn't want to use it. In view of the problems between Indians and whites, using your mother's could make unnecessary trouble for you. I think you made a wise choice. How did your parents meet, if that isn't being nosy? Were the problems between Indians and whites why they didn't marry?"

"My mother worked at a fort washing clothes and cooking for soldiers. Some of those Bluecoats are the lowest and meanest men bred; others were hardened by the war and losses twenty years past. Fighting, killing, and hating are all they know."

As he spoke of his mother, she listened closely and caught a softness and undeniable love in his tone that pleased and warmed her.

"Morning Tears, that's my mother's name, was young and beautiful and innocent; small and gentle. But she wasn't smart in some ways. Her family wanted the money soldiers paid for chores, so they forced her to keep returning there even when she had problems with them. The winters were cold and long, so supplies were needed to survive it; most raiding was halted or hindered by those same Bluecoats she slaved for. It didn't seem to matter to her family and people that she was being insulted and groped at by those crude bastards."

It sounded to her as if he was pushing the tormenting words through gritted teeth. "That's terrible, Navarro; it must have been awful for her."

"She was an obedient child, so she did as her family ordered; it was their way not to be defiant to parents and the tribe. When several of those snakes tried to crawl over her, Carl Breed supposedly rescued her by killing them. Nobody at the fort ever knew who did those murders. He tricked her into feelings of gratitude, so she became his squaw. He'd been nice to her when she'd done chores for him—I'm sure on the sly—to get her on a blanket when he could sneak away from the fort. In her eyes, he was a great and fearless warrior because he killed his own kind to save her. She thought she loved him, and maybe she did. Who can explain that crazy feeling? She made a wickiup close by for them to share. Her family and tribe ordered her to keep away from him and return home but she refused; she chose Carl over them, so she was dishonored and banished. Things could have been fine for them, except Carl was worse than those bastards who attacked her. He'd been watching her for a long time and wanted her, but not because he loved her; Carl Breed loved nobody except himself. He was mean and low, and that's no lie."

In the heavy silence that ensued, she coaxed in a gentle tone, "After she had you, he still didn't change?"

"From the time I was born till I was six, we lived on the road between odd jobs he'd do, existing as a family of worthless drifters. Sometimes we hung around dirty and wild towns near forts while he drank and gambled with his friends, using money my mother earned from sweat and tears."

His last few words sounded so cold and bitter that they chilled her to the bone. "That's no way for a child to survive; I'm sorry."

"Our lives, Mother's and mine, seemed to get better for a while when I was seven. For some reason I never learned, Carl bought—or maybe he won—a sutler store at Fort Craig. That was a pretty good time for me. We had a house, but not a real home. I had food, clean clothes, and safety from road perils. That's when I got to attend school; books and learning became my hunger and escape. I chewed into every one I got my hands on but there were never enough to fill me. The old schoolmarm was so happy to find somebody like me, she taught me extra stuff and loaned me books from her house. She was kind, giving, and honest, a real lady. I think I loved that old woman."

Beth heard the affection in his tone. "So, you were an excellent student and made all the best marks of the class, right?"

"Yep, but the other children were taught to be cruel to Indians. Half-breeds are considered even lower than Indians. Even if my looks hadn't told them what I was, seeing my mother with me said it loud and clear. They called me names kids shouldn't even know, pulled tricks on me their papas had suggested, and wouldn't let me play with them. They even gave the teacher problems because she was so good to me."

"I can't imagine why parents would teach children such wicked things. I would never do that. Hatred and bias are terrible evils. I'm sure those must have been difficult times for you to understand and accept."

"Yep, but I took advantage of that breather from trail life and shut out what anybody said or did to me. I pretended I had a hide as tough as an armadillo's. I learned all I could about the white man's world, and I learned fast. I figured getting head-smart would help me escape my father and his kind of existence." His gaze settled on her shiny black hair and he wanted to stroke it. "I don't know why he kept us, unless it was because we belonged to him and he needed us to slave for him and his friends. I couldn't grasp why Mother wouldn't leave him and return to her people. Even love can't survive some things. I kept hoping he'd ride off one day, leave us behind, and never return; or he'd get himself killed like his sorry kind often does."

"But none of those things happened?" she asked.

"Nope. The only reason I didn't run away was because I feared his revenge on my mother. I was the light of her eye, the spirit of her heart, her helper and joy: that's what she always told me."

To Beth, he didn't sound convinced of that last sentence. Her heart pained for all the things he had suffered for so long, while at such an impressionable age.

"We tended the horses, cooked meals, washed clothes, cleaned up after those bastards, and waited on them like captives, which is about what we were. The only good thing was, it taught me how to take care of myself. It also hardened me with those brutes picking on me most of the time. They loved calling me the 'Little Breed' and 'Half-Breed.' Carl didn't stop 'em; he thought it was funny, said it would give me backbone, make me tough like he was. Tough, he was a coward who preyed on the helpless. I never wanted to be like him, never. He was my father, and I hated him."

"That's understandable, Navarro, your father abused you and you watched your mother being abused by him. No one at any age wants to feel helpless and vulnerable. To be unable to fight back made it worse."

"At times, I thought I hated my mother for being so weak and a coward for letting that snake beat her child, her own blood. I couldn't understand why she endured everything he did and said to her and me. I'd never let anybody harm a child of mine. Things finally changed, but not for the better. Or maybe it was. Who knows?"

Beth felt him shrug and wondered what was coming forth next.

"After Mother had worked herself so hard and finally lost her beauty, Carl started sharing her with his friends and beating her even worse. He said she wasn't his wife or a white woman, and so he could treat a 'squaw' any way he pleased. None of the other men wanted to lay claim to her or take up for her; she was just . . . free release for them, the same kind of evil pleasure you mentioned about that slavery ring's customers.

I wanted to stick a knife in their backs every time they crawled on top of her."

Navarro seemed trapped in a temporary daze; he sounded and looked as if he couldn't halt the dark memories from attacking him or stop his agonizing words from spilling forth. Beth allowed his verbal purging.

"No man should force himself on a defenseless woman who doesn't want him. And he shouldn't threaten or beat her into submission. And no child should hear or watch his mother being raped countless times, 'cause that's what it was. Some nights when they got mean drunk, Carl or his boys roughed me up to scare her into doing whatever they ordered, and they came up with some wicked ideas when they were in those crazed moods. They'd joke and laugh as if they were just having harmless fun, like those saddletramps back at Manuel's cantina. I broke two fingers once when I jumped on Cato's back and started pounding him with my fists when he—"

All of a sudden, Navarro realized what he was saying. "Sorry, Beth, I didn't mean to sound crude or spill a wagonload of mud on you." *Shu, hombre, you didn't even tell Jessie or your two best friends such terrible secrets. Blazes, she has powerful magic to lower your guard this much!*

Beth sensed he was more shocked about revealing those dark episodes than he was about their dismaying content. "You didn't offend me, Navarro, and I'm glad you told me. I'm the one who's sorry, sorry you and your mother had to witness and endure such cruelties."

"Me, too. I was years older before I realized she was as scared of him as I was as a boy. When I was young, I thought she was crazy or weak to put up with his meanness. If I tried to defend her or get her to protect herself, it earned me another licking from Carl's belt—a wide, thick black one. He kept it just for that reason, 'cause it wouldn't go through his pants' loops. That bastard loved a good whipping better than a strong drink of high-grade whiskey or a crooked poker game."

"How could he be so cruel to his own son, a small boy?"

"He was bad, Beth, not a good inch about him. If it was winter and I got him mad, he'd lock me outside without food and cover. One time, I decided to ride for help, hoping a white sheriff would give it to a squaw and half-breed boy. I didn't get far before Carl's friends caught me and hauled me back to him across one's saddle. He tied me to a tree for three days; told me if I survived the wild animals, my punishment would be over for a while. He warned if I ran away again, it would be my mother staked out there for a week. He knew she was my weak spot, not the beatings, so he used her to get at me. I realized the only way I could escape was to take her with me. She wouldn't leave him, so I couldn't. I knew if I did, it would bring on her torture and death. Carl was that mean and evil."

Is that why you don't have a wife or sweetheart, so no enemy will have a weapon to use against you and you won't have to watch another loved one suffer? "Despite all of that, she loved him and stayed with him?"

"Yep. She believed she had no place to go 'cause she was dishonored. She was afraid she couldn't support us if we took off, or things would be worse in any job she might find. She'd had plenty of bad ones, that's for sure. And she was scared Carl would track us down and do worse than kill us. Strange as it seems, she loved him in a way I'll never understand. She kept saying things would get better one day."

Beth had a feeling he'd never told anyone such painful secrets. She didn't know why he'd chosen to share them with her today; maybe he had gotten ensnared in the past as she had with him on occasion. "Did they?"

"Nope. When I was twelve, Carl was the one who opened her eyes to the truth. He brought home a pretty *señorita* to enjoy for a while. He expected Mother to slave for his whore, too. When she defied him, he beat her bad, then whipped me until he was too tired to go on. Told her he'd beat me until I was dead if she ever balked again. Soon as she healed and he was out of camp, she took us to her people."

Beth noticed he said "brought *home,*" then "out of *camp*" . . .

"I thought I knew plenty about the Apaches from all she'd told me, but I didn't, not her particular band. She'd taught me their language and customs when Carl wasn't around, but I was in for some big surprises. First off, I learned she was the daughter of a famous thief."

"Thief or chief?"

"Thief. You see, in some bands, a skilled thief is more important than a chief. Her parents and kin were dead, but the band remembered Morning Tears and her family."

"Didn't they turn her away for what she'd done years before?"

"Nope, because for once, Mother was smart; she brought along Carl's money, supplies, and extra horses. Returning to her people as a successful and brave thief, she was welcomed back. She showed even greater cunning by giving them everything to buy weapons and supplies. That first day back, her past defiance was forgotten and forgiven."

"So you stayed with the Apaches?"

"Until I was twenty, I lived and trained as a warrior and hunter, and they tried to make a thief of me. I learned all they could teach me, and I was good. Problem was, partner, they wanted a skilled raider more than a hunter and warrior. When I didn't measure up to their demands on top of being half-blooded, I wasn't accepted there, either. It was like it had been with Carl and the whites; I was an outsider, someone to be endured, someone to show the other females why they shouldn't take off with white enemies."

Was there no end, she worried, to his past torments?

"When I was born, Mother also gave me a secret Indian name, Tl'ee' K'us; it means Night Cloud. Yep, same as my horse's name."

"Why did she name you that?"

"Because I was born at night when strange clouds were across a full moon; that's what she told me. I worked hard to support her and protect her, but she was disappointed in me because I wouldn't use my skills in the Apache way. You see, women are taught to praise victorious robbers and to scorn and tease husbands who returned home empty-handed. The young females wanted nothing to do with a failure like me. Even if I had caught one's eye, the mothers forced them to keep their distances so they wouldn't be tempted by me like Mother was by Carl. Didn't matter, 'cause none of them ever caught my eye, either."

So, no unrequited love in the Indian camp. "I'm sure your mother loved you, Navarro; she just needed and wanted to be accepted by her family and people after all she'd been through over the years."

"I think she died ashamed of me, but I do believe she loved me."

Get him off that sad subject. "When did you leave the Indians? How?"

"After a quarrel with one of the raider bands, I left camp to think. I hated to desert Mother but I hated to stay. I didn't have to make a choice. While I was gone, Bluecoats attacked; some of the band was killed and the others were taken to a reservation. Mother was slain that day."

"I'm sorry, Navarro."

"Thanks, but she was finally at peace. I think she was always afraid Carl would appear."

"Surely her people wouldn't let him take her away?"

"For the right price, you could safely bet your boots and horse they would have. Her gifts were long gone and her son was worthless. They would've been glad to get rid of us, especially me. Don't get me wrong; not all the Indians I met were like that, only Mother's small group. Some of the best men I've known were Indians from other bands and tribes. Anyway, I left Arizona and drifted alone for three years in the white man's world. I worked my way through Colorado, Dakota, Wyoming, and New Mexico territories. Spent time in Texas and California and in Oklahoma Territory. Most people seemed the same wherever I went. Few wanted or allowed a half-breed drifter to get near them, unless a skilled gun or strong back was needed. I've witnessed and experienced deceit, hatred, and cruelties on both sides. While I was drifting, I learned the white man's ways and became an expert gunslinger. Then, I ran into Carl again."

Beth felt his body stiffen and heard his voice go icy cold.

"That time, he didn't touch me; he didn't dare. I was taller and stronger, and my mood warned him I wasn't to be angered or challenged. He didn't even ask about Mother or try to recover his stolen goods. I still hated him for what he'd done to us. I wanted to prove I was a better man in all ways, prove I was nothing like him. This hunger I'd had eating at me for years grew bigger and greedier after I saw him."

Beth waited in tense silence to hear if he'd gunned down his own father.

"Carl wasn't dumb; he knew it was loco to provoke me. I could have outdrawn him and his friends with ease. I'd practiced for years to make certain nobody ever hurt me again. I stayed with him for six months to make him feel worthless and scared. I wanted him and his friends to see just how weak and low Carl was. I wanted him to live, eat, breathe, and think fear; I wanted him to worry about if or when I'd challenge him to a showdown. He got himself killed and I wasn't sorry."

"You didn't . . ."

"No, it wasn't by my hand. The best revenge I got was watching him cower in fear of me, the boy he had abused and terrified for so long. He wouldn't even bring a female to camp because he feared it would set me afire."

"You returned to drifting and working odd jobs until you met Dan?"

"I rode lots of places and did lots of things. I met some good people who turned me around, made me realize I wasn't worthless like my father."

"People like the Lanes and Matt Cordell?"

"Yep. They made me realize I'd been carrying a chip on my shoulder and daring anybody to knock if off, and that was probably why folks shied from me. I'd blamed everybody for treating me like a half-breed bastard and saddletramp when that was how I acted and viewed myself. I realized other people weren't totally to blame for me being an outsider. I was cold, hard, cocky, and bitter. The way I walked, talked, and stood intimidated people. I made people nervous and scared them away; didn't want anybody getting too close. After I took that job with the Lanes, they trusted me and accepted me. I got a hard look at myself, and I changed. Since then, I've met other good people and made other friends. Maybe that's why I understand men like the kind I once was so well."

My heavens, I can't believe you're telling me so much. Maybe you don't realize how much you're revealing. Don't stop.

"After Dan got me to work for him and the law, he became my best friend. He and the Lanes had the most good influence on me. If not for them, I'd be dead today or rotting in some hellhole of a prison. I'd give my life helping and defending any of them. I have to warn you, woman, my old self jumps on me and rides me hard and bad sometimes. I still keep to myself mostly; and I can get too wary, defensive, and cocky."

And insecure. "That happens to everyone; nobody is perfect."

Beth hesitated. "What happened to your mother is why that cantina incident provoked you, right?"

"Yep. The same was the reason with that mess at the hotel with you and that kid. I had a hard time not handling both situations differently, with my guns or fists. Learning self-control when the time's wrong was hard, *is* hard; I guess it never gets easy to . . . turn the other cheek."

"But you do it when necessary because you're a good man, Navarro. You want to help and protect the weak and vulnerable because you know what it's like for them. You shouldn't feel bad because you don't go around beating or killing every vile creature who does evil. If you did, you'd be no better than they are. You abide by the law; that's more important, and it takes a stronger and braver man to do so. Anybody can draw a weapon and take a life, but only a good man can spare one when he's crossed."

Navarro lifted his left hand and trailed his fingers over her cheek. He let his hand settle on her shoulder, and noticed she hadn't flinched from his touch. He admitted to himself she was strong and gentle, and qualified to work with him, qualified to be an agent. She had a tender, forgiving, understanding, and compassionate heart. He spoke his thoughts aloud. "You're a good woman, Bethany Wind; I'm lucky you're my partner on this assignment. Another woman would probably have trouble staying on after what I just told you."

Beth caused his hand to fall away from her body when she half turned, gazed into his hazel eyes, and said, "Thank you; that's one of the nicest things you could say to me."

His gaze fused with hers. "Sometimes, we have to practice our roles."

Beth stood without breaking their gazes. "There's no better time or place than here and now, right?" She roamed her fingers up his chest, then over his compelling features. "Our partnership will work, Navarro; we'll become good friends. We'll solve this case, and we'll do our best to protect your friends at the ranch. Maybe they won't ever have to learn you're the one who exposed and captured Matt's brother; we can try our best to keep them ignorant of that fact."

Navarro's hands cupped her face and he looked into her eyes. "That would please me more than you could know, Beth. I don't want them hurt in any way, if that's possible. Since I won't be returning there in the future, they can go on believing we're married and ranching some-where."

She was moved by his affection and respect for his friends, his loyalty to them, his concern for them. "When they see how perfectly matched we are, they'll believe our claims. We'll have to be very loving around them."

"I know. That won't be hard for you with a man like me?"

"It couldn't possibly be easier or more enjoyable with any other man alive. You're very attractive, Navarro, and you have so many appealing qualities and traits. It won't be difficult at all to play a romance with you."

"Even after all I've told you?"

"Because of all you've told me. You trust me and like me enough to open up to me. And your past made you the man you are today. Don't you see, those bad times and experiences strengthened you, and they taught you the skills and instincts you use. Without all of that, you wouldn't be the Navarro Breed standing here with me; you wouldn't be here period."

He grinned. "I never thought of it like that, but you sound right."

"I am right. Everything bad that happens to us either defeats and breaks us or it makes us better. Terrible experiences force us to move to other locations where new experiences can take place. How we accept and deal with the old ones affect what the new ones will be."

"Yep, a wise and unique woman, a real lady."

Beth smiled. "Thanks. This is for practice," she said, then clasped his face between her hands and lifted herself on tiptoes to kiss him.

Navarro arms encircled her waist and pulled her close to his body. He meshed his mouth with hers and savored the tasty kiss and warm em-brace. She wasn't mistaken; it was going to be easy to play his husband role, if he didn't allow his wayward emotions to forget it was only an assignment.

As his lips roved her face and neck, Navarro thought about what a good influence she was on him, just as Jessica Lane had been. Jessie . . . He had actually forgotten about her in the company and arms of another woman! But why did he feel as if he were cheating on her and betraying their love when Jessie was married to another man, when his marriage to Beth wasn't for love or for real or by choice? It was a strange and unsettling sensation. He pulled away, smiled, and teased, "That's enough work for today; you did fine; you told the truth when you said you'd have no trouble with our roles. I'm glad you're willing to stay and work with me."

"Thank you," she said, and forced a return smile. She hoped he didn't sense how he had gotten to her. Surely there was nothing wrong or wicked about being attracted to him, being attracted to each other, if they didn't act on those carnal impulses.

"How's the arm doing?"

"Fine, thanks to your magical medicine pouch and knowledge. We'd better get moving; the horses are rested by now."

"We don't have much farther to ride today. I just figured this was the perfect spot for telling you about my Indian blood to see if it mattered."

"It doesn't, and I'm grateful you trust me that much." *But you still left gaps in your story. I noticed when you hesitated and when you mussed your hair and your body stiffened for a moment. You've had such a hard, painful, and dangerous life. But you have many more secrets, and I wonder if you'll ever share them with me or anyone. Perhaps whomever you did with in the past used or held them against you, so you're reluctant to take that chance again. In time, you'll learn I'm completely trustworthy.*

"That full moon is so eager to show her pretty face she can't wait until dark. Nothing is much nicer than sleeping under one."

"Does that mean we're going to skip Bowie Station tonight?"

"Nope; it's a scheduled stop. You want to stay on roads and near towns during the remainder of our ride?"

"No, why?"

"Sure you want to ride through wilderness and camp in the open?"

"Of course; I have a rescuer with me if danger approaches."

He caressed her cheek without thinking. "You can trust me, Beth, because I won't let any harm come to you."

"I know." *At least not the kind of danger you mean. You're so tempting, Navarro Breed. I wonder what will happen between us when we are alone for days on end . . .*

Chapter Eight

Beth was relieved when they left Bowie Station so Navarro could stop playing his necessary role in public. His lengthy soul-baring yesterday must have been difficult and draining for him. He had been rather quiet—but polite and nice—in private last night. She hoped he wasn't worried about her thoughts and feelings about him after his shocking revelations. She would work hard to prove to him that his troubled past did not matter to her.

They journeyed along an old stage-wagon road for a while, then headed overland. They passed beyond the verdant Chiricahua Mountains and crossed the San Simon River. They rode onward into New Mexico in the Chihuahuan Desert whose landscape lacked the splendor of the Sonoran. They were fortunate it was spring, as summer heat at midday and sparse water holes were a fierce hardship in an arid region. They weaved their way around prickly pear, sotol, yuccas, mesquite, scrubbrush, and other vegetation in the almost intimidating territory. The ground was a mixture of various size rocks and brownish sand; that added to the other obstacles of nature made their progress slow and cautious. Most of the time, they rode in single file, so talk was impossible.

Beth was glad she'd donned pants, chaps, and a duster to protect herself from the harsh climate and hostile terrain. Today, Navarro's manner of dress was also different and eye-catching: fringed buckskin pants, shirt, and high-top moccasins in a chamois color and snug fit that called attention to his muscular and virile physique. The garments made him look taller and more rugged, a man matched to the current conditions. She had a hard time keeping her gaze and thoughts off him. She couldn't comprehend why it was like that with Navarro Breed and hadn't been with Steven Wind; maybe it was because she had known Steven so long and well before marrying and taking to the trail with him. Surely that was the only reason her new partner so intrigued and captivated her.

They halted for the night about forty-five miles below and southeast of Lordsburg, in the Animas Mountains. The only reason they had made a good distance was by using old trails on occasion. Navarro chose a secluded and sheltered spot far from any ranches and small towns, and near an excellent water source for drinking, bathing, and refilling canteens. She glanced at the tall peaks and steep slopes and was delighted they wouldn't have to trek over them, as her partner knew the trails and passes in this territory. As they made camp, he told her Animas was Spanish for Departed Souls.

Once more Beth's gaze scanned their surroundings and she jested, "I can't imagine any soul wanting to haunt a wilderness like this."

Navarro chuckled at her expression and tone. "I doubt they do. 'Course it's different in the sacred mountains near Phoenix."

As she unpacked supplies, she asked, "What do you mean?"

"Superstition Mountain, home of the Apache Thunder Gods. So many whites have gotten lost and died in her hills and canyons that most are afraid to ride in. They used to believe Indians picked them off and buried them in secret, until the Indians were locked away on reservations and white men still kept vanishing in there. It's not too far west of San Carlos Reservation. The Lost Dutchman Mine is located there. Ever hear of it?"

"No. Tell me," she coaxed as they cooked their evening meal. He seemed to be in a talking mood again, which more than pleased her.

"It's said two men found an old Spanish mine richer than any discovered before; they died without telling anyone where it is, if it really exists. Many people have searched for it but never found a clue or a speck, but lots of gold and silver was located nearby."

As they chatted about that rumor and ate, Navarro recalled how fragile, dainty, and feminine she'd been in Tucson and other towns along their way. But she didn't seem to mind getting dirty, sweaty, and mussed. She seemed to take the trail's demands and hardships in even stride. She appeared as much at ease in pants, boots, and saddle as she had in dress, slippers, and cozy towns. In Tucson, she'd acted frightened and distressed in the face of peril; in the open, she didn't seem afraid or unsettled by anything or anyone, even of getting wounded. She was a constant amazement, delight, and mystery. He was getting to know her better, but there was far more beneath her surface than he had seen or felt so far. Perhaps no man, and surely not one like him, could replace Steven Wind in her heart and life.

Beth was cognizant of the tight leash he kept on his emotions, a task he did better than she. Heavens, she'd be glad to be herself again, and she would be with one final change tonight . . .

"We have time for a lesson or two if you're not tired."

"I'm ready and willing to learn anything from you, Navarro."

I doubt you mean "anything," woman. "I'll show you a few tricks about knives, but it'll take lots of practice after our mission for you to get skilled with them."

He set up a target and collected their knives. "Weight and shape are important for the one you'll be throwing; been my experience, the straighter and lighter, the better for accuracy. Some men hold the handle and some the blade; I like using the blade. Grip it about halfway back between your thumb and fingers; let the side of the first one lay against the metal and spread the tips of others along the blade with the last one at the point. Grip it firm and tight for control. Pretend that rag is a man's chest or back, center is his heart. If he's a threat, go right for it. If not and you just want to wound and stop him, go for the shoulder. Throw it with force and speed, much as you can muster or she'll lose her path. When she's aimed, point your hand level with your target for a short distance and up a mite for a long trip; that takes care of any drop she'll make en route. You aim, draw back over your shoulder, sling forward, and release at the level you chose earlier. Like I said, speed and force send her straight and true. If it's necessary to use a knife, you don't want it just glancing off or pricking him."

As he talked, he demonstrated the instructions. He fetched the weapons after each bout, always recovering them from the target's center.

"You try it," he suggested, and positioned her body and weapon.

The first few knives went wild, landing nowhere near the white cloth. After a few more tries, she came closer but never touched the target. She surmised part of her problem was due to the unsettling effects of his touches, voice, and close proximity. To her pleasure, not once did Navarro become impatient, amused, or annoyed.

"As I said, takes a heap of practice. We don't want your shoulder getting sore, so you can work on it another time. Just don't try it on a man until you're trained. Riles one to get a bloody scratch." He chuckled.

"You're right; I can hear it fussing from this short spell. Now that I know what to do, I'll practice in privacy later. Thanks."

"You want some hand-fighting tips?"

"Yes, please, if you aren't too tired and it isn't a bother."

"Best to show you how to defend yourself before we shadow those snakes. Most men you'll fight will be taller, bigger, and stronger than you.

You'll have to use tricks to make up for those differences. Ever'body has weak spots you can attack: nose, throat, eyes, groin, knees, and right here," he said, tapping his hand in the kidney area at the rib cage. "You hit a man there with force and he'll buckle on you; not at first, though—takes a few minutes. Put two fingers out straight when you poke him in the eyes."

He chuckled when she blinked and jerked back her head at the unexpected action. "Quick reflexes; that's good. Just hope your target doesn't have 'em, too. With the nose and throat and groin, use a balled fist and strike with the hand knuckles, not the fingers or you can break 'em."

Beth noticed he made light contact with her nose and throat but pulled back his fist moments after it started toward her private region. He glanced at her smiling face, shrugged, and grinned about the near slip in propriety. She told him in a mirthful tone, "I get your meaning. Go on."

"Use any weapon you have: teeth, nails, feet, head, everything. Don't be afraid of getting blood in your mouth when you bite, 'cause it may save your hide just to slow an enemy for a moment or two. Gives you time to find a rock or limb to use, or to throw dirt in his eyes. Stand here a minute."

Beth watched and listened while he explained how to kick a man's knees in front or stomp the inner side with her boot heel.

"Same goes for the groin. Kick with speed and force. Never hold back, woman, or you won't disable a bigger and stronger target. Every strike has to come from all you have because you'll tire faster and easier than he will."

She waited while he spread a blanket on the rough, sandy ground.

"Lie on your stomach." After she did, he knelt beside her. "If you get him down like this, use your knee to grind into his backbone. Press hard and deep 'cause you don't weigh much. Hurts like heck and you'll have him yelping for mercy. Stand up." He noticed she always obeyed without hesitation, and he was glad. "If he grabs you around the waist from behind, use your head to smack him in the mouth or nose, whatever you can reach. Hard and fast, woman; remember that's the key to unlocking a win."

Beth felt the full length of his virile and muscular frame against hers. She enjoyed having his arms around her and hearing his voice at her ear. She hated to break their contact when he released her and turned her to him. His hands cupped her shoulders joints and his gaze locked with hers.

"If you're facing him, pretend to . . . swoon, I think you womenfolk call it. Soon as he's off guard, knee him in the groin or butt his belly with your head. Either one knocks a man down or steals his wind. You're not trying to best him, just gain time to recover or pull a weapon to even the odds. Don't get cocky and play with him or you'll be defeated. If the situation doesn't look promising, take him down by surprise, then get your feet moving to a hiding place. Show me how good you are with a rope."

Beth took the rope he lifted from the ground. She flung it over every object he asked her to snare with ease; as she was talented and experienced with one.

"Perfect. Can you lasso an escaping man or a galloping horse?"

"Take off running and you'll see."

He did and, ten feet away, found himself grabbed by the ankle and tripped. He removed the rope, stood, and grinned at her as he dusted off his clothes and hands. "You'd make a superior ranch hand with that skill. Let's see if you can do it twice."

Having retrieved and rolled the rope, Beth nodded. That time, she lassoed his chest and pinned his arms to his torso. In a slow and playful manner, she drew in the lariat with her prize, closing all distance between them. "Of course, if you were my real target, I'd have my pistol out and pointed at your belly by now. I do appreciate you not yanking and running since I'm not wearing gloves to protect my hands from burns and blisters."

"I remembered you were working barehanded, so I thought I'd better go easy on you. You gonna tie me up or release me?"

Feeling mischievous and bold, she looked him up and down. "Since you appear trustworthy, I suppose I'll let you go, this time." She watched him loosen his bond and lift it over his head, chuckling as he did so.

As they returned to the blanket and he rolled the lengthy weapon, he said, "Too bad you don't know anything about wrangling and branding; hogtying a man is a quick and ease way to capture and disable him."

"Show me, please."

"Goes like this . . ."

Before Beth could think or react, Navarro had her on the blanket on her stomach with her wrists bound behind her and her ankles secured. "See, quick and easy for a strong man."

"And an agile one. Wish I could use this trick, but that's not realistic."

He undid the knots and she turned to her back and met his gaze. "I know a few you can use. Up, woman." He extended his hand and brought Beth to her feet as he stood. "Remember that back-knee attack?" She nodded and he guided her through the movements. "If you can't snare his ankle and trip him before you use it, just slam your boot into that tender spot. While he's down, jab your elbow into his neck or skull, like so."

Beth felt his elbow make gentle contact with the sunken area at her nape. Then, he let her demonstrate everything on him.

Navarro was aroused by their touches and the way she looked at him when their gazes met. As she worked, her breathing was rapid and shallow, her cheeks extra rosy, and perspiration glistened on her face. He knew she was giving this her best efforts. Strands of dark hair escaped her long and heavy plait and fluttered with her exertions. Her eyes glowed with excitement and determination. At times, the material of her shirt strained over her breasts and called attention to her femininity. *Shu,* he'd love to stretch out atop her, hold her, and kiss those full lips. He realized he was getting too close to doing exactly that so he said, "That's enough lessons and practice for tonight. We don't want to injure that arm."

"Thanks for helping me, Navarro. This might save my life someday. Every time I use these skills, I'll remember you."

"When you're fighting a foe, woman, think only of him or you're dead."

Beth nodded. "Right now, I think I'll go wash off this trail dust and work sweat. That water I sat on the fire ring should be hot."

"Is that stream too chilly for you?" he jested.

"For washing my hair, yes. I won't take long. Keep the fire going so I can dry it and get warm afterward. Desert air gets cold at night."

"Call out if you need help, and don't go too far."

She knew from his serious tone and expression that the "help" he mentioned referred to her safety, not personal and sensuous assistance. As she sought the best spot for her task, she wondered if he'd like the change he'd soon witness, if he'd like the real Bethany Wind better.

When she returned to camp with a cloth around her head and in her nightgown, Navarro said, "I'll take a short ride to give you privacy. I won't go far and will be back soon." He didn't want to watch her dry and brush her mane, as he knew from observing Jessie how sensual that could be.

"That isn't necessary. I'm fully covered."

"I need the exercise and I want to scout the area, make sure nobody's camping too close to us. If there's trouble, fire a shot in the air."

Beth watched him swing onto his black stallion without saddling the horse, then depart. From the sound of it, he hadn't halted nearby. She shrugged and went to work on her hair. She wasn't sure if she was pleased he was preventing temptation from getting too powerful to handle or if she was disappointed that he mastered his feelings so well. His excuse for leaving camp was just that, a guileful and defensive excuse.

When her long tresses were almost dried by the heat, she braided them and covered her head with a *rebozo* to keep from chilling it during the night, as the temperature dropped in the desert after sundown. She climbed into her bedroll and closed her eyes, feeling relaxed and weary.

Navarro was surprised to find her asleep when he returned. He was quiet to prevent disturbing her much-needed slumber. Her back was to him and across the campfire but her breathing told him she wasn't faking sleep. He stripped off his shirt and removed his boots, but not his pants. He settled himself down and went to sleep.

During the night, Beth stirred and awakened when a nocturnal insect played on her hand. She shook it off and watched it crawl away beneath the illuminating full moon, pleased she hadn't screamed and startled the man nearby. She looked across the smouldering campfire to find her partner snoozing and facing in the other direction. Accustomed to the weather or used to being outdoors or simply being a hot-natured person, Navarro had pushed down the cover to cool his torso. Her eyes widened in shock: his broad back and shoulders exposed scars from brutal . . . beatings! Some, she reasoned, weren't from Carl Breed's belt or a switch during childhood. She recognized lash marks when she saw them. Her gaze roamed the marred terrain as empathy and questions filled her. Who had dared whip him and so viciously only a few years ago? How could anyone get the upper hand with this gun-slinging legend? Surely that foolish attacker wasn't still alive. Concealing that horrible secret could explain why he was always last to go to bed, first to rise, and always shirted. Why had he risked letting her make that grim discovery tonight? Or had he assumed he'd awaken and dress before she did, as usual? The sight of such cruelties prevented her from returning to sleep for a long time.

When Beth awoke later than normal, Navarro wasn't in or near camp as far as her senses could detect. She went behind some rocks to dress. She wanted to look good this morning and did a thorough grooming. She donned a medium-blue shirt and riding skirt and a tan leather vest. She brushed her hair and let it tumble free until she was ready to leave. She tied a red-and-blue bandana around her neck, then gathered her things.

"Coffee and food's about ready," he said as she approached from his rear. He was eager to get on the road, get away from the heady setting.

"Good, I'm hungry." She paused and gazed at his back where a dark shirt concealed a terrible secret. *You've suffered so much in your life, Navarro; no wonder you're so hard and tough. But you can be so gentle and tender when—*

"You gonna burn a hole in me with those powerful green eyes or come take a seat?" he joked.

"A cocky smartmouth this morning, eh? Because I was being lazy?"

"You looked and sounded tired, so I gave you some extra winks."

She murmured, "Always a kind and considerate partner. Thank you." She tossed her things onto her rumpled bedroll and sat down opposite him.

Navarro stopped pouring coffee and gaped at Beth. Her wavy tresses flamed like the boulders at Red Rock with the noon sun beaming down on them! What was she trying to pull on him with this cruel stunt, making herself a redhead like Jessie? No, not as dark as Jessie's chestnut curls— Beth's were lighter, much lighter. "What in blazes did you do to your hair, Mrs. Wind? Get that stuff off of it this minute!"

The astonished woman murmured, "I beg your pardon?"

"Why did you do that last night then hide it until this morning?"

"Hide it? I covered my head because it was chilly and my hair was still damp when I turned in. All I did was wash out the black dye I was using to look like Elizabeth Lawrence; it was part of my disguise, like the blond color I used when I was Sunshine Nellie on that slavery assignment. This is my natural color, Navarro." Why, she wondered, was he so angry? "I'm sorry if you don't like it, but it's the real me. Dan said it was all right to remove the dye after we were far away from Tucson. Besides, I don't have enough of the liquid he gave me to keep fiery roots from showing soon; that would surely be suspicious. Who's going to think to ask if Elizabeth has red or black hair? I told you that no one recognizes me after an assignment because I use disguises. Women started coloring their hair before Christ was born: Grecian and Roman women. Dan gets the ingredients I need from China and France. What difference does my hair color make to you? We're only temporary partners, so you won't have to endure it for life."

Several words stuck in Navarro's head: "Dan said it was all right to remove . . . far away from Tucson." The talk they'd had that Sunday night before he met Beth flashed through his troubled mind. His friend and superior had known her name was Wind and her hair was red. Knowing how those two facts would strike him, Dan had kept them a secret!

"I asked, Navarro, what difference does my hair color make? I accept you as you are. Do you hate redheads? Are you the prejudiced one on our team?" Beth was disquieted by the strange way in which he stared at her and how long he pondered his answer. "Well, what is it?"

"I don't dislike redheads. You just caught me by surprise changing your looks. I thought you were pulling a joke or a trick on me."

That reply confused her. "Trick or joke? I don't understand."

He lowered his gaze and finished pouring the coffee. "Doesn't matter now. Forget it. Let's eat, break camp, and ride."

"May I ask one question?"

He nodded but sent a glance of reluctance.

"Was your strong reaction because of something a redhead did to you in the past? Did my hair bring to mind a bad memory?" Once more, she received that piercing stare and lengthy silence as he decided whether or not to answer and, if he did, what to say.

"Yes, so you or Dan should have told me the truth. Drop it."

That response told Beth a lot. "In Dan's defense, Navarro, he didn't expose your secret to me. Nor did he order me not to reveal this to you," she added, touching her coppery locks. "I'm sure he thought I'd tell you about my assignments and disguises before we left Tucson. I was about to do so that day we went riding outside of town, but we were interrupted, remember?" He nodded again with visible reluctance. "Frankly, I'm glad you didn't discover the truth in Tucson because it's obvious you wouldn't have given yourself time and opportunity to get to know me. You asked me if what you exposed about yourself made me want to quit traveling with you, so I'll ask the same question. Does this matter that much to you? Will it be a problem between us?"

"Nope."

A quick answer that time. "Good. I'll get packed while you eat."

As she began doing so, he asked, "Aren't you gonna eat?"

"No. You get finished. We're running late. I'll be ready soon."

"I thought you were hungry."

"I was. Food will taste better at noon when my appetite returns."

He realized he'd upset her. "Look, Beth, I'm—"

She almost whirled from her tasks to stare at him. "Drop it, for now."

"Sure, for now. We'll settle it later so it won't interfere with work."

"I never allow anything to jeopardize my cases, so don't worry."

Navarro experienced pangs of guilt and dismay over hurting her. He blamed Dan for provoking the nasty episode. He concluded it was best to let her settle down before they had a serious talk.

As Beth prepared to depart, she held silent. Yet, she knew there was plenty to learn about his odd behavior, and resolved she would. As surely as the sky was clear and blue today, a redhead had done him wrong, and

Navarro Breed wasn't a man to cross or betray. *Curse you, witch, for hurting him so deeply after all he'd been through since birth! We were getting along so well; now, your blasted ghost has ruined things between us, made him put me in the same wicked light he sees you in! Wherever and whomever you are, I hope you're as miserable as you've made him.* Beth reasoned on the destructive female's identity. It couldn't be Mary Louise Lane because he'd called her "that yellow-haired creature." It couldn't be Jessica Lane Cordell because he spoke too highly and affectionately of her and was returning to her very home. *Who? What happened? When?*

Beth continued her chore with a busy mind. Navarro had lived and worked at the ranch for months, risked his life to help, returned to protect them after being kicked off by the owner. Had he done so because it was more than a job to him? Had there been another female living there, one he hadn't mentioned yet? Had he fallen in love for the first and only time with a woman who had chosen another man over him? Did he believe she had done so because of who and what he was? Or had she belonged to another before his arrival? Could that be it? . . . No, surely not.

While Navarro finished eating, doused the fire, and loaded his things, he worried about Daniel Withers's reason for withholding those two important facts from him. That night in Tucson, Dan had coaxed him to forget what the shaman had said or to find another woman to fit the sacred vision. Had Dan picked a female who matched it to help draw him away from Jessie? Even chose one who agreed with the Apache saying when Jessie didn't?

If Dan had tried to influence and alter his emotions, it wouldn't work because he still loved Jessie, and a man couldn't love two women. Nor could a man fall for a second female when he hadn't stood up after taking a tumble over the first one. Besides, he wasn't going to make the mistake of giving his heart and soul to another woman and risk being hurt again. Yet, it might be only a coincidence that Bethany Wind fit both descriptions. Or maybe it was just another one of life's cruel tricks on him. He wished the spirits would find someone else to taunt and harm, as surely they had given him more grief than he deserved.

As his anger faded and his wits cleared, Navarro decided it was nice of his friend to try to find him a replacement; to want him to have love, a home and family, freedom from torment. But Dan shouldn't interfere with destiny because his feelings and ties to his past couldn't be changed. He'd have to be careful not to allow Beth's red hair and last name to fool him into thinking Dan might be right. He'd soon learn when he confronted his friend if Dan had an ulterior motive for selecting Beth.

Ulterior motive . . . well, maybe he'd used one himself with his partner. Maybe he had been telling Beth all those terrible things about himself to discourage her and make her want to give up working and traveling with him. Maybe he didn't want to have her along as his alleged wife when he saw Jessie and Lane for the first time in years. He had been unable to get them and the things he was missing sharing with them out of his mind.

Were Dan and Beth fooling with his head and trying to confuse and change him, make him think crazy things and stir up unwanted feelings? That ordeal with Jessie, then Lane, had ripped him apart. He didn't want another woman messing with his emotions. True, he had taken women when a physical need arose but they hadn't meant anything to him. Now, Beth was looking and acting as if she was trying to touch his heart. He couldn't allow it because he had won one lady's love and the chance of doing that again was cactus hair slim to none. Nope, no more heart- and soul-shredding for him.

Two hours before dark, the two agents halted to camp at a location that was halfway across New Mexico.

Navarro was all too aware of the new silence and distance between them. If things continued in this bloody vein, he decided, they would never delude Jessie, Matt, or others about being in love. The Texas couple wouldn't believe they were only passing through and he wanted to introduce them to his wife to let them see he was happy and settling down, to let them know they had nothing to fear from him ever laying claim to his son. He had to convince them he was no threat to their present or future. To do so, he had to relax Beth, win her over again.

"While that rabbit's cooking, why don't you show me how skilled you are with your weapons while we have privacy for firing?"

"Sure. I'll get them. Choose the targets." As she went to fetch her arms, Beth concluded he was up to something, perhaps a last attempt to get rid of her, but she hoped not. She worried that she had permitted her loneliness over Steven's loss and an unexpected desire for this magnificent male to cloud her wits. For countless reasons, there could never be anything between her and Navarro, so she mustn't do anything to complicate her life or endanger their mission. Yet, if her partner didn't stop his weird moods and deal with his secrets, they would surely cause problems.

She returned to where he was standing. "Ready. What's first?"

"Show me how you use your pistol, then rifle and derringer."

Though nervous around him tonight, she proved her skills within ten minutes. She waited while he strung a bow from a limber sapling he'd cut before reaching the arid region. As he worked, she noticed how muscles rippled underneath his snug shirt and in forearms below rolled sleeves. He'd removed his hat and fingercombed the mussed sections. Why, she fretted, did he have to be so handsome and virile, so troubled and unreachable? She accepted the well-crafted bow and arrows he passed to her one at a time. She knew from his reaction and expression he was amazed and pleased that she and Dan had told the truth about her capabilities. Maybe she was mistaken and he wasn't trying to trip her up, only restore peace. "What about you? Do I get to test your talents?"

Beth watched him use pistols, rifle, hatchet, and whip. His lightning speed, deftness, and accuracy were astonishing. Even when she tossed two targets in opposite directions or multiple ones into the air, he never missed. She wondered if the pop of the whip made him cringe inside and if he'd chosen to master it for that reason. She told him, "As Dan said, you are matchless. It's too late tonight, but I hope you'll teach me those extra skills another day."

He snaked the whip around her waist and pulled her to him with a roguish grin. "It's a promise, and it should be quick and simple for you."

"Thanks for the compliment and confidence. How did you capture me like this without inflicting pain or damage? Those targets were ripped to shreds when you struck them."

"Control and know-how. You have to conquer its power and use it with just the right touch and force. If not, you've made a lifetime enemy."

She inhaled his manly scent as he freed her. When his gaze met hers, she knew she had to escape his pull in a hurry. "Let's eat; I'm starved."

Navarro watched her retreat toward the campfire where their meal was sending off enticing smells. The hair that framed her fair-skinned face and flowed down her shoulders was a blaze of fiery splendor, even in the dimming light. Her steps were light and agile, and her hips swayed with graceful movement. She hadn't missed a target—still or in motion— and only a few shots hadn't been dead center. He had expected her to be proficient, but not expert. Only the bow and arrows gave her difficulty but she explained she was rusty with them. Not once had the loud discharges of bullets caused her to jerk or squeal, as she had in town. She had been at ease with each of the weapons. Truth was, he'd never seen a female—or many males—who was a better marksman, and he'd told her so. At least, he had no worries in that area. But he did in another one. Her leafy gaze was guarded. She'd barely smiled or looked at him, and had used only necessary words. She hadn't flinched when he touched her, but it seemed she'd tried to avoid contact. He knew there was only one way to regain their lost rapport and to prove he liked and trusted her—to confide something personal and important. He went to join her and put aside his weapons where he took a seat at the campfire.

As he cut off hunks of the meat and put them on her plate, he asked, "Have you placed the name Carl Breed yet?"

Beth looked at his lowered head, his expression hidden by its angle and her position. His evocative tone intrigued her. "What?"

For a moment, he glanced up and let their gazes fuse. "Carl Breed, my father. You don't recognize the name?" She shook her head. "You don't go over old records and newspaper clippings when you work an area?"

"Only when I think I may find something relevant to my case. Why?"

As he served his plate, he asked, "Did you do it in Tucson?"

"Yes, but I only went back a few years to see if anything about land disputes or Harrison had been reported. I told the man at the newspaper I was trying to learn about where I'd moved and he believed me. Why?"

"Maybe you didn't come across anything about him because Carl Breed was news years and years ago, bad news. So was I, Beth. Last account would have been in early '73, so I don't suppose you went back that far."

She studied him. "No. What are you hinting at?"

"What I should've finished telling you the other day. You said you don't mind working and traveling with a half-breed bastard, but how about an ex-outlaw and ex-prisoner?" He watched her gaze widen in surprise.

"You?" She saw him nod. "But you're a lawman, a Special Agent."

"I wasn't always on the right side of the law, and I served time for that stupid mistake, lots of time. Dan and I should've told you your partner was a hardened desperado who escaped a hangman's noose by a cactus hair and almost died in an Arizona hellhole of a prison." Those big green eyes enlarged even more as she studied him for signs of deceit or jest.

"I don't believe it. You're a legend, the best, a good man."

"When I was a gunslinger and outlaw, I was also a legend, the best in those areas. I even rode with my father's gang for a while."

"Gang? Outlaw? Prison? Condemned man? Hangman's noose? You, Navarro Breed, a wanted man?" She watched him nod after each short query. She was too stunned to think or speak more words for a while. She just gaped at him as if he were lying or teasing as she shook her head.

"It's true, Beth. That's why I make such a skilled lawman. Who knows better a criminal's mind than somebody who's been one, somebody who's walked in those boots?"

"You *are* serious. When? Why? What happened?"

"Let's eat before I relate the dirty tale. I don't want to spoil your appetite again like I did this morning, and I'm sorry that happened. After I finish, if you still want to team up with me, I'll be mighty grateful."

Beth took the cup of coffee he poured and set it on the ground. She assumed his many dark secrets were the causes of his strange moods and behavior. If he'd been able to thwart their partnership as he'd attempted, it wouldn't have been necessary to share them with her. She concluded he must have despised having to do so and perhaps risk tarnishing her golden image of him. He had no choice but to confess, as somebody could recognize *him*—not her!—and expose his past identity. The fact he made the admissions proved he had accepted her on his team.

A filled plate rested on Beth's lap but it wasn't food she wanted; it was the truth. She knew she mustn't press him; he had to expose information at his own pace. Suspense and anticipation gnawed at her as she chewed on rabbit, biscuit, and beans. She ate as fast and politely as possible, then did her clean-up chores, as did he.

Navarro convinced himself he was feeding her his bitter life's story in chewable bites to win Beth's trust. He also wanted to prevent her from thinking him a liar if somebody dropped clues or facts about him later, or if somebody handed her false crumbs and made him taste worse than he'd been. There was no way, he reasoned, it was being done to hinder his dark secrets from jumping up and snatching Bethany Wind from his grasp in the future as they had ambushed and stolen Jessica Lane from him in the past. Confident those were his motives, he readied himself to confess.

"What I told you about me and my parents the other day is true, but my story had holes in it, as you may have guessed with that keen mind of yours. My father became an outlaw after his Army years. He was too lazy to do regular work but was greedy for money. He teamed up with some of his friends from the fort. Didn't take long to make a notorious name for themselves as the Breed Gang. It all made him believe he was important and fearless. They terrorized Arizona and New Mexico territories for years. Half the time, he was robbing and killing and living off his sorry deeds. The other half, he was laying low when the law got too close; that's when he'd force Mother to earn our keep."

Spellbound, Beth sat on a blanket and leaned against a rock.

"He ran that sutler store as I said, but he was finally recognized from an old wanted poster and sent on the run again. The money my mother took to her people was loot from Carl's latest holdup, a big bank job. That's why she was so highly viewed and praised by her band, forgiven and accepted so quick and easy. After that massacre in the Apache camp when I ran into him again, I rode with his gang for a while to humiliate and frighten him before his men. Six months later, I realized I was hurting myself more than him because he didn't have feelings, not the kind I was trying to reach; there was nothing inside him to provoke guilt and shame. I left him three times: at twelve, twenty, and twenty-four, but I never felt free of him while he was alive. I thought because his evil blood ran in me, I must be bad and worthless, too. Somewhere deep inside, I think I only wanted to prove to him and me I was wrong, that I was nothing like him and never would be."

Navarro crossed his legs and sat Indian-fashion. "I told myself I rode with Carl to punish him, but it was me who got punished the worst. I was in one of his old camps getting ready to leave him a final time, just ride off and forget he ever existed. He and his gang showed up with a posse eating their dust. There was a shoot-out; everybody was killed except me because I wouldn't fire on lawmen, a clue they didn't notice in all that ruckus. They didn't want to notice because three friends of theirs had been shot in the holdup and chase. I was arrested, tried in a grieving town, and sentenced to prison for something I didn't do. Would have been worse for me if the posse hadn't recovered the money. The local judge and jury didn't believe I was innocent, either. I can't blame 'em; it looked as if I was caught redhanded. The only man who could've helped me was gone when I went to trial and his report was . . . *misplaced,* so I got twenty years."

Navarro gazed toward the darkened horizon as his mind drifted back to that embittering episode. "I escaped twice. The first time was about two months after I went in. It was stupid because I was too weak from hunger and whippings to get very far. After they hauled me back, things got worse. You can't imagine what a bad prison is like. Filthy clothes and a nasty stone room that smelled like rotting flesh and old sweat. No baths; if you were lucky, you got caught outside during a heavy rain. We got lashed at the post for the slightest offense. Not much food and it wasn't fit to eat. Rats and bugs lived with you, half the time, crawling all over you. We were forced to work in desert heat with barely enough water to keep from passing out. No hats to protect our heads from the sun. We even slaved in winter when a blizzard made seeing near impossible. I saw men lose fingers and toes to ice and exposure. Didn't matter if we were inside; the cells were about as cold as the open air. We had only two thin, ragged blankets apiece and they were full of fleas and lice, filthy and smelly as a hog in soured mud. If we got sick, nobody cared or tended us, not even the other prisoners. You didn't have any friends in there unless you made 'em before you came. Plenty died and, if you were one of them, there was a fight over your belongings, if the men got to 'em before those greedy guards. If you had family or friends who'd bring you money, you could pay 'em for better food, whiskey, smokes, or another blanket. If your folks died or stopped sending money, you went back to being nobody. 'Course I didn't have anybody to help make things easier for me. If a prisoner made a bad mistake, he visited the Black Hole.''

"What kind of mistakes? What was the Black Hole?''

"All it took was riling a guard for any reason. They were determined to break every man who came there, make him crawl and cower. If one tried to stay proud and strong, he was doomed. Those brutes made bets on which of them could shatter a man, how long and what it would take. Their favorite punishment—besides that lashing post—was a deep, damp, dark hole where they'd throw you and leave you until you begged or they got tired of the joke and released you. Or you died or went loco like a few did. Sometimes, I thought I might.''

"My heavens, Navarro, how did you survive such a horror?''

"What I hated most was being locked in a small, dirty cell. I got to where I looked forward to hard labor just to get outside in fresh air and sunshine. I had seventeen and a half years to go and one guard who hated me because I was part Indian. He put scars on my back and tossed me in that hole every chance he could.''

Beth had seen those scars, added to the ones his father had put there years earlier. Her heart ached for his sufferings. It had taken a lot to change him into the man he was today. With his dark history, that amazed and pleased her. It revealed how much courage, strength, wits, and good he possessed. No wonder she found him so—

"Time came when I had to try to escape again. That bastard who rode me so hard had two of us out working one day. He kept picking on me like Carl had done when I was a kid. We got in a fight and I killed him defending myself. I think he was trying to provoke me into making him shoot me. We took off in opposite directions. I knew if I was recaptured, I'd be hanged for murder. Who would take my word about having no choice? I stole a horse, weapons, food, and clothes and got out of that area pronto. I'd set a false trail northward, so that's the road the law took. I kept on the move, didn't let anyone get close to me, and kept my eyes and ears open. Months later, I was in San Angelo and that's where I hooked up with the Lanes. I took that job because I figured a secluded ranch was a good place for a fugitive to lay low while resting and earning money to move on soon.''

Beth watched his features and expression soften, as did his voice.

"Problem was, I got to know and like the Lanes and their hands. I got tangled up fast in their troubles. Fletcher was like Carl and that prison guard: cold, mean, greedy, and cocky. Their kind preys on weaker folks. The Lanes and their hands accepted me and trusted me; I was like one of the boys to everyone there. They let me make the plans and they followed my orders without question. They respected me and liked me. They helped me prove to myself I was worth something, I was needed, I mattered. I learned to relax, smile, laugh, actually enjoy life. It didn't take long before I realized I wanted to be like them, have a good life."

Beth was baffled. "So why did you leave after you defeated Fletcher?"

"It was too late for me to grab the fresh start they offered. Fletcher had sent out sketches and queries to see if I had any secrets he could use to yank me out of his path. A true friend wouldn't stay and put them in danger of a shoot-out, or risk getting them into bad trouble. If the law figured they'd hidden me, they could've lost everything we'd saved."

"That was a very unselfish and generous thing to do, Navarro."

"Thanks, but I might as well confess my pride was involved in it, too: I didn't want a posse appearing out of nowhere and exposing me. I wanted them to remember me in a good way. If trouble came searching for me, I'd have to surrender without a fight to save their lives; stray bullets have no names on 'em. I couldn't let good folks—friends—be harmed or killed to save my sorry hide, so I left after my job was done. A few days later, I decided to risk making a go of it there if they agreed. I hoped Fletcher's scheme hadn't caught anybody's attention. I was wrong and it cost me plenty."

More than you know, partner. "I didn't get near the ranch before I was recaptured and returned to that hellhole. The only reason I wasn't hanged for murder was because the authorities didn't know I'd killed that guard. The other escapee was blamed for it after he was shot, because he had the guard's rifle in his hands; I'd let him take it 'cause he was old and weaker. I wasn't crazy enough to argue since he couldn't suffer for what I'd done. I was innocent of the charges I was sentenced for, but it was justice in a way because I had committed other crimes. By then, that bastard guard was gone and I just wanted it over so I could start fresh when I was released. I guess you could say I had hope for the first time in my life."

"How long did you serve? How did you get out early? By my counting, you still had years to go."

"I was in for two and a half years before I escaped the second time; after my recapture, I was in for five more. It was letters from the Cordells to every law office and high-ranked person they could think of that got my case reviewed and won me a pardon; actually, I was exonerated. When an investigation was started, the deputy who wasn't at my trial remembered what he'd told the sheriff about the gang having five men and five were killed during the shoot-out—and my horse wasn't hot and sweaty from a fast and long run. The bankers were questioned and admitted they hadn't recognized me after my arrest. It was decided I was innocent, so I was set free. The investigation of my case exposed what was going on at that prison and the government had it cleaned up. What the Lanes and Matt did for me at the ranch and in helping me get my freedom back made me forever grateful to them; that's why I hate to use and betray their friendship and trust. They're good people, Beth, so I know they aren't involved with Charles Cordell's crimes."

"I'm sure you're right and a good judge of character. I'm curious; during your assignments, people don't remember your name from your outlaw days?"

"I was known and convicted as Carl Breed, Junior. I chose Navarro after my mother's death because I wanted a name untainted by my father. Most of the time I didn't use a last name. Nobody who meets me is told who and what I was—except the Cordells, Dan, and another friend. You'll meet him in El Paso; he'll be our contact for a while."

"You told the Cordells before you left the ranch that last time?"

"Yep. I owed Jessie and Matt the truth about why I had to leave. The boys knew me as Navarro Jones from Colorado. When we reach the ranch, if the subject of prison comes up, I'll tell them I was framed, jailed, escaped, and didn't want them to know bad things about me when I was there."

"How did the Cordells discover you'd been recaptured? Why did they wait so long to try to help you?"

"They didn't know I was back in prison. They were trying to get my case investigated and get me cleared so I wouldn't have to be on the run all my life. They hoped they could succeed; then, if I contacted them, they'd tell me I was a free man. I was lucky those letters spurred interest in me."

She worried aloud, "Do they know what kind of work you do now?"

He shook his head. "I saw Matt after my release and told him I'd been offered a job by the Arizona governor to work on the Indian problems. Back then, Nana and Geronimo and other Indians were running free and wild. Since I was part Apache, spoke their language, and knew their customs, they thought I could help prevent more bloodshed; and they knew I'd been a scout before. Months later, I wrote Jessie and Matt with the news. Far as they know, I still work as a scout, translator, and peace-maker between the whites and Indians or that I do odd jobs somewhere."

Beth wanted to ask why he didn't make a fresh start there at the ranch after his release, with the friends who'd aided it. That was suspicious, but she decided not to probe. So many scars. So much pain from his parents, prison, and the unknown redhead. It was amazing he had chosen the straight life and become an excellent lawman. Perhaps love was the reason he'd abandoned a dark existence. And perhaps an unexpected disappearance for years had provoked his sweetheart to marry another man. That would have been agony when he returned years ago, saw Matt, and discovered his great loss. The timing made sense; she decided her speculations must be on target, or close. When she and Navarro reached their destination, if the mystery woman had been and was still on that property, she would learn the female's identity. She would learn if they still had feelings for each other. If so—

"You're mighty thoughtful, Beth Breed."

There's one more gap in your story, partner, and I wonder if or when you'll fill it in for me. "I'm . . ."

"You're what?"

"Sorry you had such a terrible life when I had such a good one. It makes me realize how fortunate I was. I could have been born in your place; or anyone could have. You've done remarkably well, Navarro. I can't think of a better partner or friend to have than you. I have no doubts, or hesitation about working and living with you."

"Are you certain, Beth? Most women wouldn't want a man with my past to touch them, and I will have to touch you to play your husband."

" 'Past' is the important word. What I told you before is still true; look at it this way, everything you were and that happened to you made you into the good man and skilled agent you are today; that's all that really matters."

He smiled and relaxed his taut body. "I like the way you look at things, Beth Breed. If you don't mind me practicing that name."

"Of course I don't, and it's a good idea to get accustomed to using it. It's late, so I'm fetching my sleeping bag. Want me to toss you yours?"

"I'll get it in a minute, but thanks." He watched her approach where they'd unloaded the horses and left them to graze. "We also need prac-tice in other areas, Mrs. Breed, romantic areas."

Before lifting her bedroll, she turned to look at him. "Does that mean you want to work on it tonight?" she asked, and quivered in suspense.

Navarro retrieved his whip and stood. He coiled it around her waist and again pulled her toward him, a grin broadening steadily on his face.

He listened to her laugh as she acquiesced to his behavior without resistance.

"Every time you do that, I'm surprised you can achieve that stunt without hurting me. Do you capture all of your women in this clever way?"

Her mirthful tone and expression were arousing, as was her captive state and nearness. "Only special ones. Others, I toss back like squirming fish too small to clean, fry, and eat."

She adored his sense of humor and mischievous mood at that stirring moment. "Since I'm the perfect size, what now, my husband?" She spoke the bold and provocative query as if it were only a jest.

Navarro was serious as he asked, "If somebody at the ranch was watching us at this minute, what would you do and say to fool them?"

Chapter Nine

When she remained still and silent, Navarro asked, "Well, Mrs. Breed, what would you do and say if we were being spied on right now?"

"Let's see, we're supposed to be newlyweds and we need to dupe our observers . . ." she murmured and pretended to think, when what she needed was time to make certain she had herself under control before getting cozy with him. "I should place my hands on your chest like this with obvious fondness, give you a tender and adoring gaze and smile like this, say I love you and how happy I am to be your wife, hug you, and kiss you."

His suspense mounted as Navarro waited for her to carry out the rest of her stirring words. When she didn't, he stroked her cheek and asked, "Would it be easier for you if you close your eyes and pretend I'm Steven?" He saw Beth's smile fade and she shook her head. He cursed his blunder.

"No, that wouldn't work because you and Steven are too different."

Navarro wished he hadn't resurrected the man's ghost so it could take a stand between them tonight. He didn't apologize because that would call more attention to his mistake.

To do what she must for the crucial mission, Beth pushed Steven to the recesses of her mind. She tried to retrieve the mood Navarro had evoked with a seductive grin, husky tone, playful manner, and enticing gaze. She placed trembly hands on his chest and toyed with the top button of his shirt. "You know, I'm very lucky to be your wife. I can't think of any man better qualified to protect me and make me happy."

As she lowered her gaze to fidgety fingers, Navarro used his hand to lift her chin. "You can't do that, Beth. You have to stare straight into my eyes and not look away. We'll be claiming we've known each other for years so we should be at ease around each other, right? By the time we get there, we'll have been married long enough that you wouldn't still be a shy bride, would you? 'Course, I don't know much about such things. I hope you do."

Beth laughed and quipped to calm them both, "It's strange, partner, but that perfectly describes how I'm feeling about now with this peculiar role. I know that's ridiculous since we aren't really married; I'll try to be more professional." She laughed again as if jesting. "Actually, this ruse could be fun and quite interesting, definitely a challenge for both of us. If we pull it off, we deserve high praise and a bonus."

"You're right; if we loosen our knots and enjoy ourselves, we'll be convincing." His tone waxed grave. "If we aren't, Jessie and Matt are gonna wonder what we're doing there. If they get leery, they won't invite us to stay." *They might even suspect I hired you to play my wife so I could see Jessie and Lane. Maybe not getting an invitation would be best for all of us.* Maybe he didn't need to spend much if any time around the woman and child he had loved and lost. He and Beth could shadow Charles after he left the ranch. The only part of the mission he'd be denied would be a chance to study Charles, eavesdrop for clues, and nose around those wagons if left unguarded. At least he had a backup plan if this one failed. He liked that his partner had promised she would do all she could to keep their objective a secret from Jessie and Matt because he'd be using and misleading them, and nobody liked that kind of treatment.

"Kiss me, Beth, as if I'm the only man you've ever loved or will love," leapt from his mouth before he could stop it.

After his silence, his words caught her off-guard. Her heart pounded. "What?"

"Do as I said, woman, and let's see if we can play lovers with as much skill as we hunt down criminals." He grasped her by the shoulders with a light grip. He trekked his lips over her rosy cheek and down her throat. He was pleased when she leaned her head back to allow him free rein. His mouth worked its way to her chin, traversed it with ease, and sought her lips. He felt Beth's arms encircle his waist and her palms flatten against his back. She swayed against him as if her strength had drained away and she required his support. Her stimulating response was more than he'd expected or needed as passion's flames licked at his body. She seemed warm and willing, as if her lonely spirit beckoned his to appease its yearnings.

Beth noticed when the pressure of his lips increased and his embrace tightened. His kiss and contact were wonderful and enlivening. As he intoxicated her senses, her heart beat at a rapid pace. Tingles danced over her flesh. Her body was as hot as the desert in summer. Her mind spun as fast as a child's top until she was dizzy and weak. She thought how glorious it would be to make love to him beneath the moon and stars, to cast all caution to the wind and take what she craved.

Navarro hadn't been kissed or held like this in years, and it was wonderful. Desire for the alluring redhead ran through him like scalding molten lead. He enjoyed how she felt in his arms, how she tasted, how she reacted to him. He became aware of his aroused state. He warned himself with reluctance this had to halt. He parted them, forced a smile, and said, "Well, looks as if we'll be able to fake it good when the time comes. Thanks, Beth, for not flinching."

Fake it? Was that all we were doing? She hadn't noticed because he had so deftly disarmed her! Nor did she share his opinion, if she spoke the truth. "You're welcome; that was a pleasant rehearsal. I'm relieved we finally got rid of our anxiety in that area. It'll get easier each time."

Easier? The only hard part was stopping us from galloping headlong into forbidden terrain. "I'm sure it will. Let's turn in. We'll make the Rio Grande if we head out early and avoid delays."

She stretched and yawned. "Sounds fine to me. I'm tired."

Remaining chores were tended and the couple took places on bedrolls spread on opposite sides of the campfire.

Beth lay on her stomach with her head facing away from Navarro. She was embarrassed and ashamed of herself for behaving so amateurish and improper and vexed with him for causing it. She'd never done anything like that with her real husband. She scolded herself for getting so immersed in their necessary exercise; it made her edgy and insecure to know he could be so . . . overwhelming. As Beth often did when she was upset, she silently talked to her deceased mate.

Oh, Steven, I miss you. Everything is so different with you gone. Sometimes I'm lonely and afraid. You and I never had problems working together. Why can't it be the same with Navarro? I know this case involves his good friends, but I suspect there's more to his worries than normal concern over hurting and angering them. Help me find the truth so it won't jeopardize the assignment and my job.

Ever since you died, Caroline and Robert have been pressing me to retire and return home. I can't move back to Denver. To do what? Find a job that won't fulfill me as this one does? To exist from day to day? I can't look for another husband just to appease my family. That's what everyone would expect. They'd be pushing every available male within fifty miles on me.

If only I could remain partners with Navarro—even though he scares the tarnation out of me at times—it would be exciting, challenging, stimulating. I'd be happy and enriched again. But this is our only mission together. As soon as it's over, he'll return to a solitary existence, the way he prefers it. Maybe in the future, another case will call for a man-woman team and they'll put us together again. At least he's becoming more open and relaxed with me. Help me, Steven; tell me what to do about him.

On the bedroll not far away, Navarro also had trouble getting to sleep. He was astonished by the easy way Beth had worked herself beneath his tough hide. He'd come to like, respect, and enjoy her; and to care about her more than he found comfortable. There was a radiance, vitality, and inner—as well as outer—beauty about her that was arresting. So was her mixture of gentleness and strength, of courage and caution, of keen wits and skills without arrogance.

With Jessie, there had been a powerful and instant physical attraction, but it had deepened fast to an emotional one that bound him to her. He and Jessie had been like troubled youths who had matured together with the help of each other. She had taught him life was precious and could be good. She had removed the chip on his shoulder, saved his hide, removed the dark cloud looming over him. She had opened him up to feelings and thoughts he'd never known. She had inspired self-worth and showed him how to make friends and earn others' respect. She had made him care about *how* he survived. She had given him herself and a son.

What had he given her in return? Anguish, fear, and near-shame. He had forced her to break her promise to him and to marry another man. He had deserted her to face torment and troubles alone. Yet, she had still loved him, forgiven him, helped him; that was the kind of woman she was. How could another female be that unique? Replace her in his heart and life?

Navarro glanced at the redhead nearby. What was Beth's magic and temptation? Her looks and personality didn't remind him of Jessie. He flung aside his cover and moved to study her. She was lying on her back now, the full moon revealing and enhancing her. He sank to one knee and gazed into her serene face. Her full lips were slightly parted. Long and thick lashes fanned on her cheeks, pinkened by sun and hot wind. Her brows, with the dye removed, were golden red. The copper hair suited her coloring better. Wavy tresses drifted from the edges of her face and flared on the bedroll, as they weren't braided tonight. Of their own volition, his fingers reached out to caress a soft cheek. At same time, Beth pushed the cover away from her neck and rested her left hand atop it, exposing a gold band that was too noticeable in the strong moonlight. His gaze glued to the wedding ring that didn't bind her to him but to Steven Wind, a man she still loved. With haste, he returned to his spot, stretched out on his back, and stared at the twinkling stars.

He didn't resist as his troubled mind roamed to tormenting days. The first time he left the ranch after that incident with Mary Louise, Jessie had told him, "I love you. I need you. Stay here and marry me. . . . Make your home and peace with me." When he'd been forced to refuse, she offered to go with him, telling him, "It's never too late. . . . Nothing's impossible." She'd been wrong, blinded by her feelings for him. No, he refuted, he'd made her wrong by disappearing that second time.

"One day you'll meet a good man and marry him," he'd said. "Forget me, Jess."

Bits of their final talk jumped forward in his mind to haunt him:

"How can I forget you? I love you. I can make you happy. You can't keep drifting forever. Please stay. . . . How can anyone take your place in my heart and life? . . . I'll wait for you to change your mind. You can't run forever. When you realize that, I'll be here."

"Don't wait, Jess. I won't be back—ever. I'm a condemned man."

"I could sell out and go with you. Surely there's someplace where we'd all be safe and happy."

He'd rattled off all the reasons she and her family couldn't go with him. "I won't stay and I won't return. I mean it, Jess."

"I love you and want you, Navarro. Don't be afraid to love, afraid to take risks to claim happiness. . . . I'll do whatever I must to have you."

"Be strong and never look back, Jess. Like the wind, I'll always feel you around me. . . . It's too late for us. It's goodbye this time."

"No matter what you say, I'll wait for you. The law can't keep searching forever. Go somewhere safe and lay low. When enough time passes, come back to me. . . . You can't change my mind about waiting. You'll be back one day, Navarro. I believe that with all my heart."

He believed with all his heart she would have kept her vow, but cruel fate had intruded; she had been forced to marry Mathew Cordell for her sake and that of the baby. After his release from prison, he had continued to believe some force would free her and they'd be reunited. Five years ago when he spied on them, she seemed content and a loving wife. But maybe she was only trying to make the best of a difficult situation. What would happen when he blew back into her life, especially if she wasn't happy or in love with Matt? Or if Matt was involved in the crime at hand or the rancher wasn't a good father to his son?

In a week, Jessie, we'll be standing face-to-face for the first time since we were torn apart; what will we think, feel, say after everything that happened between us, good and bad? Would it be easier to get over the past if we hadn't joined our bodies and didn't have a child? Will I be able to think clearly around you and Lane?

The next morning, both Navarro and Beth feigned good moods as they prepared breakfast, tended chores afterward, and prepared to depart.

While saddling his horse, Navarro said, "From here on, we play our roles as much as possible to get used to them."

Beth glanced at him. "That's a smart idea. I'll follow your orders, partner, because I'm a loyal and obedient wife. Haven't you noticed how sweet and cooperative I've been since you met me?"

He chuckled when she made a comical face. "Yep, and I'm obliged to try my darnedest to be a good husband without being too bossy. I'm glad we haven't had any problems with rank. How's the arm doing?"

She flexed it and smiled. "Fine, no soreness or infection, thanks to you and your magic herbs. But please don't make me return the favor by getting shot so I can doctor you."

They shared honest laughter and exchanged real smiles.

"Mount up, wife. Sun's getting higher and hotter."

They traveled rugged terrain that led to Texas. Last night, both had learned how fast and easy primal passion kindled between and within them. Each resolved to stay on alert against another perilous loss of self-control.

Navarro returned to camp following his bath in the Rio Grande, twenty miles north of El Paso. He gazed at Beth and asked, "What are you doing? Surely you don't keep a record of your work for somebody to find."

"Heavens, no. I'm writing letters to my sister and brother; I can post them in town tomorrow. Every month or two, I have to let them know I'm safe and well. I'm planning to visit them in Denver after our mission. Dan said I could take a few weeks off before my next assignment. That will give me a chance to see relatives and old friends again, too."

Navarro combed his wet hair, put away his belongings, and leaned against a tree nearby. He observed for a while before he interrupted her task a second time. "How do they answer? Isn't getting family mail risky?"

She met his hazel gaze as she explained, "They send letters to me at the Agency office in Sante Fe; from there, they're forwarded to Dan. When it's safe, he gives them to me to read and destroy. Since I never use my real name during cases, my identity is protected. That's how correspondence is handled for undercover agents with families." Her partner didn't have kin, that's why, she surmised, he wasn't familiar with the process. She didn't want that realization to sadden him, so she hurried on with, "It's all right to do this tonight, isn't it? If not, I'll burn them and write later."

"I see no reason you can't, no better time than here."

"Thank you. In the future, I'll ask before I take action on any matter. I wouldn't want to do anything to endanger our mission."

"That's smart, thanks."

"You're welcome, my adorable husband," she jested.

"Adorable?" he echoed with a grin and hearty chuckle.

"Well, you said to practice my romantic role all the time. I served you at supper, gave you hugs and kisses today, and stayed in my best mood."

"That you have, Beth Breed." *If you call those quick pecks kisses.*

A few minutes later, she said, "Finished; that should ease their worries for a while." She put away her writing supplies and stood to stretch.

Navarro noticed how Beth rotated her head and rubbed her neck first, then her back at the waist with a frown on her face. "What's wrong, wife?"

She laughed and said, "I sat too long in an awkward position."

"Come here."

At his husky tone, she looked quizzical but joined him. "Yes?"

"Turn around. Let's see if I can be a good doctor again tonight."

"I certainly wouldn't refuse an offer like that, my kind husband."

After she moved long hair out of his path, Navarro began at her neck with a gentle but firm massage. His strong thumbs worked at rigid muscles there. Up and down they traveled with the right degree of pressure. When those muscles relaxed, he shifted to her shoulders, kneading them with fingers and thumbs. He worked at their stiffness until they also responded and loosened. He grinned and chuckled as he elicited dreamy sighs of gratification and reflexive wriggles. He focused on her lower back, above and below the waist. He stroked until he felt the tightness ease.

"Sheer heaven," Beth murmured. "You have magical hands, partner. I could stand here like this forever."

"You mean, until my hands give out."

"Either. Both. Anything. Just don't stop yet," she entreated.

"I won't halt until I'm finished with you, woman."

Beth felt like flowing honey at those provocative words.

As he studied her, Navarro wondered if her hair color reminded him more of a red fox, new copper penny, or the boulders near the Superstition Mountains beneath a blazing sun. He decided the amount and kind of light determined that answer. And he'd never met anyone with eyes so large and expressive, or skin so soft and clear of any markings, detracting or otherwise.

Even Jessie had a smattering of light-brown freckles across her pert nose and cheeks. Maybe they had vanished over the years: ten long and lonely years since he'd held and kissed her; five since he'd heard her voice and seen her, if he didn't count looking at her worn picture in the gold pendant. Jessie had given him her pendant as a farewell gift, but a prison guard had stolen and gambled away the prize. Fate had placed it in Matt's hand months later during a cattle drive when the rancher had gone to buy Jessie a gift for their first Christmas.

Navarro had purchased the current holder in Phoenix to protect the picture he had hidden in a tiny but weather-sheltered crevice just before the law closed in on him. He'd retrieved it after his release and been stunned it was in good condition. He still didn't understand why he hadn't concealed the necklace, too; he assumed fate was responsible and had a reason for his weird action. Perhaps it was so hers could find its way home and remind Jessie of him. The locket he now wore was old and lovely, and the elderly woman who had been forced to part with it for needed money must have been saddened by its sacrifice. The only reason he didn't feel guilty about not generously returning it to the previous owner was because she was dead. He wondered if his sweet Jess had changed in looks and— "Jess," he cautioned himself to be careful not to ever call her that again.

Beth knew his thoughts had drifted far away. She reached behind her, captured his hands, pulled them around her waist, and interlocked their fingers. "Thanks, Navarro; that was wonderful and soothing." *Distract him.* She leaned her head against his broad shoulder, lazed against his body, and took a deep breath. "This is a nice time of day and peaceful spot, don't you think?"

"Yep, it is." He noticed how her slender fingers had snaked between his to curl toward his palm and nest there. Without hurting hers, he overlapped them with his. He rested his cheek against Beth's wavy tresses and cuddled her in a snug embrace. "Practice time, eh?" he murmured to make sure she knew why he was behaving in a romantic manner.

"You said to do it every chance we get, right?"

"Right. But don't get too close to me."

"I thought you said to snuggle up to rehearse our roles."

"I meant emotionally." He realized she stiffened for a moment. He asked himself why he had said such a foolish thing.

"If that interprets to—don't fall in love with you, don't worry; I'm only following orders and playing my part, nothing more."

In an attempt to pass off his mistake as teasing, he asked in a playful tone, "Aren't you gonna give me the same warning? Remind me this is only a job to us?"

"Nope, because it's as unnecessary for you as it was for me. Let's get back to work before I grab a bath to look my best when we reach town tomorrow. You said I'll be meeting a close friend of yours, and I have shopping to do. I thought I'd buy the Cordell children some gifts; youngsters love getting presents. About how old are they? Are they boys or girls?"

"Alice will be seven next month. Lance is four and a half. Lane is nine."

Beth was astonished by the way he spouted off the children's names and ages without having to stop and think. She felt him tense and heard a change in his voice. *Do you feel guilty over deluding your friends or is something else about a visit there troubling you?* "Is Lane a boy or a girl?"

"Boy, why?"

"I've met a L-A-N-E male and a L-A-I-N-E female, so I didn't know. I assume the firstborn son was named after Jessica's family. Right?"

"Yep, Lane Cordell."

If the boy was nine, that meant Jessica had wed and gotten pregnant shortly after Navarro's stay at the ranch. Had Jessica unintentionally misled Navarro and broken his heart, if she was the one who— *Heavens, Bethany Wind, your imagination is running wild tonight!* As if she'd been thinking along another line, she said, "I learned from Caroline and Robert's children that if you don't bring the same sex the same toy, it can cause jealousy and quarrels. We don't want anything to provoke problems there."

"That's smart and thoughtful."

"Last thing—"

"What?" he asked before she could finish, wanting to get away from that subject.

Getting touchy? Why? Because she married someone else and had his children? "I've been trying to think of a special name to call you during our pretense. So you won't worry when I do, I'll be calling you things like heart, husband, and dearest. All right?"

"Fine with me. I'll do the same," But not -*Tsíné*—Apache for "sweetheart/love"—as he'd called Jessie.

"Sounds nice and convincing. I'm going off duty now, boss, to get scrubbed and changed for sleep." She broke their holds and contact, gathered her things, and disappeared into some bushes at the river's edge.

You fool, why did you go and say something stupid like that to her? Still trying to make sure she won't get within a desert span of you? If you keep acting loco, you're gonna provoke suspicion and cause a breach between you two. Maybe that's what you want and need, but the mission doesn't.

Saturday before midday, they rode into El Paso. As soon as they checked into a hotel, Navarro said he was going to buy supplies for their remaining journey, send a coded telegram to Dan and one to the Cordells, and make contact with Zachariah Abernathy. Beth nodded and left to mail her letters to Denver and to shop for the Cordells' gifts.

Outside the hotel, Navarro saw his friend and fellow agent down the street. He walked in that direction as if he had nothing special in mind. He halted near the spot where Zack was whittling, but others were watching his deft hands perform, so a private talk was impossible.

"That's a fine talent you have," he said to catch the man's attention.

Zack recognized the voice, looked up, and said, "Thank ya, suh."

"If I didn't have to go purchase supplies, I'd hang around and watch. Looks mighty interesting. Maybe after I deliver my goods to the hotel in ten minutes or so, I'll return to buy something from you."

"That be real kind of ya, mister, but I'll be done and gawn dereckly. I'll be here gain tamorry if'n ya kin comes back."

"I'll try, if I'm still in town. Sure would like to have one for a friend."

"And I shore would lack to sell ya one. Make ya a good price."

"We'll see," Navarro told him and left to carry out his first chore.

Upon returning to the hotel, Zack was in the upstairs hallway waiting for him. They smiled and shook hands.

"Right on time, old friend. Anybody around?"

"Nope, already checked. This side's empty except for you two."

Navarro grinned as he noticed Zack had dropped the style of talking he used to dupe people about his identity and intelligence. "We'll stand here so we can keep an eye and ear on anybody coming, but we'd better do this quick before we're interrupted."

Zack nodded. "You ain't gonna like what I learned, Navarro. Way I got it figured, your friends are in deep trouble and need money bad. Disease killed more 'an half their stock, rustlers stole some, and a dry spell last year almost claimed their whole crop for winter feed. Most of the animals left ain't old enough for fall sale. Hay price was high and the bank's wanting its money soon."

All that trouble had struck Jessie and Matt . . . "How did you learn so much so fast?"

"I rode in as a cowpuncher down on my luck and bone tired. I worked two weeks for food and shelter. They couldn't pay me nothing, but I said I only needed a rest, vittles, and a roof for a while, then I'd move on to find a job on another ranch. No hiring of extra hands this spring, only them reg'lars there. They don't have money to replace stock and buy crop seed. With no stock or hay to sell, don't see how they're gonna repay the bank or borrow more money to see them through. Heard Cordell tell his wife not to worry, a 'solution' was on the way. They seemed like good folks to me—nice, kind, big hearts; their boys love 'em and respect 'em."

"Any word on Charles Cordell?"

"None there, but the Agency said he's en route from the Texas border. He's picking up loaded wagons and other men in Amarillo. Should arrive at the ranch about the twenty-fourth. At your pace, you two should arrive a few days afore him. I'll be riding with you far as Fort Hancock, then head overland to Nogales. Agency thinks that's where he'll leave Mexico or camp for his meeting with those renegades. I'll hang around there and pass messages. I'll be near Develer's Store ever' day from three to six, whittling and waiting for you to come or contact me."

"We'd best part before anyone sees us together too long. We can talk more on the trail. Didn't know you'd be riding a ways with us." They walked toward Navarro's room; he set down supplies to unlock his door.

As he did so, Zack asked, "I know it'll be hard for you to return after what happened there years ago. I wouldn't want to walk in your boots."

"Don't worry, old friend, there won't be any problems or trouble."

"I hope not, for you anyway. Them kind of boots are hurting tight. She's one fine and pretty lady. I can see what a big loss she was."

"Yep, but that's over. She's married and happy."

"I best get going," Zack said with a wave. "See you two outside town in the morning."

Navarro turned the knob and pushed open the door.

"Wait, I'm dressing!" Beth shrieked.

It was too late to keep the door from swinging ajar. He saw her grab a garment and hold it before her chemise- and petticoat-clad body. "Sorry, love. I didn't know you were back. That was fast work."

Beth glanced past him to the stranger standing in the hallway, a nice-looking black man with short curly hair. "We have company?"

"You two can meet and talk tomorrow. See you later, Zack."

The other man nodded at a rosy-cheeked Beth and departed. Navarro closed the door, bolted it, and put his purchases in a pile.

"That was your contact and close friend?"

"Yep, Zack Abernathy. Known him for years."

"Everything go all right?"

"Yep, tell you about his report later. This room doesn't give much privacy and we can't take any risks."

As Beth turned her back and slipped on her dress, she said, "That's fine." She wondered if he was trying to decide if or what she'd overheard.

"I thought you were gone."

She kept her back to him as she buttoned her bodice. "It only takes a few minutes to post letters and buy gifts, and both places are close to the hotel. I was freshening up and changing for supper. I thought you'd be gone longer, too." She lifted a brush and started to work on her hair.

"I still have something to do. I'll return soon and we'll go eat."

Navarro went to the telegraph office and sent Dan a message: *Forgot to tell me Red Wind news. No problem. Thanks for property loan. Will return it later.* He signed it, *Z. N. Jones* to let Dan know they'd met.

The message to Jessie and Matt related news of his marriage and asked if they could stop for a visit on the way to San Antonio so they could meet Beth and she could meet them. His motive was to give them warning but not enough time to worry. If they said no or wait until another time, he and Beth would spy on the ranch and wait for Charles to leave, then trail him.

After he returned to the hotel, Navarro took a bath and shaved in the second-floor water closet to obtain a short reprieve from Beth's charms. He also wanted solitude to ponder what Zack had told him.

In their room, Beth was glad she had finished her tasks quickly so she'd been able to overhear the men's talk. She surmised her partner was worried about the Cordells having a possible motive for getting involved with Charles's crime, and worried about seeing his old love—lost love—again.

It seemed a strain for Navarro to play his husband role tonight and it shouldn't be; after all, it was only an act, a duty, following orders. Perhaps he feared she was attempting to replace that "big loss" in his head and heart. She knew that was impossible, that he still obviously loved the mystery woman; Dan and Zack were aware of that tormenting reality, too. When, she fretted, would he realize the unrequited past was over in more than words?

Navarro entered the room and glanced at her before putting away his belongings. He noticed her sad expression. "Anything wrong, Beth?"

She cloaked her emotions and controlled her expression and voice. "Are you sure it was safe to meet with another agent in the open like that?"

"We were careful and alert. Do you mean because he's an ex-slave?"

"No, but that fact might more easily call attention to you and him."

"Just the opposite, Zack tends to be invisible to most folks. Who'd suspect a black man of being a Special Agent? When he's around, it's like he isn't there, so people talk freely around him and he learns plenty. He sits and whittles while folks watch and think he's only earning money with his skill. Searching for the right kind of wood to use gives him an excuse to be in the wilds when he's tailing somebody. You don't have anything against black folks, do you?"

"Heavens, no, but I haven't known many. Only a few lived in Denver and none were near the places I've been assigned to."

"You won't mind traveling with him tomorrow?"

"No, I'm eager to meet and chat with your friend."

"Think he'll tell you all about me?" Navarro jested.

"I thought I knew everything about you," she quipped in return.

"You know enough."

No, I don't. As she sat cross-legged on the bed and braided her long copper hair, Beth coaxed, "Then tell me all about Zack."

"He's thirty-eight, a few months older than me. He was a slave until seventeen. A lucky one if you can call it that—the property of a good man. He started off as a houseboy and became best friend of his owner's son. They knew he was smart; they let him study lessons with the son, even slept in his room as a sort of guard and companion. His master was killed during the war and his friend was murdered afterward in a raid by men dressed like the KKK. Zack knew he'd be strung up next so he moved west. He learned enough in a few years to become a lawman. Like me, he caught Dan's eye. We met on a case in Yuma and we've been close ever since."

Beth recalled how the two men were the same size, build, and height of six two. She decided Zack must be a good man to be accepted by Navarro. Too, the men had both suffered hardships and troubled pasts that provided an affinity for a special friendship. She liked discovering this side of her partner, who was turning out to be less of a loner than she'd imagined.

"What did you buy at the store for the children?"

"A doll for Alice, stuffed horses for Lance and Lane, and candy for all."

"Good thing they're not wooden horses. Since Zack just left the Cordell ranch and he whittles every spare minute, they might be suspicious if we rode in with two he could have carved. You chose well. I'm sure they'll like them."

"I also bought Jessica a shawl and Matt a knife with a carved handle."

"Why did you do that?"

"A gesture of gratitude for all they did for my husband. Remember, dearest heart, allegedly we wouldn't have met and wed if not for their influence on you and their help years ago, especially getting you released from prison."

"I guess that excuse will ride with them."

Beth was a little miffed and confused by his attitude and remarks. "If you think I shouldn't give them presents, I won't; just give the order, boss. I was only trying to make this an easy and happy event for them."

"Easy and happy" for them? Will it be? "It's all right with me."

"If we've nothing else to discuss, I'll turn in."

He grasped her dismay. "That's all. Beth . . ."

She stopped pulling down the covers and looked at him. "Yes?"

"It's a good idea. You're a kind and thoughtful person. 'Night."

She was surprised and pleased to hear that. "Good night, Navarro."

At midday on Sunday, the three agents stopped to rest and eat. After Zack finished, he pulled something from his pocket and began to whittle while he waited for departure. Beth went to sit nearby and observe as she chewed on a biscuit with fried ham from town and sipped coffee. She saw him use a sharp blade to trim slivers from the small lump. It had taken on a shape she recognized, a miniature saguaro cactus. She was enthralled and impressed by his workmanship. His long fingers moved with leisure.

"What other kinds of things do you make, Zack?"

He paused to look at her and answer, "Knife handles, hair ornaments, combs, kitchen tools, shoehorns, and toys—mostly animals, cowboys, and Indians. I give away a few; I sell others for extra money." His dark-brown gaze returned to his objective. "It relaxes me and gives me something to do during the long hours I spend alone or spying on targets."

Beth glanced at Navarro as she recalled that he made arrows during his solitude and to occupy his thoughts. As for her, she read or worked on new disguises and identities. Zack's words ceased her mental roaming.

"I also use whittling to distract people or fool 'em. Been times when it helped me get close to somebody I needed to watch or meet." He sent her a broad grin. "If I get caught by the wrong person at the wrong time, I just say I'm out hunting wood for my work."

"Does that excuse dupe them at night, too?"

"Even then, 'cause some is at its best when it's cool and damp. All I have to do is show 'em what I mean and empty my pouch of carvings and they believe me. Nobody would imagine I'm a gover'ment agent."

Beth observed how his deft fingers held and labored on the item with love and respect, as if it were a living creature. His eyes sparkled and his tone rang with zeal and affection when he talked about his hobby. For such a big and strong male, she mused, his touch was light and gentle, as seemed true of his character. "This is fascinating. How do you select the wood type and size for your craft?"

"I look for the best color, grain, and strength for what I aim to make. Certain things call for hard wood; others, soft; and some, in between. When I grasp a hunk in my fist, even if it looks dead or ugly to most folks, I can feel the life inside it and I can visu'lize its promise of beauty."

Navarro studied the woman admiring his friend's expertise. When he had held her, he perceived dormant life within her which she had buried with Steven, and he could envision its splendid rebirth.

"How do you decide what to carve next?" Beth asked.

"If somebody asks for a particular piece, I whittle it. I close my eyes, picture what it's gonna be, then do it. Or," he continued after a chuckle, "the chunk tells me inside my head what it wants to become, tells me what it's gotten hidden under its surface. I just listen and go searching for it."

Beth glanced at her partner as she compared Zack's description to Navarro's mute calls for change years ago when the Lanes heard them and brought forth his inner beauty and uniqueness with their respect and affection.

Zack withdrew a piece of exotic ebony and placed the fist-size hunk in Beth's hand. "Study the color and grain; then close your eyes and let your senses feel its strength and hardness. After you finish, tell me what you think it wants to become."

Beth's gaze glued to the specimen as her slender fingers passed over the exquisite fragment as if caressing and mentally communing with the wood's soul. "It's magnificent, Zack. Wherever did you find it?"

"Friends bring or send me samples from faraway places; that one's from India. Ebony's a devil to work with 'cause it's so hard. Looks like polished stone after sanding, maybe even a jewel. It's rarely used here."

"And I'm sure it's very expensive when it is."

"Sure is. I couldn't buy any. Thank goodness for kind friends."

Navarro knew it was time to ride onward, but he hated to halt their conversation. He enjoyed witnessing their rapport and reactions to each other. Beth seemed to have a knack for getting along with people and putting others at ease—except with him when she became too tempting. It was obvious Zack was impressed and charmed by the green-eyed redhead. He was glad the two got along so well and seemed to like each other. He decided to wait a few more minutes before saying they had to leave.

Beth glanced toward Navarro whose attention seemed elsewhere, then whispered at a level only Zack could hear, "A black wolf, a lone wolf."

The man grinned and nodded. "You have the eye and mind of an artist, Beth Breed; your choice is perfect. Just what I made with its mate."

She wished he would show her that treasure, but he didn't offer; perhaps it was lovingly carved and reluctantly sold long ago.

"Some things call for part of a limb; a few for a knot; others, the tree's very heart and soul. I keep cutting away the fat until only lean meat is left. Then, I rub my prize until it's smooth, slick as a raindrop. Don't want my buyers getting splinters in their hands." He grinned and chuckled.

Beth smiled and laughed, too. As her partner joined them, she said, "It's making magic with hard work and a special gift. Something plain is transformed into a treasure that lasts for a long time. Right, boss?"

Navarro nodded. Creating true love was making real and powerful magic, he decided, but it wasn't always beautiful and lasting, not with the wrong woman or at the wrong time with the right one. Because of lost love, he'd had ten years of loneliness and torment. He didn't want to take that risk again.

Following nights spent near Fort Hancock and Eagle Peak, Navarro and Beth halted west of the Davis Mountains to camp on Tuesday. They would reach Fort Davis tomorrow where he'd check for an answer to his El Paso telegram to the Cordells. He couldn't imagine what it might say.

After supper, Navarro sat Indian-style at their campfire. He almost had decided not to reveal his past romance with Jessica Cordell. He didn't like to expose his secrets and private life, and he'd done plenty of soul-baring with the redhead. Yet, if any slips were made at the ranch by him or anyone there, Beth's suspicions might endanger their mission and rapport. He fingercombed his hair as he reasoned on how much to say and how to begin.

Beth's fingers curled around the miniature ebony wolf in her pocket that Zack had given to her with a mischievous grin before parting. The saguaro cactus was in her saddlebag, a "lucky charm" and reminder of her days in Tucson. Both were keepsakes of meeting the man nearby. "Navarro, is something bothering you tonight?" she asked softly. "Did I do anything wrong to upset you? You've been quiet—even distant—most of the evening."

"I know, and I'm sorry, but I've got another confession to make."

Beth eyed the man whose somber gaze was fastened to the colorful flames that separated them. Her curiosity was piqued, but she hated to rush a revelation that seemed to be difficult and painful. Navarro glanced at her before staring into the fire again. It was getting late and her apprehension was increasing so she prompted, "Another confession about your past?"

"Yep, my last one," *because I'll take the secret about Lane to my grave.* "Then, partner, you'll know all about me."

Chapter Ten

Again, he went silent. Beth finished filling a half cup of coffee and sipped the hot liquid with caution. Perhaps, she mused, he needed help to begin. "Is it about a broken love affair at the ranch?" She ventured.

Navarro's head jerked up and he gaped at her. Firelight danced on her face and copper hair. A tender expression glowed in her large green eyes, and her full lips were parted. "You already know the truth? Dan told you?"

"Absolutely not: He's your friend; he wouldn't betray your trust."

"That's good to hear. I didn't believe he would. How did you know?"

"An accurate guess from clues you've dropped, and it seemed a logical explanation for why you'd need a wife as a cover during a visit to old friends. Who is she? Why didn't you two get together? Does she still live on the ranch? Is that the reason you have to tell me about her before we arrive?"

He nodded. "I can't let anything or anybody mess up this mission, and that sharp mind of yours could pick up clues and misunderstand things." Navarro ran fingers through his sable mane. "While I was working there ten years ago, Jessie and I . . . We . . ." *Spit it out and get it done.* "We were in love. We would've gotten married if I hadn't been dodging that hangman's noose and been hauled back to prison without her knowing where I was."

He saw Beth try to conceal her shock. "By the time I got out of that hellhole five years later and returned, she was hitched to Matt and they had two children. Expecting a third. I didn't know about the house fire and move, so I rode to the old ranch site. Matt was there alone checking on some things, and he laid the hard facts on me. I promised him I'd stay out of their lives and left; I've kept my word until now."

"You left without seeing Jessica? Without explaining what happened?"

"She was carrying his child; I couldn't upset her in that condition. After the baby was born, Matt explained why it looked like I'd deserted her and just vanished for keeps. Jess understood and forgave me; so did he."

Navarro poured coffee, perhaps to take a moment to compose himself, Beth reasoned. She realized she wasn't—and at the same time was—surprised to discover the mystery woman was Jessica Lane Cordell. Clues had slapped her in the face from all angles and any agent with real intelligence could decipher them. What disturbed her most was that Navarro had loved Jessica enough to marry her, had not left her of his own free will, had gone back to claim her the first moment it was possible, and had made a great sacrifice for her happiness at the loss of his own. "When she learned the truth, it didn't change things for you two?"

"How could it when she'd made a new life without me? She had a home, husband, children, a successful ranch. She'd promised to wait for me to work out my troubles, but I can't blame her for breaking her word when she didn't even hear from me for five years."

If my arithmetic is right, she didn't wait long to marry Matt. Maybe she wasn't as in love with you as you believe. "Why didn't you contact her?"

"How could I write from prison? I doubt a letter would've gotten past those guards, 'specially without them reading it. If I explained why I didn't—and couldn't—return and she wrote back without suspecting her letter would be read by those bastards, it would've connected Jess to me while I was running from that hellhole and gotten her and the others into trouble. I couldn't risk it."

As if he'd read her previous thoughts, he responded to them for her.

"When I rode off saying I wasn't coming back, I left her in a tough bind; she was still hurting bad from Jed's death, her sister's treachery, and Fletcher's evil actions. She had a ranch to run, family to protect, hands to supervise, pains to heal. She needed a strong, dependable, loving man at her side; Matt got that job while I was working on a rock pile in Arizona. I can't blame him for stepping in; he'd loved Jessie for years in secret."

Beth winced inside as she experienced empathy for him. *How can you return to such a tormenting scene? Of course,* she reasoned, *you have to prove Jessica's innocence in this case and protect her from any peril. Heaven help us if this complicates and endangers our mission.* "Is she happy with him? Does she love him? Is she over you?" She saw him wince at each question, but she had to ask them.

"That's how it looked to me when I returned."

"But you talked with Matt. How could you take her husband's word?"

"If Matt Cordell can't be trusted on any matter, nobody can."

"You have that much faith in him?"

"Yep. I'd bet Night Cloud men don't come any better than him."

"But he had a wife, children, and home to protect when you appeared out of nowhere, perhaps as a rival for them. Some men would do anything to hold tight to all they love, even a good man." *Like you. You've given up on love and marriage. You continue to let yourself suffer to protect and retain a lost dream, so you should grasp my meaning.*

"I spied on them together that night; the marriage is a good one."

The admission stunned her at first; then, she understood. *It must have been an agonizing scene to observe.* "That was smart, Navarro; I would have done the same thing."

He nodded in gratitude. "Matt had years to win her over, every day and night for five years, sharing good and bad, hard and easy, being there when she needed him. You've been married, so you know what I mean."

"While you were a traitor and black memory to her, he was her friend and right hand, her healer and sunshine. He had opportunities and time to forge a powerful bond with her during your unexplained absence."

He thought a minute then said, "I don't want you thinking bad of Jessie or Matt, because they're good people."

"I would imagine your disappearance and lengthy silence hurt and confused her. Most women, widows or rejected lovers, think the only way or best way to get over losing a man is to replace him with another one, fast."

He locked his gaze to hers. "Is that how you think?"

"No. If I did, I'd be remarried or searching hard for a new husband. I'm not." *At least I wasn't until you came into my life. Now, I'm unsure.* "A person can find new love—even better love, I suppose—but no one can take another's place. That's like . . . trying to make a docile yard dog out of a wild coyote. You said you promised to stay out of their lives and you've kept your word, but have you stolen any more furtive peeks?"

"Nope, just sent news by letter in December of '81, what I told you last time about what I was doing and where. I wrote them how they could reach me if they ever needed a hired gun again. There's an Army officer at an Arizona post who passes along any messages for me to Dan. Matt sent me a short letter after Lance was born."

"They haven't contacted you since then?"

"Nope."

Beth's heart pounded and her mouth dried as she dared to ask, "What if Jessica still loves you and wants you? Isn't it risky seeing her again for the first time during a crucial mission?"

"She still loves me, but only as a friend, nothing more."

"And Matt, how does he feel about you?"

"He asked me to step into his place if anything happened to him."

Beth gaped at him until she found her voice again. "He *what?*"

"I mean, step in to protect Jessie and his children if trouble came."

"To remain friends despite having a woman come between you is quite unusual." *If Matt isn't just duping you to keep your cooperation. We'll soon see how he reacts to your sudden return.*

"As I said, they were and they are good people, bone deep. If they hadn't been true friends, they wouldn't have tried so hard to get me a pardon, 'specially when it looked like I'd done Jessie wrong."

"You didn't do her wrong; in fact, you saved their lives and the ranch. You did far more than you were hired to do, and they must know that. They were aware you were on the run from the law and had to leave. I'm sure they realized how unselfish and protective you were being, both times."

The redhead's assessment made him smile. "Yep; that's why their actions were so generous."

"Maybe Jessica hoped a pardon would bring you back to her." Beth saw him seem to shift his position so he could avoid her probing gaze.

"Nope, she was satisfied with a letter."

Are you positive? "She'll come face-to-face with you during a visit."

"Face-to-face with a happily married man, with just you in my heart."

"That's only a ruse. I imagine Dan figured having a wife along would make things easier for all of you, and give the Cordells a credible reason for you going there. I take it from what you implied that he knows the truth?"

"Yep, but Dan doesn't have to worry about the past; what happened between us was ten years ago. It's as gone as yesterday's hours."

"Dan thinks only the best of you. Considering what took place between you and Jessica, surely the Cordells would never ask you to come and stay with them without a wife at your side, especially Matt. I'm your only hope of getting an invitation. You're a skilled lawman, but this case demands extra caution and unusual requirements. I'm lucky I was chosen as your partner. What female agent wouldn't give anything to team up with the legendary Navarro Breed and have a chance to learn from him?"

"That's kind of you to say, Beth."

"Papa said to be truthful as much as possible, even in my job, so there wouldn't be so many lies to keep up with during any fast and trying moments."

"I'll remember that suggestion; it sounds like a smart one. That other stuff I told you about the Cordells, the ranch, and my past is true. If they hadn't taken me in and turned me around, I'd still be in prison or lying dead in some dusty street or cactus patch. I'm grateful to them, all of them."

"I am, too. I'm glad they saved you from that other life and from yourself. We need lawmen like you've become."

"Thanks again; you really know how to swell a man's head." He had to make sure she comprehended the situation and had confidence in him. "After the law threw me back into that hole, it was over between me and Jess. Even though Steven's out of your life forever, you still love him and miss him; he'll always own a special place in your heart because of all you two shared in the past. Right?"

"Yes." *But Steven is dead; Jessica isn't and you'll be in her life again soon and she'll be in yours. It isn't the same; can't you see that?*

To Navarro, she looked and sounded hesitant. "It's like that with me and Jessie, too, Beth. We know it's over and we accept that fact."

You mean, over and accepted as long as Matt's alive and free. This case could change everything for you and her if he's involved, if he's imprisoned or slain. Surely you've thought of those possibilities. That's probably why you tried so hard to leave me—or any "wife"—behind. You're saddling yourself a tough horse to ride, and I can't allow you to mount it or get bucked off. This time, you could break more than your heart; you could get killed. Or you could ruin our assignment.

"We've all made fresh starts, Beth, and I won't do anything to hurt them or to jeopardize our mission," he vowed to calm her apparent worries. "I guess it was same when you lost Steven: at first, life don't seem worth much; as time passes, you see it is. You knew about love and feelings all your life; I didn't. What I learned about 'em, Jess taught me, and the boys helped. I rode away from that ranch and her a better man, a new man. I'm not sorry I took that job. As you told me, good and bad experiences make us what we are." He poured the last of the coffee into his cup and sipped it as they relaxed in meditative silence.

You still have important things to learn, partner. For a start, one can love more than one person during a lifetime; that's an unexpected lesson I was taught very recently.

When Beth had first met Steven, she'd taken an instant liking to him because of his personality and traits. He was charming, witty, fun, genial, well mannered, and good-looking. And Steven had grown on her as time passed. But with Navarro Breed, the first moment she'd turned in the Carters' store and looked into his face, she was almost struck speechless. He had an aura—a commanding presence—that made her want to be with him and cling to him. He was a consuming force that couldn't be resisted. He was power and magic and vitality, the embodiment of passion.

Passion . . . He stirred somnolent, primal urges to life, along with the new and potent desires he ignited like smoldering embers into a roaring blaze. A look, touch, or thought of him whipped up those flames within her until they burned like a perilous wildfire. They seared over her until she yearned to be engulfed. That was reckless because Navarro Breed belonged only to himself, and she could think of no way to cut through the defensive barrier he'd built around him. If she had an ounce of brains, Beth fretted, she would tell her wayward heart to avoid him like the plague. But it was too late.

Somewhere along the way, her feelings and responses were no longer pretenses, no longer just following orders. However, that changed nothing where he was concerned. He had endured so much during a tragic childhood, in a harsh prison, from hardening drifter days and ill-fated first love. When he'd given his heart, it had been broken. Until he got over Jessica, he couldn't and wouldn't respond to a woman, and she mustn't pursue or settle for half a man. She doubted she could ever have a future with him because he wasn't interested in marriage, settling down, having a permanent partnership with her. The type of assignments that required a team wouldn't appeal to him on a regular basis; nor would he want a pining female hanging around all the time. *Stick to the mission and forget these crazy hopes and dreams.*

"You seem lost in thought," Navarro said.

"I was thinking about something I read by a man named Tennyson. He wrote it about forty years ago: ' 'Tis better to have loved and lost than never to have loved at all.' Do you think he spoke from unrequited experience or a deluded imagination?" She forced out laughter to reduce their stress.

Navarro smiled as he guessed her ploy. "Most good sayings have a mite of truth in 'em." He turned serious again. "You don't have to worry,

Beth, there won't be any problems between me and Jessie or Matt. I promise."

She studied his expression and concluded he was sincere. But crazy things happened when a person least expected them to . . . "I'm sure you're not the kind of man who'd cause trouble for friends. We'll make sure the Cordells realize straight away they don't have to worry about the past, either. From what they'll witness, no couple will appear more in love, well matched, and happier than us."

If we pull off our roles and they let us come to visit. "Thanks."

"You're welcome. We'd best get to sleep. Tomorrow's a busy day."

"You're a very understanding and special woman, a good friend, and a perfect partner. My last confession wasn't as hard as I thought it'd be. I'll have to thank Dan for choosing Bethany Wind for this mission."

"That's what true friends are for, to be there when we need them. I hope I never disappoint or fail you, Navarro; you mean a lot to me."

"Same here, wife." He also tried to sound playful and calm, but his heart pounded and his body flamed as he took in her beauty and tender words. If he didn't know better, he'd think . . . *Don't be loco; she's only being nice and kind, a real lady. And ladies don't go for half-breed bastard loners. Jessie was an exception and it won't happen for you again.*

Beth smiled then rose to prepare for the night, sure to be a long one. At least he liked, respected, and accepted her. That was a splendid beginning, wasn't it?

An hour later, Beth was still awake and tense under the half moon. Things Kate Carter had told "Elizabeth Lawrence" in Tucson raced around inside her head: "Be brave, take risks. . . . Go after what you want. . . . Starting tonight."

Tonight was the last totally private evening they would share before reaching their target area where they'd be on constant guard. Beth wondered if she should attempt to gain a hold on him before he saw Jessica. She wondered if Navarro could ever give her his battered heart to heal and cherish? She understood his feelings and dilemma because after losing Steven, she thought she'd never love or desire another man. But she hadn't expected to meet someone like the overwhelming legend who had blown into her life as an unforeseen whirlwind and swept her away. While pursuing him, she could mask her true emotions behind the role she was ordered to play. Yet, that gave her only a short time to steal the key Jessica possessed so she herself could unlock the door to his heart to free him to love Bethany Trask Wind, to become the real Beth Breed.

As her quivering fingers stroked the ebony carving from Zack, she hoped it was meant as an implication she should also have the living lone wolf. It troubled Beth to admit it was going to hurt even more to lose her fake husband than it had been to lose her real one, but that was true.

I'm sorry, Steven. Please understand and forgive me, but I can't help what I feel. I've failed to resist him and avoid this predicament. I love him and want him, and I'm going to use every skill and charm I possess to win him. As for you, my beloved lone wolf, I pray the Fates dull your sharp wits so you won't see my snare coming at you until it's too late to elude it. Goodbye, Steven. I'll lay you to rest where you belong.

To capture him will be the most difficult and hazardous assignment I've accepted. This time, I'll be risking far more than my mortal life; I'll be putting my heart, soul, and spirit in jeopardy of rejection and anguish.

Beth summoned courage to put a bold and beguiling plan into motion. She flung aside the top section of the bedroll, screamed, and leapt up. As she reached for a pistol, Navarro joined her with one in his hand. She realized he had reacted with haste and agility to come to her aid.

"What's wrong?"

"Something was crawling on me." *Feelings for you,* her mind added, so she wouldn't be telling a lie. "Sorry if I woke you." *But I had to.*

"I wasn't asleep. Let me check out your bedroll." He knelt and with caution lifted the top to look inside. "Too dark to see anything in there." He lifted it by the bottom and shook it with the opening away from them. He dropped it in a pile and scanned the area with eagle eyes. "Whatever it was, you must have scared it away when you yelled and jumped."

"I don't know what got into me; I'm not usually afraid of insects or snakes."

He cuffed her chin and smiled to soothe her agitation. "You were just caught off guard while dozing."

"Maybe dreaming or a wild imagination?"

Navarro slipped an arm around her gown-clad waist and said, "Maybe, that happens sometimes when you're half-asleep."

Beth placed a hand in the middle of his back and nestled close to him to rest her head against his shoulder. "More excitement is just what we needed on an evening like this, right, husband dearest?" she murmured.

Navarro chuckled as his hand drifted upward into her free-flowing mane of copper delight and enjoyed its silkiness. She exuded the smell of fresh wildflowers. It was nice to have her cuddled up to him. He savored the way she showed no aversion to his touch, how she accepted him with such freedom and completeness, such trust. Some man, he mused, was going to be damned lucky to get this special woman.

Beth made a slight move to position a bare foot between his unbooted ones. Her arms encircled his narrow waist and she leaned against his hard and virile body. She nestled a fiery cheek to his cool, bare chest and heard his heart beating at a rapid pace. "I always feel safe and alive with you, and I enjoy your company so much. I hope this assignment lasts a long time because it's going to be strange and sad to be alone again afterward."

"I'm glad you have confidence in me, but don't go missing me till I'm gone," he jested. A dizzying swirl of sensations and observations assailed him. As if having a mind of their own, his eager arms embraced her and held her clasped to him. He rested his cheek atop her head. Her unbound breasts, their peaks taut and erect, seared his naked torso through a cotton nightgown. He heard Beth's dreamy sighs and throaty noises. His loins burned with need for her as her fingers roved the flesh of his back and her soft face caressed him. His voice was husky as he teased, "Taking advantage of the moment to practice your wifely role, eh, partner?"

"Yep. This kind of lesson is wonderful."

He stopped stroking her hair and back to cease the intoxicating pull on him. "It's also mighty late for work, isn't it?"

"Nope, never too late to prepare for something so important." She made sure her lips tantalized his bronzed skin as she spoke. She suppressed any nibbles of guilt or shame about trying to seduce him. "When I first met you, I was nervous about working with such a legend, especially one who seemed displeased to be teamed up with me."

He kissed her forehead and said, "I'm real sorry about that, but I'm used to riding and working alone, and I wasn't sure of your skills."

"It doesn't matter now because we're past that point."

He was as hot as a branding iron in a fire. Didn't she see that she and this sensuous situation were stimulating and tempting? He had strong willpower, but he wasn't made of stone. It had been a long time since—

"I'll confess: in the beginning, I was afraid this romantic part of the marriage was going to be too hard for me to perform."

"But you've learned it isn't?"

She looked up into his hazel eyes. She took one hand from his naked back so its fingers could tease over his lips. "Not since we became such good friends." She smiled. "It's actually a lot of fun. I'm grateful to you for alleviating my doubts and insecurities. Yours, too." She lifted herself on tiptoes and pretended to give him a kiss of gratitude. Afterward she teased, "You too tired for duty or did you wed an unappealing female?"

Navarro's hands cupped her expressive face. "I hope being appealing won't become a problem for us, partner."

Me being appealing or you? As he closed his mouth over hers, Beth surrendered her lips and will, and hoped he wouldn't withdraw from her.

Their tongues met, played, and mated with feverish delight. The kiss was different from those during previous practice sessions; it was long, deep, delving, titillating. One drifted into many more. Their hands roamed, caressed, and enticed as their bodies yearned to become one. Unnoticed by either, their burdened souls begged for release from troubled pasts, for a new bond to be forged in this perfect match. A cool breeze wafted over their exposed flesh but the sultry heat of passion warmed them to their cores.

A nearby coyote sent forth mournful howls that broke Navarro's concentration. He was stunned to realize he was on the verge of taking her, and she appeared willing to let him. He warned himself it was crazy to lose control like this while on duty during a tricky case and with a fellow agent. He struggled to recover his stolen wits. "That's enough practice tonight. Why don't I sleep over here and you take my spot over there in case your visitor returns to snuggle up? Can't blame him for trying."

He was halting the heady situation before it could go farther! *So much for a daring seduction scheme, Bethany Wind.* It took enormous fortitude to let him retreat without coaxing him to continue, as she didn't want to appear wanton. She was tempted to accept his offer but knew she'd never get to sleep inhaling his manly smell on his bedding so she said, "Thanks, but I'll stick to mine. If my pest returns, I'll handle it."

Navarro had seen her stare at him in what seemed to be disbelief and dismay before she lowered her lashes and head in what had to be shock and embarrassment over her careless behavior. He understood her feelings because he, too, was accustomed to having self-control and clear wits. He couldn't explain to himself or to her how they had gotten so carried away with each other, and he hoped the unfinished intimate episode wouldn't cause problems between them. He didn't want to make her reluctant or afraid to get near him or to touch him for fear of arousing him to the point he tried to lure her into his grasp. For their safety and success of the mission, she had to be able to trust him under any circumstances. As he wondered how to restore her confidence and faith in him, he went down on his knees to unfold a stubborn bottom corner after spreading her bedroll on the ground.

Beth did the same at the top, then sat on its center, which put them in close and enticing proximity as he shifted at the same time to speak to her. Before either could retreat or find a distracting tactic, the agents' gazes merged. Neither seemed able to break away. Unextinguished embers burst into new flames of desire; but this time they couldn't escape the roaring blaze that intended to consume them. They wanted . . . They needed . . .

His hand reached out to caress her flushed cheek as his eyes roved her lovely features. "It wasn't just practice, was it?"

Beth's fingers trailed over his full lips as she shook her head. *Give it one more try.* She hastened to her knees and hugged him. She buried her forehead against his bare chest and almost whispered in a ragged voice, "I'm sorry if I was forward and shameless"—she raised her head to fasten her gaze to his—"but you disarm me so fast and unexpectedly at times. I'm afraid you're a very desirable man, Navarro Breed, so don't fault me for thinking of you in the wrong way at times like this."

"Same goes here, Beth Breed, but we don't need problems."

"There won't be any if we don't allow it, right?"

He bent forward to kiss her cheek, but she turned her head and their mouths made contact. Her taste and mute beckoning cut the leash on his weakened control. His arms locked her against him. His lips and tongue explored hers with fervor. When she responded in like kind, he was lost. His body demanded and ached to possess hers and, even if he had wanted to, he couldn't resist its bold order.

Between feverish kisses, they sank to the bedroll to share an urgent union. Though she had carefully planned this seduction, what happened within and between them was spontaneous and instinctive.

They feasted on hungry kisses. Their ravenous hands explored and teased. As their mouths meshed, their appetites became greedy. In leisure, he nibbled at her lips; he trailed his over her fiery cheek, teased her earlobe, and wandered down her silky neck. As he did so, she pressed kisses on any spot her mouth could reach. Their cravings and suspense mounted. While tantalizing her with his lips, he eased her gown up to her throat. His ardent mouth trekked over her breasts, stimulating and hardening their peaks even more. His eager tongue swirled over the rosy brown points, lavishing moist attention on each in turn.

When he'd lifted himself from her to pull up her gown, Beth had taken bold advantage of the moment to unfasten his long underwear. He shifted to help her slide them past his hips. Her fingers massaged his firm buttocks, then grazed over his strong frame. She stroked his shoulders, neck, and arms as he worked magic and delight upon her body and mind. She was enthralled by the sensuous way he caressed the full length of her body with his, arousing her kindled passions to a higher level of yearning. She loved his hard, lean body flawless except for the scars. She traced several lash marks from end to end, their raised surfaces reminding her of the agony and humiliation he had endured from his father and brutal prison guards.

Her thoughts left that troubling area to seek another destination, one with a different kind of diversion. He straddled her left leg so the privacy slit in her bloomers was accessible. His deft fingers found and explored the mound between her thighs; she could hardly wait for his sweet invasion. She quivered in anticipation as he slid between her legs and guided himself within her, a contact that was rapturous and breathstealing. She locked him in place and surrendered to his raw, hot, swift, and urgent lovemaking.

Navarro was engulfed by staggering sensations. Her overtures, actions, and responses thrilled him to the center of his being where she had ignited a fire he didn't quite understand. His desire was so great that he could think of nothing except fulfilling it. He was astounded by his effect on her. She wanted him, she needed him, and she was taking him. She didn't care who or what he was or had been. He had the ability to enchant her beyond restraint, the talent to arouse and to satisfy her. She seemed to be holding back nothing from him, offering him all she was. Never, his mind told him, had he felt such a potent flood of emotions. She was as radiant and inspiring as the loveliest sunset, as fiery as the hottest desert day. He couldn't touch her soft skin enough, stroke her sensitive breasts enough, taste her sweet lips enough, or appease either of them enough to let this be their only stolen union.

Beth clutched at this magnificent man who knew how to titillate and sate her as Steven never had. Wild and wonderful feelings consumed her. She reveled in the sensation of her flesh against his. As her nightgown bunched under her arms and wadded at her throat, she realized they were so eager that they hadn't removed their few garments, just shoved them out of the path of questing lips and hands. Despite their rush, it wasn't carnal copulation; they were making love. As ecstasy captured her in its throes, she trembled, sighed, and held on tight for the joyous ride.

Navarro galloped away with her, unable to bridle his passion any longer. He knew she was moving with him, eager to reach their triumphant goal together. She was a gifted partner in and out of bed. Again, for a brief moment, he thought about how lucky some man would be to win her.

As they reached the pinnacle of pleasure, golden splendor shot over and through the breathless couple, leaving contentment—total serenity—in its wake. Unable to separate so soon, their lips and bodies remained joined as they came down to earth together.

Navarro rolled to his back and took her with him, to nestle against his side. He hadn't felt this sated and happy in years, not since . . . He kept himself from jerking upward and fleeing. How, he worried, could his wits and body be so weak as to betray his beloved when he was this close to her? He had sworn his love and loyalty to Jessie forever; he had broken that vow with Bethany Wind. He had allowed another woman to arouse and fulfill him as no other—*Don't even think such a stupid thought 'cause it can't be true.*

Beth perceived his sudden mood change. If she had been ignorant before about how powerful Jessica's hold was over him, she couldn't deny it now. Or perhaps, she mused, Navarro only feared opening himself up to another rejection and heartache. With his keen wits, couldn't he comprehend she would never betray and hurt him as Jessica had? She would love him and stay with him forever if he but asked.

Navarro propped on his side and gazed at her. She had willingly submitted to him, but he should have been stronger. She looked so serene in his embrace, but he must not mislead her. "I'm sorry, Beth; I didn't mean for this to happen. Forgive me?"

She knew—without delay—she must let him see she wasn't repulsed, angered, or upset. She stroked his angular jawline and urged, "Please don't apologize or fret. It's obvious we were both swept away. It's been a long time since I . . ." She lowered her revealing gaze for a moment and felt her cheeks flush. "You know what I mean. I hope this doesn't give you a bad opinion of me."

The astute lawman was certain she had never done anything so reckless. His self-esteem and pride were enlarged by the fact she had chosen him. She had said she found him attractive, but he was still amazed and relieved by how she viewed and accepted him. He had revealed dark and dirty secrets, weaknesses, and flaws, but she still found him desirable as a man and partner. Or maybe it was only like she said: she needed to be held, comforted, and sated tonight. Just because she was a lady didn't mean she lacked physical urges that yearned to be fulfilled. "It doesn't, and I hope you don't have a low opinion of me for taking advantage of you."

His tardy reply didn't dismay her because of the near-spellbound way he was studying and caressing her. "You didn't coerce or oblige me to do anything, and my opinion of you couldn't be higher." Ignorant bliss filled her as she presumed she had shared a part of him that Jessica never had, an intimate bond, a chance to win him. She reasoned that Navarro and Jessica couldn't have made love under the noses of her family, ranch hands, and the ever-present Matt. She smiled and snuggled up to evict any lingering dismay and doubt in him.

Navarro tapped her cheek. "What's this sly smile about?"

"I just realized this may help us play our husband/wife roles better. At least, it helped expel any mutual reservations or tension we had. It should calm us down and make us more responsive to each other before witnesses. We've both been holding back on doing our best play-acting because we were afraid we'd get aroused and something like this would occur. People at the ranch might have picked up on our caution and become suspicious. This way, partner, we won't have to be nervous about a strain tripping us up and exposing us. The Cordells have been married a long time, so they would probably sense we were bridled around each other and wonder why. We can't afford to evoke mistrust in any area of our cover story. Now, we don't have to be wary about how we behave. Right?"

From Beth's words and tone, it sounded as if she wouldn't mind making love again. She implied it wouldn't complicate their professional and personal relationships. But, he mused, was she correct? "Makes sense to me. Hadn't thought of it in that light. Think we can handle it without creating complications?"

His last question pinched her a little. "Now that we know each other so well, it should make things simpler for us. After all, partner, we're only human, and desire is a part of human nature."

She certainly spoke her mind, Navarro surmised, and she knew what to say to settle him down. He smiled. "I agree. Now we should turn in; it's late. Half the night is gone."

Beth stretched and yawned. "I thought we *were* turned in. Want me to stay over here unprotected? What if my naughty visitor returns?"

"You think we should sleep together?"

"We're already in position for it. Why not?"

"Because we wouldn't get any sleep in a small and hot bag together."

"You're right. We're both accustomed to bedding down alone."

Navarro wriggled up his lowered underwear and stood. Before going to his bedroll, he gazed down at her and smiled. "'Night, Beth Breed. See you when the sun rises."

"Good night, Navarro, and thanks." He sent her a quizzical look. "For what?"

"Giving me what I needed and not judging me wicked for it."

He chuckled and jested, "I guess I can't say the pleasure was all mine." He warmed when she grinned. "Don't worry, woman, wicked is the last word I'd think of to describe you. 'Night."

"Good night, Navarro," she repeated in contentment. *You cunning fox, Daniel Withers. Do you know us and love us so well that you tried to make a love match? If that's true, I hope your generous ploy succeeds.*

Beth was relieved her menses had taken place before Navarro courted her in Tucson. The next time it occurred, they would be at the ranch. Since it was short and light each month, the redhead wasn't worried about problems or discomforts there or on the trail later, as she was experienced in handling her monthly flow on the road.

Nor was she concerned about becoming pregnant. She had been unable to conceive a baby during a six-year marriage, so it must be impossible for her to do so. Steven had fathered a child long before meeting her; the reason he hadn't married the girl was because she vanished before he could make appropriate arrangements. While Beth was traveling with her husband, being childless hadn't mattered. Now, when she settled down, she wanted offspring; she wanted Navarro's.

Beth sighed unhappily. She couldn't give Navarro any children, either. But maybe he didn't want any after his troubled birth and youth and because they would make his current way of life impossible. Maybe it was for the best that she was incapable of conceiving; at least she didn't have to worry about getting into that kind of trouble while sleeping with him, because she wanted to do so again, as often as he allowed during their partnership.

The green-eyed redhead and half-blooded Apache reached the town of Fort Davis at midafternoon. As soon as they checked into a boarding house for the night, he left to see if the Cordells had sent a message for him.

When he returned to their room, he seemed restrained. Beth assumed it was because Jessica was a vivid reality once more, an obstacle between them. During his absence, another fact had struck her: Jessica Cordell was also a redhead. She prayed Navarro hadn't been thinking of Jessica last night. She also prayed Jessica didn't have green eyes or resemble her in any way. She wanted to assuage her doubts but thought it unwise to probe him for the truth at this early date. *No emotional pressure, Beth, or you'll send him galloping in fear and self-defense.* "Well?" she asked the silent male. "What did they say?"

Chapter Eleven

"The message is from Jessie, a letter delivered by one of her hands; a clerk at the telegraph office agreed to pass it along. I guess they didn't know if we'd be staying in town, so she sent it where she knew I'd check."

Beth watched him stare at the distracting page in his grip until she had to coax, "Don't keep me in suspense. What did they decide?"

Maybe my fate. "They're eager to meet the new Mrs. Navarro Breed. Says they'll be looking for us to arrive between Wednesday and Friday. They believed me, so they still trust me."

At last, Beth mused in trepidation, the opportunity to assess her possible rival. "That's a relief, isn't it?"

"Yep, it is."

Running scared of what you will and won't find there? Well, so am I. "We have a foot in their door; if we're clever and careful, we can wiggle our bodies inside and stay for a while. If not, we have a backup plan." *Change the topic: make him forget her for now.* "Any news from Dan or Zack?"

"Nope, they couldn't risk contacting me this close to our target. From here on, Beth, there'll be no talking or acting as anything but who we claim we are; never know who's watching and listening. Starting now, our roles are our skins. Everybody in this area knows the Cordells and L/C ranch hands."

"People also might remember their champion of years ago."

"I doubt it, except for the authorities who helped us trap Fletcher. If you recall, I was trying to avoid attention and a neck-stretching. If Jessie and Matt haven't already explained to the boys about me, I'll have to tell 'em why I'm not Navarro Jones from Colorado like I said."

"I remember everything you've told me, and I'm sure the boys will understand why you deceived them. This is it, partner, the first step of our mission. On second thought, I suppose our marriage was the first step."

The hour he had dreaded and craved was imminent. After five long and lonely years, he would see his lost love and son again. He wondered how they had changed, what they had done during that separation, and how they would feel about him. How would Jessie and Matt react to his alleged marriage? "Last chance to back out, Beth."

"Absolutely not. Until this assignment's over, you're stuck with me."

He chuckled and said, "I can think of worse predicaments."

"So can I. Don't worry, we'll be splendid together."

"You need anything while we're in town? I'll resupply in the morning. Once we leave the ranch, we can carry only so much on horse, but they'll have wagons and plenty of goods. The going will get tough and supplies may run low. If they don't move too fast, I can sneak off during the night to restock ours when we're close to a *ciudad* or *hacienda.*"

"It's good you know Spanish for our trek into Mexico. English, Apache, Spanish—do you speak other languages?"

"A little of several Indian tongues. Their sign language, too. For some reason, picking up other tongues hasn't been hard for me."

She noticed he made that statement without bragging. "How did you get so educated? Those few years you spent in school as a child couldn't be sufficient to make you so intelligent, and it's more than common sense. Like Papa, you're smart in lots of ways."

"That's a fine compliment, partner, and I'm much obliged for it." He sat in the only chair in the room and hung his hat on its arm. He saw her take a place on the bed's edge. Her gaze never left his face, as if she were probing for answers to more than the question she had asked. He suspected she was trying to distract him from the letter and its writer. After making love with him and knowing he had a romantic past with the woman they would visit, he wondered what Beth thought and felt about meeting his lost sweetheart. He'd told her it was over with Jessie, but did Beth believe him? Since she wasn't over her lost love, probably not.

During the pause, he thought how strange it was that the soul-deep loneliness he'd endured for years had subsided since he'd met Beth. Her company was enjoyable and her vitality was contagious. He hadn't felt this alive and happy since his life and body were gutted by grim fate. He owed all that to Beth. If not for her friendship and help, the personal task ahead would be difficult, if not impossible. He was glad—relieved—he had met her and was going to the ranch with a better attitude and in stronger condition.

"Why are you staring at me like that?"

"I was just thinking how lucky I am to have you as my partner and friend. It was loco to doubt Dan. I'm grateful to you for proving him right. Any other female would have resigned or been sent riding by now, because I'm hard to please and even harder to endure. I'm glad you didn't quit while I was giving you a tough time. I'll try not to do that again." He chuckled and grinned.

"Dan was right about you, too, and about us working together. I'm afraid that means our boss knows us better than we know ourselves, well enough to be certain neither of us could pull off a romantic pretense with just anyone."

They shared laughter and exchanged smiles of agreement.

"What about the answer to my previous question?"

He stretched out his legs and crossed them at the ankles, relaxed now. "While I was on the trail years ago, before I was sent to prison, I read and studied every book at every chance I had. After I got out, I looked up my old schoolmarm, begged her to tutor me, and spent a spell with her. I was surprised when she remembered me and was happy to see me. She worked with me after class and on Saturdays at her house, and that sweet woman refused to take any money for her lessons. She taught me plenty in a short time and told me how to learn by myself, gave me books and supplies to use after I left. I wanted to make sure I could fit in any place I went and on any job I wanted to take. Being a half-breed bastard and drifter were bad enough without also being stupid and ill mannered. After I signed on with Dan, I kept studying—everything, anything—because I didn't want to be given all the bottom-of-the-barrel missions, just chasing outlaws and such; I wanted to be qualified for any case that came up."

"From what I've seen and heard, you're more than talented enough to take on anybody or anything. You constantly amaze me, Navarro Breed. Someday, I hope to be as good as you are now. Heck, I'll settle for being half the agent you are."

"You value yourself too low, woman; you're already a top agent."

"That's kind and generous of you to say, but I know my limits and weaknesses. Those are what I need you to work on with me."

He leaned forward and rested his arms across his knees. "If a case comes along about something I don't know, I ready myself by reading up and talking to folks. Never take on a tricky situation unprepared."

Beth went to sit on the rug before him. She locked her arms around raised knees covered by a green dress. "What do you mean?"

Navarro felt heat rush over his body at her nearness and beauty. "If

I'm heading for a case involving mines, I study mining en route. If I'm gonna play a gambler, I practice in every saloon along the way. I request reports on the locals and the area where I'm going. If it's possible, I get recent newspapers of the area so I can see what's been happening there and who's in charge. Sort of like doing advanced scouting, or painting on a buffalo hide. You put a lot of images inside your head, like little drawings, until they make a big picture, give you clues to follow like a map. Never ride blind and ignorant into a location and case; that's why I told you all about me, because my past is part of this one. Always double check your information; some agents aren't trustworthy or they're too lazy to gather the real facts. No matter who's guiding you or supposed to back you up, in the end, you're responsible for your survival and success." He grinned. "That's lesson number one of our bargain."

After he straightened in the chair, Beth wriggled closer and propped against his muscled thigh. "Heavens, I envy your skills and instincts. Too bad I couldn't inherit my father's, or just absorb yours through my skin. I suppose nothing worthwhile is easy and quick to obtain; Mother Nature makes us toil and sweat to earn the best in life and . . ." *Don't you dare say love to him after what he's been through!* "Did that schoolmarm teach you how to dance so well?"

Navarro guessed the word she'd dropped like a hot skillet. *You're always considerate of others' feelings, Beth Breed. Except in one area; you shouldn't be tempting me with your touch and gaze, then letting me suffer in hunger.* He retrieved his hat and passed it round and round between his fingers. "Nope, Jessie did; leastwise, she got me started." That episode filled his mind but oddly didn't pain him today. "An agent's wife kindly finished my training and instructed me on table manners. She guided me on other social stuff, like holding chairs and opening doors for ladies. I surely didn't learn anything good or helpful from Carl. The only direction he sent me in was to prison. It was the same with my mother's band. If I'd become like them, I would've been slain or captured with the rest. I'd be one of those renegades we're after because I could never exist on a reservation."

Navarro caught her reaction, so he added, "Don't get me wrong; all bands and tribes aren't like that. Some of the best men I've met are Apache or from other Indian tribes; some are friends, and I still hold to part of their beliefs.

"My mother taught me a lot. There's little I can't do for myself; I have to, being alone most of the time. I watch folks and listen to them so I can keep learning. If I'm lucky, I'll learn some things from you; leastwise, I'll get to practice manners and social stuff with a real lady. I give you permission to correct any mistakes and clear out any ignorant spots. A man can't get too clever in my kind of work. Never can tell when I'll need a special skill to fool people and slide in without suspicion wherever I go."

"It must make you proud and pleased not to have to depend on others for anything. Totally independent, self-sufficient: that's what you are."

"We aren't so different in that area. You work alone most of the time, you keep learning, and you can take care of yourself."

"Only for the past year. Before then . . ."

He saw her break their eye contact, lower her gaze, and fiddle with her wedding ring—something she'd done only a few times lately. Needing to investigate her feelings about that loss, he finished for her, "You had Steven. Who was the boss and brains of your team?"

Beth smoothed away wrinkles in her skirt as she replied, "He was."

"Because you're a woman and you were his wife?"

"Partly."

"What's the other part?" When her gaze met his, he read uneasiness.

"He outranked me. He was more experienced and skilled, so it was natural for him to make the plans and decisions, give the orders."

As he looked her up and down with a playful grin on his face, he said, "I can't imagine you always riding and standing behind him or anyone."

Navarro's mood and expression warmed and calmed her. "Because I'm direct, outspoken, and stubborn?" She laughed and made a comical face as his grin broadened and he nodded after each descriptive word.

"Yep, but you're also smart and brave. I remember that day we defeated those stage bandits together. And how you handled yourself in Tucson and at other places we've stopped. Every time we talk, you have good ideas. Did you keep 'em to yourself with Steven to prevent sticking his pride and causing trouble between you two?"

"No, I told him my thoughts and feelings."

"Did he accept 'em and act on 'em?"

"Sometimes." She wondered if he was probing for personal information about her deceased husband and herself, or if he only wanted facts to aid their teamwork.

"Do you like working alone or with a partner better?"

"It's according to who the partner is and what's involved with the current assignment. I'm enjoying being teamed up with you, and I believe this mission calls for a couple for it to work best."

"Because of my past with Jessie and Matt?"

Be honest or he'll guess you're lying. "Partly."

"What's the other part?"

"What I told you before about being the perfect cover ruse."

"Are you worried I'll make a slip about what I revealed to you?"

"No."

"If you trust me to do right, then what's the other part?"

"What you said about never riding into a case and area blind, ignorant, and unprepared. Jessica and Matt's true feelings are unknown variables, so is their—or his—possible involvement in our assignment. Jessica loved you and only gave you up because she was forced to, so we don't know how she's going to respond to seeing you again. Her reaction will affect Matt's. I'm sure you don't want a misunderstanding to provoke a showdown with Matt, so you'll have to be extra careful in how you behave with his wife, or allow her to behave with you. Any surprises could tie our assignment in knots."

"Do you doubt we can pull off our pretense?"

"No."

"Do you have any doubts about me or my motives?"

"No."

"Do you have reason to doubt Jessie and Matt's friendship or innocence?"

"No."

He grinned and chuckled. "You've gotten stingy again with your words, Beth Breed. I'm doing more talking than you. Seems like we've changed places. Is anything wrong?"

"No. Sometimes I chatter too much. I was trying to control myself so I don't get on your nerves and provoke you to rush our work so you can be rid of me and my irritating habits and traits."

"Why are you worried about that?"

"Because they're your friends and nobody likes to have his friends insulted, but I thought I should point out hazardous spots. And because you haven't taught me all your tricks and talents. There's no guessing when or where I may need to use a whip or hatchet or know better tracking skills."

"Is that all you want and expect from me?"

She noted his serious—perhaps anxious—tone and expression. *Uh-oh, Beth . . .* "That was our deal: I do my best to help you solve this case without your friends getting hurt, and you enlighten me. Right?"

"Right. Just wanted to make sure you hadn't forgotten our bargain."

"You worried I'm going to chase you after what happened last night?"

"Are you?"

Navarro looked and sounded worried about becoming the object of her affection. She knew it was dangerous to distract him with personal concerns when his full attention should be on his duty. Hers, too. If they were meant for each other—and she believed they were—they would get together later, after the mission and after his feelings for Jessica were put to rest as hers for Steven had been. *Calm his fears for now.* "Even if I were tempted, it would be a foolish chase because diehard lone wolves have a knack for eluding traps," she said with a feigned mischievous grin. "Why did you ask?"

"Just wanted to be sure we understand each other." *Caray! even Jessie didn't make me act and think as loco as you do! I best be on guard against your charms or I may find myself in a painful snare.*

"Your message is clear, boss. Don't worry, I realize our mission is all we should think about until we complete it."

He couldn't tell if she believed him, and that failure frustrated him for a moment. He scolded himself when he realized he was almost disappointed she didn't argue or reason with him to change his mind. As soon as the case closed, she'd be riding out of his life, back to her dreams and memories of Steven Wind: a full blooded white man without a mark on his birth, body, or record. "It will be," he mumbled. *If I can keep my feelings corralled. And you, woman, you aren't doing anything to help me keep them under control. One look or touch from you and he wants to bust down the gate and run free, and I want to—* "We'd better get downstairs and eat. Mrs. Gray said meals are served promptly. I'm starved. You ready to go?"

She'd witnessed the odd way he was staring at her and how he mussed his black hair in wariness. *Don't know what to think and do about me, about us, right, my nervous darling?* "Lead the way." *For now . . .*

Beth looked at Navarro and said, "You don't have to sleep on that hard floor; I promise I won't attack you if you come up here with me."

"Trouble is, I can't make the same promise," he replied, chuckling.

She dared not tease. The legendary Navarro Breed afraid of anything, especially a delicate female? Maybe he just needed to be in charge of everything; maybe he wasn't ready to let go of the past; maybe he simply dreaded rejection. "As you said, I can think of worse predicaments."

"Me, too, but I don't encourage problems; breaks my concentration."

"Let me know if you change your mind." *You can't be stubborn and leery forever. You think we lost our heads last night, but what would you think if we savored our lovemaking next time? Next time . . .*

* * *

Thursday morning, Navarro was quiet as they dressed, ate, packed, and left the boardinghouse; so Beth let nature entertain and distract her. They traversed the verdant Davis Mountains. Patches of tall grasses with intermingled earth-snuggling ones covered many areas, all swaying in a nice breeze. They weaved their way past lavender and white cenizos, creamy yuccas, fiery ocotilla, and a variety of cacti. Bushes were thick and most trees were short; both were adorned with heavy jade-colored foliage. Dark-brown boulders and cliffsides jutted from the rolling or hilly landscape. Rocky eruptions created emerald humps on the surface, which they skirted. They journeyed through picturesque canyons and avoided hazardous ravines. She was awestruck by lovely red and orange paintbrush, yellow flax, green milkweed, blue sage, and white milkwort. They crossed a stream and passed Mitre Peak. Long lengths of dense grassland appeared, then rugged scrubland. It was spring, and the semi-desert region was beautiful.

As they approached a valley, Navarro slowed and murmured, "We're on Cordell land. Look over there." He motioned to where they had spooked a herd of graceful antelope. "We disturbed somebody's hunting."

She glanced upward where he pointed second to a hawk that was circling and shrieking as if fussing at them. "How far to the house?"

"About an hour at this walk. The horses need to cool and rest after taking those hills and rough terrain."

Beth liked the slowed pace that allowed them to travel side-by-side and chat, which he seemed ready to do. "Is the entire spread this rugged?"

"Nope, it's a thing of beauty. You can judge for yourself soon."

Beth agreed as they rode on. "Where is the stock?"

"What's left has probably been rounded up by now. Or they might be feeding in the south pasture if marking and counting's been done. This is one of the busiest times on a ranch. New calves and colts have to be branded and have their ears notched."

Despite his explanation, the ranch seemed too deserted for a huge and prosperous cattle empire, and wasn't at all what she'd expected. Navarro's expression and tone indicated he thought it was odd, too. "What's ear notching?"

"Putting a certain cut in a partic'lar spot; that's added safety in case rustlers change the brand. Nobody can replace a piece of ear and it's harder to change a notch to another pattern than to alter singed hide."

"Why is it necessary to also brand them?"

"Brands show up quicker and easier. Lets wranglers know which ones have been marked, and helps in separating stock during a combined cattle drive to market. Theirs is an *L* and a *C* with a slash between 'em. The males are castrated, so all they'll want to do is eat and grow."

"They remove any desire to . . . romance the females, eh?"

"Right, that's left up to the bulls chosen for the best breeding. If just any male mated with the cows, it would ruin the bloodline and lower the offspring's value. You'd wind up with a bunch of half-breeds nobody wants."

Beth caught his dual meanings and resentment. "Tell me more about branding. I take it you've done that task plenty of times."

"A team of cutters, ropers, a marker, flankers, and ironman can do everything to forty or fifty animals in an hour. I've done my share of all those jobs. Every one of 'em is a dusty, bloody, smelly, bone-tiring chore."

"Do women help?"

"Sometimes, when the ranch is big and there's lots of stock. Jessie does, or she did. She might not have time now with the house, children, and garden to tend. I've worked a few ranches where the women were too soft and squeamish for the task. You could do it without a problem."

"How do you know?"

"Anybody who gets shot and hides it can do anything needs doing." When he saw how his compliment affected her, he rushed on, "Cattle are prime sales at four years. That's a long time to tend them to have 'em go and die on you. It's a long, tough spell to ready new calves. Makes it hard to ride in tricking them when they're having a run of bad luck."

And perhaps breaking the law? "Are you nervous?"

He noticed how bright sunlight enflamed her fiery locks below the shade cast by her hat brim. He saw how her pale complexion was flushed and her cheeks were rosy. She was wearing a brown riding skirt, vest, and boots with a green shirt that enhanced the color of her expressive eyes. *"Nervous?" You bet I am, about a lot of things, including you, partner, and what we did back there.* "A little. I don't like what we have to do to them."

Beth was aroused by the furtive way he was examining her. *It scares you to be attracted to me when you think you're still in love with Jessica, doesn't it? I wonder if you're unconsciously duping yourself. We'll both know soon, won't we, dearest?* "You're eager to see your friends again?"

"Yep. Those boys are a lot of fun. I learned you can't force people to like you or respect you; either they do or they don't. I was lucky they let me fit in here for a while. When I was young and cocky, I did all sorts of crazy things for attention, but it got me the wrong kind. I had this fierce need to be superior to other men, 'specially men like Carl. I was bad and bitter, and I let folks know not to mess with me; that was stupid, since what I really wanted was friendship and acceptance. I couldn't stand for anybody to prove me wrong or make me look weak or yellow. I'm damn lucky I lived through so many showdowns and fistfights, not to mention prison."

"I'm glad you did."

Stop her from thinking in your direction. "A word of warning, Beth, watch playing with that ring so much; nervous habits can give away secrets."

She knew she had a tendency to play with her ring when she was tense and she'd tried to curb the revealing habit. She suspected that wasn't his real motive for mentioning it. He seemed to be getting defensive with her as they neared his lost sweetheart, and she couldn't allow that to happen so close to their target. "Thanks, and please keep reminding me."

He stared at her. "You aren't mad 'cause I mentioned it?"

"Of course not; partners—friends—help each other to do their best work and to avoid mistakes, right?"

"Right." He eyed her again, then smiled. "Do the same for me?"

"I will, when and if the time comes."

After they topped a rise, he said, "There she is."

Beth scrutinized the setting with great interest. From that distance and elevated level, roofs revealed the number and sizes of structures. There were two large barns, side-by-side and sharing overhangs. She saw a rectangular bunkhouse, several small cabins, and a chuckhouse where the hands ate. She noticed animal pens, well-kept yards, miles of fencing, a well, corrals, outhouses, a windmill, and a garden. The nearer they got, the more she could discern about the house that was enclosed by a wall about three feet high with an arched entrance; it was constructed in a Spanish style; and the whole setting indicated prosperity and tranquil living.

From a window, Jessica Lane Cordell watched the couple close the span between them. As they did so, her suspense mounted. After years of wondering, some of worrying and praying, she would discover today how it felt to be with Navarro. Those bittersweet days they had shared flashed across her mind: their brief and torrid romance, her torment and confusion at his loss, and her reactions to discovering the reasons why he didn't return to her. Most of what she'd become and possessed now was because of Navarro Breed—his love for her and effect on her, his help with Fletcher, and his absence since their coerced separation.

Since that day, all she knew about the ex-desperado was what Matt and what Navarro's letters had told her. At times, she had feared he might fight to get her and Lane back. Other times, she had feared losing her and Lane would create a cold and hard bitterness that could return him to the man he had been before they met. But most of the time, she had believed he would honor his word and remain a new man, and she'd lived in serenity in her fresh start.

Jessica reminded herself she had been fortunate and happy for ten years while Navarro had been unlucky and miserable, until now. She hoped life finally was being just and kind with him because he was a good man, a man she still loved and cared about in a special way and always would.

As she headed to greet them, Jessica prayed his recent news was true. From what she could tell about his appearance, he had changed amazingly little; he was still more than handsome, muscular and virile. But the same was true of Mathew Cordell. She loved her husband, children, and home with all her heart—except, she admitted without feeling guilty or wicked, for the corner Navarro owned and occupied. She had only one frightful concern, that when he saw his son for the first time he'd be unable to hide his feelings and their relationship.

She was thankful Lane's resemblance to his father had lessened over the years. With all her heart, she prayed, *Heavenly Father, please give Navarro total joy and peace. Please let this woman be perfect for him. Please let their ranch be successful. Please give him a son or daughter as soon as possible to ease his pain at losing Lane. Please don't let him have wrong feelings for me. Free him from our troubled past as you freed me. Please hear my prayer and answer it for all our sakes. Amen.*

As they reined in, Beth saw a redheaded female standing stone-still on the porch. Was Matt's wife hesitant to approach them because of her past relationship with Navarro? Was she worried over what he might have told his "wife" about them? She had assumed Jessica would be very pretty, but she was *beautiful,* a woman any man would crave. Twinges of alarm and jealousy nibbled at Beth.

Jessica looked at the newlyweds and offered Beth a cordial smile. Then, her eyes settled on a grinning Navarro and her tension faded.

As he dismounted and walked toward her, Navarro's heart pounded with anticipation and he was flooded with joy. At long last, he mused, he had returned. How different, his thudding heart told him, their reunion would be if it had taken place ten years ago, or even five years ago.

"Hello, Jess," he said as he reached her. *"Shu,* it's good to see you. You're as beautiful as ever."

Jessica was surprised at how calm they both were. "You look wonderful. It's been a long time, but you haven't changed at all. Wish I could say the same for me," she jested. "A lot has happened to us since we last saw each other."

"That it has."

"We're delighted to share this special occasion. We've always wanted the best for you, Navarro. Just as you wanted it for us. We've all done well."

His turbulent mind echoed, *"We're," "We've," "Us"* . . . "That we have, Jess. Where's that lucky husband of yours?"

"He took the children for a wagon ride; they'll return soon. We didn't know when you'd arrive or he would have been here to welcome you."

Beth witnessed as the two studied each other, their smiles broadening and bodies relaxing as they did so. As the couple stood with their sides to her, Beth observed them in dread and increased jealousy, as they seemed to have forgotten her presence. Jessica was shorter than her by a few inches, and her complexion was darker from the sun. Her hair, thank goodness, wasn't flaming red; its auburn shade was so deep, it was almost brown; the luxurious mane drifted halfway down her back in a near-riot of curls and waves. Unlike herself, the rancher had small and delicate features, but there were tiny wrinkles on her face from outdoor work and—Beth had to admit—from an abundance of smiles and laughter. Even without being very close, Beth was aware of how blue and captivating her rival's eyes were. Yet, there was a gentle, genial radiance and aura about her. Beth couldn't help but admire and respect Jessica; she'd had the generosity and kindness to forgive and aid the man whom she'd loved and lost, the courage and strength to build a new life with another man, and the wisdom to apparently let go of the past.

"You look happy, Jess; I'm glad."

"So do you, stranger, and I'm delighted. We worried about you for years. Thank goodness you finally met and talked with Matt."

"Sorry I couldn't contact you, but writing from prison would have been selfish and reckless. I didn't want you to suffer from any misunderstandings with the law. Besides, I doubt the guards would have mailed any letters I wrote, and they probably would have used them against you."

"I understand and I'm grateful you kept us out of trouble. You always did put others' needs and safety above your own. I'm so happy you're free now; you didn't deserve to be in that awful place."

"I'd still be locked up if you and Matt hadn't gotten me out."

"It was what we had to do for a good friend. It's what you would have done for us; you helped us so much in the past. We appreciated you writing in '81 to let us know you'd made a fresh start. I was hoping you would."

"I couldn't have done it if not for what I learned from you, your family, Matt, and the boys here. All of you were the first real friends I'd had." He doffed his hat and ruffled his hair. "I know you two didn't expect to see me again, but I wanted you to meet my wife and share my good luck. You don't ever have to worry about me again, Jess. We've all settled down now."

Jessica grasped his underlying meaning and nodded. She gazed at the man who had been her life, hopes, dreams, and joy ten years ago. She'd been devastated when she lost him. But after discovering the truth five years later, she'd understood and forgiven him. She was glad and relieved he'd found someone to love and to fulfill him as she had with Matt. She realized he was no longer the mysterious, wary, restless desperado she'd met years ago. That hungry, bitter, sad glint was gone from his hazel eyes. Yes, Navarro Breed had changed since their first encounter, changed because of her and his new love. Lordy, she mused, he was still a man who stood out from others, as did Matt.

If our goodbye had been different, maybe I'd be over you, too, Jessie. Maybe you wouldn't still be haunting me. Either I end it for good or I'll go on yearning and suffering. How can you be my destiny when you're so happy with Matt? If only I could hold you and kiss you to test my feelings and yours, and to make certain I've lost you and Lane forever . . .

Beth wondered if she should dismount and join them. She'd decided to give them a few more minutes alone, but was envious of their easy rapport and undeniable affection for each other. She was miffed a little at being excluded and ignored. *What if Matt arrives? Keep an eye out for him.*

Jessica's gaze traveled to the flaming redhead nearby. "She's beautiful, Navarro, and I'm eager to meet her. She's been patient with our reunion."

"Yep, she's quite a woman. I think you'll like her."

The anxious Texan whispered, "Does she know about . . ."

"No, I didn't tell her." *Everything about us or about our son,* his mind finished to assuage his guilt over the half-lie.

"That's best for everyone."

He smiled in agreement. "I'll fetch her. She's eager to meet you and Matt."

He released the hold on his first love's elbows and went to retrieve his "wife." As he helped Beth dismount, their gazes fused and searched for a moment. He gave her a smile of encouragement and reassurance he was all right and in control. The redhead smiled in return and gazed at him with such trust in him and concern for his feelings. *You're a special woman, Beth. You'd be perfect to replace— Whoa, hombre, don't get loco while you're caught in a blinding duststorm!*

"Ready?" he asked, and she nodded. He guided her to the other woman. "Jessie, I want you to meet my new bride, Beth Breed. Love, this is Jessica Lane Cordell, the lady who saved my hide more than once. As I told you, if it wasn't for her and Matt, you and I would never have met."

As they shook hands, Beth said, "It's an honor and pleasure to meet you, Jessica. I want to thank you for all you did for my husband. He told me how the stay here at the ranch changed his life." As she spoke, Beth slipped her arm around Navarro's waist, gazed up at him, and smiled. "But frankly I can't imagine him ever being anything except the wonderful man I know and love today."

As he slipped into his role, the sable-haired man chuckled and teased, "That's because you're the one who lassoed and tamed me."

Beth laughed. "I don't recall you putting up a struggle."

"That's because I was tired of roaming and wanted to settle down."

"And I just happened to be the first woman you bumped into after you made that astonishing decision?"

He cuddled her closer. "Nope, you're just the one who convinced me. Ask Jessie; she'll tell you I was a born and bred drifter."

As the newlyweds looked into each other's eyes, Jessica said, "No man is ready to settle down until the right woman comes along. It seems to me as if you two are perfectly matched."

"Yes, we are," Navarro murmured. "I'm a lucky man."

"From the way it looks, I agree. You'll have to tell me how you two met and got married and about the ranches you'll be checking out near San Antonio the fifth of next month. That's only a six-day ride from here, so surely you can stay a few days and visit. We have plenty of catching up to do."

"We'd like that, Jessie, if it won't be any extra work for you and Matt."

Jessica smiled. "Of course not. Matt and I would love to have you two stay for a while. You've traveled a long way, so I'm sure you and Beth can use a rest, good food, and a soft bed. I know the boys will be delighted to see you again. They're on the range today. They just finished branding, so they're herding the stock to the south pasture for grazing and watering. Half of them will be back later tonight; the other half will be standing guard. Who knows, we might even persuade you to help scare off any rustlers who come along or repair a few fences for old time's sake?"

"Maybe even work on a windmill? Sounds like fun to me."

Beth watched them share laughter and memories. She listened as Jessica told him a man named Big John was working in the smithy and a Biscuit Hank, who had gotten married, was cooking in the chuckhouse with his wife.

"It'll be good to see the boys again and do some serious jawing. How's Miguel and Carlos? And Jimmy Joe? And Tom? And your grandmother?"

"I'll tell you about everyone later, but they're all fine, except Gran; we lost her two years ago."

"That's a shame; she was one fine lady."

"She never forgot you and would have enjoyed seeing you again. Were you still working with the Army when you met Beth?"

Navarro realized she was trying to change a still painful subject. "No, I gave up that years ago after peace rode into the territory. I've been trying different things to see what caught my interest for permanent work."

"It appears ranching won out over your other choices."

The sound of a wagon approaching halted the conversation and all three looked toward the barn where it pulled up and stopped.

"Here's Matt and the children now. He'll be glad to see you and to meet this lovely bride of yours." Three children waved and yelled at their mother, who responded in the same manner.

Navarro watched Jessica brighten as her family came into sight, a family that could have been his. "It'll be good to see him again. You chose a fine man to marry, Jessie."

With her gaze on Matt, Jessica smiled and concurred, "Yes, I did."

Navarro was a little edgy about speaking to the man who'd taken his place years ago, who brought such a glow to Jessica's face, who might be involved in a terrible crime without her knowledge. Beth had said a desperate man might do anything to protect his possessions, but would Mathew Cordell, he worried, risk bloodshed, prison, death, and his family's loss just for financial survival? Surely not, he reasoned; Matt was strong, proud, and brave enough to start over if necessary.

"Why don't you join him, Navarro?" Jessica suggested as the children raced toward them after their father helped them from the seat and wagonbed. "You two might want to share some man-talk before supper.

The children and I will keep Beth entertained while you chat for a while."

Navarro wondered if Matt had asked to meet in private with him after his arrival. "That's a good idea, Jessie." He looked at Beth and said he'd return soon, then headed toward Mathew Cordell, whose unreadable gaze was locked on him. He made certain, when the exuberant children passed him, he didn't miss a step or stare at the oldest boy, his son . . .

Chapter Twelve

A s the two boys and little girl raced toward her, Jessica yelled, "Matt, I'll feed the children and get them ready for bed so we can have a quiet meal with our company! I'll call you before I put them down!"

Beth watched as Navarro reached the double barn and joined Matt, who nodded at his wife. She saw a big black man leave the smithy shed to take care of the team and wagon for his boss. It was obvious Navarro knew him by the way they shook hands, smiled, and chatted for a few moments. She looked at Jessica and said, "I'll be there in a minute. I want to get something out of my saddlebag."

"The kitchen is to the left, at the back. I'll introduce you to my little ones after you come inside." Jessica herded the active bunch into the house as the two youngest kept glancing back at the female stranger.

While fetching the gifts she'd purchased in El Paso, Beth stole glances at the men who walked to a corral to speak in private. The distance was too far to overhear their words but surely Navarro would tell her everything later.

The Special Agent began his difficult deception. "The last time we talked, Matt, I promised I wouldn't return and intrude on your lives; but since your ranch almost lay in our path to San Antonio, I was hoping you wouldn't mind us stopping by. I wanted you and Jessie to meet the woman I love and married. You can put to rest any lingering doubts; I know Beth is my destiny, just as Jessie is yours." Navarro noticed a gleam of relief in Matt's brown eyes. "I hope my message out of nowhere didn't worry you two. If you'd said not to come, I wouldn't have. I give you my word of honor, old friend. I won't return unless you need my help in any way."

Navarro went on. "You know what I was like before I came here the first time, so I made mistakes, plenty of them, bad ones. I never meant to tear up Jessie's life, and I'm glad she had you to love her. I know she loves you, Matt, and I think she always did. We just caught each other at bad times in our lives. Beth taught me everything that happens to us is for a purpose; we can let bad defeat us or we can use it for the good." He watched the rancher nod agreement.

Mathew Cordell studied his past rival. Unless he was a sorry judge of character, Navarro looked sincere. "I'm happy to hear such news and I'm eager to meet this woman you chose."

"She's really special, Matt. I never thought I'd find a woman like her, and I'm damn lucky I did."

Matt noticed a convincing tenderness in the man's expression and tone. The ex-desperado even had a sparkle in his hazel eyes each time he mentioned his new wife. "How did you meet her? When? Where?"

Navarro leaned against the corral and propped an arm on the top slat. He gazed across the landscape as he softened his voice. "I've known Beth for several years. Her husband and I became good friends while I was working for the railroad in St. Louis." He feigned a sad look for a moment. "Stephen was killed in a bank holdup a year ago. He's the first close friend I've lost, and it was hard for me and Beth. At least his murderer was brought to justice, swung from a rope a few weeks later."

"So you married his widow out of loyalty to . . . Stephen?" Matt asked, hoping he was wrong.

"To be honest, I realized after his death I'd been in love with Beth since I met her. But I swear to you, Matt, I never made any moves toward her while Stephen was alive; I wouldn't have betrayed a friend no matter how much I wanted her. After he was killed I gave her time to grieve before I told her my feelings. I was lucky, because she'd come to feel the same way about me. A few weeks ago, we got married in Tucson. I won't ever do anything to lose her."

"I understand; it's like that with Jessie and the children; I'd do anything for them. What made you choose San Antonio to settle down?"

"A friend told me about one ranch for sale and Beth learned about two others while she was working in the land office in Tucson. Harrison, her boss, keeps up with available property from Texas to California and Dakota to the Mexican border to help friends find homes in other places when they move. We decided ranching would be a good life for us, a nice way to raise a family. I made arrangements to check 'em over the first week of May. If we don't like any of 'em, we'll look elsewhere, maybe Colorado. Harrison also offered his help in locating the right one. Prices in San Antonio aren't too high, and I've saved plenty working all kinds of jobs. Beth's done the same, so we should be able to afford a small spread. Later, if we want, we can grow if land's available. If we do settle there and you and Jessie get over that way and want to visit, you're welcome anytime. But if you'd rather this be our last contact, I'll understand."

"Does Beth know about you and Jessie, and Lane?"

Navarro realized Matt didn't respond to his last two statements. He wondered if he was being stalled outside to give Jessie time to put their son to bed before he could meet the boy. *You planning to feed us, study Beth, and send us on our way while Lane's asleep?* "I figured it was best if that secret stays between the three of us. Women are sensitive about such things and I don't want to hurt Beth, or do or say anything to spoil our fresh start."

"So she doesn't know about your son?"

"No, and I hope to keep it that way. But he's *your* son, Matt: Lane was born as your child and he'll always be your child unless you say different. I'm sure you've done a fine job raising him. One day, he'll be a good man like you; that's what I want for him." *Unless you're guilty.*

Matt smiled. "That's kind of you to say, Navarro. You're being smart and unselfish again. I swear, Lane couldn't be any more my son if I'd sired him. We're very close. I love that boy and I'm proud he bears my name."

"Believing that is what made my decision for me and holds me to it."

"Lane will never be slighted by me. One day, he and Lance will share this ranch, as real brothers."

If you don't lose it to these troubles you're in. I'll do my best to protect this place for Lane and Jessie. "Thanks, Matt, for being a good father, and a good friend to me. You and Jessie are special. I'll never forget the times we've shared and all you two did for me. I'd be a sorry case today if you two and the boys hadn't helped me."

Matt smiled and nodded in gratitude. "I wanted to come because I didn't want you two living in dread that one day I'd return to cause you trouble and pain. Giving you peace of mind is the only way I can repay my debt to you. After we leave, you can trust me to never look over my shoulder or come after anything that belongs to you."

"We believe you; that's why we let you come. I have to admit, I was shocked and worried when I first got your message. But I realized, if you only wanted to see Jessie and Lane, you could've ridden up without asking or spied on us to catch 'em alone. I'm glad you finally found someone to take Jessie's place. You deserve to have a good woman at your side."

"The last time we saw each other, we were talking about your wife and future. It seems strange to be doing the same thing about mine today."

Matt chuckled and relaxed, nodding his head. "Yep, sure is."

"You told me about loving and almost marrying another woman when you were young. I guess that helps you understand what happened to me."

"The second time is best, sharing real love like we've both found."

"I'm delighted you came so we could meet you and see Navarro again," Jessica said, as the men talked, the children ate, and the bathwater heated. "We've been so busy this spring I've had little, if any, time for socializing." She laughed and focused an amiable blue gaze on her guest. "It'll be fun to have a woman my age around to chat with. How old are you?"

"Twenty-eight," Beth replied as she wondered if the youngsters always ate in the dining room or if Jessica wanted privacy to chat with her.

"I'm thirty-four. Matt's forty-five. I've known him most of my life; he practically helped raise me." She smiled as if to herself. "You'll stay a few days for us to get acquainted and enjoy a little diversion, won't you?"

"Are you sure we won't be an imposition at such a busy time? Navarro said springtime is hectic with roundup, branding, repairs, and gardening. Goodness, I have so much to learn about being a rancher's wife. We could camp nearby and head out in the morning."

"Certainly not. Close friends are always welcome, and I can fill your head with things you should know about your new life. It's been years since Navarro left, so we have a lot of catching up to do. Please don't feel ignored or left out when we start talking about old times. Jump right in and join us."

Beth took a rapid liking to the polite and vivacious female. Jessica seemed content in her roles of wife, mother, and rancher: love and pride glowed in those blue eyes when she spoke of her husband, children, and home. "I'm grateful Navarro worked with kind people like you and your hands." She lowered her tone. "I'm sure you know he had a hard life before your father hired him. He also told me you and Matt wrote the letters that were instrumental in his pardon. Thank you, Jessica; that was a generous thing to do."

"Navarro risked his life for us and this place more than once," Jessica responded as she checked the bath water's temperature. "He's one of the best men I've ever known. He didn't deserve to be in prison, certainly not in that awful place where they sent him. I'm happy we were able to help get him released. I'll be back in a minute; I have to get the children's tubs ready."

Lane finished eating and put his dishes in the sink. At age nine, he was old enough to do his own quick scrubbing in a water closet built on the rear porch; afterward, he hurried upstairs wrapped in a wide drying cloth to don his sleepwear.

After the younger two children completed their meals, Jessica bathed them one at a time and took them upstairs to get into their nightshirts, during which time, Beth cleared and washed their dishes and utensils, then placed those the older woman had set out for the adults around the table. As she worked, she looked inside the adjoining living room through a large archway. The heavy furniture was artistically carved from medium-shaded wood in a design that matched the Spanish style of architecture. Light-colored walls met a clean floor of interlocked pieces of stained oak. There were an enormous fireplace, a couch, several chairs, tables with elegant lamps, magnificent paintings, expensive vases filled with wildflowers, a gilded mirror, massive desk, area rugs, and other items of various sizes. Several steps led to the second floor. The kitchen and dining rooms had similar decor. All the rooms were large, airy, and well designed for comfort, beauty, and easy entertaining. She was impressed by the tidy and lovely dwelling, which spoke well of Mrs. Cordell's housekeeping skills, pride in her home, and their past wealth.

Beth recalled the stucco exterior was the creamy hue of yucca blossoms; it was all trimmed in dark red, including the roof with its *canales* for drainage. Two arched windows were in the front left dining room and two were in the right front living area. On the second floor where bedrooms were located, smaller versions were in the same places, in addition to one above the front door. A matching three-foot-high stucco wall encircled the house; inside the *yarda* were planted colorful flowers and verdant bushes. It, too, was kept neat and picturesque.

When Jessica returned, she smiled and thanked Beth for the tasks she had done during her absence, and said she'd call the men inside.

Jessica walked to the front gate. "Come on you two! The children need to get to bed; Lane and Alice have chores and school early tomorrow."

While their mother was gone, Beth chatted with the children. From the youngsters' behaviors and personalities, she reasoned that the Cordells were good and loving parents. Alice—who'd be seven next month she said—had golden red curls, large brown eyes, and a darling smile that stole one's heart. A strong resemblance revealed there was no doubt she was Jessica's daughter. The youngest boy, age four and a half, was a rambunctious child who surely required plenty of energy and wits to tend; Lance, with his brown hair and eyes, favored Matt. The oldest son, Lane, was quiet and distant, perhaps a little shy, and favored neither parent from what Beth could see, as he never faced her fully. His hair was trimmed short and, in better lighting, a smidgen of deep auburn in his almost black hair could be detected.

Lance climbed onto Beth's lap with bold confidence. He asked if she knew any stories to tell. Alice leaned against one leg and looked hopeful. Lane sat in an oversized chair away from the sofa, his gaze on a book in his hands; he didn't appear to be reading it as he didn't turn a single page during her furtive observation.

"I know a few stories if we have time to—" She halted when Jessica, Matt, and Navarro entered the room.

"I see you make friends fast," Jessica said with a warm smile.

"You have precious children, Jessica. I hope you don't mind that I brought presents for them."

"Presents!" Alice squealed. "Like on Christmas and birthdays?"

"Something like that," Beth answered with a smile. "Is it all right?"

"Certainly."

Matt put his arm around his wife as they watched.

Beth retrieved and opened a large package. She gave Lance his gift first, a small stuffed horse. Without delay, she handed Alice a rag doll. Both thanked her without a parental reminder and examined their gifts. Since Lane hadn't come forward, she walked to where he was sitting to give him a slightly larger stuffed horse. Without lifting his head, he thanked her as his fingers stroked the object. She handed Jessica a fat bag. "I'll let your mother decide about the candy; she may want to save it for tomorrow."

Lance and Alice gathered around Jessica and tugged on her skirt. "Just one piece, Mama?" one asked. "Please," the other added.

Jessica gazed at them, smiled, untied the top, and lowered the bag. "One treat, then off to bed."

"Yes, ma'am," they replied in unison as they peered inside to make their selections. Even Lane joined them to do the same, his back to Beth.

It took all of Navarro's strength and skills not to stare at his son. This was the closest he had been to the boy and only the second time he had laid eyes on his child. He wanted to talk with Lane, hug him, share with him, protect him, and watch him grow into a man. All of those pleasures were impossible; his dark past denied him those rights. At least his son had a good name, home, family, and heritage—things he couldn't have provided years ago when Lane was conceived in love with Jessica. He looked at Matt, who was gazing at him. He smiled and nodded, and Matt caught his unspoken and heartfelt message; the rancher smiled back, and said in a soft tone, "Tell our company good night and let's get you three to bed."

"Yes, Papa" was heard three times in respect and obedience.

Beth had to squat so Alice and Lance could hug her, thank her again, and say good night. She stood as Lane spoke his gratitude without looking up at her. Matt hustled them upstairs, clutching their toys.

"You have a lovely family, Jessica. You're a fortunate woman."

Jessica smiled and said, "So will you and Navarro one day."

As Navarro slipped an arm around her waist and they swapped tender gazes, Beth laughed and said, "I hope Mother Nature waits until after we're well settled, so I'll have time to enjoy my husband alone first."

"That would be nice, because children certainly take a lot of time and energy. I'll be back soon." She hurried upstairs to help Matt and ask him about the lengthy conversation he'd had with Navarro.

When they were alone, Navarro pulled Beth into his arms and nuzzled her ear with his lips so he could whisper, "How did it go in here?"

She used her cheek to caress his as she replied, "Fine. I like her and the children. She asked us to stay a while. Any problems with Matt?"

"None; he believed me. Let's be careful tonight, be real loving."

That won't be a difficult order to follow. She nodded and snuggled close. She felt his embrace tighten and his mouth place kisses on her hair.

Navarro leaned back, gazed into Beth's green eyes, and used his hazel ones to signal an observer behind them. He knew Matt was standing at the top of the stairs and watching them, so he kissed her. Matt cleared his throat as he descended the steps.

"It's about time I meet this new bride of yours, old friend."

Beth had known of their host's spying and the motive for her love's behavior. She smiled as Navarro introduced them. "It's a pleasure and honor to meet someone my husband speaks of so highly."

As the rancher took in her radiance and beauty, he said, "I'm more than pleased to meet the woman who snared this loner." He shook the hand she extended to him. "Yep, this is a special occasion for all of us. Welcome to our home, Beth Breed, and welcome back, Navarro."

"Thank you, Matt," the redhead said. "I've enjoyed myself already. Your ranch is lovely; I hope ours will be as prosperous and beautiful."

"With hard work and plenty of good luck, it will be. Navarro never was one to do a job poorly. I'm sure you two will make a fine go of it."

"All we have to do is make the right selection. Since I know nothing about land and stock, Navarro will have to do the choosing for us."

"I'm sure he's learned enough during his travels to pick a good one."

"Thanks to you, Matt, I can handle spring branding, fence repairs, rustlers, and broncbusting. I think I told you, love, Matt was the foreman when I worked here, best one I've come across. After we get our place going, we'll have to try to find a skilled man like he was to work for us."

"That's mighty kind of you to say, Navarro."

Jessica joined them with a cheerful smile. "You won my children's hearts, Beth; they could hardly stop talking about you. Thank you for being so generous. Shall we go into the dining room and eat while we talk?"

"Suits me; I'm starved," Matt said, and led the way.

The men assisted the women with their chairs, then took the end seats as the host directed. Beth was impressed and touched when Matt said a short blessing while clasping hands with his wife. *Surely you two can't be criminals.*

Jessica told them to serve themselves from bowls and platters in the center of the table: tender and juicy antelope roast, small potatoes and green beans she'd put up in jars last year, hot biscuits with prickly pear cactus jelly and freshly churned butter, and store-bought peaches from a tin can. A steaming pot of fragrant coffee sat on a trivet.

"Looks and smells wonderful, Jessie. This'll be a treat after so much trail food, won't it, Beth love?"

"Heaven. Navarro took us through towns a few times during our journey, but we camped mostly to see the countryside and to save money."

"Nothing is more romantic for newlyweds than sharing a campfire in the desert under a full moon, especially in spring," Matt said. "Once in a while, Jessie and I get somebody to watch the children so we can camp out. After you have three youngsters in the house, you'll understand why."

Children, Beth's mind echoed. A treasure she would be denied. To help mask her distress, she locked her adoring gaze on Navarro and drank him in as one dying of thirst. "Sounds like something we should do again."

"We will, love, lots of nights between here and San Antonio."

Jessica coughed politely and said, "Remember the first time you joined my family and Matt for supper at the other house? It was his first day on the job, Beth, and he was as nervous as a barefoot man in a cactus patch. It took him a while to get used to us. I think it was Gran, Tom, and Miguel who warmed him up to us and ranch life."

As she spoke, Navarro recalled what she'd done under the table that night with an unslippered foot and almost squirmed in his chair. . . . How different the two occasions were! That night long ago, she had belonged to him, loved him, wanted to marry and spend her life with him. Tonight, she was Matt's wife and future. She appeared at ease with the situation. Obviously Matt had complete trust in her and faith in their love; he didn't seem the least worried about having an ex-rival in his home, within easy reach of his wife and son. Navarro wondered if he could be as confident, generous, and calm if their roles were reversed; he doubted it. "I remember how intimidated I was by your father; he was a tough man. What's happened to everybody in the last few years?" Navarro asked.

As food was passed from person to person, Jessica answered, "I told you we lost Gran; her health was getting bad, but she slipped away without suffering. Tom's married and living in Waco with a lovely wife and four children. He owned a mercantile store in Davis for a while, but decided he'd do better in a larger town, and he has. Remember the trouble he had with his eyes and foot?" Navarro glanced up and nodded. "A doctor back East helped both problems. With special glasses, Tom can see fine; and with surgery, exercises, and special shoes his limp is hardly noticeable."

Jessica looked at Beth and said, "You should have seen Navarro with my baby brother years ago; he's wonderful with children. He kept Tom from becoming an emotional cripple. We didn't realize we were harming him by treating him different from others; we were crushing his spirit and taking away his desire to try new things. Navarro taught us to treat him the same as everyone else, even if we were scared witless he'd hurt himself. He gave Tom the courage and confidence to try anything he wanted to do. My brother was painfully shy and embarrassed about his disabilities until Navarro worked on him. Then, Matt took over after his departure."

Beth locked gazes with her "husband" and smiled; she knew he had no choice except to return her tender gesture.

Jessica looked at her ex-lover and picked up where she had left off. "I wish Tom lived closer; I know he'd be thrilled to see you. He missed you terribly after you left. If you get near Waco, be sure to look him up."

"I will; I'd enjoy seeing him. I'm glad life's been good to him."

Jessica's eyes twinkled as she asked, "Would you believe the talented doctor who helped Tom is Mary Louise's husband?" She saw Navarro stop eating and look at her as if it was the first time he'd heard that news.

"My baby sister straightened herself out and made a good life with a fine man; they live in Philadelphia with their children. Amazing, isn't it?"

"I'm happy for you, Jessie; I'm glad she got herself turned around."

"It took some trouble to clear her head, but she admits it was worth the pain. As for the boys, Miguel got married and kept having so many little cowpokes he decided to start a ranch of his own. Pretty soon he won't have to hire seasonal hands because he'll supply all he needs.

"As a wedding present, we gave them ten cows and a bull to begin their herd. Our hands bought them chickens, pigs, and two horses. We let a couple of them take time off to help Miguel and Annie get their place going."

"Who did he marry? He didn't have a sweetheart when I was here."

"Annie came to work for me while I was pregnant with Lane; Matt found her and hired her as a surprise. She was smart and sweet and a hard worker. I hated to lose her, and still haven't replaced her. Let's see; who else? Hank married a widow from Davis, and Jefferson found himself a good wife. They still live on the ranch and work for us. Rusty is foreman, and Carlos is assistant foreman, and Big John is still our blacksmith and carpenter. As for Jimmy Joe, he hasn't changed; he keeps us laughing and watching our backs for his jokes." She looked at Matt to ask, "Did I cover everyone?"

The rancher nodded. "Better than a cozy blanket. You best eat before food's either gone or cold."

"I'll catch up while Beth tells us how she and Navarro met and married."

Beth stopped eating for a while to tell the cover story that Navarro had told Matt earlier. "After Navarro and I bumped into each other in Tucson, we spent all our free time together, fell in love, and got married; all in one week."

"How exciting and romantic," Jessica murmured with a genuine smile.

Navarro reached out, grasped Beth's hand, and jested, "I wasn't about to give her time to think twice about marrying a drifter and loner like me or she might have come to her senses and refused."

"There was no chance of that happening, dear heart."

"Right, because I was determined to corral you, woman."

"What have you been doing since you left here, Navarro?"

The agent released Beth's hand so she could return to her meal. "You know me, Matt, I had dust in my boots. I've been drifting around from place to place and from job to job for years. I guess I was searching for what I finally found." He glanced at Beth and smiled. "I met plenty of nice people and did plenty of interesting things. I even worked other ranches and roundups and cattle drives, mostly in Dakota and Colorado. Dakota's beautiful country, but it has long and harsh winters; not a place I'd want to take a wife to live." He mentioned states and jobs he had tried, or alleged he had, and he threw in a few amusing tales and interesting adventures.

"Tell them about tracking that mountain lion," Beth coaxed. After he finished the tale, she murmured, "Isn't he the smartest and bravest man alive?"

Matt glanced at Jessie and grinned before he said, "I thought you were working for the Army all this time."

"Nope. Years back, the Indian problems were settled, except for roving renegades here and there or when some of them broke from the reservation and stirred up trouble. Didn't seem like much need for a scout, translator, and peacemaker anymore. Since I wasn't busy on tasks I was hired for, they kept giving me lousy orders I didn't want to obey. When my agreement with them ran out, I left to see what else I could find."

Jessica lowered a fork to her plate. "Lucky for you and Beth you did, else you wouldn't have met."

"After roaming for so long and so far, settling down will be quite a change for you," Matt added.

Navarro looked at his partner, captured her hand on the table, and squeezed it for them to notice. "Yes, it will. It just took a long time to find the right woman to convince me that's what I wanted." He let his amiable gaze drift back and forth between the Texas couple. "You two have done well for yourselves. Your ranch is still the prettiest I've seen. I'm sure running one this large takes lots of time and sweat."

Matt sighed and said, "We've had a few hard times but things are getting better."

Navarro knew from Matt's reaction he hadn't intended to make that slip. He leapt on it fast. "Anything I can help with, Matt?"

"No, but thanks for the offer."

Navarro pretended not to notice the odd expression in Jessie's blue eyes before she lowered her head and pretended to use her napkin. Matt also seemed tense and wary. "You know, old friend, if you ever need my help again, all you have to do is ask, just send for me and I'll come. I owe you two plenty, more than I can ever repay with words."

"That's mighty nice of you, Navarro, but we're fine. More coffee, please," the rancher requested as he held out his cup to his wife.

The two agents perceived that everything was anything but "fine" for the Texas couple in the financial area.

As they ate, Beth gave furtive study to the two men who loved Jessica. Both had dark tans, though Navarro's had a bronze tint. Both had white teeth, full mouths, and arresting features, but her partner's were more captivating to her. Both were strong, muscular, virile, proud, and hard-working. They had similar builds, but Navarro was several inches taller. Both had brown eyes, but her love's had lots of green flecks. Both had sexy, appealing smiles; but Matt's came easier, stayed longer, and danced in his eyes. Both were handsome and rugged, but they didn't favor each other in the least, and their personalities were nothing alike. The rancher was nice and charming; not her choice between the two, though she was thankful the foreman had been Jessica's choice years ago.

Matt ended the silence. "Navarro always was one to help out friends in trouble, Beth. He taught us plenty about defeating men like Fletcher and his boys. It was a good thing Jessie located him in San Angelo, brought him home, and persuaded Jed to hire him."

"The sheriff and Army couldn't stop that snake from striking at us, so I told Papa we needed an expert gunslinger to help us battle him. I went searching for one and found him, thank heaven." Jessica laughed before adding, "Or rather he found me."

Navarro jested, "I found what I thought was a young and helpless boy being attacked by a man, a big bully."

"And rescued me from a certain beating or death. We had to flee for our lives with his brothers on our trail in hot pursuit. We fought them together; then, Navarro agreed to accept my offer of a job."

"I had no choice after I got shot and you hauled me halfway home while I was out cold. You made the ranch sound like a perfect hideout."

"It was for a while. We helped each other out of some tight spots."

"That we did, Mrs. Cordell," Navarro concurred, struggling not to stare at Jessica while they chatted about old times; times that had brought them together, then torn them apart forever.

Beth knew how her partner must be feeling, so she used the conversation to delve for clues both about the Cordells and Navarro. "However did you convince your father to let you go search for a gunslinger to hire? It's so dangerous."

Jessica locked a merry gaze with her husband's matching one. "Matt helped me. Papa was a proud, tough, independent, and stubborn man; it was hard for him to accept he couldn't handle the problem alone. But things grew worse every day. Matt and I knew Fletcher wouldn't stop at anything to get our land, even murder. He was attacking at our busiest season—during spring roundup and crop planting. The boys couldn't work and fight his gang at the same time. I got Matt to work on Papa because he always trusted him and listened to him. Matt and I are much alike. We believe in doing whatever's necessary to protect our home and family from .evil. We worked hard for what we have, and nobody and nothing will be allowed to take it away."

Would either of you break the law to get what you want or to defend family and possessions? "Why did this Wilbur Fletcher want your ranch so badly? Navarro said he'd backed himself against mountains and needed your property to expand his empire; he also said you had better grazing land and water sources. Was that all there was to it?"

"No, we learned the truth later for his greed and evil. He planned to bring a rail line from up north down into Mexico with spurs to Fort Davis and to silver and gold mines in the Chinati Mountains. He needed a route across our land because of its ample wood and water for engines and easy terrain for laying tracks. If his scheme to push us out had worked, he'd have been a powerful and rich man. I still get angry when I think of the blackhearted things he did to us."

"What exactly did he do? Navarro rushed over the details."

"You could say he started simple: undercutting our prices and scaring off seasonal hands we needed. When those tricks didn't work, he got dirty and dangerous. He ordered his gang to set fires, stampede herds, lock foxes in the chicken coop, cut fences, destroy windmills, rustle cattle and horses, kill or maim stock and pets. Twice he tried to frame us for crimes, but failed. They shot some of our hands, injured or terrorized others into leaving, and attacked our home with gunfire. He even had my father murdered in cold blood."

"That's horrible, Jessica. I'm so sorry you all had to suffer so much. But why couldn't or wouldn't the authorities stop him?"

"He had everyone fooled but us. He was rich and powerful, well known. He was so cunningly devious he could probably charm a blind man out of his cane. He made sure no clues pointed at him. His men were so scared of him and his other hirelings, jail or a rope looked better than betraying that sidewinder. I hated him and wanted him destroyed. With Navarro's guns, training, and brains, we did just that."

"Why didn't your father hire an ex-lawman or detectives to obtain evidence against Fletcher, or employ a large band of men to battle such a snake?"

"Men bound by law wouldn't do what had to be done—fight back in the same ways he was attacking us, the only talk a man like that understands. Navarro had the guts and know-how to do it and he taught us. He gave us the courage, wits, and aid we needed to win our bloody range war."

"But the law finally stepped in. Isn't that what you told me, dear heart?" Beth asked Navarro, who only nodded.

Jessica nodded, too, and replied, "Yes, the day that bastard and his men ambushed us and were killed. Pardon my language, Beth, but I've lived and worked around rough men so long, their naughty habits have rubbed off on me."

As Jessica sipped coffee, Beth queried, "Did you ever have trouble with Indians before they were brought under control?"

"Not much. Papa made truces with them right after he moved here. Sometimes they rustled a few head but not enough to fight them over. Once in a while, renegades still take a few steers for food. As long as it's not too many and they don't do any killing or property damage, we ignore it."

What about renegade rustling now that you can't afford to lose any stock? How far would you two go to protect your dwindled herd? "What if they broke from the reservation and became a threat?"

Navarro knew Beth's motive, so he kept silent. He despised this type of questioning but felt, as she must, it was necessary. If Jessica and Matt had fallen prey to Charles's deceit, he'd have to rescue them. If they weren't involved, and he didn't believe they were, he had to clear them of any false charges of collusion and prevent backlash from any foes or the law.

"We'd let the Army deal with them if the band's too large for us to defeat," Matt responded. "Did you see or hear about trouble on the way here?"

"No, thank goodness. But after I moved to Tucson, I heard frightful tales of past horrors. And Navarro told me about the old Comanche War Trail twenty miles east of here where we're heading. I hope there aren't any dangerous renegades around San Antonio."

"Don't worry, love, there aren't," Navarro pretended to calm her worries. He was sure the questions coming from her, a female, wouldn't arouse suspicions; and she'd done a skilled probing job so far.

"But if any trouble comes, your husband is capable of dealing with it, even singlehanded. We couldn't have defeated Fletcher without his help. We'll always be grateful to him and call him friend. After we did in that snake, we tried to get Navarro to stay on, but he couldn't."

"It's a good thing I didn't stay, Matt, and you two got me out of prison or I wouldn't be sitting here with Beth."

Jessica smiled and said, "Fate has a way of putting us where we should be for good things to happen to us. We may think a problem is terrible and painful, but it moves us into another place and rewards us for our strength and courage to go on. Never let trouble destroy you."

"You're right, Jessica; and if one's lucky, one has good friends to lean on for assistance in hard or dangerous situations. We're both grateful for all you two did for Navarro, so if you ever need anything, let us know, please."

"You're most kind and generous, Beth, like your husband."

She continued her probing. "So what happened to the railroad and Chinati mines?"

"The railroad·used another route, and the Fletcher brothers' mines supposedly played out almost immediately after Wilbur's death. They sold out using trickery, but the joke was on them." She paused to laugh. "New and bigger strikes were made. I wish we'd purchased that property, too; the earnings would be a godsend in hard times. You'll face some harsh times, too, but don't let them come between you two or get either of you down. Matt and I don't; whatever happens, we stick together."

"We'll take your excellent advice, Jessica."

Matt changed the subject. "Seems this is a week for surprise visits."

Navarro kept his tone light as he asked, "What do you mean?"

"My younger brother Charlie is coming soon. Haven't seen him since I left Georgia after the war, twenty-one long years. He wasn't but fourteen when it started, but he fought to the end. I hear from him every few years, but I can't write him 'cause he moves around a lot, like you did, Navarro."

"I'm sure you two will have a fine reunion after being apart so long."

"I'm sure we will. Why don't we go in the other room, Navarro, while Jessie clears the table. Beth, you can keep her company if you like."

That idea suited the fiery redhead just fine, as it would give her privacy to cull crucial information from Jessica, on several matters.

Chapter Thirteen

Matt and Navarro went into the living room to talk about "ranching and old times" as the two women began clean-up tasks.

Beth was intrigued when Jessica closed the kitchen door. As she helped put away leftovers and empty plates of uneaten bits into a bucket for pigs, the Special Agent wondered if that action was to give the men or them privacy, or was only done to soften the noise of their chores. Beth knew she must establish fast rapport with her target so she would relax enough to speak freely. If she must play a besotted bride who was so in love she couldn't think straight or control her tongue and so indebted to the people who had made her marriage possible, she would. It was her job to do or say anything necessary to succeed with the important assignment. She was cognizant that victory would save many lives and prevent much property damage for innocents. If the Cordells were involved, despite being Navarro's friend and lost love, they must be stopped. Those personal connections also meant she must pay extra attention, as her partner might be too distracted by or too loyal to the couple to do so.

As Jessica washed dishes and Beth dried them, the slightly older woman remarked, "You and Navarro seem very happy and well matched; I'm glad. He deserves every handful of love and happiness he can grasp."

"Words like those from a close friend of his warm my heart."

"Believe me, Beth, they're true and sincere."

"We appreciate them and your hospitality. Navarro speaks highly of everyone on the ranch and his days here, so I was eager to visit. It didn't take long for me to grasp why that time in his life is so special to him. From what he's told me, you and Matt saved his life. If all of you hadn't turned him around, we wouldn't have met and gotten married, so I also owe you a large debt." Beth put aside a saucer and reached for another one as she chatted. "When Navarro says how grateful he is, you know he would do anything for you two. You and Matt can call on him any time and he'll come and help; me, too, if necessary."

Jessica stopped scrubbing a plate to look at the radiant redhead. "You're a very special woman yourself, Beth Breed. Too many people are selfish and greedy these days. It's nice to find somebody who isn't."

Beth twirled the cloth inside a cup. "I've learned life can be short and cruel sometimes. I'm fortunate I was given a second chance at love and happiness, especially with a unique man like Navarro." She gave the dish in her hand a dreamy stare. "When I looked up that day in the Carters' store and there he stood after all that time and torment, my heart almost leapt from my chest. I must confess," she murmured with a sparkle in her green eyes, "it was hard not to jump into his arms and cover his handsome face with kisses. I'm sure that brazen behavior would have shocked the Carters and their customers."

Before Beth continued in a serious tone, she laughed, as did Jessica. "Stephen's loss and two distant moves in less than a year were difficult. Being reunited with Navarro made me come alive again; to be frank, more alive than I'd ever been. Some mornings when I wake up, I can hardly believe he's lying beside me, he's my husband." She furtively observed Jessica as she spoke. "It's amazing how life and people can change so fast under certain circumstances. My feelings are different: they seem so much stronger and deeper. It's as if Navarro was meant to be my true and lasting love. Second chances like this don't happen often. I hope I'm not sounding silly and girlishly romantic."

"Not at all, Beth; I understand and agree. It's rare for a woman to find two wonderful men at different times in her life. When we're young, we don't know much about those kinds of feelings. First love chooses us and carries us away like a captor, and we sort of lose ourselves in that person. The next time, with good luck, we choose it and travel side-by-side; we become a half of a perfect whole; we find ourselves."

Beth halted her chore, widened her gaze, and looked at her target. "That's a perfect way to describe it, Jessica. You're smart and intuitive. With Stephen, it was like . . . a fire that burned fast, hard, and consuming. He ruled me and our roost, and I never said or did anything to alter the situation. That was how I was reared, to be an obedient wife. After being on my own for almost a year, I couldn't have stepped back into those slippers. I didn't have to with Navarro. He's my other half, a partner. I'd known him for years. But that day in Tucson, it was like I was really seeing him for the first time as a man, if that makes sense."

As Jessica finished washing the utensils, she said, "I know what you mean. Matt lived under my nose from the time I was seven, except for two years when he went off to war in the South. Papa hired him when he was eighteen and made him foreman in '66. We became friends and family. He helped raise and train me. But I grew up as a tomboy, as Jed's son; I was taught and did everything he and the hands knew and did. I was Papa's heir and had to be ready to take over when he was gone, so I lived as a boy, then a man. I've worked as hard on this spread as Papa and Matt and all our hands." Jessica paused to add hot water and more soap to the dishpan before attacking greasy pots.

Beth smiled at Jessica and coaxed, "So how did you two get together?"

Blue eyes glistened with joy and love as she answered, "I was twenty-four when I realized I was a woman and decided I wanted to look, act, and live as one. Most folks considered me a spinster, but it hadn't mattered until I started thinking about love and marriage, a home and children. I had to work on my appearance and behavior to let people know I was a female."

As Jessica laughed softly, Beth subtracted dates to confirm the timing of Jessica's enlightenment: Seventy-six when Navarro came . . .

"Thank goodness Matt hung around all those years and gave me time to grow up, to clear my head."

Beth mused, *Of Navarro's pull and magic?*

"We spent thousands of days and nights together working and laughing, sharing and learning, drawing closer and closer without my awareness. I'd come to see Matt as my best friend, my older brother. Somewhere along the trail, our friendship bloomed into love. He's been the most wonderful thing that's happened to me, the rock of my existence."

"It must have stunned you when you realized you loved him as a man."

"It did, and it didn't. When I was a young girl, I was infatuated with him. I guess he became familiar, comfortable, and I took him for granted. Matt used to be so soft-spoken and serious, and he still is but in a different way. He was always easygoing and hardworking, always there like the next day. He's the most unselfish, gentle, tender person I know. Some people think a man with such traits is weak, but Mathew Cordell is as strong and tough and brave as they come. He can stand shoulder to shoulder with any man, and heads above most. He's a man who'd never run out on his family and friends even at the cost of his life. He's as honest as the day's long, as near to perfect as possible, an expert rancher, devoted father, and priceless husband. If necessary, I could support myself and the children and defend us and this ranch, but I wouldn't be complete and happy without him. His loss would be the worst agony I'd have to endure."

As if realizing she hadn't replied to Beth's question, Jessica added, "It was that trouble with Fletcher and inheriting the ranch that changed me, made me see life, the future, and Matt differently. The same is true for him; he'd always loved me and wanted me but never let on. Coming so close to death and losing me showed him he had to speak up and take a chance I'd accept, which I did, of course. Amidst an evil mess, we found each other, found something wonderful. So did Navarro. And my brother and sister, too. Lots of good came from that snake's wickedness."

Beth had no doubt Navarro's disappearance was a crucial factor in opening Jessica and Matt's eyes and pushing them together. "Fletcher affected many lives in ways he never intended. I'm glad everything worked out for all of you."

"Matt and I have been blessed. You and Navarro will be, too. He's a special man, Beth, and I'm glad he found you to share his life."

"Thank you. I have to admit he's totally irresistible and perfect, just as Matt is to you. We're two lucky women to have husbands like them."

"And they're two lucky men to have wives like us," Jessica quipped.

They exchanged smiles and shared laughter.

While putting aside the last pot, Beth knew she was being studied. She kept her body relaxed and expression genial. She pondered the auburn-haired beauty's praise of Matt and words about Navarro. She wondered if Jessica was so in love with Matt and so disarmed by her, a stranger, that she could be this open about her love and marriage. Or was Jessica only trying to paint a pretty and innocent picture of Matt, herself, and their existence? Was she trying to prove the past with Navarro was over and hoping she'd share that fact with him? Beth had worked many assignments, involving many people. It was her opinion that Jessica was being honest. Until Mrs. Cordell gave her a reason to think otherwise, the agent decided, she'd labor under that premise. She'd do her best to protect these people who had helped Navarro so much. If they were entangled in some mess, she'd try to extricate them as repayment.

Beth watched Jessica wipe the counters and kitchen table, then dump the used water. "Where do the children attend school?" she asked. "Is it far away?"

Jessica dried the dishpan and hung up wet cloths as she responded, "No. We and some neighbors built and funded a small school where our ranches meet and hired a wonderful teacher. Hands' children also go there. Jefferson used to drive ours over in the buggy and pick them up in the afternoon: Big John does it now because Jefferson is needed more on the range. That's a romance to tickle the heart: Jefferson fell in love with our schoolmarm and they got married. He and Maria still work for us. Maria's Mexican, but she was born and raised in Texas. She's as smart and nice as folks come, and the children love her. She has a special and clever way of getting them to do their best work. I've had to fill in for her twice when she had her babies; let me tell you, Beth, educating youngsters isn't an easy job."

"I've learned that no task that's done right is easy."

"True. Well, that's it. Thanks for the help and company. I enjoyed our chat, even if I did most of the talking. It's been too quiet around here lately."

"I enjoyed it, too. I hope you'll tell me more about Navarro and old times while I'm here. And teach me all you can about the challenges and work I'm facing. I'd appreciate any advice and guidance you can give."

"I'll be delighted to share anything I know about ranching. I haven't had someone like you to talk with since Annie moved. Blazes, I miss her. I think we'll become good friends and have fun during your visit."

"That would please me greatly, Jessica. I didn't know many people in St. Louis because Stephen and I lived so far from town and were so busy with the farm after moving there. When I was in Tucson, I didn't get close enough to anyone to relax and talk like this. It feels good."

"Yes, it does. We'd better join our men or they'll wonder what's taking so long in here."

Matt looked up as they entered the room. "I was about to poke my nose in there and see if you two needed help. I hope Jessie didn't talk your ears off, Beth," he joked as his wife sat down on the oversize arm of his chair, leaned against his shoulder, and nudged him playfully.

Beth took a seat close to Navarro on the couch and he rested his hand on her thigh. "She didn't. We had a wonderful time. She's promised to educate me on becoming a rancher's wife. It sounds like a big job."

Matt wrapped an arm around Jessie's hips and tucked a thumb in her dress pocket. "Can't round up a smarter teacher in that pasture. There's nothing my little woman can't do and do it better than most of us cowpokes."

Navarro agreed. "Take his word, love; I've seen Jessie at work on and off a horse. She's a top hand, right, Matt?"

Matt tugged on Jessica's hair. "Nothing could be closer to the truth."

"Stop bragging about me, you two, or my head will swell."

"It sounds as if you deserve the praise you're getting, Jessica."

"Thank you all."

When Jessica leaned over and kissed her husband's cheek, Navarro looked at Beth and said, "Matt's been telling me how much work and skilled planning a spread takes. He was just getting to know how to pick stock and breed 'em. Go on, Matt; this part is important to us."

The rancher stretched out his legs and complied. "Longhorns can take heat, thirst, and hunger the best, but they're leaner, have tougher and stringier meat than purebreds or mixes. We mated ours with Durhams, Booths, Galloways, and Herefords. Next, we plan to use Angus. Herefords made our choice blend so far; meat's top grade and brings a high dollar. Just make sure you check their noses, ears, mouths, eyes, and hooves like I told you, else dishonest and greedy sellers pass off old or ailing stock."

"Thanks for the warning. I remember having to check navels, noses, and any wounds for screwworms every summer; and I recall how to treat infected ones. What else do I need to be on the watch for?"

"Rustling and drought; you can slow or stop the first one, but there's little a man can do to fight bad weather except build yourself plenty of windmills and tanks and keep 'em whirlin' and filled to the brim during hot and dry spells. Might carry you till it decides to rain if you're lucky."

Two troubles mentioned, Beth mused, but what about the third and biggest? She was pleased when her partner delved for it.

"Anything else to watch out for?"

"Hoof-and-mouth disease: it's bad, spreads faster and easier than a flash flood in a dry wash. Strikes with about as much warning, too. Makes blisters in the mouth, 'tween the toes, and on udders and teats. Gets in the milk, droppings, and spittle. Catch it quick and you can steer off big trouble by getting healthy stock away from sick ones and killing infected ones pronto. Ain't no medicine or cure, just clean-up. Seen it before?"

"Yep, once. We had to kill and bury almost a whole herd to keep the rest from getting it. Had to burn off the pastures to make 'em safe again. He couldn't sell for two years until buyers were sure the meat was good. Nearly broke him in spirit and pocket. He told me goats and pigs can also get it, so I'll be careful with them, too. Anything else might attack me?"

"Infernal cattle plague!"

Navarro read the bitterness in Matt's mood as those words leapt from his mouth before he could stop them. The perceptive agent saw Jessie glance at her husband as if in disbelief that he'd let a . . . *secret* slip out. He also detected his old friend's annoyance with himself for being careless. Acting as if he hadn't noticed anything unusual, Navarro said, "Haven't run into that before. What is it?"

"Something you don't wanna mention to others or you'll be ruined when they panic and cut you off from sales and stop you from riding across their land to get to market or railhead. It's a devil disease from a foreign country; don't have it in America except by accident. Least Doc hadn't seen or heard or read about any cases like mine so he didn't know what was wrong when it attacked here. He believes it's an offshoot of hoof-and-mouth, just different from ours 'cause it came from imported bulls. Kills 'em in a week or less. They burn up with fever, their innards go to water, and they get sores on the body and in the mouth. First thing we noticed was this . . . slime coming out of their eyes, noses, and mouths. They got so weak they laid down and died. All we could do was burn carcasses and kill any that was in contact with those devil beasts that week. Fired the west pasture where they grazed. It's fenced off; I ain't taking no chances that grass and water ain't still bad. We got a few head roaming there to test it, but had no sickness or deaths for months. 'Course, Doc had to tell the Cattlemen's Association to warn others not to buy and import any. You can imagine what that news did to our market. What stock we saved can't be shipped and sold until next year— that's if we don't have more losses. Doc's to watch us and give them a report. We have to account to him for every head on the ranch. Can't get rid of any animal's body, no matter how it died, until he's examined it."

"*Shu,* Matt, that's bad. But you said there are no new signs of the disease?"

"None, and the ones trapped there are doing fine. Gaining weight and playing like spring calves and colts. Eyes clear and shiny. No sores."

"How did your stock get infected with something we don't have here?"

Navarro and Beth watched as Matt removed his arm from around his wife's shoulders and leaned forward to brace both on his hard thighs. They saw his anguished gaze settle on the floor. His tone was near sullen and his voice was hoarse when he finally answered.

"A . . . friend sent me a few bulls from Brazil. Thought they'd improve my bloodlines. Give mine a taste and quality that'd demand highest dollar."

"Have you told this friend what happened? Is he going to help you out?"

"Yep, he knows and he's got a way of settling up with me."

"Let's move to a more pleasant topic, please," Jessica suggested.

Matt nodded agreement. "Why don't I fetch that bottle of wine we've been saving for a special occasion and toast these newlyweds?"

"That's a marvelous idea. I'll get our best glasses."

Navarro and Beth didn't talk as Matt got the wine from a nearby cabinet which Fletcher had built in as a bar. They didn't even glance at each other to prevent suspicious expressions from showing on their faces that Matt might notice in the fancy mirror over the bar. Jessica returned and placed the glasses on a square table near their chair.

Matt opened the bottle and served the wine. He held up his glass and said, "To our old friend and our new friend, may you be as happy as Jessie and I are."

All four sipped the tasty liquid and smiled.

"Thanks, you two, for everything."

Beth retrieved her package once more and said, "These are my way of thanking you two for what you did for Navarro."

Jessica admired the ecru chantilly lace shawl with its pattern of flowers and ribbons on a spotted background. "It's beautiful, Beth; you shouldn't have. It's much too expensive."

"It's from France, handmade. I hope it will always remind you of how kind and generous you are and remind you of our friendship and gratitude." She turned to Matt. "This is for you, with the same sentiments."

The rancher accepted the knife with a decorative scrimshaw handle of a wolf pack in a forest. He examined it with eyes and fingers. "It's the finest and prettiest one I've ever seen. Thank you, Beth, Navarro."

"I'm glad you like it; I wasn't sure what to get you."

"This is perfect, but you didn't have to bring us anything."

"Yes, I did, because you two gave me the best gift alive."

"Before she gets to praising me too high and swells my head, we'd best get moving. It's late and I know you have to be up early for chores and to tend to the children. If you don't mind, Beth and I will camp nearby in the grove."

"You will not!" Jessica refuted with a smile. "One of the cabins is empty, so you two will stay there. It's more comfortable and private. I've already cleaned it and made the bed. Matt will show you where it is."

"That's too much trouble, Jessie, and you're expecting company."

"It's no bother, Navarro; and Matt's brother is family, so he'll use one of the rooms upstairs. You don't have to be in San Antonio until the fourth, so you have plenty of time to visit. Besides, Big John has already put your belongings in there, along with your gear and saddles in the tackroom and your horses in the corral. This is the least we can do to repay you for all you did for us. Right, Matt?"

The rancher appeared to experience no qualms about Navarro's motive for coming. "She's right, and you know it's impossible to argue with Jessie Lane when she makes up her mind about something."

"I remember," Navarro said with a grin and chuckle. "Thanks."

"Our pleasure," Matt responded. "You keep saying how much you owe us, but the other boot to that pair is how much we owe you for past help."

Both agents told Jessica good night at the front steps and followed the rancher to a nearby cabin in a group of several where the foreman resided and newly married couples stayed until better arrangements were made for them in the rented houses at the old Lane homesite.

Navarro and Matt shook hands at the door and the rancher left.

Inside, Navarro said, "If I haul in my bedroll, it'll look strange, so we'll have to sleep together. If you don't mind." He hung his hat on a peg.

"Of course not; we can't risk arousing suspicions. They're nice; I like them. I can't imagine them being involved in our case by choice."

"I'm glad you agree, because I'm convinced of their innocence. I just don't like what I heard about disease and drought almost ruining them."

As she glanced around their new setting, she asked, "You also think the 'friend' is Charles, don't you?"

"Yep. Question is: was it an innocent mistake or was Matt's brother being devious, using them?"

Beth began to unpack her things. "A man as wicked as this Charles seems to be might do anything to get his way. There's another possibility . . ."

Navarro stopped unbuckling his gunbelt. "What?"

"That was done intentionally to give Charles an excuse to come here to apologize in person and to repay Matt. That's worth checking out after he arrives. Seems cunning and plausible."

"You might have something there, Beth. Thanks."

"Was it as hard seeing her again as you imagined it would be?"

Navarro draped his weapons over a wooden chair. "What made you think it would be painful for me?"

"I didn't say painful, just *difficult* to see your first love happily married to another man and with a lovely home and fine children. And in trouble."

He removed his chaps and tossed them over the same chair as he answered, "I think Jessie always loved Matt and didn't know it. When I was living here, every time he was mentioned, her voice and expression softened. I missed that clue to trouble. What did you two talk about for so long?"

Beth brushed over their conversation.

"See, it doesn't bother her to be around me again. Matt, neither."

"And it doesn't bother you to be around her again?"

"How would you feel if they were Steven and his wife?"

That's a fast and sly sidestep. "I guess why and how I lost him would determine my feelings. If you and Jessica had parted of free will, it—"

"We shouldn't be talking like this. Somebody could overhear us."

"Sorry, and you're right again. I'll get ready for bed. You should, too."

As she turned her back to change, Navarro wondered why he didn't speak his mind and appease his partner's worries. He had experienced a strange and contradictory mixture of emotions upon discovering Jessie seemed to have gotten over him and the past: relief and disappointment, joy and sadness, calm and tension. It was obvious Jessie wasn't the same woman he'd known years ago. She had matured, flourished, and mellowed under Matt's loving care. Even her appearance had altered; her hair was more brown than red, and the shorter sides and top she'd cut for her masculine ruse in San Angelo were now the same length as the locks that curled wildly halfway down her back when unbound. She had gained weight and filled out, but was still dainty and shapely. In her sky-blue eyes, he had read only friendship, pure and innocent love, and total tranquility. The old Jess, a firebrand of a girl who had loved him passionately, was gone, and in her place was a serene parent and mate. In his mind, he had kept her as she was in looks, personality, and feelings ten years ago. It was an odd sensation for an illusion, a golden dream, to crash into reality.

For a moment when he first saw her, he had wished he could return to the past when they'd first met, if he could do so as a free man. Yet, he couldn't help but wonder, if they and circumstances had been different, would they have fallen in love? In all honesty, he couldn't answer, and that indecision troubled and surprised him. For him, time had halted like a stopped watch, but Jessie's had continued to run, marking time and creating new hours, leaving old ones in the past forever. It appeared as if his Jess was as much of a ghost as Beth's lost love.

Beth . . . She had won over Matt and Jessie with charm and ease. She had done a good job tonight. Maybe the reason he didn't explain the truth was because it might give her the wrong idea, that he was available, especially with a night of fiery passion and a curious attraction lingering between them. He wasn't accessible and never would be. Love was too hard, too painful, a risk he didn't want to take again. Besides, it was probably futile with her. She was only obeying orders, nothing more. She had surrendered to him that reckless night out of need and loneliness and a brief loss of self-control, all things he understood and felt at times.

He shifted his thoughts to another loss: Lane, a handsome, smart, and special boy, his boy, his son, but in birth and blood only. What he wouldn't give to be rearing Lane on a ranch with—

"Ready to put out the light?" Beth asked for the second time. Her heart ached at what she assumed he was feeling. She warned herself once more to restrain her emotions where he was concerned or she'd come away from this assignment with an anguish too great to endure. Yet, she wanted to comfort him and herself for a moment. "How about a friendly hug to calm us down? We've been under a strain for hours."

As they embraced, each sought solace, encouragement, and strength from the other. Both felt the tension from recent episodes ease away. Both felt desire chew at them but sensed this wasn't the time to succumb to their hungers. With reluctance, they released each other and smiled.

You're a fine friend and partner, woman, and maybe more . . . "You did good today, Beth Breed; more than good, excellent. All we have to do now is make sure they keep us around until Charles arrives."

"Thanks. I'll do my part as best I can." She climbed into bed as she told him, "Good night, boss. That was nice and I admit I needed it."

"Me, too. 'Night, partner." He doused the lamp's flame, shucked his boots and garments, and took a position on his left side. He realized she was doing the same on her right one, putting them back-to-back but still close to each other on the bed. *Shu,* he fretted, it was going to be a long and hard night with a tempting woman so near in body and so far away in spirit.

Navarro was up and dressed when Matt knocked on the cabin door; Beth was grooming herself while he tried to keep his eyes and thoughts off her. He opened it enough to go outside but still guard her privacy.

"Morning, Matt."

"Morning. Thought you might wanna eat with me and the boys in the chuckhouse, then ride the range a while. They're eager to see you."

"Sounds good to me. Let me tell Beth where I'm going."

"Jessie said for her to come to the house when she's ready."

Navarro went back inside to pass along the quick messages. He wondered if Matt's intention was to keep him away from Jessie and Lane as much as possible, at least until they all adjusted to being together again. He was eager to see the range and herd to learn how bad things were. He headed to the cookhouse where his old friends were waiting to greet him.

When Beth was ready, she walked to the house and found Jessica in the kitchen. "Good morning. What can I do to help?"

"Grab yourself some coffee and take a seat. I'll have our food ready in a few minutes. Our husbands are eating with the boys so they can chat. Lane and Alice have already done their chores and left for school. Eat up, Lance."

After pouring coffee and sitting down, Beth looked at the little boy sitting at the table. "How are you this lovely morning, Lance?"

"Mama cooked me johnnycakes" was the four-year-old's reply.

"He'd eat them every day if I'd let him," Jessica said with a laugh. "Don't forget your milk, son, and slow down or you'll choke."

"What chores do the other children have before school?"

"Lane milks the family cow in the morning and evening; Biscuit Hank, the boys' cook, does the other two. Alice feeds the chickens and lets them out to scratch for the day and pens them up at night, except for those sitting on eggs. Do you know about those chores?"

"I've done those two, but Stephen chose which nests and birds were allowed to sit and make hatchlings."

"I'll teach you how to do the choosing later. Matt hays the stock in the morning and I gather the eggs for us; Hank, for the men. Big John slops the pigs for me from the bucket I sit on the back porch; he mixes it with their feed and water. I'll teach you about that, too. Until you hire help, which is a big expense, you and Navarro will have to do the chores yourselves."

As they ate breakfast in leisure, Beth queried, "Lane is kind of quiet and shy, isn't he? He doesn't seem outgoing like Alice and Lance."

"His best friend just moved away and he's sad and lonesome, hasn't had time to get over the loss. But he's still a mite quiet and serious, just like his father used to be. I suppose Lane is mature for his age. He was our only child for years, so he spent a lot of time around adults—me and Matt and the hands. He was on a horse before he could walk and helping with chores as soon as he could. He's a lot like my brother, loves to read and learn. I won't be surprised if he wants to go off to college like Tom did. Every time my brother visits, they talk about it constantly."

"Lane doesn't want to become a rancher like Matt?"

"We don't know; he doesn't, either. We'll let him make his own choice about what he'll do and where. Nothing makes a person more miserable than being forced to do something they don't love and respect."

Beth wondered if Jessica's words referred to more than her son.

"If you're finished, Lance, why don't you play in your room with your toys? Miss Beth and I will be right here working if you need me."

"Yes, Mama."

Jessica washed his face and hands and helped him from the chair. Her adoring gaze followed the child until he was out of sight.

Beth heard his footsteps on the wooden stairs. "He's precious. I can't wait until we have one like him." She laughed and refuted, "Yes, I can. I hope it's a ways off to give us time alone and time to get established."

"You love children, don't you?" Jessica watched her nod. "You're good with them. I'm sure you two will make wonderful parents."

Beth reasoned the woman might wonder why "Elizabeth Lawrence" didn't have any children after being married for several years, so she asserted, "I hope I don't have trouble getting pregnant when the moment comes. I lost two babies before they could be born when I was married to Stephen. The doctor said I was fine and the losses were nothing more than results of accidents. We crashed in a runaway carriage the first time and I took a bad fall during the second one. He said not to worry."

"I'm sure everything will be fine for you and Navarro. I've often heard of such things happening. I had a hard time with my first child, especially problems with his birth. Matt delivered Lane and saved our lives because the doctor couldn't get here. Mary Louise, my sister, had difficulty conceiving; her husband's a doctor and there was nothing he could do to solve their problem. She and John were about to give up hope when she got pregnant; now, they have a passel of children."

"That's encouraging news." *Except in my particular case.*

"Beth . . ."

The agent's curiosity was piqued when Jessica paused. "Yes?"

"It's none of my business, and I won't mind if you say so, but . . ."

"What is it, Jessica? You can tell me and I won't be offended."

"If you haven't told Navarro that fear, I'd keep it to myself for a while, just in case it takes you a long time to conceive. You don't want him to worry about you and having children while you're still getting close and starting a new life together. Men can be . . . sensitive about such matters if they want a child of their own badly. When a man Navarro's age settles down, he wants everything fast—wife, home, children, and success—because he waited so long to get them. I guess it has to do with male pride, fear of losing their . . . virility, afraid of failing you and himself, and having no heir."

"You're right; it'll be our secret for a while. If the doctor hadn't assured me I'm fine, I would have told Navarro the truth before we wed."

"I think you did the best thing for both of you, so don't worry."

"I'll keep praying and believing. Thanks for the advice." *But why do you look and sound so . . . concerned and mysterious over our future baby? Is it because you want him locked "firmly into his new existence"? I can't blame you for wanting to protect all you have from trouble.*

They cleared the table, washed and dried dishes, cleaned and put on two hens to boil, and did some light housekeeping. Jessica told Beth that after the fowl cooked and cooled, she'd remove the meat to make chicken and dumplings for supper. As they worked and Lance played in his room, they chatted about many things.

"You must be very skilled, Jessica, for your father to have let you take on that gunslinger mission all by yourself."

"I didn't start out without help; I had a big, strong hand with me. He was killed in an accident on the trail. I buried him with rocks and took off."

As they finished in the kitchen, Beth gazed at the dainty female. "So you continued alone?"

"I had to; I was too close to town and we needed help bad. It was silly to return home because none of the other hands could be spared. I cut the top and sides of my hair short, then hid the rest of it with my hat. Banded my breasts—what little I had then—dirtied my face to mask my sex, disguised my voice, and kept my head ducked, never looked anybody in the eye. I'd lived with and as a male for so long it was easy to play one. I searched the town and checked the saloons because San Angelo was a known hangout for gunslingers. Those kind of men have a crazy streak of loyalty to men who hire them and fierce pride in jobs they take on. I was scared and nervous, but I was careful and alert. Still got into trouble." She laughed.

After hearing those facts, Beth concluded Jessica Lane Cordell would have made a clever agent. If Navarro had been with the Agency long ago and she'd taken off with him, they would have been an excellent team. With haste, she dismissed that intrusive thought. "What happened?" she asked, making sure she sounded curious.

Jessica used a damp cloth over a homemade brushbroom to clean the wood floors. "I was questioning a saloon girl when one of the town's bullies took offense when she tried to get rid of him and stay at the table with me. Before that drunk arrived, I ran into some scary moments convincing her I didn't want her upstairs services. It's funny now, but, at that time, I had to do some fast and clever talking not to insult her or expose my identity."

While Beth dusted furniture, she laughed and said, "I imagine so. Yep, you'd have to be cunning and quick to outwit them as you did."

"That brute wouldn't settle down. He attacked me, yanked me right out of my chair, and roughed me up. I was lucky Navarro arrived and rescued me 'cause nobody else would challenge any of the Adams boys. I'm sure he's told you about his childhood troubles, so you can understand why that incident with the young boy he took me for provoked him to intrude."

She saw Beth nod. "I must confess: Navarro looked like the tallest, bravest, and handsomest man I'd seen when he stepped between me and that huge beast. He tried to talk Adams out of a fight, but it didn't work. I couldn't believe anybody would go against a man who looked, moved, and spoke like Navarro in the old days. Adams was a cocky fool and drew on him. I've never seen any man clear leather as fast and easy as Navarro." Jessica smiled and said, "I guess you could say, I knew I'd found my man."

In more than one way. So, you were smitten and fascinated by him the first time you met, just as I was. I'll bet Navarro has that arresting effect on all women. With little effort, he could win any female he desires, except the only one he loves and wants.

"You married a special man, Beth. You'll always be safe with him."

"You're right, and thanks. Was it hard to persuade him to take your job? I mean, with him being a fugitive on the run."

"That's why he finally agreed, but he said no at first. That saloon girl told us we'd better git pronto 'cause Adams had mean brothers. We didn't hang around to see if she was right. Turned out, she was. News traveled swift and they came after us and attacked. Navarro tried again to talk his way out of a gun battle with about as much success as he'd had with their brother. Even in his old days, Beth, he didn't kill unless he wasn't given a choice. Anyway, he was wounded and I saved his life, so he thought he owed me, least he used that excuse to accept my offer."

Jessica worked her way into the dining room with Beth following. "I believe he accepted because I saved his hide and because I promised him food, shelter, a new horse, and good pay; and because Fletcher sounded like a worthy challenge to him, a mean bastard like his father. I didn't learn the truth until he had to leave. By then, we were friends, so he trusted me with the real reasons he'd come and couldn't stay. He did far more for us than just fight Fletcher. We hated to see him go; he was one of the best hands we'd had, put him to hard labor on branding the day he arrived."

I'll bet his confession and loss were hard on you, so you turned to Matt for comfort. I'll bet you never expected or planned to fall in love with your foreman, or your hired gunman. I wonder what happened between you and

Navarro during that long ride home with you doctoring him . . . "I imagine he was shocked to learn you were a girl, a young woman."

Jessica filled the room with merry laughter. "He was. Angry, too."

"Angry? Why?"

"Because Papa had let a tiny female go after a dangerous gunslinger. Since I was in big trouble when we met, Navarro didn't think a woman could protect herself or be as good as a man at anything."

"But you proved him wrong in a hurry after he got shot. I'm sure you won his respect and friendship fast. He was lucky he found you at a time when he desperately needed help and friends."

"I don't believe Navarro was ever a bad man; he'd just had bad luck for a long time and too much of it. Once he was in good surroundings with good people, he had a chance to let the real Navarro surface. After he did, there was no going back to his old self and existence. He's proven that by how he's lived and the way he is now. He was always searching and hungering for peace, respect, acceptance, and love—even though he'd denied such yearnings to himself. It's hard for a man born and raised like he was to give free rein to his feelings. You'll be good for him, Beth, and I doubt you'll ever regret loving him and marrying him. I'm overjoyed to see him so happy and relaxed; and I'm proud we played even a small part in bringing about such changes for him."

You know him well. "So am I, since he's settling down with me."

As they did tasks upstairs, they continued their genial chat. Jessica related her normal routine for the day, week, and each season. She spoke of gardening for daily food consumption and canning extras for winter. She gave suggestions about drying, curing, or pickling items such as fruits, meats, vegetables, berries, and spices. She talked about churning milk into butter, making soap and emergency candles, keeping the wood box loaded for cooking, sewing, and washing and ironing, tending sick or injured animals as well as children, and helping with ranch work when necessary. Jessica cautioned her not to let chores and children "keep you from giving your husband plenty of time and attention because he'll still be around after young'uns are grown and gone." During the ten years she had been married, she said she'd made certain she kept romance alive, their relationship exciting and fulfilling, and communication flowing freely.

Beth realized the woman had wed Matt *very shortly* after Navarro's departure. Had a love-blinded Navarro been mistaken about Jessica's feelings? No, Navarro had told her Jessica promised to wait for him. So why hadn't she, at least for a longer period? Jessica didn't strike her as being cruel and devious, nor a vixen who would dally with a man's affections. Perhaps, Beth mused, she had recoiled after Navarro was compelled to abandon her. But why hadn't she just thrown herself into ranch work and her family while she healed? Yet, the union with Matt had succeeded; they were happy and in love. The contradictions in words and timing baffled Beth. It was as if a vital puzzle piece was missing.

After Lance went to sleep, the women began to debone and demeat the chickens. "He gets up so early that he's sleepy by one. I'm so glad he still takes naps. It gives me time to do chores faster, especially gardening and ironing. Things are a little different at present. Some of the hands are pitching in to help with chores while we entertain our visitors. Matt told you Charles is coming soon."

"I'll bet you two are elated about his visit after being separated for so long. We should go when he arrives to give you privacy for the reunion."

"That isn't necessary. You two must stay, at least until Wednesday. That'll leave you time to reach San Antonio for your appointments."

"Must stay?" "But—"

"You don't have to cut short your visit because of him."

"Cut short your visit?" "Is something wrong, Jessica? Don't you like Charles? Aren't you looking forward to seeing him?"

"I don't know Charles, never met him, never had the chance."

"You don't look or sound as if you want to, either."

"To be honest, Beth, I don't. I'm angry with him," Jessica began, then halted to glance out back and front to make sure they had privacy.

Chapter Fourteen

Beth halted the work on her hen and looked at her companion. She queried the reason for Jessica's unexpected words and mood.

"He's the one who sent those diseased bulls to us. This ranch has faced all kinds of perils and hardships but we've always been able to defeat them. That evil predator was unlike anything that's attacked us. There was no way to fight it, Beth; we were helpless, almost destroyed. If we'd been in deep debt, everything we own and have worked for would be gone."

Sounds as if she wants to talk. Draw her out slowly and carefully. "Matt's brother is responsible? He's the . . . 'friend' Matt mentioned?" Beth read sadness mingled with anger in Jessica's gaze as she nodded; then, a gleam of distrust filled those heavenly blue eyes.

"He's never sent the children or us anything in the past. When he finally gets a very tardy 'generous' streak, this is the result!"

From the corner of her eye, she watched Jessica frown, yank pieces of fowl from a chicken's thigh, then toss the bone in a refuse pan. The woman's knee bumped the cabinet in a rhythmical cadence that indicated agitation. *Go easy, Beth.* "Matt must feel terrible, since it's his brother."

"He does, but he won't blame Charles. He says it was an accident because Charles supposedly doesn't know anything about cattle and their diseases. Matt knows now he should have kept them separated from our stock for a while. Only a week would have changed everything! But he was so excited about having a breed no one else did that he couldn't wait to see if our cows showed any interest in the new boys and see how the new ones mingled and got along with our herd. From all the glowing things Charles wrote him about those blasted beasts, Matt was like a child at Christmas with a new toy. When Charles said it would make the L/C Ranch prosperous, Matt believed him; it was his brother talking, and Charles had been everywhere, seen and done everything, to hear him tell it. Well, *he certainly didn't know everything, or we wouldn't be in this mess!* Matt feels so awful about his mistake, I haven't mentioned my worries to him. I don't want to hurt him and shame him by telling him what I really think."

"Worries?" Sounds like suspicions to me. Beth knew from all she'd learned that Jessica wasn't a coward or a weakling, nor did she appear to have lost faith in or respect for Matt; she was being compassionate and protective of her love. "I think you're right to keep silent, at least a while longer, like you advised me to hold quiet about having children. Men's pride can be enormous and difficult to handle at times, particularly when they make an error or one involves their family or a close friend. The animal doctor couldn't do anything to stop that disease's rampage?"

"He'd never seen rinderpest and knew nothing about it. He's sort of a self-trained doc, no real schooling in medicine. As Matt said, he thinks it's a foreign strain of hoof-and-mouth, and that's what he told the Cattlemen's Association. We haven't confessed the truth, and that's probably terrible of us. If there was any risk to other ranchers, we would, honestly. They've been warned not to import stock so that should be enough to protect them. If they learn it's a new disease to our country, we would be avoided worse than that evil plague. We can't risk losing everything, Beth, we just can't."

"Don't worry, Jessica, we won't mention it to anyone. The threat is over and you've done your duty to others, so you mustn't feel guilty. You two have suffered and lost more than your share, so you made a wise decision. How did you discover it was this . . . mysterious rinderpest?"

"After Matt telegraphed Charles with the bad news, Charles wrote and enlightened us. Said he'd checked out the problem with the seller. But he asked us not to tell anyone, warned it might cause us more trouble and start a panic if the Association and other ranchers learned the truth. He said the seller told him we had dealt with the matter in the only way possible and the disease had been conquered and wouldn't return. So far, it hasn't. It may have been foolish and selfish, but we took his word. He must have told the truth because every sign of it has vanished."

Beth noticed that Charles "wrote" and didn't telegraph his response. "I'm sorry it didn't work out as Matt hoped. I know it must have broken your hearts to watch your cattle suffer and die by the hundreds."

"Thousands, Beth, by the thousands. I don't know if I'll ever forget this horror or forgive Charles. I hate the thought of him coming into our

home and onto our land after what he's done to us, what he's cost us."

"Matt hinted that Charles is going to settle up with him over the loss. Is his brother a rich man? Can he repair such heavy damage?"

As she put the hen's carcass aside, Jessica said, "I don't know. He wrote he has a big surprise for Matt that will solve our problems."

"But you don't know what that 'surprise' is and you don't trust him, right?" Jessica nodded. "Has Charles given you any reason to doubt him?"

"Not really. It's just that . . ."

"Just that what, Jessica? Since he's Matt's brother, I understand why you don't want to discuss any misgivings with him. But you can trust me. Let me help you like you helped my Navarro."

Jessica almost flung the hunks of meat into the broth pot. "It's just strange that Charles would suddenly send us such an expensive gift. I mean, he only writes Matt every few years and he's never been to see us. He doesn't even know what his sister-in-law, nephews, and niece look like! He's never even asked Matt to meet him somewhere for a visit."

Beth watched Jessica wash her greasy hands, then lean over to fetch a flour container to make the dumplings. As she straightened and grasped the tuffed end of a thick auburn plait to toss it back over her shoulder, Beth murmured, "That does seem odd. But perhaps this Charles is simply an odd person. Why not wait until you meet him to decide if you like him and believe him? I know it's easier for me to form an accurate opinion about somebody in person. Looking into eyes and listening to a voice usually tell me if a person is being honest and sincere."

"For Matt's sake, I hope he is. I'm going to try my best to be nice and give Charles a fair chance. But it'll be hard, blasted hard. That's why I'm hoping you and Navarro will be here as a distraction in case I don't like him. I'm not good at hiding my feelings with Matt."

"We'll stay as long as possible. But we have to leave no later than Wednesday."

Jessica continued the talk as she mixed, rolled, and cut dough while Beth cleaned up after their other task. "From the message in his last telegram, he should arrive Saturday or Sunday, Monday at the latest. He's only going to be around for two or three days; I hope that's true. I think it's mostly a rest stop during a business trip to Mexico, not a real visit. If we didn't lay in his route path, I doubt he'd be coming this time."

Take the opening, Beth. "What type of business is Charles in?"

"Apparently he dips his fingers into all kinds of barrels, any kind with money at the bottom. It's supposed to be a secret, this time, but he's delivering arms and ammunition to the Mexican government. It seems they can't get weapons in by ship or hauled overland because of bandits and renegades. He told Matt the weapons will help stop raiders from crossing the river to rob us, so he claims he's doing us a second good deed."

A claim that doesn't hold water with you. "Do you have many problems with outlaws and Indians crossing the border and attacking here? Will it be like that in San Antonio, if we decide to settle there?"

"No, not in years for us, and very little in past ones. The same is true for where you're going, so don't worry. Charles doesn't know what he was talking about or he wouldn't have made such a stupid statement. Please stay as long as you can to help me get through this; I'll be ever so grateful. Besides, I'm enjoying your company and having help around the house. It's been a long time since Annie left. As I told you, I've missed having a close friend for talks and chores. Annie's loss helps me understand Lane's feelings over his friend. This visit is good for all of us for lots of reasons."

"You're right; I can't recall when I've enjoyed myself or another person more. Of course that doesn't include my new husband," she added with a dreamy smile. To keep Jessica from becoming suspicious of her, Beth didn't ask any more questions about Charles or the couple's financial problems. She sipped coffee as Jessica put the meat mixture on to simmer.

"Blazes, I miss having good beef! But we can't slaughter any of the steers we have left, for money and health reasons. I usually serve meat only at supper, and vegetables and bread at midday. We'll also have canned butter beans, beets and dried fruit tonight. I hope that tempts you."

Beth licked her lips as she noticed Jessica and Navarro often used the same expletive. "It does. You're a good cook. I'm watching every move you make in here so I can steal your ideas and learn your talents."

"Best I remember, Navarro cooks as well as I do, at least on the trail. He should be very helpful in the kitchen; he's used to doing such chores."

"He's been that way so far; I hope he doesn't stop."

"Matt helps me, too. If husbands want wives to have enough time and energy left over for them and . . . diversions, they should help out."

They shared merry laughter and more genial talk.

When the children came home from school, Lane disappeared up the stairs before Beth saw him. But Alice joined her mother and Beth in the kitchen and chattered like a squirrel about the teacher, her lessons, and friends.

Two of the youngsters joined them for the evening meal in the dining room which had a larger table and more chairs. Matt sat at one end and Lance was placed at the other. The boy insisted on Beth sitting beside him. Alice took a seat next to her mother, across from the visiting couple.

Matt glanced at his wife and asked, "Where's Lane?"

"He's upstairs. He isn't feeling well, he says."

"He's writing to Joey," Alice disclosed. "Miss Maria let us play Joey's favorite game and it made Lane sad. Made his tummy hurt."

"I put my horsey on the bed with him to make him better."

"That was nice of you, Lance."

"He's good, Mama. He gave me this."

Lance drew an amulet from under his shirt and held it out for all to see, and Jessica questioned, "Lane gave you his Indian medal?"

Alice jumped in. "He said the magic doesn't work for him."

Beth gazed at the artistic amulet. "It's Indian, isn't it?"

Matt nodded and said, "Yes. Last summer, a few Apaches camped west of the old house site; they'd escaped from one of those reservations. I gave 'em a few head to butcher for food and let 'em rest up a couple of days before they crossed the border into Mexico to hide out. Can't blame 'em for hating those places; most are downright awful. Lane wanted to see what real Indians were like, but I figured it was best to leave 'em be, so he sneaked out of the house during the night and rode over there. He doesn't usually disobey, but his curiosity chewed on him too hard. An old medicine man found him spying, said he was brave, and gave him that necklace. He's worn it ever since."

"It's mine, Papa; Lane said so."

"If Lane gave it to you, it's yours. But if he changes his mind after his sadness over Joey goes away, it would be kind to return it. When we love somebody, son, we aren't selfish; we show 'em how much we love 'em by doing nice things for them and being nice to them."

Navarro was warmed by the way Matt dealt with the children. It seemed the rancher was an excellent father, the kind he'd like to be.

"Do I hafta give it back tonight? Can I keep it a few days?"

Alice jumped in again. "Lane said he never wants it back. He said it was bad luck for him because he got it disobeying you, Papa. He said Joey's father had to go away the day after he got it. Then, Mr. Cooper came and took Joey. He don't want it back, Papa, never, I'm sure."

"We'll see" was Matt's tender but unconvinced response.

"Sarah won't ever go away, will she, Mama?"

"I don't think so, Alice."

"If my best friend moved like Joey, I'd be sad and crying."

Matt said in a gentle tone, "Eat, children; it's nearing bedtime. You can talk and play tomorrow when there's no school."

"Will you play with us, Miss Beth?"

"Of course, I will, Lance. We'll find some wonderful games."

"Will you tell us stories?"

"If that's what you want, Alice."

"Yippee!"

Everyone laughed at Lance's exuberance and began their meals.

"While I clean up and Matt gets the children to bed, Navarro, why don't you take Beth for a walk? She's worked hard today. She deserves fresh air, a change of scenery, and private time with her new husband."

"That's a good idea, if you'll excuse us."

"See you in the morning, Navarro. You wanna ride along again?"

"Sure do, Matt. See you in the chuckhouse at sunup. 'Night."

"Come over as soon as you're up and ready, Beth. I rise early."

"I will, Jessica. Good night, everyone."

The agents left the house and strolled around the lovely area. When they weren't holding hands, Navarro had his arm around her waist or shoulder as if snuggling her close. Beth was introduced to the wranglers they encountered; the men all smiled and spoke a minute but didn't detain the romancing couple. She was quick to notice how they liked Navarro.

At the corral, Navarro halted Beth and pointed to horses in a nearby pasture as he pretended to be talking about them. "We're being watched; Matt's on the front porch, so be careful how you act."

Beth turned to him and fiddled with his collar and shirt buttons as she kept her gaze on those areas. "Is he spying on us? Is he suspicious?"

Navarro lifted two sections of flame-colored hair from her chest and put them behind her. "Nope, just getting fresh air. We'll talk here because we're too far from anyone to be overheard and we can see anybody coming in any direction. Anything to report?"

Without meeting his hazel gaze, she began, "Last night, the reason I asked if it bothered you seeing Jessica is because—"

"This isn't the kind of talk I meant, if you don't mind."

She fused her gaze to his and persisted, "This is about our work, not your feelings or your past with Jessica. That's none of my business, unless it intrudes on our case. I asked you that question because you seemed too distracted to pick up on crucial facts. That isn't like you, Navarro, so I assumed the reason was—"

He was surprised, but intrigued. "What clues do you think I missed?"

"The disease's timing and symptoms."

"I don't catch your drift, partner. What's strange about them?"

"I didn't want to press the annoying matter with you until I checked out my suspicions. Jessica and I had a long and serious talk today, a very enlightening one. She practically swore me—us—to secrecy. I doubt she'll tell Matt about our conversation and she's kept her worries from him."

Beth was cognizant those last statements seized his interest. His grip on her forearms tightened for a moment and he was on full alert. She related the conversation with his lost love before giving her speculations. "So you see, Matt never intended to make that slip to anyone. Jessica is suspicious of Charles, but she won't tell her husband, and I doubt Matt would believe the dirty truth. It was no risk for Charles to murder their stock because he's no rancher and can claim ignorance and innocence. I'm not familiar with ranching, either, but I realized Matt wasn't describing the same disease as hoof-and-mouth. I was right; rinderpest is different. Charles was clever to tell them what it was and to swear them to secrecy for their own good. He knew if Matt and Jessica or that doctor checked out rinderpest, he would be exposed. He probably assumes, since the danger is over and no one discovered the whole truth, his vile deed is safe forever."

Beth smiled and caressed Navarro's jawline to dupe any unseen observer. "I didn't ask Jessica how the cattle reached them because I didn't want to appear overly nosy. But even using the fastest ship available these days from Brazil, then traveling from the coast up the Rio Grande or overland by train, lots of cattle had to be sent to get only a few here alive and healthy-looking enough to fool a skilled rancher like Matt and his hands. It's my guess the culprits kept infecting one or two at a time during the voyage and final trek to the Cordell property. In case Matt didn't instantly mix them in with his herd, those he received had to be infected at the last minute to prevent them from showing warning signs before he did put them together. It wouldn't surprise me if those culprits hid out nearby with more sick cattle to make certain their plot worked. It would have been easy for them to sneak in additional ones that would be overlooked on a spread this size and with thousands of animals and lots of wranglers on it. When the Cordells' steers and cows started dropping like flies, who would think to count the others and realize there were more dead foreign cattle than Matt had received?"

When she paused, he coaxed, "Keep going; I'm listening."

From his tone she surmised he hadn't grasped her meaning yet. "The disease attacks and kills in a week or less, Navarro. A week or less," she emphasized. "If the Brazilian seller shipped only the bulls that the Cordells received, those four beasts wouldn't have reached here alive." She reiterated certain points. "I don't think Jessica comprehends exactly why she's distrustful; Matt certainly hasn't figured it out, and the local animal doctor wasn't knowledgeable and qualified enough to catch on."

"Matt, Jessie, and the boys are experienced and smart, so I can't understand why none of them caught that timing flaw. On the other hand, neither did I. I'm glad you're riding this trail with a clear head. Trust me, woman, my mistake won't happen again now that I'm wise to it."

Despite embarrassing or vexing Navarro, she had to report all her conclusions. She did so in a gentle tone and with a sweet expression. "Doc and the hands didn't think it was odd because they believe it's a foreign strain of hoof-and-mouth. Doc said the imported cattle reacted slower because it wasn't a new disease to them and they probably had inbred resistance. But the Cordell herd was vulnerable and susceptible, so it struck them fast and hard. Doc compared it to disease-resistant whites spreading lethal and swift epidemics to defenseless Indians. Or a rabid animal showing no warning signs and dying later than its victims. After Matt and Jessica learned about rinderpest, Doc's earlier theory still made sense, at least to Matt. Remember, they still haven't told Doc and their hands the truth about what really killed the stock. It's obvious they hate to lie but don't believe they have any choice, and they've done all they can to protect other ranchers and the rest of their herd."

"That's smart thinking, Beth, good investigating."

She was relieved he didn't seem angry with her for catching his error. Pride appeared to glow in his eyes. "Thanks. I suspect rinderpest always ravages fast. Dan or the Agency could check it out to see if I'm wrong. If I'm not, we'll have proof this destruction wasn't an accident. That could help us build our case against Charles. And it could help you win the Cordells' understanding and forgiveness if they learn about our mission and deceit. The truth will be hard on Matt, but it's better for him to hate and blame Charles instead of you."

"I'm grateful you always think of others, especially your partner. I'm obliged you're keeping me from staining my reputation."

"A tiny lapse under these trying circumstances is natural. If you were perfect all the time, I'd never been able to impress you and surprise you.

I appreciate you unselfishly giving me opportunities to earn my salary."
She winked and laughed, and he chuckled and stroked her hair.

"We'll have to wait until after we leave to send Dan or the Agency a
telegram; it's too risky from here. My assessment may sound farfetched,
but Charles probably thinks he needs a valid reason for visiting when he's
never done so before and he's heading straight into Mexico. Another
point to consider: his dirty ploy cost plenty of money and time, so this
scheme is bigger than the Agency realizes. Either Charles is rich and paid
for it, or he has wealthy supporters. It also required plenty of help: men
in Brazil, men on the ship, and the deliverers. That calls for a huge payroll
and a large amount of hirelings to hold silent."

As Navarro absorbed her words, Beth added, "He could have begun
a terrible plague in America if those infected beasts had come into
contact with other herds along the way. How could a man do something
this wicked to his own brother?" She saw Navarro stare at her strangely,
then learned why.

"Shu, woman, you're smart and alert and good-hearted. I think you're
right about all this, so I'll get Dan on it soon as possible. I'll tap into the
first telegraph line we spot. I have a key in my saddlebag and I know the
codes." He watched Beth smile and relax, then look eager.

"Can you teach them to me during our long ride through Mexico?"

"Yep, but never use 'em except in an emergency. Draws attention to
the receiver and your location if the company realizes it isn't coming
from a station. All it takes is one . . . 'tiny lapse' in procedure or using the
wrong code or breaking into the line when it's in use. Dire emergency
only. And you'll have to get your hands on a sending key and have a
reason it's in your bag if you're caught with it. I say I'm a line-checker;
got old papers to back up my claim. I have hiding places in my saddle
for other identifications. I'll show you later and I'll get a man I know to
make you some."

Navarro motioned to the honey-colored palomino with flaxen tail
and mane that was grazing with the Cordells' horses. "You've got a
beautiful mount, Beth, and you two ride as one; that's important."

"I thank you and Sunshine thanks you," she said with a grin.

He tapped her forehead. "Put this clever brain to working on something else: what the Apaches have to trade for guns and bullets to make
this exchange so important to Charles and his friends, worth such an
expense. There haven't been any large robberies we know about. They
aren't raiding any one area enough times for a victim to spend so much
to get rid of them. Mere hatred of Indians or a hunger for revenge
wouldn't warrant provoking the Army against the renegades. I don't see

how Geronimo and his band could have or could steal anything so valuable to use for trading. I guess we'll find out what the bait is when we reach the end of our journey. Anything else?"

Beth related other things Jessica had told her. "She trusts me and feels free to speak her mind and heart. I understand now what you meant about feeling so guilty and ashamed for deceiving them. I like her. I like Matt and their children. They have something very special, so I hate to see any part of it destroyed by greed and evil. If I ever settle down, this is what I want for myself. It would be a tragedy for them to lose all of it. I hope we get enough evidence on Charles before he leaves to have him arrested and convicted. If he's planning to use part of the payoff from his sorry deed, the Cordells are in a bad fix because he won't get it."

"I'll see to it they aren't hurt if Charles fails them during his visit."

Beth wondered if she grasped his meaning. "You have enough savings to give them such a large gift? Enough to replace thousands of cattle?"

"Give them money, no, and they'd never accept it, too proud. Loan it to them, yep. They'd repay me so I wouldn't have a financial loss. Besides, I won't be using the money I've saved to settle down, least no time soon. I owe them and they might need my help to keep this place."

Make them a huge loan out of gratitude, or out of love for Jessica to protect her holdings and happiness?

Navarro cupped her face between his hands and kept her gaze captive to appease her worries about thinking him distracted from duty by Jessie. "Once and for all, Beth, Jessie is happily married; you've seen that for yourself. What happened between us years ago is over for her."

What about for you? You still have unresolved feelings, don't you? Beth dared not press him at this premature stage, especially after he'd just made a point about not settling down. "Let's get inside. It's been a long and tiring day. Ranch life starts early. We need our sleep."

They walked to the cabin and entered it as shadows blanketed the land under a waning quarter moon. Navarro kept his back turned while Beth changed into a nightgown.

"Finished. Thank you, kind sir." She reclined on the bed on her stomach and propped up her chest with folded elbows. She lifted bare feet into the air and crossed them at the ankles. "What did you tell your old friends—the hands—about your name change and sudden departure?"

Navarro sat to remove his boots; he'd taken off his weapons and chaps before going inside to dinner. "Told 'em I was on the run from the law after being framed for a crime I didn't commit. Said I'd escaped from prison and was hiding out here. That's why I couldn't stay and why I lied about my name and where I was from. Told 'em I was cleared five years ago. Handled it just like I said I would on the trail from Tucson."

"They believed you?"

He looked over at her and nodded. He noticed how the lamplight danced over her coppery tresses and soft flesh. Her hair looked as if it held imprisoned fiery flames that were trying to break free. Those unbound locks spread around her shoulders and they kissed the bed and caressed her body, as he craved to do at that moment. Lamplight also played in her cactus-colored eyes, causing them to sparkle and shine. There was a radiance about her, a seductive glow, a flush of emotion on her cheeks. She was beautiful and tempting, and his loins concurred eagerly with his troubled wits. "Like you said, stick close to the truth and no worries."

Beth pretended not to notice how he was staring at her, and she tried to conceal how it aroused her. "They must like you very much." She rolled to her left side, cocked her right shoulder backward and rested her right hand over her side at the waist. Her left forearm supported her torso and her fingers spread out over a pillow, which she stroked to release mounting tension. Her right knee against the mattress braced her as it lay half across her left thigh. She turned her head sideways until her chin was almost touching her left shoulder and her dreamy gaze locked on the lamp. Steven had told her once that the position was stimulating and that being close to soft light flattered her coloring. *If you want him, go after him as Kate Carter advised. Teach him that second love is possible.*

Shu, woman, what are you doing to me! These tight confines are dangerous. You make a man feel drunk just looking at you or being near you! "Seems that way." As he peeled off his shirt and pants, she didn't turn her back to him or appear embarrassed. He tossed his garments over the chair, as there was no longer a need to hide the multiple scars on his back.

"I can understand why. You're a very likable person, Navarro Breed."

He focused a roguish gaze on her, then grinned and warned, "Careful, Beth Breed, or you'll swell my head too big to fit in our bed."

Her playful gaze drifted to him. "Conceit isn't a flaw or weakness of yours, partner. To hear Jessica tell it, that cocky, sullen, embittered desperado of long ago is gone forever."

Attired only in the bottoms of his long underwear, he walked toward the bed as he asked, "And what do you think?"

"Me?" Beth's unbridled gaze roved his bare chest, then his handsome face where a devilishly sexy grin teased at his full mouth.

He placed hands on hips and stared down at her. "Yep, you."

Why are you asking? So you can stress your loner tendency again? And why and when did you remove that locket you always wear around your neck? Why only the Apache amulet tonight? She struggled with the covers and wriggled under them as she murmured, "Does it matter?"

Navarro doused the lamp and joined her. "Yep, 'cause we're partners and friends. Least I hope we are. Just want to make sure all the bad things you're hearing about me from Jessie isn't changing your good opinion."

"It doesn't and we are," she vowed as she rolled to her back.

You're an amazing woman, Beth Breed. Shu, *did I measure you wrong in Tucson! You've been a big and steady surprise, a real nice one. I've never teamed up with anybody better.* He knew why he didn't say those things aloud; they'd sound romantic and serious. "Well?" he pressed as he propped on his side and gazed downward.

"Well, what?" She felt his warm breath on her face and neck, causing both to tingle and warm. She couldn't see him in the darkness but knew his gaze was locked on where he knew she was lying in close proximity.

"You're being evasive, woman."

Beth laughed. "A trick I learned from a legend, a man matchless in certain skills." She asked herself if she dared to show him he could desire and respond to another woman. Could she entice him to forget his lost love's existence for even a brief while? Could he make love to her again? Particularly here? This time with clear wits?

Navarro was reasoning along similar lines. If he took Beth again, would it convince her it was over between him and Jessie? Surely making love to her this close to Jessie would—

If you really want an answer, you'll get it. "She's right."

"What?"

"I think Jessica has you figured right, that you're just about perfect as a man and a partner. I think we make a good team. I think we'll succeed in our assignment because we're compatible and determined. I think we'll try our best not to let these people get harmed. I think we're having a good time here with them, actually a good time together because we've become friends. I also think we've forgotten to practice our roles better, that we're going to get rusty if we don't return to our lessons. I think your wife might enjoy a kiss and a little attention, if you catch my drift."

Think fast, hombre!

She felt him lift his hand, then movement indicated he was ruffling his hair. *Back off or proceed with reckless abandon?* "Well?" The word escaped her lips and heart before her head could make its own decision.

"Well, what?" he mumbled to stall for thinking time.

Let it go for now, Beth. "Good night, Navarro."

"Good night?" he echoed. "What about my answer?"

"Didn't seem as if you were going to give one. Are you?"

"Only way I can answer tonight is like this." His mouth captured hers and his arms imprisoned her body. What the heck, he wanted and needed her, and it was obvious she felt the same when she returned his kiss and embrace. It felt good to touch her this way in bed, and felt good being with her out of it. The ex-fugitive's heart and body pounded in desire and wavered in confusion. If he was still in love with Jessie, why did Beth move him like this? Reach and stir him in a way that implied more than physical urges and attraction? Was he ready to give up forever on Jessie? Ready to take another risk with another woman, with Beth? Since he didn't know the answers to those questions tonight, should they—

Let her choose. "We don't have much time together, Beth; we go our separate ways when this case is over. I have little but this to offer a woman, so it isn't fair to let you believe otherwise. Think about that fact for a minute before we get tangled up by our desires. Much as I want you this way, you're a good friend and a fine woman; I don't want you getting hurt."

Are you warning me or yourself not to fall in love? Are you scared you'll weaken if I do? Are you afraid of risking another rejection and broken heart? That wouldn't happen with me. Does it trouble you to desire me under Jessica's nose, to make love with me so close to her? If not, doesn't that tell you something important?

While Beth was making her decision, Navarro also gave the matter serious thought. When he'd met Jessie, his heart had been frozen; his life, dark and empty. Jessie—like a flaming summer sun—had softened and melted him, brightened and filled his life. Losing her had frosted him. Now, Beth—another fiery, perhaps hotter, sun—was trying to thaw him and change his life. But a second loss, a third freeze, would damage his emotions forever. Thought of returning to the cold, hard, bitter man he'd been scared him. It was best not to let his feelings gallop wild and free until and unless he was ready.

Beth lifted her hand and stroked his prominent jawline. Her thumb moved back and forth over his lips, and he pressed stirring kisses to it. Her heart beat fast and hard as suspense filled her. She yearned to kiss him, to feel his flesh against hers, to be locked in his captive arms, to make passionate and unrestrained and deliberate love to him, and to have him in her life forever. She hadn't felt this way about Steven or any other man. "Isn't this what we both want and need tonight? What harm could it do? We can give each other something scarce and enjoyable while we're a team. This kind of relationship is all either of us has to offer for now."

"I like you and care about you a lot, Beth, I don't want to mislead or hurt you. I don't think I have it in me to give you—or any woman—what you need and want, or what you may expect afterward if I don't make myself clear at the start. I want to be friends, even lovers. You're a desirable and special woman. But I don't have more to give than that, and I doubt I ever will. Make sure you understand and accept that harsh and selfish fact before we go any further. It's not because I'm waiting for a second chance with Jessie; that's over for us. I've been a loner and roadman most of my life; I can't see myself changing."

Say what you must. "What *I* mean, Navarro, is sharing a bond of friendship, getting a closer and better working rapport, and enjoying our mutual attraction, not love and marriage. I don't know how I gave you that false impression, and I apologize for making you nervous. I realize they aren't our destiny. Yes, I do like, care about, and desire you, too; but that doesn't mean I expect you to fall in love with me and marry me. I don't want to mislead or hurt you, either. I thought we both understood and agreed to a . . . relationship like this only for as long as the mission lasts; then, we go our separate ways, but still remain good friends. Just because I'm a woman and I've been married before doesn't mean I want or need to be a wife again. And just because we're lovers doesn't mean I have serious or permanent claims on you, or you on me. Even if by some unforeseen miracle I fell in love with you, I would never make demands on you. By the same token, I would expect the same behavior from you. How can I be any clearer?"

"I agree with what you just said but make certain it's more than just words you're hearing and saying. I won't guide you into a box canyon with pretty lies and a false trail like most men would do to get what they want, and I do want you."

Well, Beth, she mused, *do you ride onward into possible peril in search of his love or retreat to certain safety?*

Chapter Fifteen

Beth's heart urged, *Teach him he can have a bright and happy future with you if he dares to accept it. Prove to him you and new love are risks worth taking.* "I understand how you feel. Don't you realize it's embarrassing and hard for me to practically be forced to cajole and seduce you every time we want to go to bed together? You've made your position crystal clear and so have I. Well, do you want me until this mission is over, or do we call a permanent halt to our affair to assuage your worries about me pursuing you later? I won't have this talk again."

He couldn't summon the wits or strength to retreat. "You're right, Beth, so no more talk. But I will say I haven't cared this much about many people in my life. That's why I want to protect you from any harm and do what's right for you. If I didn't care, there wouldn't be a problem."

"If we didn't care about each other, there wouldn't be this situation."

"You're right again," he murmured, and kissed her. When Beth laced her arms around his neck and responded in an ardent fever, she removed any thoughts except for those about her and this stimulating episode as he chased a wild and wonderful Wind.

Beth's hands roved over his strong shoulders, crossed his scarred back, and caressed his taut buttocks before she brought them up so her fingers could play in his midnight hair. *Yield to me, my love, and I'll never make you sorry you did.* As if he heard and agreed with her dreamy thought, she felt his embrace tighten and heard him groan in rising desire that matched her own. *Can't you see and feel how perfect we are for each other? Don't you realize this must be more than physical desire?* Her body flamed at a swift and uncontrollable pace, one she didn't want to slow or halt. She quivered at the force of their shared passion, as did he.

Navarro's pulse raced. The contact with her was more potent than any Apache *tiswin* he had drunk in the past. As their kisses became deeper and more urgent, his mouth trailed over the soft and warm surface of her face before traveling down her neck, then returning by a different path. He nuzzled his chin against her fragrant locks and relished their texture against his skin. His hands roamed up her arms and drifted into her fiery mane where wavy strands surrounded his questing fingers. He wondered if passion and friendship were all she wanted from him, all he wanted from her. He craved her like mad, but he couldn't afford the distraction of turbulent emotions in the midst of a crucial case. Whatever might happen between them must take place later, if they both allowed it.

Beth grasped his head and guided his mouth back to hers. She took and gave countless kisses until they were both breathless and trembling. Her fingers sought the pulse point in his neck; she could feel his heart pounding in desire *for her*. She felt it gaining speed with each minute he held her close and pleasured them. She was so elated she wondered if her heart could burst. She had known deep inside he was the perfect man for her the moment they met. If only *he'd* grasp that truth. He needed convincing, and she was giving that task her best efforts. Soon, they would be endangering their lives when they challenged Charles Cordell and his cohorts. She'd lost her mother, father, and husband. She would feast on every morsel of affection he shared with her. Once they were bound in bodies, hopefully unity in hearts would follow. Then, he would never release her, never ride out of her life as he had done with Jessica.

It was difficult for Navarro to believe he could touch Beth so deeply. It was clear she didn't care who or what he had been or was. She liked, respected, admired, and trusted him. He was glad she was honest and brave enough to take what she desired, and he never wanted to make her sorry for that decision.

Navarro meshed his mouth to hers as his shaky fingers unfastened the buttons of her gown. He was relieved when she peeled it over her head and dropped it to the floor. His hands trekked her satiny flesh with arousing leisure. They reached and covered her breasts where they savored the firm mounds. Her nipples hardened into taut buds as he caressed them while kissing her mouth. His head began to lower as his lips journeyed down her throat. He brushed them over the straining peaks and lavished sweet nectar upon their pinnacles.

Beth felt his hands shift to her bloomers. In case he didn't know how to loosen and remove them, she assisted him. His hands ventured over her naked body, stroking every part he could reach. Afterward, they traveled over her hips to the very center of her passion. With skill and tenderness, he caressed her moist and silky region. She moaned and squirmed in delight, her body sensitive and receptive to everything he did. She wanted to touch, pleasure, and tantalize him, too.

Beth unbuttoned his underwear bottoms and Navarro lifted his hips so she could push them out of the way. Her hand closed around his maleness. She heard him suck in air and stiffen a moment when she did so. She smiled at his reaction and continued. Her fingers worked their way up and down his hot, hard, smooth length. Her mind was trapped by a wall of fire around them. Her body was engulfed in passion's flames, a blaze of splendor she wanted to consume them and mold them into one.

Navarro guided himself into her welcoming heat after she parted her thighs. Once inside, he halted a moment to establish self-control before he began to move inside her.

Each time he thrust within her and she matched his pattern, it was sheer ecstasy. Their hearts throbbed in unison as they moved with urgency, aching for release from sweet torment. Both were torn between wanting to claim their reward and wanting their magnificent quest to continue, as it could be their last, at least for a long time.

Soon, there was no choice for them to make. Their desires ran wild and untethered. Unable to wait another minute, they climbed upward at a rapid pace to a level they hadn't visited before. They grew breathless as ripple after ripple of wondrous pleasure washed over them then remained cuddled and quiet for a while as contentment embraced and held them.

Finally, Beth murmured, "I'm glad you made the right decision. It was worth changing your mind, wasn't it?"

"Yep, if we don't get too caught up in this new role; distractions can have bad consequences. None of this on the trail after we leave."

What else, Beth fretted, could she say except, "You're right, boss," with a sad reluctance? "This predicament is your fault; you're so attractive and appealing. Your skills cover every territory."

As he pulled his underdrawers into place and secured them, he mumbled, "That's my problem: *you're* too darn hard to resist."

To relax him, she forced out merry laughter. "How can something that sounds so amusing be that bad?"

"As I said, anything distracting is too hazardous to allow, even a ride as nice as this one. I'm just a man, Beth, so I think and feel like one. I get carried away when an arresting woman like you leans in my direction."

Distracting and arresting? "Then, from now on, we should try to control ourselves when the time and place aren't right."

"I think that's best. And please don't let yourself get hurt by me."

"Don't you trust me by now?"

"Of course I trust you. Why do you ask?"

"Then believe I'll honor my word and promise to obey your orders." She heard him sigh in relief. She retrieved her gown and replaced it, but not her bloomers. She yawned and settled herself, then said good night.

The next morning, Beth awoke to find Navarro staring out the cabin window. He was leaning against the wall, positioned so he wouldn't be seen by others. He was so engrossed by something he was viewing he didn't hear her rise and approach. She must have been in a deep sleep because she hadn't known when he had gotten out of bed and dressed. She gazed beyond him to where Jessica was helping the two oldest children do their chores. Irrational jealousy and vexation chewed at her nerves, especially after the glorious time in his arms last night. *I'm not the dangerous distraction during this assignment, Mr. Special Agent; she is and your lingering feelings for her!*

Navarro's thoughts were troubled this morning. He told himself he shouldn't be taking a risk of getting Beth with child as he had done with Jessie. If that happened, he'd wed the mother of his child this time, even if he had to hog-tie Beth to haul her to the altar. He'd give their baby his name and be a good father to it. He would never let Beth go through the anguish and fear Jessie had when she'd discovered her condition and he was unreachable. But that complication shouldn't occur since his partner seemed to know how to avoid it, as she'd had no children with Steven in six years.

Another topic plagued him: Matt's possible involvement in Charles's plot. He didn't want to believe it was possible, but things Beth had learned raised small doubts. If the ex-foreman couldn't bear to destroy and lose a ranch Jessie's father had created and left to her, he might take a reckless and desperate path to protect it for his wife and children. If something happened to his old friend, weren't his first responsibilities and loyalties to Lane and Jessie, not to himself and his "wife"? Until he made certain things were all right for his loved ones, he shouldn't ride off and desert them again. And he positively shouldn't walk toward another woman.

Beth was worrying along a similar line: Navarro had said he didn't think Matt was involved in Charles's crime, but he might not really believe his assertion. Matt was years older than both Navarro and Jessica;

perhaps he was waiting for something to happen to Matt so he could replace the rancher. Maybe her lover didn't truly believe Jessica was lost forever; maybe he was still hoping and dreaming deep inside he would have her again one day.

"You're still in love with her, aren't you?" She watched Navarro react to her startling voice, then listened to him reply without turning to her.

"That was a long time ago, before she married Matt. It's over."

"Does true love ever die? I don't think so." *Subside, but not expire.*

Navarro suddenly halted watching his son. He had to quell his torment before he faced his partner and she read the feelings written on his face. He assumed she was referring to Steven Wind, and that conclusion had an odd and irritating effect on him. "Maybe it doesn't die, but it changes when you have to find and ride a new trail," he muttered as he turned to her.

She feigned an inquisitive look. "Does it? How so?"

"It better jump off your shoulders or you're in for a hard and bitter time riding doubleback with a carcass weighing you down."

Her tone was soft and her gaze was tender when she ventured, "Nobody knows that better than you, right?"

"Unless it's you." He grabbed his hat and left to end the conversation. He had been a prisoner of his past for ten years, had been convincing himself he still loved Jessie in the same way he had long ago. He'd told himself over and over they would always be bonded through their child and he should remain available in case something happened to Matt and they needed him. Well, the time had come when he could no longer deny the truth or keep fooling himself. Jessie was doing fine, and so was Lane. He was the one who needed to get on with his life without them. Yes, he still loved Jessie, but he wasn't *in love* with her. Those feelings had changed, and he wasn't sure when or where it occurred. Maybe he had only needed to see her again to prove it to himself, and he had. Maybe time had healed him as it was said to do. Or maybe Beth had changed his mind and heart! That would be a cruel joke if he found new love just as his old one needed him most!

Beth, he reasoned as he walked to the chuckhouse, was still locked in her past with her lost husband and there was no chance to win her until she pardoned herself. He knew from experience only the captive person had the key to unlock an emotional cell. He was shocked to catch himself thinking maybe he had found second love only to lose it to his foolishness, or to ties to his past, or to a dead man. How did a half-breed bastard loner, a flesh-and-blood man, fight a ghost? If he tried, after almost ordering and warning her to keep her distance, would he be risking another tormenting rejection?

Beth stared at the door after he almost stalked out of the cabin. She had riled him by questioning him on such a private matter. She wished she had kept quiet until he was ready to deal with his weakness. Much as she loved him and wanted him to be happy, she had to make sure he didn't frame Matt so he could recover Jessica. Beth scolded herself for thinking such a terrible thing. No, Navarro Breed would never do anything like that. She had to admire him for leaving the couple in peace for ten years, until it was necessary to return this week in the line of duty.

Beth bathed, dressed, and brushed her hair before securing it into a long and heavy plait. She made the bed and straightened the cabin. As she positioned a chair in one corner, she noticed an object lying on the floor. She retrieved the locket Navarro always wore around his neck. It must have fallen out of his shirt or pants pocket when he flung his garments aside last night. She couldn't imagine why he hadn't noticed that noise, so perhaps the keepsake had slipped out during night while he was asleep. Or while he was making love to her . . .

With trembling fingers, Beth opened it and looked inside. As feared and suspected, there was Jessica Lane Cordell's lovely though faded image. If his love for her was over as he claimed, why did he keep her picture close to his heart? Why had he removed it? Was he afraid someone might glimpse it and want a peek inside? Or could it be a good omen from fate that it was time to let go of the past? Maybe Navarro had left it behind as an unspoken message, one she couldn't decode: I'm over Jessica, or I'm trying to get over Jessica, or I'm not over her and you don't stand a chance of replacing her . . .

Questions! Questions! Questions! Leave them be, Bethany Wind!

She put the treasure on Navarro's pillow beneath the cover so no one could possibly notice it lying on the bedside table. *Let's see what you say when you discover it missing, find it tonight, and realize I've seen the evidence and guessed your deepest secret: you still love her.*

Jessica looked up from her task, smiled, and said, "Good morning, Beth. I saved you some coffee and ham biscuits; they're in the warming oven. Sit down and eat while I finish the dishes."

The redhead did as suggested. "Where is everyone? Am I late?"

"You don't have a schedule, so just rest and have fun. Lance and Alice rode over to the old homesite with Jefferson to play with his kids; that's where we have some houses for married hands. Lane went riding with the men. After range chores are done, they're going fishing and picnicking. The children will be back this afternoon and it'll be noisy again, so enjoy the quiet."

The women shared laughter before Beth asked between bites, "Do all of your children ride?"

"All three were in the saddle before they could walk steadily. They have their own ponies and help take care of them. It's good training."

They chatted while Beth finished her breakfast and they completed kitchen chores. Then, she helped Jessica change bed linens.

"I wash on Mondays. If you want to toss in your laundry, that's fine."

"Thank you. Washing them here will be easier than on the trail."

"I have mending to do this morning while the children are gone. Active youngsters are rough on clothes, so is a working man. You can sit with me and chat or do whatever you prefer."

"I have some sewing, too, so I'll join you if that's all right."

"Of course it is."

"Jessica," Beth began hesitantly, "if you need or want privacy while I'm here, please tell me. I know you aren't used to having another woman underfoot. I don't want to intrude on your schedule or take advantage of your kind hospitality; don't feel obligated to entertain me or include me in on everything. I won't take offense if you need time alone; I'm sure my presence is disruptive."

"Are you teasing? You're no bother at all, and you're being lots of help. I'm the one taking advantage of you. This visit is what I needed and I'm having a wonderful time. Just don't let me talk off your ears or bore you."

"I promise you don't do either one. I must say, Jessica, I'm having a wonderful time, too."

"Even with a wonderful husband and children and good hands, ranch life can get lonely on occasion. I have the hands' wives and neighbors, but that isn't the same thing."

"I know what you mean; we all need good friends, a special friend. We need to be able to say what we think to someone who understands and who'll hold our confidence. I didn't make that kind of friend in St. Louis or in Tucson, so I didn't have anyone to share with until now. I'm glad I met you, Jessica Cordell. I'm going to miss you like you miss Annie and Lane misses Joey."

"I'll miss you, too, Beth. But we won't be far apart if you and Navarro settle in San Antonio. Maybe we can arrange visits once in a while."

"That would be nice." As Beth went to fetch her mending, she cautioned herself not to be annoyed with her target because the man she herself loved still loved Jessica. Yet, nips of envy troubled her. Jessica was indeed a special woman, so Beth comprehended why Navarro loved her. It was too bad this was a mission, as she'd like to remain friends with her. She wished her ruse was true. She hadn't expected to become emotionally involved with the Cordells or with her partner, and she mustn't allow either to distract her from duty.

Later, the women's conversation and sewing was interrupted by a knock on the door. After Jessica answered it and returned, she beamed with joy.

"The mailman brought a letter for Lane from Joey. Maybe this will brighten up my sad son; he's sorely missed his best friend. Your firstborn is very precious to you, Beth, particularly if you almost lost him during birth."

The agent smiled, then focused on her sewing to conceal her pain. A child conceived in love was a beautiful dream she would never experience in reality. She could imagine the joy and pride of holding her lover's baby in her arms and— *Stop it, Beth, don't torment yourself with can't be's.*

When the task was done, Beth went to put away her repairs. When she went back to the house, Lane was home and Jessica was upstairs.

"Look, Miss Beth, a letter from Joey! The magic's working!"

Beth glanced at the exuberant boy's hand as he shook the page he was holding. "What magic is that, Lane?" she asked him.

Lane withdrew an Indian amulet from beneath his shirt. "Mr. Breed gave it to me this morning. He said it was because I was . . . gen-ner-ous to my brother and should be rewarded. He said it would protect me and help me. He told me friends ain't never lost. He ain't seen Papa in five years and they're still good friends; like Joey and me. Joey's coming to stay with his grannie when school's out and we'll be together again. Ain't that wonderful? See, the magic is working just like Mr. Breed said. He called it a *Yuu':* that's Apache for amulet. This one is . . . *Nzhu 'izee':* Good Medicine. I learned them Indian words from him this morning. He's smart; he knows everything. I'm gonna be smart like that when I get big. He's nice, Miss Beth. I like him. I hope you and him visit a long time."

Beth was astonished by Lane's mood and personality change, thanks to her lover. His sunny smiles could light up the darkest corner. With his prominent bone structure and features, the Apache amulet looked as if it belonged around his neck. As he ruffled his silky near-black hair and his hazel eyes danced with glee, he reminded her of . . . Beth's heart pounded faster and harder by the minute. Her pulse raced as if liquid fire filled her veins, then, a chill attacked her very soul. Her mouth and lips dried. Her chest and throat constricted. With Lane close and looking straight into her face for the first time, she realized who he favored, and it wasn't either of his parents. "You're nine years old, aren't you?"

"Yes, ma'am. My birthday was last month, March thirteenth. Joey's ten," the boy added before focusing his attention on the amulet.

Beth glanced at it as Lane's fingers traced the intricate and colorful design. Was it a gift of love from father to son? Had Jessica also given a special gift to his father, a farewell gift of herself? Or had the two been secret lovers during his stay at the ranch? Whichever was true, something had compelled a hasty marriage to Matt after her lover disappeared. Lane was the reason Jessica hadn't waited for Navarro's return after promising to do so! The timing was undeniable; Lane's birth had occurred nine months after Navarro's departure, with prison making his return impossible for five years. Since Jessica and Navarro were in love at that time, she wouldn't have slept with Matt in June of '76, and she wasn't married until later to the ex-foreman. Beth had no doubt as to who had fathered Lane.

Beth recalled Navarro's odd reaction when the Cordell children were mentioned on the trail, and his sullen behavior this morning. Had he been watching Jessica and Lane, or only his lost son? Her heart ached at imagining the agony Navarro had endured five years ago when he learned the truth, as surely Matt had told him everything. It must have been hellish for her partner to find and lose a son in almost the same breath, to hear he bore Matt's name and Matt had reared him as his own.

Beth's heart also pained at how this reality affected her. She no longer had to imagine how discovering the bond between Jessica and Navarro would make her feel; without mercy, the truth had buried her alive. She hadn't given Navarro something Jessica never had. In fact, it was the opposite, and would remain that way forever since she couldn't have children. Surely Navarro would want a child one day to fill the gap Lane's loss had created. She must accept that she couldn't replace Jessica and Lane, and that Navarro would never be free of those powerful bonds. There wasn't a rope around her rival to cut; there was a thick and wide metal band around him and his love and son. It was foolish and self-defeating for her to think she could sever it.

Beth glanced at the amulet that still held the boy's concentration. It was a symbol of father and son's shared Apache heritage, a closely guarded secret. Lane Cordell would never know about his real father, what the man had endured and the sacrifices he had made. Navarro must be pleased and relieved to see them happy; he must realize he made the right decision years ago. Yet, none could ease the total anguish of what could have been. She masked her own anguish, as Jessica would return soon. "That's a wonderful gift, Lane; I hope you'll always keep it and treasure it."

"I will, Miss Beth; I won't ever lose it or give it away. I'm hungry. I'm gonna go find Mama and see what time we eat." He hurried upstairs.

"Miss" was what the children called her, and that's what she was; the marriage to Navarro wasn't real and would never be real. Beth had the urge to cry, to scream, to rant, to flee; she did none of those things. She reminded herself she was a Special Agent on a crucial mission. She was here to do a job. She wouldn't blame or hate Jessica for what happened in the past; it must have been torment for her when she lost Navarro and when she discovered her condition. It was a miracle Matt still wanted her, carrying another man's child. No wonder all three were so nervous about seeing each other again. No wonder Navarro had stayed away from friends for years. But things seemed to be going fine because Navarro had a "wife" and he was no longer a threat to them.

But is that true, my love? Will you stay out of their lives now that you've seen them again and your hungers have returned? Can I ever become more than a friend, partner, and lover to you? I rode into this box canyon with my eyes open, so I shouldn't have any regrets. I suspected you still loved her. But God help me, I never suspected this obstacle. If only—

"You ready to eat, Beth?"

She turned to face Jessica and smiled. "Sounds tempting to me. Lane says he's starving. He's got to build up his strength for playing with Joey."

Lane hugged his mother and almost squealed, "He's coming back, Mama! I can't wait. Six weeks," he grumbled.

Beth said, "They'll pass quickly, Lane; you'll see. Work hard in school and do your chores and June will be here before you know it."

Later, Lance and Alice returned home and began playing in the front yard with the toys Beth had brought them. She and Jessica strolled to the porch to check on them. When the mother noticed that the youngest boy had both stuffed horses, she asked if he had Lane's permission.

"He said I could, Mama."

"Then, it's fine." To Beth, she said, "Lance and Lane are very close, thank goodness. They rarely squabble. They're the same way with their sister. I'm lucky my children give me so little trouble."

"Yes, you are. I've seen some fight like starving animals over meat; and some tease each other without mercy. Yes, you're very lucky. But you're also fine parents, Jessica, you and Matt; that's why they're so good."

"That's one of the nicest things anybody could say to me; thanks. I'm going to put on tea to boil. Want to join me or relax here for a while?"

"I think I'll visit with the children. I'll keep an eye on them for you."

Beth sat on the porch and placed her feet on the step. She propped her elbows on her knees and rested her chin between cupped hands. She watched Lance and Alice play make-believe; as she was doing with Navarro, she mused. Soon, Lane came out of the house and sat down beside her. Beth looked at him. "Your mother says you love to read. What are your favorite books?"

Lane related many titles Beth recognized. "You like to read?" he asked.

"Yes, very much. By reading all kinds of books, you can learn many things, let your mind travel to faraway places and times long past, share adventures with the characters, and get to know what other people are like without leaving home."

"That's why I love to read. Uncle Tom and Aunt Mary Louise send me books from where they live. Uncle Tom went to college and got real smart. I want to go to college, too."

"You don't want to become a rancher like your father?"

"Yes, ma'am, but I wanna be a *smart* rancher."

"That's a wonderful goal, Lane; I'm sure you will be."

Lance joined them and worked his way into Beth's lap. She laughed and asked, "Do you like books, too, Lance?"

Alice came to sit on Beth's other side as Lance asked her to tell them a story. "Have you heard *The Princess and the Pea?*" After excited coaxing, Beth related the Hans Christian Andersen fairytale, using voices of the characters and animated sounds and expressions.

Jessica peeked out at the scene and didn't intrude. It made her heart warm to see her children cuddled around her new friend. She decided that Navarro couldn't have chosen a better wife. She observed for a moment, smiled to herself, and went to see if there were any remaining chores to be done.

An hour later, Navarro and Matt arrived, carrying a large mess of fish. Both men witnessed the same scene Jessica had and experienced the same emotions. As they entered the enclosed yard, Beth was completing a story for three enrapt children. When the redhead looked at the men, the youngsters' gazes followed her line of vision.

Alice leapt to her feet and hurried to her father. She hugged his legs as she said, "Papa, Papa, Miss Beth told us lots of stories. She tells them better than anyone, even better than Miss Maria."

Lance had wiggled from the female's lap and joined the newcomers. "You don't have to put a pea in my bed, do you, Papa?"

"What?" Matt asked in confusion. He leaned over and scooped up Alice, who explained without delay, and the rancher chuckled. "No peas in your bed, Lance." With a child on each arm, Matt headed for the porch.

Lane told him, "Miss Beth knows lots of stories, Papa. She reads books all the time like me, all kinds of books. Can she visit a long time?"

"We would love to have her stay a long time, son, but she and Navarro have to leave soon. They're going to look for a ranch to buy."

"A ranch like ours, Papa?"

"Not this big, Alice," Navarro answered with a chuckle.

Lane widened his eyes and told his siblings, "Mr. Breed used to work here with Papa. He told me when we were riding this morning. He gave me this," the boy said with pride as he showed his amulet once more. "Mr. Breed knows plenty. He's smart like Papa."

"Maybe you'll grow up to be just like your papa; he's smarter than I am; he can run a big ranch. I'm just learning how to do that with his help; that's what good friends do for each other."

Beth wondered if Navarro used the word "Papa" instead of "Father" so Matt wouldn't doubt to whom he was referring.

"You're his teacher, Papa?" Alice asked in awe.

"I guess you could call me that. I'm helping him learn ranching stuff.

"You kids need to play by yourselves while we get this fish cleaned and cooked for supper." Matt lowered the two he held to the ground, and then all three of them headed to a shady area of the yard to amuse themselves. Matt turned to Beth and said, "I'm much obliged to you for being so nice to them."

"They're easy to be nice to, Matt. You and Jessica have done an expert job rearing them. They're precious, delightful children, and a lot of fun."

"Good practice for when you and Navarro have some of your own, eh?"

She smiled as anguish assailed her at knowing she'd never have that experience and it might cost her Navarro.

Jessica came outside and greeted the men. "Let's get those fish around back where we can clean them. You boys had good luck today."

"I'll help," Beth offered.

Matt looked over at the dainty redhead. "That isn't necessary, Beth; you don't want to get dirty and smelly."

"I don't mind. I'm good at scaling and gutting, but not frying. I have a bad habit of getting the grease and fire too hot and burning the fish."

"Why don't we all work together and we'll finish sooner?"

"Navarro's idea is the best," Matt announced, and they all laughed.

After the cleaning was completed, Jessica and Beth took the fish inside to prepare and fry them. Matt and Navarro scrubbed the wooden table they had used and went to get rid of the fish entrails, heads, and scales.

As they walked to the back porch to wash up in a basin located there, Matt observed, "Beth's face lights up every time she looks at you; that's how it should be. Seems to me you made a perfect choice for a wife and helpmate."

Navarro smiled and replied, "Beth's a real treasure; she makes a man mighty glad he found her and darned lucky to win her."

"She appears to take to ranch life and seems to love kids."

"That surely makes me happy since I'm wanting both. With her at my side, Matt, I know I'll be as lucky and happy as you and Jessie." Navarro glanced around to make sure no one was within hearing distance of them. "I hope you don't mind me giving your son that amulet. I should have asked permission first."

"It was fine. He seemed kind of dejected; what you did g ive him back was his spirit and faith. Kids need to believe in magic sometimes. He'll always remember you kindly. So will me and Jessie; you know why."

"I'll never forget what you've done for your wife and son."

"Let's get inside now and see if our women need more help. I'm sure the children are getting hungry and sleepy; been a long and busy day for them."

For all of us, Navarro's mind added.

After the meal and clean-up chores were completed and the children put to bed, the two couples joined the hands near the barn. Carlos, the assistant foreman, entertained them with a trick rope display. Jimmy Joe did the same with a series of hilarious jokes. Rusty, the foreman, was content to observe and chat. Biscuit Hank, the chuckhouse cook, and his wife visited for a while, then turned in because they began their work at dawn. Big John, the blacksmith, talked with everyone before he also headed for his bunk.

Beth witnessed the genial personalities and good rapport between all of the men, their bosses, and their old friend. It was easy to grasp why Navarro had enjoyed this place and these people and how they had had such a potent effect on him. She was stimulated by the way her "husband" treated her before the others—happy, proud of her, and in love. She also played her role with skill and success.

Navarro laughed and joked with the men. Yet, he wasn't calm inside. He couldn't forget Jimmy Joe's slips about how bad things were on the ranch and about how he didn't see how Matt was going to make it through this crisis. Even Rusty had remarked on what a shame it would be for the Cordells to lose their spread. Navarro himself had seen enough to worry him, too. Then, there was Lane and Beth . . .

"It's time we were turning in, Jessie. We have church tomorrow."

"You're right, Matt. Good night, everyone. See you at seven, Beth."

"Good night, Jessica, Matt. Thanks, boys, for a pleasant evening." Navarro guided her to their cabin by a snug grasp on her hand. He realized she didn't curl her fingers around his as usual.

Once inside, Beth withdrew it immediately. She closed the curtains and began to change into her nightgown, without asking him for privacy as usual. She hung her skirt and shirt on pegs, removed her petticoat and chemise. "It's been a long day, boss. Good night."

Navarro stared at her as she undressed with her back to him. He had the feeling something was troubling her. "Are you all right, Beth?"

She glanced at him over her shoulder and said, "Of course. Why?"

"You're mighty quiet." *And you're not smiling and relaxed.*

"Just tired. Nothing new to report. I didn't ask questions today to avoid arousing suspicions. I only played my part; I hope that's enough."

He noticed she didn't ask if he had made any new discoveries, which seemed odd to him. "You couldn't be doing a better job, so don't worry."

"Thanks." She pulled down the cover on her side of the bed, eased under it, and nestled her head on the pillow with her back to him.

Navarro shrugged, undressed, and uncovered his pillow to do the same. He saw the locket glittering in the lamplight. His widened gaze rushed to Beth's face; her eyes were closed, but he knew she wasn't asleep. Though he had worn it for almost five years, he hadn't missed it in his pocket where he had placed it after removing it yesterday to avoid it being seen and misunderstood. He worried that she'd peeked inside and misunderstood the situation. He clutched the pendant in his hand and decided it was best not to discuss the matter tonight. He walked to the chair and put it in his pocket. He returned to bed and doused the lamp. "Night, Beth."

"Good night, partner," she murmured in a passive tone.

Sunday morning, they attended a small church located miles from the ranch. Navarro and Beth watched the Cordells mingle with friends and acquaintances. They witnessed how well liked and well respected the ranchers were, despite their recent troubles. Most of all, they both noticed what a close-knit and happy family they were.

Afterward, they enjoyed a dinner of cured ham, canned corn, canned tomatoes with okra, and several trimmings. When the meal and chores were finished, the children went outside to play and the adults took a ·stroll.

Aware now of the missing puzzle piece, Beth furtively watched Navarro who was careful not to be caught furtively eyeing Lane. She had decided, for the good of their mission, the wisest course of action was to act as if she didn't know about his son, his secret feelings for Jessica, and the locket's contents. To prevent suspicions in the Cordells and Navarro, she made certain she played her part as usual. She realized this wasn't the time or place to allow personal emotions to interfere with her duty. With luck, maybe her partner believed she hadn't invaded his privacy.

Navarro couldn't get thoughts of Beth off his mind today. She looked beautiful and arousing. He had learned what a hard worker she was in any situation. She was skilled in her job as an undercover agent, was far more than a worthy partner, and a good friend. She was charming the boots off Matt, Jessie, the children, and the hands. She fit in no matter who she was with or where she went. She made others feel at ease and delighted to be in her company. What was more, she played his wife with a talent he found amazing in view of her concealed feelings about him. She had to think the lowest of him after viewing Jessie's picture in that locket.

If she did, his heart argued. Maybe she hadn't peeked! She surely didn't seem angry or hesitant with him today. Perhaps she had been only fatigued last night. Or was he fooling himself? If she was ignorant and he asked her, she'd discover the truth then. If she wasn't and he didn't mention it, she'd think the worst. He decided he would wait until she broached the subject. That was it: wait until she told him she knew, then he'd explain.

The moment after he made that choice, Navarro reasoned it was foolish not to deal with the matter at once, as his worry over it was creating a problem with his concentration on the assignment. Charles Cordell could arrive at any time, so he needed to be on full alert. If he got Beth alone, he could pick which path to take: a silent trail or a revealing road. "Matt, you and Jessie mind if I take my wife for look-see of your ranch? Might give us ideas for things to do with ours later. Besides, this is beautiful country for a romantic ride."

"Sounds like a good idea to me. You two need some time together."

"Beth?" Navarro hinted.

"I'd love to have a tour. Since you used to work here and Matt's refreshed your memory in the last few days, I'm sure we won't get lost."

"Not for long," he jested with a sexy grin. "We'll be back before dark."

Navarro saddled Night Cloud and Sunshine while Beth changed into casual garments. She joined him, and they galloped from the corral.

Soon, Beth was mystified because he *was* giving her a guided tour of the property! When they reined in to rest the black stallion and palomino, she asked, "Is this outing for business or pleasure, boss? Did you learn something about the case you needed to discuss with me?"

"Nope, just figured we could use a little privacy. Staying on constant guard gets a mite snug after a while."

"You're right; constant pretense can cause a strain. Thanks. You're very thoughtful." She let her impassive gaze travel the landscape. "This ranch is huge and lovely. I've enjoyed myself here. Jessica and I have even become friends. I hate what she'll think about me when this assignment is over. None of my previous targets discovered I was involved. I hope the Cordells can be kept in the dark, too, but I have an awful feeling we won't be that lucky if this case is as big as I imagine."

"Maybe we'll be lucky. We're a good team of skilled agents, so we'll do our best to keep our work and identities a secret."

"That means you can't visit here again, or you'll have to find an excuse for losing your wife and for not buying a ranch and settling down."

"Yep. Anything we need to talk about before we head back?"

Sidestepped that angle with ease, didn't you? She pretended to ponder his query for a minute. "I don't think so. Any new orders?"

He gazed at her and urged, "Just be careful."

"I'm doing my best not to arouse suspicions. Have I made a mistake?"

"Nope. I meant, be careful with your safety. Charles Cordell is cunning and dangerous. He has lots of men traveling with him. I don't want him guessing what you are and coming after you for revenge."

Or provoking a shoot-out at the ranch where your loved ones could get trapped in crossfire? She smiled and murmured, "Thanks for caring."

He guided his horse close to hers and she sent him a quizzical look. "I do care about you, Beth, honest."

"And I care about you, Navarro. We'd better get back to work before we . . . get carried away with too much caring." She laughed playfully. "Wranglers could be roaming the range and catch us being improper."

He reached out and caressed her flushed cheek and hoped it was a reaction to him. "How can a husband and wife do that?"

"There's a time and place for everything, remember?"

"I do believe you have a shy and modest streak after all, woman."

Beth laughed again. "Before the wrong eyes, absolutely."

"If I can't tempt you to be daring, let's ride."

"Lead the way, boss."

As they neared the ranch Navarro halted them and said, "Come over here with me. We'll ride in together." Before she could respond, Navarro scooped her off the palomino and settled her before him on his mount. "You're as light and soft as a rabbit. Snuggle up," he told her as his right arm encircled her waist; his left one passed under hers to hold the reins. He didn't inch backward much to keep their bodies in contact.

As they trotted away, Beth was too aware of Navarro's hot loins at her buttocks, his hand stroking her side, his stirring breath near her ear. She was relieved the distance was a short one or, she fretted, she'd be too stimulated to face anyone who greeted them when they arrived at the barn.

Navarro halted his stallion, helped Beth dismount, and joined her at the fence where he secured the animals' reins. "The boys are watching from the chuckhouse porch," he whispered. "Let's fool them good." He pulled her into his arms and kissed her. He knew it wasn't a ruse; he had to taste her lips.

When he nestled her face against his chest and caressed her back, Beth saw Jessica and Matt at the chicken coop, just barely visible from their position. She pretended she didn't see them, and knew Navarro hadn't. If the couple's worries about him weren't over, Beth resolved, she'd end them right now. She gazed at her "husband," smiled, grasped his head, and lowered it to fuse their mouths once more. She feasted on him as if ravenous for the treats he had initiated to dupe the hands.

Navarro was taken by surprise and responded with a sudden fever of desire to do more than embrace and kiss her. He wanted to sweep her away to their cabin to make passionate love to her. But it was too early, only five o'clock and still light, with supper looming ahead.

Beth managed to part them without appearing to resist him. "We're being watched by the Cordells, but we don't want to overact. We—"

Jimmy Joe galloped into the outer yard with a cloud of dust trailing him. He halted near the ranchers and announced to Matt, "Riders comin', boss. Must be your brother and his friends. About five minutes back."

Navarro and Beth exchanged looks that said, *Get ready; he's here!*

Chapter Sixteen

Big John approached the couple and offered to curry their horses. Navarro thanked him and agreed. He let his protective stallion know it was all right for the black man to touch him.

As they headed to join Matt and Jessie, Navarro quelled his fiery desires and he murmured, "Be careful, love; this is the beginning of the dangerous part."

She met his gaze and whispered, "You, too. I don't want you getting hurt in any way." She smiled at Jessica as they halted nearby.

Navarro asked, "What's the excitement about?"

"My brother's almost here. Be coming in sight any— There he is!"

The undercover agents noticed Matt's elation and saw him head toward the entrance gate to his home to be ready to greet Charles. Jessica glanced at Beth, forced a smile, and followed her husband. Navarro and his "wife" joined them at Jessie's coaxing.

Charles Cordell rode into the clearing that surrounded the house and other structures. He dismounted with a broad grin, but his friends stayed on their horses and hung back at a short distance. The agents noticed how those three men remained silent and alert and checked out the location. All three appeared tall and muscular, and were well armed. The brothers embraced with an enthusiastic hug and gave each other a light slap on the back.

"Welcome to our home, Charlie. This day's been too long in coming. Lordy, it's good to see you. Any trouble finding the place?"

"None, your directions were simple to follow. I rode ahead of my wagons to give us time to visit before they get here and I have to move on to my appointment. Should allow us two or three days leadway. Which one of these beautiful women is my sister-in-law?"

Navarro watched Charles eye Beth and Jessica with annoying rakes of mud-colored eyes that glowed with a light he found offensive. As if sensing a threat, he placed an arm around Beth's waist.

Matt grasped his wife's hand and tugged her forward. "This is her, Jessica Lane Cordell, the best woman in the world."

Charles grasped her hand while murmuring, "Pleasure and honor to finally meet you, Jessica. I can see my brother has excellent taste in women and land. He's one lucky ex-Reb, luckier than the South was years ago."

"Thank you for the flattery, Charles, and welcome to the *Lane/Cordell* Ranch. Matt's been eagerly awaiting your arrival ever since you wrote you were stopping by."

"Took me long enough to get out this way. Every time I planned a surprise visit, something came up and prevented it. Is this your sister?"

Navarro was getting more vexed by the minute as Charles appraised Beth with undeniable interest. He had noticed Jessie's comeback to Charles's compliment on *Matt's* choice of land; in truth, the property had been selected, settled, and owned by the Lanes. He also grasped she didn't say she, too, had been "eagerly awaiting" his visit.

"Nope, this is Navarro and Beth Breed. He's a longtime friend of ours, used to work here years ago, one of the best hands we ever had. They just got married a few weeks past. They're visiting until Wednesday, en route to San Antonio where they're buying a ranch."

"Ah, newlyweds. Congratulations. I hope you're enjoying your new marriage and visit. Glad to meet you, Navarro, Mrs. Breed."

"A pleasure," Navarro replied as they shook hands. He warned himself not to break the man's fingers over his suggestive tone and grin.

Beth gave him a genial "Hello" and a polite smile in response as the children rushed forward to check out the commotion.

"This is my family: Lane's the oldest. Alice is nearing seven, and Lance is halfway to five. Kids, this is my baby brother, your Uncle Charlie."

"He's too big to be a baby, Papa," Alice said amidst giggles.

Charles squatted and said, "You're right, Miss Alice. What a pretty little lady you are." He ruffled her curly hair before standing. "A fine-looking family and ranch, Matt. Makes me envious of you." He lifted and opened a cloth sack he'd dropped on the ground and handed the children gifts.

"More presents!" Alice squealed as she clutched another doll. "Thank you, Uncle Charlie; she's pretty. Look at her dress, Mama."

"It's very nice, Alice."

Lane and Lance accepted accurately carved and sized wooden pistols with leather holsters, and both thanked their uncle. Lane assisted Lance before strapping his own gift around his waist. Navarro's son asked Charles questions about the wooden weapons.

Beth used the distraction to study their new target. He had a medium-size build on a frame just under six feet. His eyes and hair were brown, as were a short and neat beard and thick mustache. A dark tan implied he stayed outdoors much of the time; the deep shade caused healthy teeth to appear snowy when he smiled or grinned. She knew from Jessica he was thirty-nine, six years younger than Matt. He favored his older brother but he wasn't as rugged or good-looking. Charles didn't have Matt's appealing personality and charm; nor did he possess Matt's honesty and honor; Charles was a cunning deceiver and betrayer. Beth didn't like him and she didn't trust him. Neither did Navarro judging from his snug grip on her!

"Can we go play with them, Papa?" Lance asked.

"Sure. You can visit more with Uncle Charlie later."

After the children ran off toward the backyard, Charles handed Jessie a package, which revealed a pearl-encrusted gold brooch when unwrapped.

"You shouldn't have, Charles; it's much too expensive, but thank you."

"Consider it a combination wedding-lots of missed birthdays-and ten-years-worth-of-belated-Christmases present. Beautiful women should have beautiful things. Isn't that right, Matt?"

"Right. Put it on, Jessie, and let's see how it looks."

As she did so, Charles said, "This is for you, big brother."

Matt took the Spencer lever-action repeater rifle and studied it. "A fine weapon, Charlie, good weight and multiple firing. Thanks."

"Might help you keep rustlers and renegades away. Has your name and the date she was made engraved on the butt plate. I have a case of ammo for you in one of my wagons; it was too heavy and awkward for horseback."

"It's nearing time for the children to eat and bathe, so let's all go inside," Jessie said. "They have to get to bed early for school."

"We'll go wash up after our ride and give you all some time alone for a proper reunion," Navarro told the group.

"Supper will be in thirty minutes, so hurry," Jessie coaxed.

"I'll be back in about ten minutes to help get the food ready."

"Thanks, Beth. I'll round up that busy brood of ours, Matt, while you take Charles in the sitting room. You two can chat while I do my chores."

In the cabin, Beth asked, "Why did you bring us in here? We need to observe Charles, don't we?"

"Yep, and we will. I didn't want to appear overeager to be around him every minute. We don't want to make him skittish. Let's get cleaned up and head back to the pit to see what we can learn about our slick-talking snake."

They ate leftovers from the large Sunday dinner and chatted about family, the ranch, and other neutral topics. Afterward, the three men retired to the sitting room to converse while Beth did the dishes and Jessica bathed the children to ready them for bed; Charles's friends had eaten where they camped near the barn. Charles had told the group the men were employees of his and guards, and not to be included in the family meal and reunion.

After the children hugged their uncle and told him good night, Jessica and Beth put Alice down on a pallet in the couple's room. Lane and Lance always shared a room, and Charles was to use the little girl's during his stay.

Jessica closed the upstairs doors to prevent voices from disturbing the youngsters' sleep. She whispered to Beth, "What do you think of him?"

"I'm not sure, yet. He seems a little too . . ."

"Flirtatious and false?"

"I . . . really shouldn't speak wickedly of him; he's a stranger, family."

"He's Matt's family, not mine; and I don't care for him or his behavior. How dare he bring my boys real-looking weapons! And that doll for Alice, it's too fragile for everyday playing. And this trinket, it's . . . it's an unappreciated attempt to win me over after he almost destroyed all my family created, what my father died to preserve. I must sound terrible, but he reminds me of Wilbur Fletcher. He gives me the shudders."

"Me, too, but we'll have to be nice to him for Matt's sake."

"He can't be gone soon enough to please me. We were having such a wonderful time; now, he's spoiling our last few days together."

"Maybe he'll spend time on the range with Matt and the boys."

"Blazes, I hope so. I guess we have no choice except to join them."

When they went downstairs, they didn't have to endure Charles very long before he said he was going outside to smoke a cigarillo and get fresh air. He asked Matt to go with him.

Navarro stood and said, "We'll say good night. See you tomorrow. Been nice meeting and talking with you, Charles."

"Same here, Navarro, Beth. Have a pleasant sleep."

"Good night, everyone," the redhead said, and followed her partner.

Inside the cabin, Navarro pressed Beth against the closed door and whispered in her ear as he pretended to nibble on it. "They can see us through the window. Let's do some quick kissing, then douse the lamp. I wanna sneak out and spy on 'em." His mouth closed over hers and he wished he didn't have to rush away when she responded with ardor.

Following two fiery kisses, he guided her to the bed and put out the lamp he had lit earlier to prevent returning in the dark. He yanked off his shirt, belt, and boots.

"What are you doing?" she asked.

"Not much of a moon, but this light-blue shirt could catch the wrong eye. The boots and belt could make noise. Just precautions. Don't worry about me. I'll be back soon as possible."

He sneaked out the door, around the cabin, and to the stucco wall. He slipped in the near blackness as close as was safe to Charles and Matt. He listened in suspense and rising worry:

"That's a fine rifle you gave me, little brother."

"It's one from our shipment, the best made."

Navarro heard Charles's lips draw on the cigarillo and smelled the smoke he exhaled. *Our shipment,* his keen mind echoed.

"This is also for you, little brother. You don't need to count it tonight; it's more than enough to settle us up for that trouble you endured for me. I'm sorry it had to be done this way, but I had no choice. The money should make it up to you."

"Don't worry about it, Charlie; everything will be like it was as soon as I use this to restock my herd. There won't be any trouble; nobody knows the truth; Doc doesn't even suspect what happened to those steers."

"That's good; we don't want him or anybody getting hotheaded and coming after us. Does Jessica know about this?"

"I haven't told her."

Know about what? Navarro fretted.

"That's best; she might not understand or agree."

"I can handle Jessie, so don't worry. It's late and we start early around here, so we'd best get to bed. We'll talk more tomorrow. Just be alert around Jessie; she's still upset about the cattle."

"Everything will be settled soon, Matt, and we both may come out of this situation rich men. That wouldn't bother you none, would it?"

Matt chuckled and replied, "Nope, it surely wouldn't. I just hope your dangerous idea works and you stay out of trouble down there. You change your mind about coming back this way after it's done?"

"No, but I'll be back later to make sure we're settled up."

Navarro listened to the brothers' return to the house. His exposed broad back rested against the cool stucco wall. His arms lay across his raised knees, bare feet supporting them. What he'd overheard didn't sound good for Matt and caused him to think it was possible he'd misjudged his old friend. If so, Jessie and the children were in for heartache. He hoped with all his might that Matt wasn't guilty and he wouldn't have to arrest the rancher. If he did, remaining days and nights with Beth were numbered, a thought he found unsettling and saddening.

Navarro worked his way back to the cabin, entered, and bolted the door. He wasn't surprised to find Beth still awake and wanting answers. "I'll tell you later, after I sort it out in my head. I don't want to go jumping to conclusions, but it didn't sound good." He shucked his pants and joined her in bed. He rolled close to whisper, "While you were busy in the kitchen, he didn't say anything about diseased cattle; it's supposed to be a secret, remember? He didn't explain his reason for going to Mexico or tell what kind of business he's in. When we're sure of our privacy, we'll go over this in detail. I don't like the looks of those men with Charles, so let's be careful with our talk."

She cuddled closer to whisper, "You're the boss."

Navarro inhaled her sweet fragrance before she rolled to her back. She was so intoxicating and enchanting. He was captivated by her potent allure. She had stolen his peace of mind and self-control; she'd worked her way under his tough hide; she was almost stealing his heart.

Beth listened to Navarro's breathing and knew he was disquieted about something important. She was relieved he didn't seem happy about discovering the possible collusion of Matt; no doubt because the rancher was an old and trusted friend. If Matt was guilty, Navarro was lost to her, because he would be back in Jessica and his son's lives faster than she could blink. Even if Matt was innocent, that didn't mean she could win the man she loved.

And I do love you, Navarro Breed. She had never lost herself in the smoldering depths of any man's eyes or experienced an overwhelming urge to wantonly surrender to a man, not even Steven Wind. Perhaps she was embarking upon a reckless and futile adventure, but she could not stop herself from going, did not want to stop.

Navarro wondered how she had the power to make him ignore all else except his yearning for her. He murmured, "I want you, Beth."

When she turned to face him, he gently grasped her chin and pulled it toward his to seal their lips in a heady kiss. He was too near and too compelling to refuse. There could be so little time left to explore their feelings and to strengthen their bond. Her heart rebelled against the loss of him. His embrace was strong, comforting, enlivening. His mouth left hers to nuzzle his chin against her hair. His lips claimed hers with hunger and possessiveness; they burned those sweet and forbidden messages across her unsteady senses and hazy brain.

Unruly desire attacked Navarro as his hunger for her increased. He felt enthralled by her, by a desperate need of her; it was one prison from which he didn't want to escape.

Beth perceived Navarro's gentleness. His body was lean and hard, but his skin was soft and almost hairless. His broad shoulders were followed by a flat waist and narrow hips that led to supple thighs. She'd never imagined any male could be so devastatingly magnificent, so overpoweringly attractive. She was like a piece of soft wood in his hands, ready and willing to be whittled into any shape he wanted, a treasure he would keep forever as the ebony wolf and the saguaro cactus Zack had carved and given to her.

Navarro pushed strands of coppery red from her neck so his mouth could journey it without obstacles. "Am I being selfish and unfair to you? I didn't even ask if you wanted me tonight."

Beth chose her response with caution. "You're honoring the bargain we made and so am I. We aren't children or dreamy-eyed youths. If we're both in agreement, no problems are involved." *If only I could give you a child to replace Lane, maybe. . . .*

He noted her anxiety, but misread its cause. He must use his talents to rekindle the fires between that his query had doused. From her response, the answer should have been obvious: she wanted him, too. His head lowered once more. His deft tongue plundered her mouth.

Beth could not resist that summons. His masterful lips seemed to brand her mouth, cheeks, and throat—every inch of her face and neck. Any restraint vanished. Potent feelings took control and guided her toward total submission as flames of passion leapt and burned within her. She wanted and needed this to happen again, and tonight. She was glad her menses was a little late this month.

Navarro trailed his tongue over her parted lips, nibbled at them with his teeth, then tasted the sweetness of her mouth again. With her help, he removed her gown and bloomers and tossed them to the floor. His lips trekked over the flesh he had bared. His fingers quivered as they moved over her shoulders with leisure and delight. His hands caressed and fondled and stroked silky areas as he set out to tantalize, stimulate, and pleasure her and to give her the same satisfaction that he received. His mellow tone whispered soft and stirring words into her ears. "You're wonderful, Beth Breed, and I enjoy you every time I touch you. I get all fiery sometimes just watching you or hearing your voice. I hope this is a slow mission so I can keep you around for a long time."

Beth trembled within his arms. She thought it unwise to tell him how his words affected her or to respond to them, as he might not realize how they sounded to her and may not mean how she took them. She might reveal her true feelings, might expose her lie about not wanting love and marriage. His embrace and romantic onslaught were blissful. A curious mingling of languor and tension surged through her. Her mind was dazed by a fierce and rapturous longing for him and what lay ahead. She never wanted those breathtaking sensations to halt.

With lips fastened to hers, Navarro wiggled out of his long underwear and cast them to the garment pile. *"Shu,* woman, you set me afire too quick and easy. That's some magic you possess and use on me. A man don't stand a chance of escape when you set those arresting eyes on him. If I'm not careful, you'll be leading me around like a bull with a nose ring."

"Don't worry; I won't risk enticing you to break free and deny myself such pleasures. I want to take selfish advantage of you every chance I get because I'll never have another partner like you." Beth stroked the virile body touching hers. Its strength and beauty titillated her senses. His hands were strong, skilled ones, and gentle. From his sable head with arresting hazel eyes to his firm middle to his warm feet, her "husband" was appealing. His actions were slow and deliberate, as if he were memorizing every inch of her body. Never had her breasts been this sensitive to touch and kiss. Her body and mind throbbed with mounting urgency.

As Navarro's lips nuzzled her breasts, Beth's tension was laced with anticipation. She was eager to explore and to gather all treasures of lovemaking with him. Her hands played in his midnight hair and stroked his bronzed frame. She enjoyed the way his muscles moved beneath her fingers. When his mouth returned to hers, she murmured between heady kisses, "You amaze me, Navarro Breed. You sap my will and wits. When you touch me and kiss me, all I can do is respond; all I want to do is respond." .

"Are you sure you aren't too tired and sleepy for this, love?"

Her voice was constricted by desire as she replied, "Never, never with you." Without shame or reservation, she entreated, "Teach me all you know in this area, too; I want to experience every sensation possible."

That plea captivated and thrilled him. "You will, Beth." His fingers caressed her flushed cheek as he told her, "All you have to do is relax and enjoy yourself, *-Tsíné.* Do whatever seems natural or pleasing. Later

I'll teach you anything you don't know or learn along the way." She was eager to savor everything with him, and he wouldn't disappoint her.

She responded to and devoured each kiss and caress, every unspoken promise of what was to come. Her hands roamed his neck and shoulders. Her fingers played in the black curls at his nape, then traveled his hard, muscled back. Navarro's body was splendid, too tempting not to investigate. The bud of her womanhood tingled and pulsed with pleasure as he stroked it. Every spot he touched was alive and aflame. Navarro was pure passion and raw power. He was blissful enchantment and scorching fire. He was verdant earth, gusting wind, and glorious sky. He was brilliant lightning and refreshing dew and colorful rainbow. He was like all of the forces of nature combined, and he was assailing the core of her being.

Navarro had difficulty breathing, thinking, and mastering himself. The range of emotions he experienced astonished him. When his lips and hands aroused her to writhing and coaxings, his knee parted her thighs to connect their bodies.

Beth arched to meet his approach. As he entered and withdrew many times, a curling tension built within her. She clung to him and responded at an increasingly feverish pitch.

Navarro moved with caution and gentleness, but he didn't know how much longer he could control his passion. His rhythmic strokes were sending her along an upward spiral, but he was traveling just as fast as she was. He took her with an intensity that was new and stirring. He scaled heights he had never reached before this night and this woman.

Beth moaned as her climax seized her and carried her away in a flood of ecstasy. Her breath caught in her throat as the powerful sensations assailed her body and stole it. She clung to him and savored his kisses.

Control deserted Navarro. He plundered her mouth and womanhood until every ounce of need was sated. The release was so powerful and stunning that he trembled from the force of it.

A golden aftermath settled around and within them as she lay in his arms, as breathless and tranquil as he was. Navarro continued to trail kisses and fingers over her flushed face and body, and she did the same to him.

"Whew, woman, that was something. Thanks."

Beth was confused by his tenderness and gentleness. How could anything this powerful and special, she mused, not be real? "I should be the one thanking you. I never expected anyone like you to come into my life, partner. I hope you don't leave it too fast. I hate to think about finishing this role and mission."

"The same goes for you, woman."

"Maybe we'll find a way to visit between assignments so we can share some more wonderful and satisfying times."

"Sounds good to me." He cuddled her against him and said, "We'd best get to sleep; we have a criminal to investigate tomorrow."

After breakfast, Matt told everyone he and his brother were taking a ride alone, just the two of them, so they could chat; but the agents noticed that their target's three men trailed them at a distance. Jessica said she was going to begin her Monday chores and went to gather her laundry.

Before Navarro left to help Big John in the blacksmith shed, he whispered to Beth, "There's no way I can saddle Night Cloud and follow them without being seen, so we'll miss this chance to study them together and pick up clues. Just be on alert for anything Matt told Jessie since his arrival; she may confide it to you. It's for sure Charles must have enemies or he wouldn't need constant guards in a safe area. I'll see you later, love."

"I'll be helping Jessica with the washing and ironing. Put anything dirty on the floor by the bed and I'll fetch our clothes in a minute."

"That isn't necessary."

"Yes, it is. We'll be hitting the trail soon and need everything clean. Besides, how would it look if I washed my own clothes and not my husband's?"

"You're right, as always. Glad you have a smart and clear head, Beth."

"Except for when you daze my wits, Mister Breed," she jested.

Navarro grinned and caressed her cheek. "I'll try to remember to do that only at safe times." They laughed before he headed for the cabin.

As the two women worked over wash and rinse tubs, Beth said, "I hope Charles doesn't try to talk Matt into accepting another hazardous gift. He shouldn't be making suggestions when he knows nothing about ranching; that would be like me trying to convince Matt to buy cows as steers. I'm sorry, Jessica, but he makes me nervous. I don't think he's trustworthy. Men who live by schemes and daring ideas are deceivers."

"I agree. I told Matt not to be taken in by his brother again."

"You told him you're suspicious of Charles?"

"Not exactly. I only mentioned something similar to what you just said. I'm sure Matt would never repeat a mistake like his first one."

"Let's pray Charles doesn't suggest a second one that sounds too appealing to be resisted."

"I doubt Matt would make any new decisions without asking me."

Beth realized Jessica didn't sound convinced of that statement. "I hope you don't mind me making this offer, Jessica, but I can loan you the money to replace your cattle. Stephen left me plenty; it's in the Tucson bank. I never touched it because I thought I might need it in my old age or if I got injured and couldn't work. Navarro has enough to pay for our fresh start, so my savings are available to you and Matt as a loan."

Jessie stared at her. "That's much too generous, Beth. Why?"

"Because I like you and your family and this ranch; you're the best friend I've had in years. I don't want Matt being susceptible to any more of his brother's wild ideas just to recover from your losses. Please accept my offer. I know you'll pay it back when things are normal again."

"We couldn't, Beth; Matt's too proud to take money from anybody except the bank."

"If the bank won't loan you what you need, please let me help. It's the least I can do to thank you for my happiness and Navarro's life."

"I'll think about it, but only if it comes to that."

"Agreed, and we won't mention it again unless you change your mind."

They chatted about other things as they completed the task. After the clothes and linens were hanging out to dry, Beth said she was going to wash her hair and let the sun dry it before the others returned.

She lathered her long and thick tresses near the well so she'd have an ample water supply at hand. As she was doing so, she didn't know Navarro was in the kitchen speaking in private with Jessica while Lance was playing with Biscuit Hank's wife near the chuckhouse.

"I wish Miguel could see you now. He wouldn't believe his eyes. I recall what he told me about you after our return from San Angelo."

Navarro leaned against a cabinet. "What was that, Jess?"

"He said that you were a man with a troubled spirit, one who'd kill to survive, who'd been hurt many times and in many ways, a man from two worlds who fit in neither, the kind of man who destroyed himself."

"He was right, Jess."

"Back then, but not anymore. He said you couldn't survive if you changed and you'd never find what you were searching for. You proved him wrong."

"If I hadn't met you, Matt, and the boys, he would still be right."

"Miguel really liked you. He respected you. From the start, he believed you'd never break your word and you'd fight to the death for us."

"I would have."

"I know. I hope you understand what happened after you left. I hope you forgive me for hurting you. I never meant to do that, Navarro, never."

"You did what was best for everyone, even us."

"I realize it was hard on you and I'm sorry you had to suffer so much, a lot of it because of me. I'm glad our past is settled."

"You really didn't mind us coming for a visit?"

"I'm delighted you did. Beth is a wonderful person, perfect for you."

"Thanks. I can see you and Matt are perfect for each other, too."

"We are. Thanks for letting us make a fresh start."

"It was worth what we lost to gain what we have now, right?"

"I believe so. We helped each other through some rough times."

"The reason it took me so long to get over what we had was because I didn't get to explain what happened or say goodbye. That haunted and worried me for a long time; that's why I never gave another woman a chance to get to me until I met Beth."

"It all worked out as it should; it made you wait until she came along."

Navarro captured her hand and gazed into her blue eyes. "This will be the last time we see each other, Jess; that's how it has to be for Lane and Matt's happiness. Unless there's trouble and you need me. If that happens, send for me fast, pronto. I'll come and stay only long enough to help, then be gone again; I promise."

"Don't worry; we'll be fine, all of us. There is something I want to tell you while we have privacy: I'm not sorry we met and shared those few months. You'll always have a special spot in my heart and life, and I'll never forget you. I want us to remain good friends."

"Me, too, Jess, and the same is true about you."

Their gazes locked. They smiled, recalling the best days of their past together, and embraced. Each knew they were sharing a final farewell.

Beth entered the house to tell Jessica she was going to sit on the cabin porch to dry her hair and would return afterward to help with chores. As she reached the archway into the dining room, she halted and remained out of sight. From the way the two doors were positioned, she noticed her lover and friend embracing in the kitchen. They didn't know she was there, and her partner's wits were too dazed by his love, it seemed, to detect her presence. The two shared a brief kiss and hugged again. With silence and dismay, Beth sneaked from the house and tormenting sight.

"Be safe and happy, Navarro," Jessie murmured.

"You too, Jess. This time we can say goodbye in the right way, without pain and suffering and confusion."

They hugged again, then shared another short kiss; it proved to both that the fiery passion they had once shared was gone. Their hearts and bodies now belonged to others. They smiled and nodded in acceptance of the reality.

"It was kind and generous of Beth to offer to loan us money to replace our herd. You won yourself a real prize in her, Navarro."

"She didn't mention it, but that's a good solution to your problem."

After chatting a few more minutes, Navarro went to locate Beth. He found her sitting on the cabin porch.

Her head was bent over and she was brushing tangles from her damp locks.

He placed his boot near her hips and leaned against a wooden post. He tipped back his hat and observed his partner. "I was just talking with Jessie. She told me about your loan offer. What was that about?"

"So she and Matt wouldn't become desperate and get involved with Charles's schemes. You can't offer a loan; I thought mine would stall any problems until you can."

"It won't be necessary; Charles gave Matt money last night."

Beth halted her task and looked up at him in befuddlement. "He hasn't told Jessica; I'm sure of it. I wonder why."

"I don't know, but I don't like it." He related the talk he had overheard last night between the brothers.

"It looks bad for him, but maybe there's a logical explanation."

"I hope so for Jessie and the children's sake."

Do you? "So do I."

He reached out his hand and played with a wet curl. "Beth?"

"Yes?"

Navarro ruffled his hair and said, "Never mind. I'll see you later."

Beth watched him return to the smithy shed. She pondered what it was about him that made her feel so alive, desirable, feminine. Navarro had an overwhelming and wondrous power over her, but it wasn't only a physical attraction, yet that facet of their relationship was splendid. With Navarro, she didn't experience even the smallest fear for her life and safety; she had total faith in him. But there were two obstacles between them and she feared those barriers were too strong to shatter. How could she battle his desire for his love and his son? If only Navarro would realize it was possible to love more than one woman during his lifetime.

By the time her hair was dried and brushed and braided, the brothers had returned and everyone had a light meal before Matt left to check on fence repairs. The rancher took Rusty, Carlos, and Navarro with him.

While Jessica was putting a tired Lance down for a nap, Beth went outside where Charles was smoking, to see if she could learn anything.

Chapter Seventeen

Beth decided, if necessary, she would be coquettish to evoke clues from the offensive man. Someone as cocky as Charles should make slips while trying to impress her. She halted, smiled, and remarked, "I'm sure you're enjoying the rest and fresh air after your long and dusty trip."

"This is a peaceful place my brother has here, and nice friends."

"I'm glad you came to visit. Jessica and Matt needed cheering up after all the problems they've had in the last months. Drought and disease must be horrible things to endure. It takes so much time and money to recover from them. I've heard many ranchers and farmers never do. I can't imagine losing everything one owns. I hope that doesn't happen to them."

"It won't; I'll make certain it doesn't."

"You're a good man and brother, Charles. Matt's lucky to have you."

"Thank you, ma'am. To be honest, I feel partly responsible for their trouble since I'm the one who sent those bad steers that killed theirs."

Probing for how much I know? "You? Matt said a friend did it, but he didn't mention your name. You must feel terrible about such a mistake."

"I do. Hoof-and-mouth gives ranchers nightmares and heartache."

"I don't know about such matters. Navarro is the knowledgeable and experienced one in our family. It seems I have a lot to learn about ranches."

"I doubt you'd have a problem learning anything, Beth. You have a smart head under that flaming hair. If you don't mind my saying so, those are the most enchanting locks I've seen on a woman; makes a man want to run his fingers through them. Sure does set off those lovely green eyes and perfect complexion. Navarro's a damned lucky fellow he snagged a beauty like you."

"That's a nice compliment." She pretended to be uncomfortably warmed by his admiration and to seek a distraction. "You shouldn't blame yourself for an accident, Charles; surely Matt and Jessica don't fault you for an error. In their place, I wouldn't."

Charles mashed his cigarillo with his boot. "Matt doesn't, but I'm not sure about his wife. She hasn't warmed up to me yet."

Beth donned a mask of surprise. "I'm sure you've misread her. Jessica is just tired and preoccupied with company and spring chores; that's why I've been helping her as much as possible while we're here. A ranch, home, husband, and children are a lot of work. She isn't the kind of person to be unfair or ill-mannered. If you're right, though, I'll bet she warms up to you before long, so don't worry. I know you're family, but you two are strangers, and she is under a big strain these days."

"She has a right to be annoyed with me over that fiasco. I thought I was doing something good for them, but it turned out the opposite."

He shifted his position to put him closer to her, but Beth didn't retreat an inch. "What made you think of cattle as a gift?"

"When I was in Brazil on business, a friend of mine talked as if his breed was magic and money on hooves. Since I was planning to visit my brother soon, I thought it would be a nice surprise."

"It would have been a wonderful present if they hadn't gotten sick and died; you couldn't have foreseen such a tragedy."

"Matt was luckier than my Brazilian friend; he lost his entire herd before he could handle the problem. His cattle grazed free on distant hills, so the disease went unnoticed too long and every animal got infected and died. He said he tried to send us a warning; it didn't reach me until it was too late for Matt to destroy those contagious steers I sent him. I move around a lot, so I'm hard to reach."

Beth grasped that he never mentioned his alleged friend's name. "You don't have a home or office anywhere for messages?"

"Not really. I sold both years ago. Caught drifter's blood, I guess. A man should have his adventures before he's too old or settles down."

"That's a wise decision, because wives dislike roaming husbands. I'm looking forward to putting down roots myself."

"Matt said you two are looking at ranches in San Antonio next week. I hope you find one you like. A beautiful woman like you deserves a good life."

"You're too generous and charming. You swell a woman's head." She saw him smile. "If we don't find what we're seeking here in Texas, we'll look elsewhere. We have a friend in the land business in Tucson who's helping us locate the perfect place. What business are *you* in, Charles?"

"All kinds, mostly the buying, selling, and transporting of goods."

"What types of goods?" she asked as he brushed an insect from her shoulder, then let his fingers drift down her arm before removing them.

"Whatever somebody needs for resale, or wants for himself."

His chocolate gaze grew bolder by the minute. She felt as if he were mentally stripping and fondling her. The ploy she was using was working too fast and too well for comfort, but she must continue it. "You said you're going to Mexico on business. The kind you mentioned?"

"Yep. This time, I'm delivering arms and ammunition to *Presidente* Diaz's troops. That's isn't for public knowledge, so don't repeat it to anyone."

Trying to awe me with claims of friends in high places and beguile me by sharing a secret? "A mystery! I love them. Your work must be fascinating and stimulating, and sometimes dangerous."

"Why dangerous?"

"Road bandits and such. Surely you've had freight wagons attacked by men trying to steal your goods."

"I keep too many guards around for my loads to tempt outlaws. How much do you know about Mexico's history and problems?"

She sent him a quizzical look. "Practically nothing. Why?"

"For decades the country was plagued by revolts. Diaz fought in several of them, even ousted three *presidentes*. He's a powerful and feared man. He has a firm grip on most areas and citizens, but he's harassed by large and vicious gangs of *bandidos*. Sometimes, he's annoyed by renegades or rebels, but they're not much trouble to capture or destroy."

Beth knew the last sentence was untrue, especially where it concerned the Apaches, who had been thorns in Mexicans' sides for numerous decades.

"Gangs strike, flee, and hide before his troops can reach a location after getting a message. Roads and trails from the west coast to the interior are favorite raiding areas for outlaws and renegades. That's why Diaz's men are in a tight bind, getting themselves slaughtered in ambushes and shootouts; they need weapons and bullets, but their supplies can't get through. I told him mine could, and asked a nice price for success. I'm meeting one of his units in Chihuahua. We hope to sneak in our delivery before those outlaws or Injuns return to raiding the overland routes in the eastern half."

Beth widened her eyes. "You see, your business *is* hazardous. Are you sure you can make that journey without getting injured or slain?"

"That's why I have so many guards. My men are far better with guns and cunning than any outlaws, renegades, or soldiers. Two of them— Blue and Evan—can smell or hear an enemy coming from a mile away. My men are fearless and loyal, and deadly to foes. If they're lucky, those *bandidos* will be kicking up hooves in the western section."

Remember those names, Beth. "If *they're* lucky? What do you mean?"

"If they tangle with my men, they won't have a grain of luck; good luck, that is. The few who were crazy enough to attack were left in the dust as buzzard food or they galloped away licking their wounds."

"At least you'll be well protected in the face of perils. So, en route to Mexico, you got the chance to visit your brother. That's fortunate for both of you. Matt seems thrilled to see you, like a child at Christmas."

"We were close as boys, but we got separated when he moved west. I surely missed him after our parents died. The war came and things were bad for . . . everybody."

Am I hearing resentment toward Matt for leaving his family? "That's over, thank goodness. Matt's done well with his move. He and Jessica have a lovely spread and wonderful family. You've never been married?"

"No, never found the right time, place, or woman to tempt me to settle down. I envy Matt and Navarro for finding two ravishing women. Utterly charming, well-bred ladies are hard to come by."

"Thank you again. Will you be able to stop by on your return trip and visit longer?"

"I'm not sure. Diaz might ask us to use another departure route to conceal our meeting with him. Don't want *bandidos* trying to pick us off."

"Please be careful in Mexico. I would hate for Matt to lose his only brother to fierce outlaws in a foreign country."

"His only kin. The rest died during the war after Matt left home. It's just me and him now."

Again, she thought she heard a ring of resentment toward his brother in his tone. "Then it's good you're back together. Families should live close to each other when possible; life can be short out here, or anywhere."

"Truer words never came from prettier lips. Actually, what I'm doing might be beneficial to Matt. If the *Federales* use my shipment to get rid of their bandits and renegades, they can't cross the border and attack my brother's land and family. From what I've heard, they used to ford the Rio Grande and raid down Laredo and Brownsville way."

"It's a good thing you're arming the Mexican soldiers against such criminals. I hate to end our pleasant conversation, Charles, but I promised to help Jessica with the ironing this afternoon. I'll see you at supper."

"I hope we get a chance to chat again, Beth; you're a charming woman."

"I hope so, too, Charles. I would love to hear about some of your adventures. Not many men have the courage, intelligence, and means to confront such challenges. I'll bet you could entertain me for hours with your exciting experiences."

"That I could, Beth. It's too bad you're taken or I would be tempted to hang around longer to get better acquainted with you."

"As you said, one doesn't meet many unique people."

"I hope that refers to me and it's a compliment."

With temerity, she murmured, "Yes, it does and it is." Beth was overjoyed when she felt an uncommon blush heat her cheeks; but it came from rising anger about the constant grazing of his fingers over her hands or arms. "I have to go now and get busy." As she said those words, she feigned modesty and an improper slip-of-the-tongue.

Charles caressed her fiery cheek and grinned. "Yep, I would be more than tempted to stay here a long time if you weren't leaving."

What about if I weren't married, you snake? "I'd better go now."

"Don't forget: my business is a secret. I wouldn't want you innocently mentioning it to anyone during your journey who might be tempted to head out to rob us. Criminals or not, I don't like killing unless it's necessary."

"I understand; a secret it shall remain. See you later."

She knew Charles was raking his lustful brown gaze over her entire body as she returned to the Cordell house. She also knew he assumed she was attracted to him and was feeling uneasy and embarrassed about it. At least, by his trying to charm her and her faking interest, he had dropped some information, though mostly false. Dare she use her wiles to try to extract real clues from him? No, she decided, that was too risky.

Beth spent part of the afternoon ironing clothes—hers, Navarro's, and some of the children's. She played with the youngsters after Lane and Alice came home from school, and particularly had fun with her lover's son. She helped Jessica with the evening meal of fried chicken, rice with gravy, canned blackeyed peas, canned fruit, cactus jelly, biscuits, and drinks.

Following a later than usual meal due to Monday's chores, the children were put to bed soon after they finished eating. As Beth helped her, she noticed with delight that Alice preferred the doll she had brought over Charles's expensive one. Since she and Jessica didn't want to spend time around Matt's brother tonight, both said they were tired and were going to bed. Jessica added that would allow the men to enjoy masculine talk. Beth added that she needed to rest up for their impending journey.

The men took a walk and joined the ranch hands at the chuckhouse. The Special Agent noticed that Charles's friends still kept to themselves in their makeshift camp, probably ordered not to put themselves in a position of being questioned. Navarro had seen his target chatting and laughing with a blond-haired man. It was too bad he couldn't find an excuse to meet the tall, thin gunman with piercing steel-gray eyes so he could delve for clues.

After Navarro reached the cabin, he found Beth asleep. Her breathing sounded as if she was exhausted, so he was careful not to disturb her when he got into bed. He wished she was awake so he could get a report about what, if anything, happened with Charles.

When he arose, Navarro left Beth sleeping and went to tell Jessica she'd be in later. "Since we're leaving tomorrow, I thought some extra winks might be good for her."

"She's been a big help during your visit, and I'm grateful."

"She's enjoyed her stay here; thanks for being so kind to her."

"I know you two will be very happy, Navarro."

"I have no doubts," he replied, and wished that were true. "I'm heading to the corral to see if the boys need any help. You know me, I never was one to laze around."

"I remember; your mind and hands had to stay busy."

"Remember, too, Beth's loan offer was genuine if you need it. I have more than enough to buy our ranch and stock and get things going. Never spent much on the trail all those years, so I saved most of what I earned. Some jobs paid big wages, like guarding gold or silver shipments."

"Matt said he'd figured out a way to settle our bank debt and pay for all our needs."

"Maybe Charles is planning to loan him money; he seems a rich man."

"I hope not!"

"Anything wrong, Jessie? That answer sounded like trouble."

"I just don't like or trust that man, Navarro, and I don't know why. He guessed the truth from what he said to Beth yesterday."

"What do you mean?"

"Let her tell you; I hear them coming. Fetch me water."

Navarro slipped out the back door and obeyed, as if that was his reason for returning to the kitchen. "Here you go, Jessie. Anything else I can do to help before I join the boys?"

"That's all. Thanks." Jessie turned and smiled at the brothers.

Charles asked Navarro, "Where's that lovely wife of yours?"

"I was letting her get some extra rest for our long and dusty ride."

"Traveling and camping in rough terrain can be hard on a gentle lady. Too bad there isn't a railroad between here and there. On the other hand, it gives you newlyweds romantic privacy. You're one lucky fellow, Navarro; she's beautiful and charming."

"Yep, she is. Thanks for the compliment about her."

Matt added, "Beth and Navarro are a perfect match, like me and Jessie."

"Maybe I'll be as lucky as you two boys one day."

"You can't meet a woman like our two on the trail. You'll have to settle down some place to scout for one. You aren't getting any younger, Charlie; if you want a home and family before forty, best get busy looking."

"You sound like a real matchmaker, big brother, just like old lady Tims was. I'm sure you remember her. Paired up more couples than Cupid."

Navarro noticed how Matt nodded but looked uneasy.

"If Jessica and Beth were available, I'd stick around and let you do that job for me. Any more angels around like those two?"

"Not that I know of, little brother."

Navarro shrugged and shook his head. "Me, neither."

"Too bad, I could use me a superb wife."

At two o'clock, Charles's wagon train arrived and set up an overnight camp near the other three men. The two couples and Lance stood with him in the outer yard and observed the commotion from a distance.

"Ten wagons, you must be making a big delivery."

"They aren't full, Beth. I pack lighter than most transporters; makes a fast pace if trouble strikes and better time. Extra men and wagons don't cost as much as lost business if you can't reach customers quicker and with more goods than other companies. I also have to haul supplies and water for the men and feed for the stock when no grass is available. I carry extra wagon and harness parts and two repairmen to handle breakdowns. Even have my own smithy and equipment in case a horse throws a shoe."

"I never realized there was so much to the freight business. It takes a very intelligent owner and excellent planner to be safe and successful."

"Thank you, ma'am. I've learned those precautions from experience."

"Can I go look at the big wagons, Papa?" Lance asked.

Charles said in a hurry, "That isn't wise, boy; those horses and wagons aren't toys. I don't want you getting hurt."

With a nod Matt added, "He's right, son, so stay away from them."

Navarro studied the types of carriers: two schooners with tall canvas tops and eight freighters with boxed-in beds. All were loaded and covered so nothing inside was visible. He counted twenty-six men and one dog.

Matt, Navarro, Charles and some of his hirelings, and Rusty rode off an hour later for the rancher to show his brother the best route to the border. Other cohorts took team horses to a nearby river to treat them with fresh water, lush grass, and rubdowns. A few remained behind in camp.

While most were gone, Beth played chase and hide-and-seek with the three children. As they raced about amidst laughter and squeals, she let Lane get near one of the schooners without relating Charles and Matt's cautions to Lance not to do so. As she pursued Lane around the last one in the group, the large dog began to bark in a loud and near wild manner. Beth came to an abrupt halt. "Stay back, Lane; he looks mean and angry. We shouldn't be—"

A man jerked aside a canvas curtain at the rear, stepped onto the gate, and shouted at them, "Whatcha doin' around here?"

Beth sent him a wide and innocent gaze and jumped as if he'd startled her. The fact was, she'd heard his boots approaching on the wooden base. As she spoke, she kept glancing at the enraged animal beneath the wagon as it continued to growl, bristle, and eye them in a menacing way.

"Callarse, Bruto; *sentarse."*

She grasped Lane's hand and pulled him behind her for protection if necessary, but the dog obeyed his master's Spanish commands to be quiet and sit down. "The children and I were playing chase. I was about to catch up with Lane and tell him we shouldn't get too close to his uncle's wagons. We must have disturbed the dog's nap or surprised him with our voices."

"Best play elsewhere; ain't safe here for kids. They could git hurt climbin' on wagons or spookin' that critter. He's trained to guard us."

Now that the creature's threat was past, Beth took advantage of her and the stranger's position to steal furtive glances between the man's legs. "I apologize for intruding, sir; it won't happen again. But please keep him secured like that; I wouldn't want the children to get bitten by accident."

"He stays tied up around folks. Just don't tempt 'im to break his rope. I seed him do it afore. Ain't no pretty sight when Bruto finishes off a man."

If she'd known about or even suspected Bruto's vicious streak, she wouldn't have allowed Lane to get near him for any reason. She would have been agonized if the boy had gotten injured while she sought clues. And Navarro and Jessica wouldn't have forgiven her for taking such risks with their child's safety. She was thankful nothing had gone wrong. "Thanks for the rescue and warning," she said to the gruff and chilling man. Beth and Lane were joined by Alice and Lance before they took many steps. Still within the man's hearing range, she passed along instructions in a gentle tone, "You heard the gentleman; no one comes over this way again. It's dangerous, so your papa and uncle would be mad at us."

"I'm sorry, Miss Beth; I didn't mean to cause trouble."

She smiled and grasped his hand. "You didn't, Lane; don't worry. Let's go play on the other side of the house where it's safe. Thanks again; goodbye," she looked back and told the scowling villain. She chatted with the children as she guided them to the other location to continue their games. But she had glimpsed something frightful behind the man . . .

Jessica had prepared a special farewell meal for "you and Navarro, not for Charles," she mouthed to the redhead while they set the table. As they put baked turkey and dressing on platters and other dishes in bowls in the kitchen, Jessica whispered, "I'll be glad when he's gone, but I'll miss you two. I hate it that you have to leave at the same time."

"We have no choice. Departing tomorrow will give us only enough days to reach San Antonio to make our appointments. We'll miss you, too, and Matt and the children. I'll write after we make our choice and get settled."

"I'll be eager to hear all the good news."

"I'll be just as eager to hear from you that everything's back to normal. I wish I could show you the wedding presents our friends in Tucson gave us. I left them in my trunks there until we get settled and I send for them. If you need to reach us, send a letter to us in care of Henry and Kate Carter at Carter's Dry Goods there. They'll forward it to me with my trunks."

"I took your advice and I've tried to be nice to Charles. I'm glad you told me he was offended. I wouldn't want Matt annoyed at me."

"Charles seems to want everybody to make a fuss over him. I bet he tries to beguile every woman he meets, married or single. He was much too flirtatious with us. Speaking of offending people, who is that 'old lady Tims' Charles mentioned? That seemed to trouble Matt."

Jessica brushed over the story of Matt's first love in Georgia when he was eighteen. "Sarah dropped him a week before the wedding and married another man three weeks later. Mrs. Tims was the one who convinced her she was making a mistake and got Sarah together with her nephew. It was mean of Charles to mention that episode today; Matt told me he had. You see, Charles was always possessive of Matt; he was bitter and angry when Matt left home when Charles claims the family needed him most. He's the one who persuaded Matt to return and fight during the war. I'm lucky he didn't get my husband killed or maimed. I think he might blame Matt for their family's deaths and loss of property."

"Perhaps that's why he sent the cattle, as a peace offering," Beth hinted, but didn't believe that was true. Neither did Jessica from her expression.

Beth said her good nights early so she could pack for their departure before going to bed. She left Navarro in the house with the men so he could gather any clues Charles might drop in a final conversation. There hadn't been an occasion to relate her findings to Navarro, but she would when he came home. *Home and husband.* Her anguished mind echoed those lovely and wishful words as she loaded her saddlebags.

Before returning to the cabin, Navarro told the ranch hands goodbye, as many would be on the range when they left in the morning. He went to see if Beth needed any help. His packing was done and his weapons ready.

"Can we talk?" she asked in a low voice.

Navarro pulled her into his arms, placed his cheek against hers, and whispered, "Let's not chance it. We'll go over our plans tomorrow when it's safe. With a new moon tonight, darkness would conceal any spies outside. I was hoping to use it to sneak a look in one of those wagons, but Charles has them too well guarded for taking risks. He even uses an attack dog. Let's turn in. We have a long, hot, dusty journey ahead. From here on, we become part of the land: no fires, baths, noise, or . . ." He leaned back to gaze into her upturned face. "That's the only precaution I'll miss."

Beth smiled. "Me, too. I've packed all except last-minute things. Good night, husband dear." She caressed his strong jawline as she took a deep breath. "You're about to retire from that confining role."

"Yep," he murmured, a part he'd gotten used to and enjoyed.

They separated to undress and get to bed. They hadn't been there long when they turned toward each other at the same time and whispered the other's name. They shared muffled laughter.

"You thinking about and wanting what I am?"

"If I'm reading you right, yes. You said no playing on the trail, so it's our last chance. It would be a pleasant farewell to our marital roles."

"Yep, proper goodbyes are important; makes separation easier."

Is that what you were doing in the kitchen with Jessica? Were you two only sharing a bittersweet and final farewell because you never had the chance to do so in the past? I hope so. Please, God, make that true.

They removed their garments and nestled together, bare flesh making stirring contact. At first, they shared slow and short kisses and gentle caresses. As passions mounted, those actions increased in speed and depth and urgency. Their mouths meshed, their tongues played, and their hands wandered and pleasured. Soon, they crossed the border into blissful surroundings, savored their visit, and headed for serene terrain. There, they went to sleep in each other's arms, naked and sated.

Beth removed the linens from the bed, tied them in a bundle, and left them lying atop it. She straightened the cabin, packed the rest of her belongings, and went to join the others.

"I was hoping I'd get to say goodbye to you, Mrs. Breed."

Beth shook Charles's extended hand, smiled, and said, "It was a pleasure to meet you. Maybe we'll all visit again at the same time. I wish you a safe and successful journey."

"I hope yours will be as profitable as mine." To Navarro, Charles said, "You locate this little woman a very special ranch; she deserves the best."

"I'm sure we'll find just what we're looking for."

Charles and Matt hugged affectionately and said their last goodbye.

The two couples, Lance, and a few ranch hands watched the wagons pass through a wide gate and head southward across the pasture.

"I hate to rush, but we best get on the trail, too, while it's still cool. It's been a good visit, Matt, Jessie. I'm glad we stopped by."

"So are we," Matt replied as the men shook hands.

Navarro told his other friends farewell. Two gave them wedding gifts: Big John handed him a large wooden sign for the new ranch with their names burned into the surface; Biscuit Hank and his wife presented Beth with a packet of their best recipes and some trail snacks; and Jessica gave them several embroidered pieces for their new furniture.

Beth embraced and thanked first Matt then Jessica. She lifted Lance and gave the little boy a hug and kiss. Lance responded by repeating the action with her and begging her to visit again. She had risen early to see Alice and Lane before they left for school, as had Navarro. She surmised how difficult it must be for her love to say a last goodbye to his son.

Navarro suspended the cloth sack loaded down with gifts around his saddlehorn. He knew he'd have to conceal it somewhere in the rocks at the border to prevent it from being extra weight and noise. He also knew he'd sneak back later to recover it. He approached his past love, smiled, and embraced her as the friend he now was. "Goodbye, Jessie; I wish wonderful things for you, Matt, and the children. Before you two know it, this place will be like it was before trouble came." He pressed a parting item into her hand while Matt and Beth chatted with Lance, and mouthed, "For Alice." Aloud, he said to her, "Thanks for the food; we'll enjoy it for the next few days."

More well-wishes were exchanged before Navarro and Beth mounted their horses and rode eastward toward the sun. The ranch hands returned to their tasks, and Lance hurried off to play in the front yard. Matt put his arm around Jessica and cuddled her close to him.

Jessica held out her opened hand for Matt to view what Navarro had placed there: her old and worn picture. "It's over for him, my love, as it should be, thanks to Beth. He's happy and free; he won't be back again."

"For all of our sakes, love, I'm glad he found her."

"So am I, Matt. Now, let's see about solving our problem."

Matt withdrew the packet of money and said, "That's over, too, thanks to my brother. With this, we can rebuild our herd and pay off the bank."

Navarro glanced back once for a last look at Matt and Jessie and their homesite. He was glad he had seen Lane before the boy left earlier. His son had thanked him again for the amulet, then hugged him and said he'd never forget him. That had warmed and comforted him, made his loss endurable.

As soon as they were out of sight, Navarro slowed the pace so they could ride close and talk. "We'll head this way another few miles in case anybody trails us, then turn south. Travel eastward of them; use the landscape to conceal our presence. After we reach the Rio Grande, we'll ride upstream to drop in behind them; then let their tracks mask ours."

"It's good you know this area so well and know such clever tricks."

"Yep. We'll stop later to change clothes; didn't want anybody seeing us in our disguises. I'm glad you have something tan to wear and you're riding a palomino; the desert swallows up those colors. Just in case you didn't, I bought you some buckskins and moccasins in Benson; hope they're the right size. They're cooler during the day, warmer at night, and protective against cactus and prickly bushes and trees. Comfortable, too."

"That was thoughtful and smart. What amount do I owe you for them?"

"Nothing; they're gifts to my partner." As he looked at her and smiled, he cautioned, "Be sure to keep that flaming head covered; it would stand out against a blue sky like a beautiful sunset. After we close the distance between us and them, I'll coat Night Cloud with dust so he isn't noticeable. Now, tell me what you learned."

After Beth gave most of her lengthy report, Navarro murmured, "You took some risks, but they paid off. From the way Charles was eyeing you, we want to make certain he never gets his dirty hands on you. He was so dazed by you he didn't watch his tongue."

Surely you aren't jealous . . . "We know he isn't heading to meet with President Diaz in Chihuahua, so he thought he was duping me."

"What he said about those *bandidos,* rebels, and renegades is mostly true. I guess he figured if you'd heard any of that stuff you'd believe him."

"I was suspicious of every word that left his lying lips. He has so many men and that blasted dog, Bruto. What do *callarse* and *sentarse* mean? That's what his master shouted at him."

"Spanish for 'Be quiet' and 'Sit down.' If I'm going to get near their camp to spy, I'll have to get rid of Bruto first. That won't be easy, but I will."

"It's a good thing you know Spanish. We also need to be on alert for two men called Blue and Evan. Charles claimed they could 'smell or hear an enemy coming from a mile away.' The one he spent time with at the ranch is named Jim Tiller. Matt says that's his best friend. He supposedly didn't join us any time because he's a loner. Charles bragged to me about all of his men being skilled gunslingers."

"We shouldn't have to challenge his gang, just follow and spy. When they make contact, I'll send word and we'll get help to capture them. Main thing we're supposed to learn is if he's in on this alone or has partners."

"I'm sure Matt isn't involved, no matter what we heard and saw that seemed to incriminate him. Besides using Matt for cover, I think Charles had a little spite in mind when he sent those cattle. I told you what Jessica said and how Charles acted with me yesterday."

"Could be. Lots of brothers part ways and have trouble." *I hope that never happens with Lane and Lance.*

As he glanced the other way, Beth assumed it was to conceal the expression on his face which must have to do with his son and Lane's half brother. "Last thing: I saw a Gatling gun in one of the wagons when Lane and I had our near run-in with Bruto and his master. While that villain was standing on the tailgate and fussing at us, I saw it between his legs. If that weapon falls into the renegades' hands, many soldiers can be cut down with one sweep, maybe even ranchers or farmers or townfolk. There could be a second one in that other covered wagon, perhaps more. If he's loaded with repeating rifles like the one he gave Matt and has plenty of ammunition, put those two forces together and it's going to be a long and bloody war if we don't stop him."

"We can't arrest him for transporting guns and ammo across the border. We have to catch him breaking the law redhanded before we can move in on him. All we have so far are suspicions and our eavesdroppings. Accusations this serious about a man as rich and respected as Charles Cordell will demand indisputable evidence. Else, he could find a cunning way out of the charges. We need more than the words of an Apache half-breed bastard and his beautiful 'wife.' Don't worry, we'll stop him."

"What if Charles makes contact and turns over his load in Mexico? We can't challenge him, twenty-six gunmen, and a band of renegades. We're skilled and determined, partner, but those are heavy odds against us. Our evidence would be gone; we'd have only our word about what we witnessed. What if he's heading for that Apache stronghold Dan mentioned to you, the one in the Sierra Madres where the Indians were captured last month?"

"I doubt it because Goyathlay and his braves are raiding in southern Arizona. Zack told me that bad news when we talked in El Paso. I must have forgotten to mention it to you."

Beth noticed he used Geronimo's Indian name. "That was twelve days ago. Couldn't they be there by the time Charles reaches it?"

"Yep. But if Charles was delivering goods there, he would have started his journey from Arizona or New Mexico. That would have been closer and easier and faster, and he could still do it on the sly. Nope, I think he's going to cross over the border into Arizona as if he's coming from Mexico. This should be far enough away; let's stop and change and head south."

They reined in, dismounted, and donned buckskins and moccasins. They folded and put away their departure clothes.

Beth eyed the garments she was now wearing and high-top footwear as she rounded the palomino. "I like them. Good protection from sun and vegetation. Sunshine and I should blend right into the desert. Thanks, boss."

Navarro caught her left arm in a gentle grasp and shifted her about to examine his choices. He sank to a knee, lifted one foot at a time, and checked the Indian boots. As he rose, his hazel gaze journeyed up her body with leisure and satisfaction. "Perfect fit. Looks good on you, woman."

"Feels good, too. How did you guess my sizes?"

"I didn't. I borrowed your shirt, riding pants, and slippers to use."

"You're sneaky and clever, partner."

He grinned and murmured, "When I have to be."

"You're also wonderful and considerate, Navarro Breed."

"I can be if I work at it hard enough, can't I?" He chuckled.

Beth's green gaze roamed his muscular physique. She decided his outfit had been specially made for him, as it almost molded to his frame. "You are even when you don't work at it," she quipped in return.

"Watch it or my hat'll soon be popping off a swollen head."

"Then, I'll hush because I don't want any changes in this handsome face and captivating mane."

As she trailed fingers over his jawline, then fluffed the sable hair at his left ear, Navarro was tempted to carry her off into the nearby bushes and make love to her for hours. He couldn't; they had work to do. "Any chance you'll go to a town where you'll be safe and comfortable and let me finish this part of the assignment alone?" He saw her expression alter after his first three words. Maybe she had expected him to say something else . . .

"No. I'm not your cover now; I'm your partner, your backup, an agent on duty. If you try to shake me, I'll follow or do my own trailing."

"I figured as much," he said with a grin and chuckle as he tugged on her thick braid in a playful manner. "Tuck this in and let's ride."

After they mounted, he waited for Beth to conceal her hair. She pulled a tan hat close to her eyes to shade them from the sun's glare. With the differences in their heights, the hat's position caused her mouth to be most noticeable. He wanted to kiss those full pink lips and—

Beth lifted her head and looked at him to say, "Navarro, be careful when we catch up with them. I don't like the looks of Charles's hirelings."

"That's why you're not getting near them, woman. At the first sniff of trouble, you're riding for safety, like it or not. Understand?"

"But—"

"Don't start refusing orders now, Agent Wind; I'm in charge."

"Yes, sir."

"If I say to get moving, woman, I'd better see your backside fast."

"What about you?"

"I'll be right behind you, just don't halt or look back or we'll both be in deep trouble. I can get myself out of any tight spot, but not while I'm trying to protect you. Don't endanger us with defiance."

"I won't disobey direct orders; I promise. But don't send me riding just to be rid of me or to protect me and put yourself in peril."

"I know your skills, so I'll use them to the last minute. Agreed?"

Beth realized he, the one in charge, didn't order her to stay behind and that pleased her. "Agreed."

"How's the arm?"

"My wound's healed. If not for a tiny mark, you'd never know I got shot. I hope you won't have to tell Dan or put it in your report."

"No need, partner, and I won't let you get harmed again. Let's go after that sidewinder."

"I'm ready."

Chapter Eighteen

Beth familiarized herself with the surroundings as they traveled across a rolling terrain of grassland that was splashed with scrubs, ball-like trees, a variety of vegetation, and hills of many heights and sizes. Mountains and peaks loomed at a distance on all sides, appearing purplish or brown in the morning light. She noticed how multiarmed chollas branched like jade candelabras with hot-pink flames. She glanced at ocotillas that sent spiny limbs reaching in all directions from their bodies. She inhaled the mingled fragrances of mesquite and tamerisk with their enticing blossoms that attracted countless bees and other insects. She saw buffalo gords slithering over green foliage. Yuccas grew in abundance and often studded hillsides, as the saguaro did near Tucson, their ivory offerings rising upward toward a serene blue heaven. Outcroppings of prickly pear and other cacti with well-guarded blooms were scattered about. Wildflowers in white, red, orange, blue, lavender, and yellow added a profusion of beauty to the picturesque setting.

The ride was easy and steady, even when they were required to skirt an occasional ravine or gully. They encountered few barren, sandy spots in the verdant region. Antelope, rabbit, hawk, and other animals and birds foraged for food and reveled in freedom. Navarro pointed out a mountain whose formation was shaped like a cathedral or a medieval castle, then one that resembled an elephant. Time and miles passed as they traversed the Cordell Ranch near the Santiago Mountains.

Navarro made certain they stayed out of sight of any observer. He kept fieldglasses suspended around his neck and used them frequently to keep a close watch on their target. When the wagons were halted to rest and water the teams and men, he told Beth he was leaving to tend a problem. "Just stay here, be still, be silent, and wait for me. Don't use those fieldglasses unless you do it through bushes, or a reflection might give away your location. Get some rest and shade. I've done this kind of trick before, so don't worry. And don't dare leave this spot until I say so."

"Yes, sir, I hear you."

"I'm serious, Beth Breed, not a peep or a step. I'll return before you're ready to mount again." He took some things from his saddlebag, discarded his pistols, and placed a knife at his waist.

As he tied a bandana in a fusion of green and brown around his head in a scarf fashion, she asked, "What are you doing?"

"Had it made and dyed for this kind of situation."

"I meant, why are you leaving your pistols? You'll be defenseless. Please don't do this, whatever you have in mind."

"If I don't make it back, you can have Night Cloud and all my other possessions," he murmured with a roguish grin.

"Don't joke about something so serious and dangerous."

"Then kiss me for certain good luck." He bent over, grasped her face between his hands, and took one before she could respond.

Beth watched him sneak between trees and bushes as he made his way closer and closer to the temporary campsite. Even at her distance, she heard Bruto when the dog began barking. Her heart felt as if it were about to jump into her throat and leap from her body when she saw the vicious creature take off in Navarro's direction. He went toward a ravine and was out of sight. Minutes moved by like hours as she tensed forward to hear her love being attacked.

Her fear heightened when the animal's master began yelling for him and walking toward the place she had last glimpsed her partner. Bruto raced into sight, joined his owner, and they returned to the wagons. Within ten minutes, the long line started to depart.

Beth used his fieldglasses to study the area where the agent had vanished: nothing. "Where are you, Navarro?"

"Right here."

Beth almost screamed when he startled her from behind. She whirled and stared at the grinning man who was sitting Indian-style on the ground.

"Bruto won't be a threat by tomorrow morning."

"How do you know?"

"I fed him poisoned meat."

She asked in amazement, "Where did you get poison out here?"

"Stole it from the ranch. Big John had some to use on rats and such."

"That vicious beast ate from your hand without biting it first?"

"Nope. I tossed it in his path as he came my way. He stopped dead and gobbled it up. Real sweet-tasting stuff, I hear. Were you on full alert?"

"Yes, why?"

"That proves my point; I can sneak up on somebody without being seen or heard, so now you know you don't have to worry about me next time I take off like that."

Beth had no choice except to agree about his skills, but she knew worries would still plague her each time. "As Dan said, you're the best."

"Thanks, woman. Let's get on their tails again."

They mounted and returned to shadowing their target.

Mesas and buttes appeared. The countryside made a slow change into drier, scrubbier, and harsher topography. The mountains ahead loomed closer. Green amaranth, future tumbleweeds, became a common sight. Cactus and ocotilla increased in number. Where there wasn't a water source, as there had been many so far, windmills supplied the life-sustaining liquid needed by stock, but none was pastured today in this region. Hills began to ascend gradually.

They reached the Chalk Mountains on their left. The inclines and declines became even steeper. Rocks of all sizes were abundant. They rode through passes with craggy peaks. Gorges and ravines knifed the terrain on both sides. They crossed flash-flood sections in current dry washes. Dense clusters of ocotilla formed near forests and caused detours around them.

At dusk, Charles and his men halted to camp in a low area of the rugged wilderness. Navarro and Beth did the same but at a higher elevation for easy observation and safety. He left the horses in a canyon where there was grass and a seep, as he knew Night Cloud would guard Sunshine.

In serious tones, he instructed Beth, "You'll have to eat your supper without heating it; no fire, no coffee."

"Water's fine, and the weather kept Jessica's gifts warm." As she unpacked the meal and gathered their canteens, Navarro watched the men.

"I guess Bruto isn't feeling too good about now; I don't see him."

"He was mean and dangerous, but I hated for you to poison him."

"Didn't sit well with me, either, but I had no choice."

They ate in silence as Navarro continued his task. Finally he said, "I'm going to get a little closer while I have something to use for concealment. See what I can learn. Charles and Tiller have their camp off from the others, so maybe they'll do some talking. I should reach them about the time they finish their meal and start settling in."

"There's no moon tonight. How will you see to move around? What about snakes and tripping on jagged rocks? It's too risky."

"I'll be fine; I promise. I'm skilled and experienced in these things. If I'm not back by morning, you head for Fort Davis and contact Dan. You know the code. I have to do this, Beth; it's my job; it's important. A lot of lives depend on us succeeding. I'm not going to abandon you here. Get some rest and sleep. I won't let any of them head up this way without stopping them." He watched her give a reluctant nod.

Beth didn't argue when he took his precautions this time and left her sitting alone, to wait and worry again until his return. She knew if he was caught, they would kill him. Yet, she couldn't be foolish and disobey—or see in total darkness without any moonlight. She stayed on constant alert to make sure he didn't sneak up on her a second time as a test. She reasoned that if he could do it, so could an enemy.

Navarro headed toward the location which Charles and Jim Tiller were approaching. He pressed himself against a boulder and listened.

"We're on our way to riches, Charlie. Sure was cunning how you got Diaz to order rifles and a Gatling gun, then changed the numbers on those papers and got Ben to pay the balance for our scheme."

"Yep, old friend, one Gatling gun was easy to change to a four and one thousand rifles to four thousand."

"That's 'cause you made him write his order in English so you could mark over his numbers without trouble. Hell, Charlie, you made him a deal he couldn't refuse."

"I had to give him a cheap weapons and delivery price so he'd take my bait and cover us with the law. I think they got on to us after that trouble Blue and the boys had last time. That mess scared some of them; they don't like to challenge those government agents."

" "Wouldn't have been no trouble if Grady hadn't panicked and fired on 'em. I had a gut itch we shouldna hired him."

"Well, it's too late to change what happened, but nothing came of it. I offered the boys high wages for this trip, so I insisted Diaz settle up with gold coins and he agreed. That's enough to pay the boys real good. We don't need to make a profit off Diaz, not with what we're getting from that Indian and not having to repay Ben. We send old Diaz his two wagon-loads and continue on with our secret haul. After the boys make the exchange, they'll rejoin us near the Carmen River, and old Diaz won't know he's been used. He's happy; the boys are happy, and nobody's the wiser. Even the law's fooled. Nice of that agent they stuck up our noses to get himself killed. His friend didn't know we saw him spying and knew he'd report that fall as an accident; our hands were as clean as a baby's after a bath. If they did any more investigating, we came out just as clean. Thanks to old *Presidente's* signed papers, everything looks legal and innocent."

"Nobody's spied or trailed us since that agent got tossed off the case. We're safe and we're gonna stay safe; these fools will guard us with their lives for their hefty shares of those goin coins. All they want is lots of money, so they'll do their jobs and they won't turn on us. They all agreed: any man dies, they split his share; any man tries to rob us and escape, they hunt him down and kill him real slow and painful and take his share. We don't have to worry about that deal tempting 'em to kill off each other, least not before their job's finished. They know they might need all gun hands if we have trouble with bandits or soldiers or Injuns either side of the border."

"We'll have our share as soon as we reach Morenci."

"Smart of you to set up the exchange there so we can check out that Injun's offer before we turn over such a big load to him."

"He was more than willing to receive them there; that way he can show those San Carlos brothers of his how many guns and bullets he has so they'll join up with him and say farewell to that barren reservation."

"You think he told Blue the truth?"

"Yep, I do, Jim, my friend. Those messages he left for us are real sweet. We're lucky he ain't got killed or captured before we could get our load made and delivered. He knows we're on our way, so he's being extra careful to stay safe and alive and on the loose. Ben's supplying his band with food and stuff so they won't have to risk raiding. If he can keep his braves under control while they twiddle their thumbs, we'll be rich."

"It's a good thing old Geronimo ain't in on this deal; I doubt we could fool that sly fox into paying such a price. Think he'll give us trouble?"

"I doubt it; he's doing his own romping around. He's taking the attention off us. While the soldiers are scouting and chasing him, we'll be supplying the chief who'll make Geronimo look like a tamed wolf. We'll head on to our planned crossing point. If there's trouble in the area, we'll change it."

"What if there is trouble at the border? Soldiers patrolling it."

"We'll talk our way out of any complication there. We'll pretend we decided not to deal with Diaz, say he was planning to use the weapons against peasants accused of being rebels, say we didn't want to get involved in killings of innocent people. I'll tell them we're heading for Fort Apache to make a deal with the Army for battling those renegades we read about in the newspapers. Later, we'll claim we were attacked by Geronimo's band, robbed, and barely escaped with our scalps."

"You sure that Injun will keep his word?"

"Yep. He wants what I have real bad, and what he has means nothing to him, not confined to no reservation."

"What about Ben? Still planning to put him in a pine box?"

"As soon as he's served his purpose, you arrange a convincing accident for him. We needed his money to finance this deal and keep those Indians supplied and out of mischief. His part's about over. Before he's gone, I want you to make sure he doesn't have any clues laying around to point at us."

"You amaze me all the time, Charlie; you must have the smartest brain in the country. You think your brother's smart, too? Think he suspects anything?"

"No, Matt's too trusting; he believed what I told him. If he'd been home where he belonged and hadn't run off like a coward after that whore scorned him, those bastards wouldn't have gotten to me. He shoulda been there to protect me or kill those sons-of-bitches. You saved my life, Jim, and I'll never forget it was you who did it. I would have bled to death if you hadn't come along. Not many men would have tended that kind of injury. Ruined my life. Can't ever have kids or even bed a woman again. It's hell when the wants attack you and you can't do anything about them. I'm glad you killed those Yankee bastards. They had no right to do that to a young boy; hell, I weren't but sixteen."

"Why'd you give that traitor money to buy more cattle?"

"To keep him duped and quiet, put him off guard."

"Why didn't you let him be destroyed? He earned it for deserting you and your family. They'd be alive and you'd be whole if he'd been there. It was best I didn't get around him or I mighta put my knife in his chest."

"I know; that's why I told you to stay clear until we left. Soon as we get rid of this load and claim our reward, we'll have everything we want. I may even find a way to get that redhead for my wife. Even if I can't hump, I'll need the perfect female for show."

"You really liked her, didn't you?"

"She's just what I need for my new status."

"Matt's wife is a real prize, too, from what I saw."

"As soon as I finish off my brother, you can have that vain twit. When you're done with her, I'll take the kids as mine. They favor Uncle Charlie as much as Papa Matt. Raise 'em as mine and nobody will be the wiser. Or maybe I won't take those irritating brats. Maybe I'll let you father a child for me with the redhead; it'd be more like mine than his would. We'll think on that possibility, old friend. Beth Breed Cordell . . ."

Navarro was furious at hearing those dark plots against his loved ones. It told him how crazy and evil Charles was, and how doubly dangerous. He listened a while longer, but the two men were talking about nothing of interest to him as they turned in for the night. He sneaked away to rejoin his woman and to protect her from harm.

Navarro had memorized the return path, so he traversed it without a problem. He used keen wits, deft hands, and agile feet as his eyes. His partner's breathing told him she was still awake, and a change in it revealed she had detected an arrival. "It's me, love," he whispered to prevent startling her again.

"I'm over here. I have your bedroll ready."

He inched his way to her and lay down on the roll she had spread next to hers. When she pried him with questions, he told her to go to sleep and he'd tell her everything tomorrow during their ride.

Through fieldglasses at dawn, Navarro's gaze followed the moving man who held his dead dog wrapped in a blanket. It appeared Bruto's master was taking his pet's body into the hills to bury it, hills opposite and south of their location. The agent looked at Beth who was sleeping peacefully and knew she was safe where she was. He prepared himself and went to intercept and slay one of Charles's men.

Navarro reached the site just as the stranger finished his task. He couldn't understand why the man carried the dog atop a high rise to bury it. He sneaked up and clubbed him on the temple with a rock, then shoved his body over a cliff. With haste, he concealed his actions and set up false clues. He finished in the nick of time to elude the two men who arrived.

"Evan! Where the hell are you? Evan! We're ready to pull out. Leave that stupid dog be and git your ass back to camp. Evan!"

"There he is, Blue, down there."

"Well, shit in my face if the fool ain't done got hisself kilt."

"You think he jumped or was pushed?"

Blue studied the ground and said, "See those loose rocks and skids? He got too close and tumbled over. No other tracks. Dumb bastard. Been crazy since that mean dog took sick yesterday. Never seed him act loco."

"Think he's dead? How we gonna git him outta that gorge?"

"We ain't. Don't matter if he's still alive; he'd be all busted up. You know the rules: you git hurt, you git left behind. Grab his horse. Let's go."

Navarro stayed hidden until the men were back in camp and distracted by departure chores before he sneaked to Beth's side. He thought about how cold-hearted Charles's hirelings were. It astonished him to learn how different the Cordell brothers were from each other. He reasoned it would hurt Matt bad if he learned the truth.

Beth looked at Navarro as he entered their camp. "Where have you been? Did you creep down there again this morning?"

"Nope. Evan left camp and I got him. Made it appear an accident."

Beth stared at him. "How do you know it was Evan?"

"Blue told me."

"You're confusing me even more or I'm not wide awake yet. I thought we were going to hang back until the border."

"I changed my mind. Or you could say, they changed it for me."

"What do you mean?"

"I figured, if Charles and his friend were going to do any boasting or plan changing, they'd do it first chance they had real privacy away from the ranch; that was last night, and I was right."

"Darn it, Navarro Breed! Do I have to drag every scrap of information out of you a crumb at a time? What happened?"

"Sorry, Beth, my mind drifted."

"It's no wonder; you've gotten little rest and sleep."

"I've gone on a lot less of both when I had to. My mind was sorting what I heard. They're pulling out in a few minutes. We'll talk first, then catch up. At least we have a few clues to go on now."

Beth listened intently as Navarro related what he'd done, what he'd learned yesterday and this morning, and what his conclusions were.

"That deal with Diaz gives him a sly cover I hadn't expected. And his claim about heading for Fort Apache might sound logical to a judge and jury if we moved against him too soon; at least, give 'em too much doubt to convict him. Charles can be clever and a smooth talker; look how he's tricked and duped his own brother. We don't want him turning on a persuasive innocent act we can't destroy with solid evidence."

Beth nodded agreement but didn't interrupt.

"We have to learn who this Ben is before Tiller gets rid of him; he could've recorded facts we'll need as proof. He's somewhere near Morenci, Arizona, and he's rich; that's a copper district, so he may be a mine owner. When it's safe to send Dan a message, I'll get him to assign an agent to nose around there. I also want to let the Agency know Geronimo isn't involved so our men won't be chasing the wrong shadow. If Dan gets hold of the list of Indians on San Carlos Reservation and who's escaped, we can use it to come up with possible suspects. At least, Charles thinks he's safe with Jake gone; that was smart of the Agency not to put another one of our men in his gang or on his tail. For now, he's lulled and cocky."

"That other trouble he mentioned concerning Blue and Grady, do you think it was about Papa and Steven?"

"Could be. He had on gloves so I couldn't see if he had X's on his hands. After I get him, I'll check for you."

"I want to help, not sit in camp every time you challenge them."

"You can help soon, I promise. I'm skilled at what I'm doing at this point; you aren't."

"I never will be if you don't take me along and teach me."

"I can't let you get that close until I train you to be as quiet as a shadow and as invisible as air. There's no time for learning and practicing here. Before we cross the border, I can't watch after you, do what I must, and cover both our tracks. If you tagged along, you'd endanger our mission and our lives. After the dog, Evan, and Blue are gone, they'll be wary and on alert for a while. That's when we hang back, rest, and I train you. His load to Diaz will head straight for Chihuahua. We'll have to be extra careful those men don't ride up on us when they head to join up with Charles again. Our easiest and safest terrain is west of them, and that'll put us right in those boys' path to the Carmen. Charles is crazy, but he isn't a fool. I'd bet my best boots he had campsites scouted for available water and grass and ready defense. He probably knows just when and where to watch for trouble."

"So, you do all the work and take all the chances while I simply keep you company?"

"For the time being, yep. Later, you'll do the same as me. Before that day comes, woman, I want you trained to handle anything that comes up."

Beth smiled as she accepted his strategy. "I'll work hard and I won't disappoint you."

"Just bear with me a while and obey every order."

"You don't have to worry so much about me; I'm not stupid or rash."

"I *do* have to worry about you, partner; Charles has a bad itch for you. As soon as his journey's over, he's planning to get rid of your husband and take you as his wife."

Beth noticed a cold glint in his hazel eyes and a razor edge to his tone. Even so, she murmured, "You're teasing me, right?"

"I'm serious. Matt, Jessie, and the children are in danger, too."

Beth was horrified as she listened to that part of his report. "I didn't mean to entice him to such ideas."

"It's never safe to make any man a tempting offer, then withdraw it."

She couldn't tell whether he was scolding or cautioning her. "Even in the line of duty, Agent Breed?"

He removed the bandana, ran fingers through his hair, and put on his hat. Charles's vile craving for her and threat to Jessica, Lane, Matt, and friends provoked an unfamiliar fury and panic—and hatred?—that could cloud his judgment and wits if he didn't control them. He had wanted to jump over that rock to tear out the beast's deadly claws and fangs. For a minute, he had thought, *The mission be damned! I'll kill you to make sure you never harm any of them!* And the first person who'd come to mind to protect was Beth Breed. *Beth Wind,* his distraught mind corrected.

In his unsettled state, he muttered, "Everybody does reckless things in the name of duty to ourselves, or others, or good causes. I'm no different. I can't chance messing up the assignment. Maybe sometimes we do have to choose between arresting a criminal and taking justice into our own hands so he can't do worse. If a man lacks honor and integrity and loyalty, he's worthless. Guess it comes down to when and where we draw the line between 'em."

Or the reason for needing to draw a divisive mark. So, she mused, it wasn't jealousy concerning his or Charles's feelings for her that had Navarro riled and alarmed, and he was calling her "Beth Breed" only by habit. "We'll make certain he doesn't get near any of the Cordells."

"Not even if I have to kill every one of them barehanded."

How I wish you could feel such love and loyalty to me, Navarro.

The couple traveled east of mountains and hills that screened their presence in a region that was too barren and dry to traverse in the open without exposing themselves. The caravan threw up dust clouds that were seen from far away, and the two agents avoided doing the same thing with their path.

From the old and rocky road the villains were using, Navarro knew where they'd be crossing the Rio Grande. Without heavy burdens to slow their pace, they reached the river long before their target. They rested, ate, and cooled off in the bluish green water where ample trees, rocks, and thick vegetation would keep them from being seen by foes.

"You stay put while I check out our snakes. But keep alert and ready to ride; I showed you places you can lose them."

"How do you know they'll stop here or any will leave the others?"

"It'll be eating, resting, and watering time. Since Evan's gone and Blue's their best scout, he'll come to study the area for signs of danger."

"Heavens, you're so intelligent and cunning. After this mission is over and we part, I hope I remember everything I'm learning from you. Thanks for not getting irritated when I ask so many questions."

"Keep asking and learning, Beth, and I'll do my part to help. I want you to come out of this alive and unharmed. Yep, just as I figured," he murmured from behind his fieldglasses. "Real nice of Charles to send Blue and a friend ahead to study the terrain. This'll be quicker and easier than plucking fruit off a prickly pear." He handed Beth the fieldglasses. "No reflections with these. I'll be back later." He gave her a quick kiss on the lips and hurried off to confront peril alone.

Beth packed the fieldglasses with her things, though she was tempted to observe him through them. She resaddled Sunshine and loaded her gear to be prepared to escape if trouble came calling. Navarro's things were concealed in bushes, as he rode bareback and took only his Indian weapons.

Navarro positioned and readied himself amongst jutting boulders that seemed to be tossed from sky to earth in a haphazard manner. Ranges of several mountains enclosed the area and prevented any long-distance spying by the wagon train heading in the direction where crossing would be easy. Floral scents from tamerisk, mesquite, willow, and wildflowers drifted into his nose, as did the odor of dried dirt. Since he was wearing moccasins instead of telltale boots, he didn't have to worry about disturbing moss and lichen that grew on rocks. He had covered his black stallion's hooves with thick cloths to imply an unshod animal was used when tracks were found later. To protect his hands and face from painful pricks, he made sure he didn't get too close to dagger plants, cholla, or ocotilla. He was on guard for real snakes, in particular the rattler who frequented this rugged area. He also was careful not to walk into dozing or foraging javelinas, as their noises and movement would attract unwanted attention. As he waited, a few animals came to drink from the river but most were avoiding the noon heat.

The two targets came into sight, dismounted near the bank, and studied the ground. They walked in opposite directions as they continued their search to unearth any problems. When the stranger reached Navarro's hiding spot, the agent jumped him from behind and slid his knife across the villain's throat. He shoved the body into a gully and waited for the second one to approach. When Blue called to his companion, Navarro made muffled sounds and groans as if an accident had occurred.

Blue grumbled, scowled, and stalked toward him. "Where are you?"

Navarro leapt off the rock and onto Blue's back. Before the man could react, the agent's right hand side-pinned Blue's gun arm so he couldn't draw a weapon to defend himself or fire a warning shot in the air. His left arm came over Blue's shoulder with speed and he drove the blade into the evil man's heart with force. He flung the body to the ground, flipped it over, and yanked off Blue's riding gloves to check his hands.

Navarro removed from the two bodies any possessions that might tempt a thief, then he fired an arrow into Blue's stomach. Afterward, he broke off the shaft and tossed it aside as if Blue had done so before engaging in a lethal battle. The lawman scuffed up the ground to indicate a fierce struggle. He hurried to the men's horses at the river and whistled for his stallion, who responded without delay to his beloved master's summons.

Navarro stroked Night Cloud's neck, and the animal nuzzled his owner's hand. "Run 'em downriver, Night Cloud, and stay." He slapped the two sorrels on their rears and his stallion chased them through the water away from the site. He concealed anything he didn't want found and finished setting up the scene to mislead Charles and his hirelings.

When the group arrived to find no one around, Jim Tiller took several men and scouted the area. After the bodies were discovered, a warning was rushed to Charles, who joined them in the rocks.

"What happened, Jim?"

"Looks like they spooked some Injun. One set of moccasin prints and one unshod horse. Robbed 'em and took off downriver with their horses. Probably long gone, dry as this blood is. Want some boys to go after him?"

"No, let's take a break and move on. If he's got friends nearby, he could be going after them. Keep the boys close to the wagons and on alert. Just make sure that redskin don't follow us; himself or with a band. We don't want to lose any more men."

Navarro didn't leave until after the wagon train crossed the river and was rolling onward toward their next campsite. Knowing the caravan's noise would cover any he made, he whistled for Night Cloud. The stallion responded within minutes, splashing water as he raced toward his master.

Beth sat in the shade of a cottonwood that did little cooling in the midday heat. Perspiration rolled down her back and between her breasts under the buckskin garments. Moisture beaded on her face for only a moment before the thirsty air drank it. Her brain felt as if it were being roasted in an oven. She dared not remove her hat and allow fiery hair to show; that color would be visible for a long way against the dull shades and greens of this region. She hated to imagine what it was going to be like to ride deeper into the Chihuahuan Desert. She knew she needed to be careful of being lulled into dazed wits or attacked by dehydration.

Navarro's return elated her. She smiled and hugged him before questioning him.

He related his successful actions and reminded her they'd hang back for a while. "I'll hide the gifts we got at the ranch in those clefts over there and cover 'em with brush. I'll fetch 'em after we finish this assignment."

As they rested in shade, Navarro began a reluctant topic: his ghostly rival for the redhead's love. "Blue was the man who killed Steven, maybe your father, too. He had those knife scars you mentioned, two X's right where you said they'd be, between the thumb and first finger on his left hand. You've got your justice and revenge, Beth. Those marks tie the two cases together just as Dan suspected they would. Charles is out three men and that guard dog, but he still has twenty-three mean *hombres.*"

Beth let it all settle in a moment. "Justice and revenge." Navarro had gotten them for her. That link to her past was over. Unless . . . No, she reasoned, Navarro wouldn't lie just to take her mind off of searching for her family's killer. "Thanks. I . . . I have to be alone for a while. I'll be back soon."

"Watch out for snakes and such."

"I will," she tossed over her shoulder.

Beth reached a private spot and leaned against a slanted boulder. Even with a hat pulled down to her brows, her eyes squinted in the brilliant light. Her heart raced as a whirlwind of thoughts and feelings assailed mind and body. Unbidden tears stung her heat-dried eyes and threatened to flood down her cheeks.

Rest in peace, Papa, Steven; you've been avenged. Now, I have to get on with my life without you two. If only . . .

Navarro watched Beth almost lose the battle not to cry, weep over the husband she had loved and lost, *still* loved, it appeared to him. He knew from his tormenting experience with Jessie, no one could force a lost and lingering love from another's heart and mind. Until she released herself from an emotional prison, new love couldn't bloom and flourish. Since he wanted to win her, he must have patience while she freed herself.

Navarro pondered the talk they'd had at the ranch. He'd alleged he had nothing to offer except friendship and desire; that was no longer true. His warning was foolish, and perhaps had damaged any budding feelings for him. He wished he could erase what he'd said. To expose his love now was just as reckless; it was too soon after his "break" with Jessie for Beth to believe such a claim, and Beth wasn't ready to hear it or to respond to it. He sneaked away to allow her privacy to master her anguish.

They camped that night on the Rio San Antonio in Mexico, miles northeast of Charles's chosen site. Until darkness engulfed the land, Navarro used a tall peak for spying on their enemies to make sure no one was sent back to check their flank. They ate cured ham in biscuits and dried fruit furnished by Jessica and sipped tepid water.

Shortly before all light was lost and he was assured of safety, Navarro allowed Beth to strip and bathe in the river. After she finished and while she stood guard, he did the same. Soon, blackness encompassed them because a quarter moon rode so close to the sun's coattail. That situation prevented her from seeing his face, which was stubbled with five o'clock shadow. "We can't see a thing coming at us without a campfire for light."

"That's good since I look a mess," he joked. "I won't cut my hair or shave while we're on the trail; it'll help disguise me when I go into a village or town, in case any of Charles's men head in for some reason. They'd be sure to recognize me without a beard and mustache. You, woman, there's no way we could hide your beauty and identity. You aren't afraid of the dark, are you?" he teased across the scant space separating them.

"No, are you?" she quipped.

"Nope. Good thing we aren't because we can't risk a fire or snuggling. I hope you don't have any visitors again like you did that night on the trail." He knew he didn't have to clarify which seductive night he meant.

Beth clutched the ebony wolf carving in her hand. They couldn't chance any contact that could distract them, but she wished he would wrap his arm around her and let her sit next to him. She wasn't frightened; still she craved his touch and solace. They hadn't talked much today. At least the sun's demanding heat was gone and cool desert air wafted over her. Crickets and frogs nearby didn't seem troubled or silenced by the impenetrable darkness. She sniffed with delight the night-blooming cactus that perfumed the area. The horses had grazed and drunk and were quiet except for their breathing. That's all she heard from her partner, his steady breathing.

Two wagons—one schooner and one freight hauler—kept heading west for Chihuahua and a rendezvous with Diaz's soldiers. Four men on horses rode with them as escorts. The other eight wagons and hirelings turned northwestward toward the Arizona border as Navarro had overheard.

They journeyed all day through the hilly and mountainous section. After their leaders halted for the night, Navarro guided Beth onward a few miles to camp on the Rio Conchos. He wanted privacy to teach her more self-defense and knife tactics, and did so until light began to fail them beneath the quarter moon. Dusty and sweaty from practice, each stood guard while the other stripped and washed.

"Few things feel better than a bath under these conditions," Navarro observed. "Besides, I enjoy the view when it's your turn."

"You don't even steal a peek at me, Navarro Breed, and you know it."

"Are you sure?" he jested with a roguish grin.

"With your skills, I would never argue with certainty against you."

"Wouldn't it be nice if we could scrub each other?"

"Sheer heaven, but far too distracting and perilous. Maybe later."

"That's one promise I'll be sure to remember and collect."

"Did I make a promise?"

"You implied one; that's the same thing. And don't go withdrawing it."

"I won't. And if you forget, I'll remind you of your vow in return."

Vow . . . Wedding vows . . . He wished theirs were true.

So did Beth as she settled on her bedroll to search for sleep.

They journeyed through the Sierra de la Tasajera region with its mixture of high and low topography. On occasion at a distance in a valley, they saw small villages where peasants labored with crops or sheep. On a section of grassland, they noticed two ranches where *vaqueros* wrangled cattle and horses on nice spreads with watermills and large *haciendas*. West of their location was the Sierra Madre Occidental, one of Mexico's two *cordilleras,* a mountain range that Geronimo favored when he fled America for rest and regrouping. The landscape was much like what they had left behind in their country: dry, rugged, and wildly beautiful. Vegetation was much the same, too—cactus, agave, mesquite, scrub brush, and cassava. But added to the familiar wildlife were pumas and wolves, two creatures almost nonexistent across the border.

Teaching her some Spanish along the way, Navarro told her the territory was called *tierra caliente,* meaning "hot land."

When they set up camp on a stream miles from their targets, Navarro thought it was safe enough for bow and arrow practice. "This canyon won't let our sounds go beyond its walls. We might need to use these weapons if things change between here and the border. You said you'd used them but you're rusty. Let's get you all clean and shiny again."

* * *

An hour later, Navarro said, "You're good with that bow, woman."

"In a pinch, I'd do all right as backup. But you, total accuracy."

"What I taught you helped; all you need is a little more practice. You learn fast, Agent Wind. You're getting as good on the trail as I am."

"Only because of all you've shown me and told me. I wish . . ."

"You wish what?"

"I wish Papa and Steven had possessed skills like yours so they'd still be alive. Or if I'd had them back then, I could have saved—"

"No, Beth, you couldn't have. No man, not even me, could escape an ambush with odds like they rode into. If you'd gotten there sooner, you would have prayed for death before men like Blue and his friends finished with you. Never blame yourself for not being there."

Like you don't blame yourself for not being there when Jessica learned she was pregnant and needed you? It was mean and wrong to assuage one's guilt and anguish at another's expense, so Beth refused to let that cruel and rude retort leave her quivering lips. "I'll try. If I forgot to thank you for dealing with their murderer, I'll do it now; thanks, Navarro."

"You don't need words; you say it with actions and expressions. Now, if you want to get that dust and sweat off, best do it before dark."

"I think Sunshine would love a soothing splash, too. If the stream's deep enough, I'll give her a rub in it."

Beth guided her palomino to the water where rocks and trees shielded them from sight, but not by intention.

Back at camp, Navarro was too engrossed in fantasies of Beth to realize peril was about to strike . . .

Chapter Nineteen

Beth finished currying Sunshine and tethered the palomino nearby to graze until she could take a bath. Her soap was missing; she assumed she must have dropped it earlier and began to retrace her steps to find it. She didn't get far before she saw one of Charles Cordell's hirelings spying on their camp where her lover sat in deep thought with his back to the villain. It appeared a preoccupied Navarro was oblivious to the peril.

With haste, Beth concealed herself and scanned the surroundings for other foes; she saw and heard no one, and was relieved. She reasoned on the hazard and a course of action; the villain could either ambush and kill Navarro or leave to bring more threats to challenge them. The sandy-haired man hadn't drawn his pistol but she surmised he could in a flash. It was up to her to disarm the enemy, as any attempt to warn Navarro would alert and panic the gunman.

The agent's recent instructions flooded her mind: "Don't step on rocks, twigs, or leaves; and don't drag your feet. If you're not wearing moccasins, take off your boots or shoes and go barefoot. Even if you step on a cactus or jagged stone, ignore the pain and never yell. Keep the sun or moon in your face so you won't cast a shadow. Keep the wind blowing into it so he doesn't catch your scent. Hide anything that might grab attention, like that flaming hair and pale skin; you can smear dirt or mud on your face and hands, and cover your head with a cloth. Control your breathing and keep it dead silent. Remove anything that makes noise, even a squeaky holster or belt. Don't let your thighs rub together or let your arms graze your ribs; that makes more noise than you realize. Try to take him from behind. Movement is harder to mask coming at him from the front or side. Take quick glances at the ground to plan your next step. Advance slow and easy; if you rush, you'll be sighted or you'll make a mistake. Choose a silent weapon you're skilled at using. Keep yourself loose; if you hold tight, you can't move fast or react quick enough to trouble. Always be aware of the closest available cover in case it's needed for hiding or protection. Be ready to act in the blink of an eye; sometimes, that's all you have between life and death. If you're soft-hearted and strike too light and gentle, you won't take him down or you'll only wound him; he'll come to and kill you. Don't get many opportunities for second chances. If you're cutting down odds, make the attack appear a selfmade accident or blame it on somebody who'll take suspicion off you."

Beth eyed the problem once more as she reviewed Navarro's tips. She wasn't wearing anything that would create noise. A breeze blew into her face, and what light was left from a setting sun danced on hot cheeks. Since the fiend was between her and camp, there was no difficulty in gaining a rear approach. Her pistol, derringer, and knife were on the stream's bank where she'd removed them for a bath. Only the blade was safe to use as a silent weapon, but there wasn't time to retrieve it. She selected a rock that was the right size and weight to avoid a strain on her shaky hand. Her gaze examined surroundings for possible cover if needed. Hardest to obtain was quiet breathing as her heart pounded and pulse raced. She wanted to flex her body to release its tautness but that would be unwise.

Beth began a slow, wary approach. The only time she took her eyes off her target was long enough to glance at the ground for objects to avoid. She crept closer and closer to the culprit. She realized from the way he shifted, he was about to check his security. She slipped behind bushes and peered through foliage without disturbing leaves as he first looked to his right rear and then to his left.

As he did so, the remainder of Navarro's instructions came to mind: "If it's quiet, you have to be extra careful because any sound is picked up by your target. Even if there's noise, don't be fooled into thinking it'll cover any you make because a skilled man shuts out the normal like he shuts his eyes, but his ears are still open and he hears what's unusual. Don't know what kind of rules you and Steven had, but me and my partners, when I use one, have a main rule that can't be broken: if the partner goes down and you can't get to him safely, he's left behind to use his wits to escape or to face his fate. No rescue, no matter who's involved, is allowed to endanger your life or the mission. It's loco to let futile heroics get you killed. Never confuse courage with rash daring. Never let guilt or pride sway your judgment or cloud your wits."

Beth recalled she'd promised to obey those orders. But, she mused, could she desert her lover if he got wounded or pinned down? Could she gallop off and leave him to endure Charles's evil? She didn't have to worry about guilt or pride or conceit swaying her, but love might if she wasn't careful. She observed the cur nearby as he completed his search for peril. Satisfied he was safe, as there was only one horse in camp to match the one man in sight, he resumed spying.

Beth was relieved he wasn't in a rush to attack her unsuspecting lover, or to go for help or to fire a warning shot in the air before they could escape. She was glad Sunshine's saddle was obscured by rocks and that the palomino remained quiet at the stream. She prayed those observations stayed the same so she could reach and disable the villain. She proceeded to stalk him with caution. Within a few feet of her prey, his hand started to inch toward his pistol. Beth ordered herself not to panic, but did increase her pace.

The trembling redhead lifted the rock and struck the miscreant's temple with enough impact to cease his threat temporarily. After the villian was questioned, Navarro could get rid of the blackguard. She could slay in self-defense, but ambushing in the back left a bad taste in her mouth and was a last resort.

The strange sounds caught Navarro's attention. Within seconds, the ex-gunslinger was on his feet and facing that direction with pistols at the ready. He saw Beth standing behind a low boulder with only her head and the top of her shoulders in view. He noticed she was staring at the ground and standing motionless. Her expression and behavior told him to join her in a hurry.

Navarro took in the facts within moments. His hazel gaze journeyed up the redhead's taut body and focused on her face. He knew the flush there was a result of more than desert sun and heat. Her green eyes were nailed to the downed man with bloody temple. The crimson-splotched rock was held in a tight grip at her right thigh. Her breathing was quiet and rhythmic. For a few minutes, he ignored his lover to scan the area.

Beth looked up at him. "He's the only one I saw or heard when I went searching for my lost soap. I couldn't warn you without giving away my presence. Perhaps you should teach me a bird or animal sound to use as a signal to get your attention the next time there's trouble."

There won't be a next time; shouldn't have been one today. "You saved my life, Beth; thanks."

"You'd do the same for me. What now? His cohorts are bound to come looking for him when he doesn't return soon. How do we make this appear an accident? Or whom do we frame for it before we take off? I assume we can't stay here and certainly we can't leave him alive."

To see how much she'd learned from him or past experiences, he asked in a pleasant tone, "Got any clever ideas?"

Beth pondered the situation, then suggested, "What if he tripped and fell, or something spooked his horse and he was thrown, struck his head on a rock in the stream, landed facedown, and drowned?"

Impressed with her wits, Navarro smiled. "Perfect."

"He isn't dead. At first, I thought you might want to question him; then, I realized he wouldn't regain consciousness before we have to get out of here. Will you— Never mind, I'll handle it. I shouldn't have left him alive."

"You chose your weapon and action right. To make it look convincing, let the water finish him off when I place him facedown. You saddle our horses and pack our gear while I handle this sneak. Use the stream to ride northwest. We'll camp over that ridge."

Beth's gaze followed the direction in which his finger pointed.

"I'll cover our tracks and catch up. Should be just enough light left for us to do our tasks. Give me that rock to use at the stream so I won't have to make another one." He eased it from her grasp. "See you in a while."

Beth settled herself on the bedroll to relax. She looked at Navarro as he sipped water from his canteen. "Do you think Charles suspects he's being tailed and he ordered scouts to look around?"

"Our spy probably wanted a breather, so he took a ride in the wrong direction and stumbled on to us by accident. Actually, stumbled on to me. Good thing you were out of camp and you lost that soap and caught him snooping. Guess you're disappointed in your legendary lawman?"

"If you were perfect, Navarro, you wouldn't be human. And if you never require backup or assistance, I'm unnecessary baggage and may as well go home. I really needed something to boost my confidence and justify my presence, prove I'm a valuable part of this mission. I also needed it to practice and test my new training, and your lessons worked. In a way, saving my new partner's life makes up for being unable to save my old one's. Please don't be embarrassed or irritated with yourself, or begrudge me a small amount of glory and reassurance. Isn't it worth a smidgen of hurt pride to let me feel worthwhile?"

"You're right. But in the other saddlebag, I wouldn't be human if I weren't concerned and riled over making a stupid and dangerous mistake. You did good, woman; better than good. I'm proud of you, Beth

Breed. Never doubt you're valuable or needed by me and this mission."

He watched her glow with joy and relief. "Don't worry about stepping on my pride; even if you do, you aren't heavy. Besides, I'd rather be a live fool than a dead hero. Just so I'm not one too often and tarnish my golden image too much in your pretty eyes," he added as if jesting and chuckled to insinuate he was. "Let's bed down. We're safe now. I promise I won't shed my guard skin again."

"I know. Rest assured, Agent Breed, I trust you and have no fear for my safety. Your image couldn't be shinier, and making a tiny error once in a while prevents perfection from making me feel intimidated and insecure."

Sunday evening, the couple camped in a secluded canyon that would be difficult for others to find but only a few miles from the wagon train. After unloading their possessions, Navarro filled their canteens and watered the horses at Rio Torreno. Before eating a cold and dry meal, he backtracked and brushed away any signs of them. From a high peak, he observed the gunrunners until ominous clouds drifted overhead and revealed a storm was impending. He witnessed the villains' hurried preparations for bad weather, and halted his task to do the same.

"If I were you, Beth, I wouldn't use my bedroll. Once they get soaked, it takes a mighty long time to dry. If it sours, it smells and itches until it gets a good washing. I'll wrap the weapons and food in our slickers and tie 'em snug. We can't wear 'em tonight. If the wind whips up and pops 'em, they'll make noise that'll carry too far. Same reason we can't make a cover with 'em. Can't chop brush to make a *ramada,* either. We're gonna get drenched and chilled, so be prepared to snuggle for warmth. No fire again."

Navarro glanced at his partner who appeared to be taking the bad news in stride. "You may want to tend any business before that rain comes. When she does, she'll be fast and hard and biting."

Beth smiled and said, "Thanks. I'll return in a minute."

Navarro scowled when he almost started whistling. *Shu,* that woman had a way of making him feel good from head to foot! Not once did she take offense to his suggestions, requests, reprimands, or orders. Not once had she complained about hardships or white-hot heat or slowed their pace or been frightened of dangers. Not once had she shirked her duty or been a nuisance or burden or been reckless. And, not once had she tried to entice him or tempt him into seducing her. On the trail, she was a professional, a total delight, a rare . . . treasure.

He grinned as he recalled teasing her about that word for a special woman; her response that day couldn't have been truer. She was a rare and exquisite prize, one he wanted to earn and keep forever.

"What's so amusing?" Beth asked in a cheerful tone.

"That was a happy smile, not a humorous one. I was just thinking about what a perfect partner you've been and what a good team we've made."

"Shocked and relieved, eh? I tried to tell you in Tucson I wasn't as troublesome and unskilled as you imagined and feared. I admit this is the toughest trail I've ridden to date, but it's been educational. Even been fun at times. Make that, lots of times."

His gaze softened and smile widened. "Much as I dislike being in error about anything or anybody, I'm glad I was wrong about you; that should teach me not to make snap judgments before I pocket all the facts. I hate to imagine what kind of mess me and this mission would be in if it was another woman standing here instead of you."

Beth was pleasured by his sincere compliments, and warmed by his caressing gaze and husky tone. "Thanks for giving me the opportunities to prove and improve myself. Your respect and friendship mean a great deal to me, Navarro."

"Yours mean a lot to me, Beth, more than you realize. I haven't gotten this close to many people, partner, and it feels good with you. I doubt you know how much I care about you and our friendship."

Beth threw caution to the wind for a minute to hug and kiss him.

As their lips parted and he embraced her another time, he drew a deep and ragged breath. "This is your only flaw, Beth."

She leaned back and gazed into his face. "What is?"

"Being too tempting at the wrong time and place. On second thought, that's *my* weakness instead of yours. Best I recall, you haven't tried to distract me a single time with your many charms. I can't fault you for being irresistible, only myself for not having stronger willpower. It wouldn't take much to persuade me to shuck these clothes and—" He went silent and stiffened as a noise caught his attention. He glanced toward bushes and gave a soft chuckle. "Just an armadillo foraging." His gaze roved her face as he asked in a roguish manner, "Where was I?"

"You were about to order me to control a hazardous situation."

"Read my mind, eh?" He glanced upward and observed, "It's raining. Thank goodness, because I need cooling off, pronto."

"Likewise." As he prepared for bad weather, her mind shouted, *Mercy, what I'd give to hear you say you love me! At least your opinion of me improves every day. And your desire and affection seem to be increasing. But I must remember not to press you too hard and rapidly. I don't want you to panic, whirl, and gallop in the other direction. I need you to keep riding toward me, away from Jessica.*

"We'd best get settled before the downpour starts."

They sat on a blanket he'd placed near rocks. The palomino was tethered near the black stallion who kept her calm and still as they grazed and ignored the brewing storm. Within minutes, they were all soaked, as huge and swift drops pelted them. They nestled together with only hats and buckskins for protection against the often stinging rain.

If not for the warmth of Navarro's body, Beth knew she would be shivering. Her face lay on his chest and she listened to the steady beating of his heart, and yearned to own it. He rested his chin atop her head and held her in a tender embrace she savored. Water dripped off his face and tickled her nose. An otter swimming in a pond was drier than they were, but she didn't care. Being with him was sheer heaven.

Navarro felt serene and elated with Beth willingly in his arms. He wanted to be more than a partner and friend to her, more than comfort for a lost husband. He wanted to fill more than temporary needs; he yearned to fill every one she had. He wanted the place in her heart and life that Steven Wind had possessed.

The ex-desperado feared that a man who had been born and reared and lived as he had would not be a choice she'd make for a second husband. Beth probably wanted an easygoing, even-tempered, untainted, pure-blooded man—as Jessie had selected in Mathew Cordell. He was convinced Beth desired and liked him, but could she love him, love him enough to marry him? He wasn't ready to seek that truth, in case the answer was no and asking it frightened her away from him. He had promised not to make demands of her if the "miracle" of love occurred, if she was serious about preventing it. He must glean that fact before he broke his vow and acted with unwise haste.

The storm's fury increased. Bushes were yanked to and fro. Grass was whipped about by forceful gusts. Water raced down rocks. In some places, it formed rivulets and moved like tiny streams. Thunder pealed and boomed overhead and lightning zigzagged across the darkened sky.

As Beth cuddled closer and tightened her arms around his waist, he asked, "Storms make you nervous, love?"

"No. In fact, I enjoy them. But not particularly outside," she added.

"Sorry I couldn't get us to cover. If I hadn't spent time this morning and during breaks teaching you those Indian trail signs, we could have—"

Beth raised her head and lifted her fingers to his lips. "Don't worry about me; I'm fine. We're getting closer to where the Indians hide out, so it's important I know those signs, especially since you'll be away soon."

Navarro's hand grasped hers. He kissed and nibbled on her fingers. He watched rain drip from her hair and lashes. He saw drops roll down her face, and his mouth also demanded to be that close to her. He kissed her eyes, her nose, and cheeks. His mouth captured hers and let their tongues dance to a heady beat. He longed to make her his in more than a physical way.

Navarro shielded her face with his as he gazed into her eyes. "Do you know how deep you get to me, Beth Breed? How much I want you?"

"I know how much I want you here and now."

"None of our targets will leave camp in this weather, so if you're willing—" He went silent as she wiggled from his arms and stood. His heart thudded in dread of her recoiling from his weakness. Before he could apologize for losing his head while on duty and for trying to coax her to surrender, she extended a hand to him. He stared at it a moment, took it, and came to his feet in confusion. Until she began to lift his shirt to remove it . . .

"You sure about this?" he asked in mounting suspense and delight.

"If you are," she replied, her answer almost muffled by thunder.

"I am." *With all my heart.*

Escaped strands of hair were glued to their faces and necks. She struggled to remove the saturated garments as he did the same with his. Naked, they embraced and kissed in a near wild frenzy for each other. Her fingers roved his slick back and broad shoulders as his captured her taut buttocks and pressed her closer to him. He guided her to the soaked blanket and lay atop her as their kisses and caresses grew bolder.

Not even cool air could squeeze between them or chill their fiery desires. Her hands played in ebony hair while his buried themselves in flaming tresses. Their thirst for each other enormous, their lips met over and over in fervent rapture. His mouth trailed down her throat and captured a straining rosy brown bud. As he tantalized her, Beth sighed in contentment and growing desire.

Beth's unbridled response heightened Navarro's passion. Her ardor inspired him to hold nothing back. Love's flames engulfed him in a blazing glow. His lips and hands brought her to uncontrollable tremors of desire. She uttered moans of feverish encouragement as she became breathless and rigid with need for him.

Intoxicating sensations washed over them as did the pouring rain. The storm with its thunder, lightning, and endless drops went unnoticed because the storm of their passion was more powerful and real. Neither was bothered by inhibitions or modesty. Neither thought of anyone else.

Navarro kissed her deeply as he entered her. The mingled sounds of rain and thunder seemed to urge them onward to a faster pace. The heavens rumbled. Dazzling lights clawed across the sky. There was no time left to explore, to seek, to tease before their flash flood swept them away in powerful currents.

She arched to meet every thrust. She wanted the tormentingly sweet stimulation to continue, but she wanted delicious release more. When she murmured, "Now, my love, take me," her senses whirled in delight, as did his.

Navarro whispered in a ragged voice, "I will, *-tsíné*, I will." The lawman's heart drummed with joy when she writhed in overpowering release. He cast his control aside and joined her.

They continued to kiss and caress as their bodies calmed. With the flames of their desires extinguished, they were aware of the chilly rain beating against their naked flesh. Every so often, nature lit up the area and they could see each other for a moment. Then, near blackness returned as clouds concealed a moon that hadn't quite reached its half-luminous state.

"You're wonderful, Navarro. You continue to amaze and please me."

He was overjoyed to hear he gave her such pleasure. "How about if you hire me as your private pleasurer?"

"Think I can afford your expensive price?"

"I'll make sure you can."

"Then, you're hired until our mission's over." *Then, I want more.*

Navarro misunderstood her meaning and took her words as a gentle and kind reminder they would part after the assignment. "I accept."

Why couldn't you say you want that job for life? "While it's still raining hard enough to rinse us off, I think we should use nature's bathwater and get dressed. I have goosebumps atop goosebumps."

They let the rain shower them and they struggled into their clothes.

"Next time, my new hireling, let's do this inside or when it isn't storming. Buckskins don't like coming off or going on when they're soaked."

They resumed their earlier positions and endured the weather without complaint, as it had enticed their wanton behavior. Beth went to sleep in the warm confines of his arms; but Navarro only dozed as he planned how to keep her safe and in his life. Even if he failed to win her during this case, he resolved, he wouldn't give up. Ever.

*   *   *

Beth stirred as Navarro eased from their position at dawn to study their enemies. "Go back to sleep; it's still early and you need more rest."

Drowsy, she sank to the wet blanket in his warm spot and obeyed.

Navarro watched her for a few minutes, his heart bubbling with hope. *Take a risk with me, Beth, and we can be happy together. Don't let Steven's ghost stand between us. Don't be afraid to trust me and accept me. Allow what you feel for me to grow into something beautiful and special. I won't reject you or betray you or hurt you. I won't ask or expect you to change into someone else. I want and need you as you are for my wife.*

His hand reached out to awaken her to say those things. He drew it back and balled it into a fist. *Not yet, hombre; it's too soon to press her. Give her time and patience. Show her how you feel before you blurt it out and she thinks it's cunning talk to keep her on your bedroll. Let her see you want her, not Jessie or another woman. You've roped her with friendship and good loving; now, pull her to you slow and easy.*

Sees-Through-Clouds' words filled his head: "You not walk alone forever, Tl'ee' K'us. Woman with hair burning as flaming rocks will walk at your side. Much stands between you this moon; it blow away when you chase the wind." The old Apache saying filled it next: "Wherever the Spirit Wind blows, a brave and cunning warrior must chase it and capture it. If he does so, he will have the powers of nature in his grasp, the powers to be and to have all he desires."

Navarro smiled. Everything Daniel Withers had said about her was true. Dan did know him better than he knew himself. Because of meeting Beth, he'd stopped riding backward toward a futile past and could see what was around and ahead of him. *I owe you a big debt, old friend. She's the woman in the shaman's vision; she's my destiny. All I have to do is convince her of that fact and remove any obstacles. I'll capture you, my sweet Spirit Wind; I will.*

Following the wagons' departure, Beth donned clean bloomers and a tan shirt, vest, and riding skirt in order to continue blending in with the landscape. She went to the river to wash her underdrawers and the buckskins she'd worn for days. She secured the garments to her cantle and left her thick hair unbound to dry en route. As soon as their possessions were loaded, she followed Navarro's lead northwestward.

It didn't require long for the hot desert sun and wind from their movement to absorb the moisture in her locks and garments. Since they traveled with obscuring hills and mountains between them and Charles's group, Navarro said it was fine not to conceal her red hair this morning. When they halted for a rest and water break, she brushed those free-flowing coppery tresses and braided them into one long and thick plait. She knew her companion kept glancing her way with an odd expression on his face and a matching gleam in his eyes. Since he said nothing and she couldn't read the unfamiliar mood, it made her a little nervous.

Upon rising, he had given her a brief kiss on the cheek, a cheerful "Good morning, *amiga,*" and a roguish grin. As they ate a breakfast of dried meat and nearing stale bread, he tested her on Indian trail signs. He praised her highly for passing it with ease. She wondered if his mellow mood and tranquil expression simply indicated he was content with her as a worthy partner and an exciting lover.

At least, she mused, he didn't deceive and ensnare her with false words of love and pretense of a future together. She was convinced he cared about her, but Jessica and Lane still owned his heart and first loyalty. During their sojourn, he might let her borrow them for a while but he'd return them to his first love after the mission.

It always came back to Jessica Lane Cordell. Perhaps similarities between his past love and present partner explained why Navarro was attracted to Beth Breed; perhaps those were the reasons she appealed to him. Her troubled mind listed those matches; they had met during missions and fought a villain together; he was reluctant to take both jobs, but had reasons to relent; they had shared romance and adventures on the trail and at the ranch; both women were redheads, though Jessica's hair leaned more these days to dark chestnut; both saved his life; both had become his partner, friend, confidante, and lover; both had helped him deal with personal troubles and tangled emotions; and both had loved and wanted a future with him.

Beth couldn't decide if Navarro comprehended those facts. If so, the truth could make him even more wary of her and their relationship. If not, she shouldn't mention those similarities and worry him. If she wooed him slowly and easily, maybe she could win him. But she mustn't push too hard and fast and panic him into fleeing. She should drift closer to him to see how he responded and reacted. Then—

No, Beth, you can't! Navarro deserves more than you can give him. He deserves a home and family, a child—a son—to replace Lane. You can't give him that gift. If you truly and unselfishly love him, you must let him find a woman who can replace his loss. Enjoy him until the end of the mission, then let him go. Maybe the romance with you will teach him he can make a fresh start with another woman. Don't let him learn you love him or give him false hopes of a life with you. Make it appear the only bond between you and him is friendship and physical attraction. Never give him a reason to think you're leading him on and, afterward, you've rejected him. Never let him imagine for a moment you can replace his two losses.

It isn't possible. You know he'll want a son one day. It isn't fair to let him believe you could give him one. Even if he came to love you and said it didn't matter, some day he'd realize he was wrong and that situation could evoke resentment. You can't deny him the joy and pride of having and rearing his own child, someone to carry on his name. Don't do that to him, Beth; he's earned the right to a full life.

That afternoon, the caravan and trailing agents crossed the Juarez-Chihuahua road at different times and spots. Both parties were careful to avoid travelers on horseback, in stages, and with two-wheeled carts. So far, neither soldiers nor bandits nor renegades had troubled either group.

Between that road and Rio Carmen, the men who had left days ago to rendezvous with Diaz's troop reunited with their boss and cohorts. They had returned on horseback as the transport wagons had been left behind as hampering speed or as part of the delivery. Navarro and Beth used his fieldglasses to watch numerous canvas bags of payment and fresh supplies being hauled into a schooner. The mules that had carried those burdens were tied behind tailgates in case they were needed later.

"Those gold coins make them a tempting target, partner. What do we do if somebody attacks to steal them? Our mission will be wrecked."

"You can bet your boots the exchange was done in secret and those men made sure they weren't followed. But they're on alert for trouble, so we have to be extra careful. Let's ride ahead and make camp earlier. I want to find you the perfect hideout before I leave you behind. I also need to catch a nap before I head for Dublan to send Dan and Zack messages."

Beth looked at him from their prone positions on the elevated ground. "You aren't going to ask if I'll be all right alone?"

He locked his gaze with hers and grinned. "Nope, because I know you will. You've learned enough to do what's best and safe. I trust you to stay put after dark and to hang back tomorrow. Follow the route I showed you and make camp; I should join you before dark."

"What if you run into trouble in Dublan? Or you're delayed?"

"I'll be in and out before any of Cordell's hirelings can reach there by getting a good jump on them now."

"I meant, what about other kinds of trouble?"

"I'll avoid any, so don't worry."

"You know I will until I see this handsome face again," she jested.

"And I will, too, until I see this beautiful one of yours. Promise you won't . . ."

"I won't what?" When he shifted in uneasiness, she smiled and hinted, "Get too close to Charlie boy and tempt him to snatch me away from my protective and possessive partner?"

"Don't force me to break my own partnership rule by having to gallop into his camp to rescue you."

"I'll obey your orders just so you won't have to risk your neck for me."

"I'm serious, Beth."

"I promise I won't budge from where you hide me. If trouble comes snooping around again, I'll use all you've taught me to escape. But if I'm captured, don't you dare risk your life or our mission by doing something reckless. Trust me to find a way to talk myself into release or I'll escape the first chance I get. Swear it, Agent Breed."

"No, because I'd be lying to you."

"If you don't swear it and mean it, neither will I."

"That's different."

"How so, when you say I'm almost as well trained as you are? The rules apply to both of us or to neither of us."

He studied the stubborn set of her chin and mouth and the resolve in her gaze, then scowled. "All right, it's a deal."

You're duping me. I can detect it in your voice and eyes and that hair-mussing habit of yours. "You swear on your life and honor? Cross your heart?"

He frowned and exhaled loudly. "You win this time. But you'll have only three days to escape any trap before I come after you. *Comprende?*"

"*Sí, amigo,* I understand. You can look for me after three suns, too."

He didn't want to point out he wouldn't be alive that long if he was captured but that she would. Thoughts of what Charles could do to her scared him, and he didn't taste fear often. He had given the impending separation intense deliberation and reasoned she was safer in camp alone than going with him where she would attract too much attention and interest from any low-bellies hanging or hiding out there. Much as he hated to leave her alone, he had no other choice; the mission and his duty insisted on it; peace demanded it. Besides, *Agent* Wind would not let him shirk his responsibilities and disobey orders for personal reasons.

Navarro observed their target a few more minutes, then said, "Let's mount up and ride, woman."

As Beth followed his almost gruff command, she was relieved he didn't make her swear on a lie, because it would be one. She had no doubt Navarro wouldn't survive Charles's evil for more than a day or a night. She had to obey his orders to avoid putting him at risk with worrying or fighting.

They rode for two hours through valleys between summits that loomed in all directions and concealed their presence. Some pinnacles had razorback ridges which reminded her of pictures she had seen of prehistoric animals. They skirted furry-looking cholla, prickly pear clusters, multi-branched ocotilla, other cacti, and a variety of scrub brush. Intermingled at times were vivid yellow and hot pink wildflowers.

As they neared a sierra chain with craggy spires and steep cliffs amidst tall mountains, the landscape became greener and lusher, indicating, Beth assumed, either a recent rain or nearby water in this area. Short trees were ample, and sections of the region were adorned with orangish-gold poppies. Beth was amazed by how fast the terrain could alter its face and features at certain locations. The desert was harsh and demanding but it gave beauty to those who noticed it.

Navarro pointed upward to a verdant slope. "That's where I'm hiding you as soon as the horses are watered."

"Where?" she questioned.

He pointed again. "Where the vegetation is greenest and thickest."

"With trees and bushes growing along water lines?"

"Yep. Learn that life-saving clue from Steven?" She nodded. "Usually there's a stream or seep near such spots, especially after a rain."

"With the ground so dry, how can you tell it also rained here?"

"See those ocotillas and *amapolas?*" She nodded again. "Only time they have leaves or flower that much is after a rain."

"You know about everything," she complimented him.

"Thanks, but I'm not perfect. Remember?"

She smiled and shook her head. "Forget a rare mistake, partner."

"Can't, 'cause it's rare ones that get me into trouble."

I hope you aren't implying you're afraid I'll be a problem when parting time arrives. "If you're going to have time for a nap and rest, lead on."

Guess that means hush up, hombre.

The horses were tended and they trekked up the gradual incline. At the top, he guided her around boulders, piles of fallen rock, and towering formations until he found a small clearing he liked, and dismounted.

Beth glanced at nature's magnificent display surrounding them. Some brought to mind enormous tree trunks with exposed roots and rough bark. Others favored gigantic candles with melted wax that formed rippling patterns on their sides and at their bases. Weeds, grass, wildflowers, and cacti seemingly sprouted from spaces between rocks or crevices in them. She climbed a boulder and peered through a narrow opening. From that lofty height, she could see for miles across a splendid setting. She looked at Navarro as he approached her. "It's so beautiful here."

"Come down before you fall. No climbing while I'm gone. Can't risk a broken leg or arm or busted skull."

She laughed and teased, "Have you forgotten I was a tomboy and could best my brother Robert and his friends at such games as this?"

"You never took a spill from a horse or fence? From a rock or tree?"

"Exposed," she quipped. "I get your point, boss. I'm coming down."

"Let me help so you won't slip."

Beth stared at the hands uplifted to her. Contact with those arms, fingers, and body would be arousing. If their gazes meshed en route, it would be a perilous temptation. If he kissed her, she would melt like ice in the desert heat. "I can make it, but thanks, partner."

Navarro noticed her strange expression and her hesitation. For some reason, she didn't want to touch him or have him touch her . . . He stepped backward to give her room to descend in safety. After she did, she headed for where he had unloaded their possessions. He went to join her.

"You want to nap or eat first? I'll be mouse quiet while you do."

"I'm not hungry or sleepy, so I'll rest a while and head out. That'll give me more light for riding. After I leave and cover our tracks, stay put until morning. No fire and no noise. Got the travel directions clear?"

"They're as clear as today's sky. I'll be good, partner."

"If you are, I'll bring you a surprise."

"What?"

Her radiant smile and sunny exuberance warned him. Maybe he'd misunderstood her look and mood. "If I tell you, it won't be a surprise."

"If you tell me, I'll have a better incentive to behave myself."

"All right then, I'll tell you."

Beth waited in anticipation for his news . . .

Chapter Twenty

Beth stood on the boulder again and watched her partner conceal their tracks on the slope and from the stream. She flattened herself against the formation to her right as he suddenly twisted in his saddle and scanned the crack with his fieldglasses; her movement was too swift to reveal her eyes spying on him.

She remained where she was for a while, then climbed down without taking another peek; she suddenly realized the setting sun must have her hair shining like a blazing fire and not only Navarro but foes might be able to spy her in the cleft.

She strolled the clearing as she reflected on his parting words. Hot and fresh food would be a wonderful "surprise," but it wasn't the one she wanted.

Tears filled her eyes and rolled down her cheeks as anguish, like a hungry beast, bit off hunks of her heart and chewed them in leisure. "Oh, Jessica, how lucky you are to have won the love of two good men who would do anything for you." Beth wiped away the moisture that stung her sun- and wind-blistered skin. "You have Navarro's love and his son, and I can't hate you or resent you for those treasures. I have to settle for the only part I can have of him for a while longer."

Yet, Beth realized how swift that awful day was approaching. Within another week or two, the mission would be over and they would part. She did resent missing spending today and tomorrow with him, two precious days lost forever. She stroked her lower stomach and wished his child could take root and grow there, uniting them with a bond she craved.

Stop dreaming, Beth, it isn't going to happen, ever. It has to be your problem because Steven fathered a child but not with you. I can't let

Navarro suffer because of my cruel fate, he's endured too much torment. I can't deceive him into thinking I can replace Lane's loss, and I can't lie to him later and claim I didn't know the truth. Maybe he suspects my terrible secret and that's why he won't surrender his love. "Of course he suspects; how else could I be childless after six years of marriage?"

Beth stopped pacing and sat on a rock. *Unless he thinks it might be Steven's fault. No, he thinks it's me, so he won't be tempted to take a risk it isn't. You're just edgy because your menses is late this month. Be glad it gave you a ten-day reprieve so you and Navarro could share those stolen moments. Pray it doesn't come for the next few weeks so you can share more of them. If only its tardiness meant something else, something beautiful and wonderful; but it's come late before, and it came to naught.*

Beth ate an unappetizing meal from cans and sipped tepid water. She spread her bedroll and stretched out with a book. She tried to distract herself with reading but the attempt failed. She lay on her back and stared at the sky as day slipped into a black cloak. At last, she went to sleep.

Noise awoke her at dawn. She bolted to a sitting position and listened. She leapt to her feet and climbed the boulder to peer over the lower terrain. She sighted the trouble at the stream: a sleek cougar had charged a band of peccaries and caught one. Others were scattering in all directions. The piglike creature squealed, hissed, and thrashed until it was dead from a bite on its throat. The tawny cat half carried and half dragged its lifeless prey toward the formations left of her location.

Beth observed in dismay. If the puma's den was over there and she was infringing on its territory, she was lucky it hadn't discovered her last night and decided she or Sunshine would make a nice meal. She had been so tired in mind and body, she had slept deep and heard nothing until this morning. She decided she mustn't tell Navarro about the incident and worry him about placing her in danger.

As Beth glanced toward her palomino, she laughed softly and relaxed. *You panicked woman. Sunshine would have warned you of approaching peril. Get ready to leave in case you have to do it in a rush. If the wind shifts, that cat might come hunting again.*

She straightened her clothes and strapped on her weapons. She placed the bow and two arrows within easy reach while she ate and packed. "If you sneak over this way, my beauty," she warned in preparation, "I'll need a silent weapon to deal with you. There's no telling how close Charlie is or how far sound from gunfire can travel. I hope you don't force me to kill you or give away my presence."

As if she jinxed herself with those words, Sunshine soon became restless, then agitated. The palomino whinnied, pranced, and shook her head. Beth went to calm Sunshine with pats, strokes, and a soothing voice, but nothing worked to pacify the wild-eyed animal. The redhead's eyes and ears soon detected the cause of her mount's panic. Throaty rumbles compelled her to turn slowly. The cougar leapt to a boulder and paused there to stare at the human and horse; its ears and nose twitched as if searching for clues to the situation, its muscled body crouched low to the rock as if ready to pounce or flee at a moment's notice.

"Steady, Sunshine; it's all right, girl," she murmured. With caution and without taking her gaze from the peril, Beth's hand sought the weapon nearby. *No sudden and threatening moves.* She lifted the bow and nocked the arrow; she hated to slay him. If she shot him in the foot, she realized, his teeth could pull out the tip later. But could she hit that size target? Would the big cat remain still long enough for her to try? If she missed or it didn't deter him, would she get a second chance to defend their lives?

The tawny creature seemed content to linger. As she and the beast exchanged stares, her heart pounded and she trembled. Her knees shook and her mouth dried. She prayed for the threat to depart.

Beth saw him flex his claws and tense his body. She had to use his deliberation time to seize an advantage. She drew back the bowstring and released her first arrow. The whiskey-colored animal flinched at the sound but didn't move quick enough to prevent being hit in the leg where Beth imagined his ankle would be if he had one. It let out a guttural noise she took as a reaction to the pain and surprise. Beth readied the second arrow with haste and aimed it as the cat shook its paw and bit at the offender. The shaft snapped off and the cougar made a rushed exit from the clearing.

Beth ran in the same direction to watch the creature lope across the terrain and vanish between rocks in the adjacent hills. She went to the palomino and comforted the horse, who calmed within minutes now that danger was out of sight. She swayed against a tall formation, relaxed the tension on the bowstring, and lowered the weapon to her side. Safe, she closed her eyes and took several deep breaths.

After striking camp, Beth rode until she reached an elevated section high enough to spy the wagon train or its dust from a lengthy distance. She left Sunshine to graze while she scrambled up the slope and found a safe spot. Nothing unusual was in sight, just desert and sierra chains. The sky was blue and clear, and the temperature was still pleasant. She waited and observed, lying on her stomach, for over an hour. As she did so, small birds chased insects while larger ones pursued them. She noted how the landscape was dotted with greenery and bright floral colors. She watched a hawk try to grab a rabbit with its claws, but several swoops failed as the scared creature darted from one protective shield to another until the predator gave up its goal. She noticed other critters scampering about in search of food or a resting place before the heat became almost unbearable. Spiders, bugs, and lizards busily worked and played, a snake slithered over the warming ground and wiggled into a cluster of rocks. The region was filled with all kinds of life that had adapted to its rugged demands.

Just as she must do the same with her life. Beth frowned and pushed personal worries aside to concentrate on her task. She was positive she had camped farther west than the caravan would travel yesterday and had departed this morning earlier than they should have. Surely, she reasoned, they weren't ahead of her. She couldn't ride into the clearing between the ranges to see if fresh ruts were there, not yet.

She gave them another hour. Just as she was about to head down the slope to check for tracks, her target came into view. She saw the dust clouds before she sighted the wagons. *You need fieldglasses of your own, Agent Wind. Buy some as soon as possible. If you'd had a pair, you could have seen them sooner or seen there were no tracks down there.*

Beth turned to her back and rested for a while, as the caravan seemed to take forever to reach and pass her location. She sipped water from her canteen and let Sunshine lick some drops from her cupped hand. When she decided the culprits were far enough ahead, she mounted and trailed them, using a slow pace to hinder raising dust and an obscured route southwest of them.

They forded the Rio Santa Maria, halted for rest and the midday meal, and crossed a wide stream. Ever so often, she sought a peak and spied on the villains. Without the aid of fieldglasses, she couldn't see much at the distance Navarro had ordered her to keep.

But at midafternoon, she didn't require their assistance to see the train's escorts pair off and ride in different directions as if scouting for trouble. *Damn! Do I backtrack southeast, or head south, or try to conceal myself? If they see our tracks, Sunshine, we're in big trouble. What would Navarro do?* She pondered a moment, then nature gave her an idea.

Beth covered the palomino's hooves with cloths and walked the horse through an arroyo. After leaving the dry gulch, she headed toward a thick covering of brush and cacti. She dismounted and tethered her horse out of sight. "Easy, girl; stay quiet and still." Sunshine's head nodded as if the tawny mare understood, and obeyed. Beth gingerly approached the concealment she needed and readied herself.

As the riders came into view, she waited until they were almost within a few feet of her before she roused and flushed the slumbering javelinas. The startled and angered creatures hissed and chattered like rattlesnakes. After she poked several with sharp arrow tips, they squealed and raced from their cover, nearly darting into the path of the oncoming horses. The hirelings' sorrels panicked, reared, whinnied, and retreated a few steps as the noisy herd took off in the opposite direction.

"Sonofabitches! Scared hell outta this stupid horse! You damn coward! Yo're ten times bigger than them roasters. Behave yoreself or I'll beat ya loco!"

"Let's git afore we spook more javies and git ourselves throwed and busted. We don't want them other boys splittin' our shares of them coins. Ain't nobody around or them wild pigs woulda let us knowed. Hellfire, I'm more 'an ready to git outta Mexico and head to Gilas where it's safe."

"Cordell's loco for takin' us all this here long way around jest to send Diaz two measly loads. Rest of us shoulda headed straight for . . ."

The two men were out of hearing range before Beth could catch the remainder of that sentence. She moved from the crevice that had protected her from the peccaries' sharp teeth and outrage. Thank goodness, her relieved mind concluded, Navarro had taught her how to sneak up on man or beast without being noticed. She also was grateful she had observed that last critter slip into the bushes to join his group.

As Beth retrieved her horse, she grinned and congratulated herself over her cunning victory. The taste of danger was blood-stirring, and eluding foes was stimulating. Her success told her she could take care of herself; she had done her job with skill.

But don't get cocky as that provokes mistakes. Stay alert and careful.

The elated redhead mounted and shadowed the criminals until they halted and camped near another stream. She guided Sunshine onward for miles and located the site her partner had pointed out on a map and told her to use. Not wanting to be caught by surprise or offguard by Navarro or enemies, Beth took precautions so neither would occur.

Navarro walked his horse toward the rock-enclosed area. Beneath a half-moon, he saw the palomino grazing and Beth's possessions on the ground. A bedroll was spread and a shapely hump filled it. He almost sighed in relief to find her there, then scowled as he made a stealthy approach to give her a lesson on carelessness. If he were an enemy or wild animal, she was putting herself in great peril by lowering her guard so much. He hadn't stopped worrying about her since they parted, and he couldn't bear the thought of her being injured or slain. Even if she were exhausted, she shouldn't take such a risk. She—

"Don't move, stranger, or I'll fill your backside with lead."

Navarro felt a pistol barrel pressed against his spine. He chuckled and turned. "That was a sneaky trick, woman; fooled even me." Her radiant smile warmed him and her soft laughter was like sweet music.

Beth removed a hair-cloaking dark bandana and dry wiped dirt smudges she'd used to mask a pale complexion. "I had a good teacher, this matchless legend I came across in Tucson. Did I pass your sly test, boss?"

His mirthful gaze danced over her glowing locks and exquisite face. "Yep, couldn't have done better myself. Glad to see you here in perfect shape. You missed a few spots." As he spoke, he fetched his canteen and pulled off his own bandana to wash away those grimy traces. "That does it. School's over. Agent Wind, you've passed your grade."

"No, it isn't. You have plenty more secrets and skills to teach and I want to learn all of them."

"Suits me fine." He unsaddled his stallion and left him free to graze at will. He tossed his belongings in a pile. During those tasks, he queried, "How did things go?"

"I didn't leave that hilltop until I broke camp this morning. I waited for them to catch up, then trailed them at a distance. After they camped, I rode here as ordered in case they checked their flank and sides. No fires and no noise. As you said, Agent Breed, if I obey orders and use my wits as taught, I stay out of trouble. So, where's my surprise? I'm starved. I waited eating supper until your arrival. You didn't forget, did you?"

He chuckled at her playful tone and expression. "Nope." He handed her cloth-wrapped Mexican food. "Eat while I give you a report."

He watched her savor the meal while he related the coded message to his friend in Nogales and the coded one to his superior about Geronimo; he also related the other clues they had gathered. "When I meet Zack in Fronteras, maybe he'll have answers about this Ben in Morenci and their Indian contact. I told Dan to get the Army to help us by leaving a crack at the border door for Charles and his wagons to slip through. If Charles is halted or harassed there, it could jeopardize our mission, stop us from getting the solid evidence we need against him. We can't let anything or anybody make him bolt and run. We have to get the names of his financial partner and that renegade leader. If Charles doesn't fill their needs, they'll only find somebody else who will."

Beth had to reveal the additional fact she had gleaned by accident, but she wouldn't expose the cougar episode. If she did so, he'd think she was in constant peril when apart from him or blame himself for placing her in danger and he'd be reluctant to leave her alone again. "There is something I need to tell you. I did have a little problem on the way here." She told him of the scouts and how she'd handled them. "Do you think Gilas is a place or a man in Arizona?"

He was astonished and impressed by how she had dealt with the predicament. "In my opinion, it's the name of the Gila Mountains near Morenci; they edge the reservation on the south end. Must be their rendezvous point. We'll know soon. You did well, Beth; I'm proud of you. A few more days in Mexico and a few in Arizona should wind up this case. In a week, partner, two at the most, this black threat should be over, and Charles will be tasting prison food. What are your plans after we finish this assignment?"

"I thought I'd mentioned I'm visiting my family, relatives, and old friends in Denver for a couple of weeks. I'm looking forward to enjoying a nice rest and seeing everyone. I miss them all terribly if I go too long without a visit. They don't know when to expect me because I didn't know how long this mission would take. I wrote them I'd probably arrive in June or July. That would be excellent timing with my nephews' and nieces' school schedule."

He saw her eyes and face glow with love and with eagerness to see her kin. "You ever think about making a family of your own?"

"When I'm tempted, I tell myself all the reasons why it won't work for me. I guess I've become a drifter at heart, like you. I love adventure and travel. I love using and honing my wits and skills. I even love the danger. With this successful mission on my record, I should be able to get more exciting and challenging cases. That is, my legendary agent, if they don't think you did all the work and took all the risks and give you all the credit."

"I'll make sure that doesn't happen. I'll tell Dan you did your share, sometimes more. I'll put everything in all my reports."

"Thanks, I can use the praise on my record to forward my career."

"You earned it, woman. When you mentioned your brother's and sister's kids, you sounded as if you deeply love and enjoy them. I got the same impression with the Cordell brood at the ranch. Is it just them or all children?"

If he's testing your feelings and intentions, test his in return. "Most children are a delight, but I couldn't be a mother. I can't change myself or my life. But I enjoy borrowing other people's for a while."

"You aren't planning to ever have any?"

"No, but you sound as if you would love to have some."

"You're right. Some day I want at least one daughter to spoil and one son to work beside me after I retire and buy my ranch."

"So, you *are* planning to become a rancher like Matt. I didn't think that claim was just part of your ruse. I can envision you working your land with a wife and little Breeds beside you. Makes a pretty image, doesn't it?"

"Yep, very pretty. You're not even tempted a tiny bit?"

"I can't have that kind of existence. A true-blooded agent and trail woman wouldn't make a docile wife. Think I'd be happy nailed to one spot?"

"How do you know what you like unless you try it?"

"I don't have to die to know I don't like death."

He stared at her. "That's an odd comparison: marriage to death."

"Not with my bad luck."

"It could change if you met the right man. Maybe you will on your next assignment." *Because your next case is going to be with me, partner, if I have to make Dan search high and low for one that needs a team like us.*

Beth laughed. "I can promise you I won't find a husband during a case. This temporary relationship between us happened because of temptations arising from our romantic ruse and because we both needed somebody for a while. I have thoroughly enjoyed our . . . situation and you, but I ordinarily don't get involved with men during my assignments."

"Maybe it happened this time because we like each other so much and get along so well."

"True, we have become good friends and satisfying lovers. I like and enjoy being your friend and partner, Navarro. I hope we'll always be close and I'd be more than willing to partner up with you again. I like the added benefits of you being my boss."

To Navarro, it sounded as if she was telling him that was all she wanted from him, now and in the future; she was letting him know not to say anything serious or disquieting. She was telling him *no* with words and hints, and he wondered why. He had gathered and hoped she was coming to love and want him as much as she obviously desired him. He asked himself if he was mistaken, if he had misread her clues, or missed vital ones. Was he riding headlong and blind toward another loss?

Despite good intentions to retreat from him, Beth was disappointed he didn't argue her points or try to persuade her to change her mind. If he had his sight aimed on her, it didn't show. Frankly, she was stunned by his revelations about love, marriage, and children. It seemed to contradict what he'd told her at the ranch. She couldn't deduce his motive for that change of heart and future plans, and certainly not his reason for telling her.

On Wednesday, they crossed the Rio Janos, neared the northern tip of the Sierra Madre western chain, and camped on the Rio Casa Grande. Both realized there was only one more night to spend before leaving Mexico, then three days or less to Morenci and the completion of the case.

After they ate leftovers from Dublan, Navarro handed Beth his locket. "I want you to have this as a friendship and farewell gift, something to remind you of me and our work together. I could forget to give it to you later if things get crazy in Arizona. I might even get you a picture of me to use until you replace it with your husband's or child's—that is, if you change your mind about marrying and having them. If not, you can put your parents picture in it; that shouldn't be suspicious if you forget to remove the necklace during a mission. I bought it in Phoenix years ago."

"You shouldn't part with it."

"You've earned a reward, partner."

Beth opened the pendant and looked inside; it was empty.

When she lifted a quizzical gaze to his, he grasped her awareness of what had been there until not long ago. "I returned it to Jessie before I left the ranch. It's over between us, been over a long time, but I didn't realize it until I saw her again. I still love her, Beth, but I'm not in love with her." *In case that's what has you worried and hanging back.*

"That's good, Navarro. Now, you're free to get on with your life as she did with hers. You can find yourself a mate, marry, and have another son."

"What do you mean by 'another son'?"

Beth cursed that slip. *If you loved me and trusted me, you would have confessed that secret by now so I could understand you and the past situation better.* "Lane Cordell is your son, isn't he?"

Navarro didn't hesitate before responding, "How did you know? Who told you? Dan? Jessie? Or accidental eavesdropping?"

"I only had suspicions until just now when you confirmed them."

"How did I give away that secret? Something I did or said?"

"A logical conclusion to a curious riddle. Being pregnant explains why Jessica didn't wait longer for your return and why she wed Matt so fast after your departure. She's a strong and brave woman so she wouldn't have betrayed you for spite or broken her promise without a good reason. A son also explains why it was so hard for you to get over her and why you avoided them for years. I assumed there was more to the past than what you told me because something didn't add up. For starters, you didn't return to the ranch after prison either to see the Cordells and hands or to seek a job; your requirement of a wife and ruse in order to visit old friends was odd; and you seemed worried about more than danger to them from Charles. I didn't fit Lane into the puzzle until our third day there. Lane and I talked many times and he told me his birthday was March thirteenth. That meant Jessica conceived him while you were at the ranch fighting Fletcher and before she married Matt. Since you two were in love in June . . ."

She knew there was no need to clarify. "Another puzzle piece: Lane resembles you more than either Jessica or Matt. That isn't noticeable unless you two are together, so don't worry about exposure. I can only imagine the anguish you've endured over their losses. He's a fine boy, Navarro, even has some of your traits; you're lucky to have him. I'm sure you love him and you're proud of him."

"I am. But he was born and raised as Matt's child, so he'll always be Matt's son. I owe Jessie and Matt that much for sparing him the shame and torment of being viewed as a half-breed bastard like his father. I owe Lane, too; I wasn't there for him because of my sorry past and mistakes. I didn't know he existed until after my prison release and that talk with Matt five years ago. I'm damned lucky Matt loved Jessie so much and was there to clean up the mess I left behind. I swore to him I'd never intrude on their lives, and I wouldn't have if this blasted case hadn't come up. I'm convinced they're in love, a happy family. That's why I needed you and our ruse, as an innocent reason to go there for a visit."

Dan is the one who believed you needed a wife with you to prevent temptation and trouble because he knows the truth . . . "I'm sure the past was hard on all of you. Maybe Jessica and Matt are at peace now; I hope so. They're good people, Navarro; they'll rear Lane right. You can't ever replace a special boy like him, but you can have another son or lots of sons and daughters. You can have children who'll bear your name next time and you can raise them on your ranch, watch them grow, be a crucial part of their upbringing."

"First, I have to find myself a perfect wife. By perfect, I mean one who can accept what I am and was, and put up with a hardcase like me."

"You're a prize, Navarro, so keep looking and I'm sure one will come along someday. Any woman would be lucky to grab hold of you." *Argue with me. Say you've already found the one you've waited for and it's me.* He didn't. "Now that you're over Jessica, that task should be easy." Beth held out the locket to him and said, "Shouldn't you save this as a wedding present for your wife? It's valuable and precious to you. She could put her love's picture in it and wear it close to her heart as you did for years."

I'm a "prize," but not one you want to collect? His hands captured her open one and closed her fingers over the shiny oval. "I want you to have it for what you mean to me and all you've done for me. Put your first child's picture in it, because I'm sure you'll change your mind one day."

"No, partner, never."

"You're that sure about having no children? Ever?"

"Positive." *But I wish I weren't. If I had the slightest doubt, I'd beg you to give me a chance to prove I'm perfect for you. But I'm not perfect and my flaw will remain an obstacle between us. Now I understand why it's so important to Jessica for us to have a child. How I wish you could say; it doesn't matter, Beth, I want you anyway, but you can't and won't.* She yawned and stretched. "Been a long day. Good night."

"See you tomorrow, partner."

Navarro lay on his bedroll. His troubled mind contemplated the woman nearby, their relationship, and her feelings about many things. He knew she loved her job; yet, she couldn't remain an agent and on the road forever. Why was she so set against having a husband and children? Did Steven still haunt her? Was she afraid to reach out to another man, to him, to risk another loss? Or was it him she didn't want permanently? She could think badly of him for doing Jessie wrong, even though he'd been trapped in a bind and couldn't help what happened long ago. In view of his and her past experiences, Beth could be afraid to trust him, afraid he'd do the same or worse to her. She could lack all respect for him in that personal area. Maybe she just didn't want a half-breed, ex-criminal, bastard, ex-prisoner for a husband and the father of her children. Beth could believe he was still emotionally yoked to Jessie and Lane, and she'd only be second choice. She could be under the mistaken impression he was after her because he wanted a wife and children. Maybe she was reluctant and scared to get strapped down while he remained an agent on the road, which he wouldn't. She could even think it was his way of convincing Jessie he was out of her life so his lost love could truly be free and happy.

Navarro pondered ways to change Beth's mind about a future and family together, things he craved with all his heart. If she was being honest with herself and him about not wanting children, could he pursue and accept her under those terms? Could he change her mind later? If not, would having her and a ranch be enough to fulfill him? If there was a good reason behind her reluctance, maybe so.

During the journey the next day, two culprits left the wagons and rode ahead as fast as the terrain allowed. Navarro suspected that they were going to check out the next stopping area for soldiers or to get news from somebody who was prearranged to meet them there.

They traveled onward until late afternoon when they reached the north branch of Rio Bavispe; they halted at that river. Navarro told Beth they were fifteen miles below the border, straight south of Arizona's Chiricahua Mountains. As the agents observed from a concealed position, Charles and his hirelings appeared to be setting up camp.

"What's he up to now?"

"I'm not sure, Beth. Maybe he's taking a short break before heading on into Arizona. Maybe he's ahead of the rendezvous schedule, so he's letting the men and horses rest a spell. Maybe he wants to make sure it's safe to cross the border. Whatever his motive, he isn't pulling out tomorrow or he wouldn't be putting up that small tent or building those *ramadas* for shade."

"This gives you more time to meet with Zack and make our plans," Beth observed.

"I'll head on to Fronteras as soon as I have you hidden and Night Cloud is rested. Zack should be there by now. Hope he's got good news for us."

"You're sending Dan a message?"

"Yes. This beard and mustache should protect me if any of Charles's men ride off, too. I'll change out of these buckskins into regular clothes to keep from drawing attention to me. You be careful while I'm gone."

Beth sat in the quiet and lonely camp in a concealed canyon; she was fast becoming tense and frustrated. If Charles was up to no good at this very minute, Navarro wasn't there to discover it. She was a trained agent, so why must she sit in hiding like a frightened or helpless woman? On any other case, she would be in the thick of danger and busy investigating foes.

Her decision made, Beth took precautions and sneaked toward Charles's camp. His tent was far enough away from the wagons and men's campfires for privacy but not enough to place him in danger of a surprise attack. Using dense scrubs as cover and with a stealthy pace, she crept toward her target. Only moments before making a terrible mistake, she noticed a thin cord running low to the ground and tied from bush to bush, with suspended bells obscured in their foliage. If she'd tripped over it, the noise would have exposed her presence. With added alert, she watched for more ambushes and avoided those clever snares.

As she reached Charles's tent, so did his best friend, with steaming coffee and a hot meal. She heard Jim Tiller say he'd return soon with some for Charles. She didn't have to wait long before the man kept his word.

"This looks tasty, Jim; that cook you hired is talented on the trail."

"Thanks. I told him I'd chop off his hands if he didn't feed you right."

Beth listened to them share laughter and trivial conversation. Then, the talk became interesting and informative.

"How about a dash of whiskey in our coffee?" Charles offered and Jim accepted. "Not much longer, old friend, and we'll be eating the best food available in the finest restaurants and sipping whiskey in the best saloons with beauties hanging on our arms."

"That redhead gonna be one of 'em?"

"Soon as I get around to collecting her."

"You want me to kill that husband of hers for you?"

"Maybe, or maybe I'll do it myself. I didn't take to him."

"Because he kept putting his hands on her ever' chance he got?"

"That, and he's a sly one, dangerous. I want to be sure he's dead and buried before I convince her to marry me."

"Think she will?"

"One way or another. If she's smart, Jim, she won't turn down a rich man. So, what time you leaving in the morning for your meeting with Eagle Eye?"

"I'm pulling out at first light to get in fast travel while it's cool. This damn desert saps a man and his horse. Gimme another splash of that whiskey. I should make Grey Peak in three, maybe three and a half, days. After I set up the time and place with that Injun for the exchange, I'll see Ben on the way back to join you. Should be gone a week."

"You know where to locate that peak?"

"Ben sent a good map; not far beyond Morenci. Won't be hard to find."

"You shouldn't run into Geronimo and his band. Tully said he's raiding below Tucson. I'm sending a few boys to Fronteras tomorrow to see what news they can gather. They'll telegraph Ben to get a message to Eagle Eye you're on the way. You be more than careful, old friend."

"Always am, Charlie. You, too. Hate leaving you here without me."

"I'll be fine. I'll have some boys scout the border, too. We don't want to stumble into any patrols. We want our luck to hold out longer."

"This area seems safe, but it's wise to use guards while I'm gone. Though I set out those traps, it wouldn't hurt to be double careful."

"I told Tully to handle it after supper."

When Beth heard those words, she decided it was time to get moving before the sentinels went on duty. Careful of the warning devices, she made it back to her camp safely.

There, she paced and pondered her next course of action. She reasoned she should follow Jim Tiller to gather more clues. It was possible she might learn who and where Ben was, the date and place of the exchange to prepare a better trap, and the hideout of Eagle Eye. It was clear she, Navarro, and Zack could not challenge the separate or combined bands of Charles Cordell and the Apache leader.

Time was crucial, and she assumed her partner would be away for too much of it. He could be delayed by business or trouble, especially with Charles's hirelings heading for the same town. If Navarro was injured or—God forbid—slain, she would be of no help to the case while stranded in camp or even while trailing the villains' wagons. At least being in Arizona and after gathering facts, she could wire Dan and they could still carry out the trap. If she did nothing and something happened to Navarro, Charles would succeed with his evil crime and would go unpunished because no one would know when and where to lay and spring the trap.

Bethany knew she wasn't being reckless or cocky by not staying put as ordered by her partner; she would only be doing her job, her duty, carrying out her assignment. Yes, she would shadow Jim to Grey Peak. To ensure a safe start, she should get a jump on him and the border scouts by leaving before dawn. She readied supplies and a disguise. She wrote Navarro a message about what she'd discovered, where she was heading and why, and a warning about the snares Charles had placed around the camp. She told him she would trail Jim up and back and spy in between. She reminded him she had proven herself, promised to be extra careful, and urged him not to worry.

The redhead removed the locket and placed it with his belongings, having asked him in the note to keep it until her return in a week. Thanks to his lessons, she would be able to mark her trail with Indian signs, in the event he insisted on following her and leaving Zack behind to watch Charles.

Beth tried to get a restful night's sleep but suspense and anticipation often intruded. Before dawn she was dressed, additional precautions taken, supplies packed and loaded, and canteens filled. She mounted Sunshine and skirted Charles's camp with the intention of lying in wait for Jim.

Chapter Twenty-one

Upon entering town two hours after dawn, Navarro stabled Night Cloud to be curried, watered, and fed. Except for rest and nap stops, he had ridden all night. He passed a main-street saloon and nodded to the black man whittling nearby. He headed for a small hotel and registered under a false name. Soon after he was in the room, Zachariah Abernathy sneaked inside to join him.

The two agents shook hands and exchanged broad smiles. "Glad to see you, old friend. Looks like we both made good time."

"I kept a check at the telegraph office in Nogales. After the clerk handed me your message and I saw it was in code, I told him, 'Is cain't read, boss. Wills you tells me whut it says?' in my best southern drawl."

"You're good at hiding your wits and identity behind that clever ruse."

"Yowsiree, boss, sir." Zack chuckled. "Where's your partner?"

Navarro sat in a chair and motioned for his friend to use the bed as one for himself. "Hiding in the hills close to our target."

Zack's brown gaze widened. "You left her alone back there?"

Navarro grinned, doffed his hat, and dropped it to the floor. "She'll be fine. Dan didn't paint her large enough. She's as skilled and as smart as we are. Been more than a pleasant surprise to me. If anybody can take care of herself and trouble, it's Beth Breed."

Zack caught the last name his close friend used for his partner. "Must be high caliber for you to leave her behind. Learned anything new?"

"Just that they're heading for the Gila Mountains soon and, for some reason I haven't figured out, they're camping for a while about thirty miles back. What about you and Dan? Any answers to my questions?"

Zack propped his shoulder against the headboard. "Geronimo's riding like the wind and being about as easy to spot and catch as a northern gust. He's been raiding from Tucson to a few miles over the border since he escaped Crook in March. Killed two men outside Nogales last month. Ambushed a unit of soldiers, killed some, stole horses and supplies, and got away without a scratch on 'im or his band. He did some attacking on ranches, even killed some kids, reports said. 'Course we both know they can't always be trusted to be fact, not with folks so riled up against 'em. Might not have been Geronimo's band; got other renegades on the loose."

The black man frowned before continuing his revelations. "General Miles is hot to get him. Army's got springs and passes under guard trying to snare him, but that fox avoids them like a 'dillo does the sun. Suspicion is Geronimo saw heliograph signals jumping mountain-to-mountain from Arizona to Sonora, got spooked by those flashes, and took off out of their message range. You know Indians, Navarro, they're real superstitious about what they think is magic. Doesn't help any the newspapers are terrifying and stirring up folks; according to them, Geronimo is everywhere at once, making raids that'd require a band a hundred times the size of his and claiming he's done all kinds of tortures and murders. When he's finally trapped, he's in for big trouble. Wouldn't surprise me if he isn't strung up on the site. Better not happen if they don't want more renegade trouble."

"You're right, Zack. If they hang him, tempers will flame, the reservation will empty, and blood will flow fast from both sides. He's a beloved legend. If the Army really wants peace, the government should make the Apaches a fair offer. Geronimo's smart; he'd accept. I wonder who his secret rival is."

"We don't know. Dan's going over the San Carlos list. Could be he was never captured or gave a fake name or was on another reservation."

"We'll know soon. What about that man named Ben?"

"He's about as hard to unravel as that Indian mystery. There's a Benjamin Murphy about fifty years of age who owns a copper mine near Morenci. Report said he isn't a likely suspect. Good reputation and seems to be a nice man. Well liked and respected by the locals. What some call a true southern gentleman. There's a Bennett Smith about the same age who owns a silver mine not too far away and lives in Morenci. Said to be cold, hard, greedy, and despises Indians. Miners hate him but he pays good so they endure him. Last, you got Benson Jeevers, fortyish. Owns a lotta businesses. Rich, arrogant, greedy, and hates Indians. All answer to the name Ben."

"Shu, three rich Bens in the area," Navarro scoffed as he mussed his sable hair and frowned in disappointment.

"We haven't opened President Diaz's eyes; we don't want him sending troops after Cordell or making a try for the rest of those weapons. Might be best for his pride and for peace to keep him ignorant he's being used."

"I agree. Anything else?"

"There's an Army captain in the hotel down the street you're to see. Dan got 'em to cooperate with us about the border pass and our mission. You're supposed to set up signals and a schedule with him before we leave town. Make sure we get us a thick mirror and don't break it."

"That won't be a problem since we both know Morse code. As soon as Cordell begins to move again, we'll flash them to clear a path for that snake to slither across the line. I'll be sure to tell the captain to pass my signals the long way around to his contacts so Cordell doesn't see 'em and get spooked like Geromino did. Could be one or more of his men know Morse code, too, so we don't want to tip our hand. I'll go wire Dan and meet with the captain before I eat and grab a few winks."

Navarro retrieved his hat and stood. "I wanna head back to Beth by noon, so meet me outside town about that hour."

Zack exposed snowy teeth as he grinned. There was a twinkle of playful mischief in his chocolate eyes. "Miss her real bad, huh?" He saw his friend's gaze soften; then, the white man furrowed his brow.

"Sometimes too much for thinking straight; that's dangerous for her and me. One thing's for sure, she's leading me on a long and hard chase. I got a lotta miles of tough terrain to cover if I'm gonna overtake her, if I can."

"I've never known Navarro Breed to give up on anything, so you will."

As they entered the canyon about six o'clock, Navarro reined up and halted Zack. "Something's wrong. Her horse is missing. It's too quiet."

"Maybe she's tricking you again like you told me she did before."

Navarro's senses heightened as he studied the abandoned location. "Not this time. My gut feeling is bad, old friend. Move slowly and easily."

At their campsite, Navarro found the dismaying message she'd left for him: a little rock, atop a medium one, atop a larger one—trail sign for *Attention!*—and another small, sharp-ended rock that pointed north and was placed on a big, flat one to reveal the direction she had taken. "She's gone. Looks like on her own choice or she wouldn't have had time to leave me this message."

"Why would she take off by herself and with you gone? You two have a quarrel before you left camp? You been . . . chasing her that hard?"

Navarro caught his meaning. "Nope, I haven't offended her with unwanted attentions; we get along fine; couldn't be much better."

"Think she only went to spy on Cordell or take a ride?"

"I hope not; he's tricky and dangerous. Besides, there are no signs saying she was planning to come back. But she wouldn't leave without telling me more than her direction." He dismantled the three-tier stack and was relieved to find a note, until he read it to himself in silence, then aloud to Zack.

"She spied on those snakes and took off to trail one? Lady has grit."

"Just wait until I get my hands on her for being so reckless! She should have stayed where she was safe. When I returned, I could have gone after Jim Tiller and gathered any clues he might drop. *Shu,* they're almost a day ahead of me! She could be hurt or in danger this minute."

"Simmer down, old friend; she's an undercover agent and she's only doing her job like she says. You told me she's as skilled as us. We woulda done the same thing if this chance was tossed in our laps."

Navarro crumpled the paper in a balled fist. "But she's a woman, Zack, and those bastards are dangerous! Charles has a bad itch for her and I don't want him getting the chance to scratch it if she's caught."

"You're letting worries cloud your thinking, if she's as good as you say. She's probably doing just fine."

"Even the best agents run into trouble and she's got no backup man."

"Didn't you tell me she usually works alone?"

"Yes, but . . ." Navarro paced around to release his tension.

"Didn't you tell me she'd worked the trail like an expert?"

He stuffed the note into his pocket. "Yes, but . . ."

"But what, old friend? You love her and you don't want her killed?"

Navarro halted his movements and looked at Zack. "That's about the size of it. Never expected to get lassoed again, but I did, good and tight. Fact is, tighter than Jessie ever roped me. Hardest part about this mission has been keeping my mind on it with her around day and night."

"Beth tied up in that love knot, too?"

"I'm not sure; she keeps those kinds of thoughts and feelings to herself. She got a bad knock-down like me and I don't think she's picked herself up yet. Hasn't been the right time to help her do it. We got real close playing husband and wife, and I want her to stay Beth Breed."

"What about Jessica Cordell? Things go all right with her at the ranch?"

Navarro smiled. "Couldn't have been better, thanks to Beth. All it took was seeing Jessie and her new life to realize it was over, been over for both of us a long time. I just had been fooling myself. Jessie and Matt are happy, perfect for each other. Got a fine life together."

"That's good news, Navarro, for you and Mrs. Cordell. I wanted to ask what happened but figured it was best to wait until you mentioned it. I like Beth; I'd be happy to see you two get together after this assignment."

"So would I, if she doesn't get herself killed being a heroine and doing her duty. She doesn't know where she's headed or how big that renegade's band is. If she tried to get close enough to overhear their talk, she can put herself into a trap. Grey Peak isn't in the Gila Mountains, so something's either changed in their plans or Charles lied to his men. Maybe he didn't want his hirelings to know the real location in case one got captured or turned traitor. You stay here and watch Charles while I go after her, and don't forget about those snares if you do any close spying. I'll stop at Bowie to send Dan a wire; tell him about Eagle Eye, Grey Peak, and Ben. Maybe he can learn more from Charles's Fronteras telegram if he can find a way to get its message; may give us an evidence tie between Cordell and Ben. I'll remind him we can't put agents on those clues and risk spooking any of our targets. If Charles doesn't wait for Jim and starts moving northward, you send that mirror signal to our Army friends."

"You pulling out after her tonight?"

"Still got hours of light left. Since I know where Grey Peak is, I'll use roads and trails when possible to make better time and maybe catch up."

"Need any help preparing? Or want to borrow anything?"

"She hid my stuff in those rocks. I'll fetch what I need."

"How do you know?"

"She used a brush to cover her back-and-forth tracks," Navarro said, and pointed out his meaning. "Rocks and trash turned over from here to those scrubs. 'Sides, she'd travel light and quiet."

"You got a keen eye. Looks fine to me. Who woulda noticed but you?"

"An Apache or somebody trained by one. They taught me good, Zack."

The black man followed Navarro as he fetched supplies. "That's why you're the best; you can track a trail that isn't there. If she leaves you signals like those rock piles, she could expose herself. Most of those Army units use Indian—Apache—scouts. If one comes across her signs, they'll think they're on to a renegade band and follow her. She'll lead them straight to that secret meeting, spook 'em, and bust our case."

Navarro noticed she took his fieldglasses, bandana, and two canteens. He was impressed by her precautions. He pushed the pendant into his pocket and was eager to replace it on her neck. "Beth will realize the same thing and drop that idea. She'll also guess I know where Grey Peak is, so no trail markings are necessary."

"*If* she guesses you'll come after her."

"She will, 'cause she knows you're here to watch our target."

"Unless I didn't get your message to me in Nogales or got hurt. Or you got new orders from Dan in Fronteras."

"If she doubts I'll pursue, I hope she doesn't get into trouble and lose hope of a rescue or try something crazy to escape."

"I'm betting my best carving wood you'll meet her on the way back here. Yesiree, Dan's gonna be mighty surprised about his matchmaking."

"I doubt it. I have me a suspicion he chose us for each other."

"Did a darn good job at it. Watch your backside, old friend."

"You, too, Zack." He mounted his horse. "See you in a week, either here or there. You know what to do."

With the borrowed fieldglasses, Beth observed Jim Tiller as he halted to make camp. For hours, the Chiricahua Mountains had loomed before them as an oasis between the Sonoran and Chihuahuan deserts. Foothills drifted into forest-covered ridges and magnificent formations of spires, pinnacles, balanced boulders, and columns of rocks standing on end. The mingled scents of pine, juniper, and spruce wafted on a soothing breeze. Stream-fed glens and canyons wandered through the region and provided great beauty. They also offered homes for a variety of birds and animals.

Beth was overjoyed by the location Jim selected for the night and was relieved to escape the arid and rugged demands of the surrounding terrain. The sun was setting, but daylight would linger for a while. A waxing quarter moon had been visible on the low horizon for the last few miles so she wouldn't be cloaked in total darkness in the woods, where she rode a little deeper than her target to avoid being seen. She dismounted and let her palomino drink and graze while she replaced the clipped fringes from her buckskin garments, dangling them over her waistband in case they were needed to make a trail.

Beth chewed on dried meat and Mexican bread Navarro had brought from Dublan on Tuesday. She sipped fresh and cool water from the stream and splashed her pinkened face. So far, she hadn't encountered trouble or extreme hardship, and she hoped her task would continue in that vein.

* * *

Saturday, she walked her horse near the edge of the forest and hid behind a gathering of boulders. It wasn't long before Jim came into view, leaving near dawn as suspected. She shadowed him for hours as they skirted Fort Bowie, crossed the rail line from Lordsburg to Wilcox, and journeyed the San Simon Valley. She was thankful Jim clung to its side hills instead of riding the center grassland where several ranches and settlers lived. Gamma grass and bushes swayed in the wind and doves took flight with frequency. Antelope grazed alone or with stock. The Gila Mountains appeared in the distance. The landscape added an abundance of cacti, and chipmunks played amongst them. At the northern boundary of the valley, Jim made camp; so did Beth.

As she watched several armadillos browse for food at dusk, the agent kept her tan hat on until darkness shielded her flaming locks from anyone's attention. Again, she chewed on distasteful dried meat and appeased her mouth with bites of dried fruit and more *pan de campo*.

She snuggled into a bedroll and leaned against a rock. She decided that was safer than lying down where she might sleep too soundly. Her mind filled with some of the countless things Navarro had told her about the Apaches during their trek across Mexico. Those revelations helped her to understand him and the Indians better. She concluded that if the government took action to correct the hardships, cheating and swindling, and harassment on the reservations, escapes would cease, hatred would lessen and peace could reign at last. So many frauds and deprivations were alleged by the Indians and their supporters among the whites and military, and few abuses—if any—were examined and halted.

Perhaps, Beth thought before drifting off into a light sleep, she could ask for her next assignment to be an investigation of those allegations. As a matter close to Navarro's heart, perhaps he would partner up with her.

Sunday evening, Beth camped far downriver from Jim and southwest of Morenci. During their ride, she had sighted many snakes, hawks, lizards, and even a roadrunner with its mate. She had weaved around and between bloom-laden mesquite that buzzed with activity, tall sotol, multi-fingered cholla, glorious yucca, odd-smelling creosote with greenish-yellow flowers, and countless prickly pear with exquisite sunny blossoms. All flourished in harsh soil and beneath a blazing sun that could blister through garments if the material was too thin.

The swift and muddy Gila River was not water she cared to bathe in, or even drink until dirt settled and the top portion was cleared. Sunshine didn't care and guzzled mouthfuls after the long and hot trip. The palomino enjoyed the shade of taller and thicker trees along the bank, as did Beth, who also found them helpful for concealment.

The terrain above Morenci was more arduous than Beth had imagined when she watched Jim head toward the Coronado Trail. As the road went upward in elevation, the temperature lowered from the desert heat as the numbers of pine, aspen, piñon, and juniper increased. The abundance of prickly pear and mesquite continued and mingled with agave about to bloom. Bunch grass and sacahuista, which the Mexicans used for weaving baskets, was blown about in a stiff breeze.

When she had climbed higher, Beth glanced down into huge copper mines for which the area was known. Seeking and removing the ore left chasmic locations barren, almost ugly. What reminded her of steps descended into deep pits where transport trails were as winding as the one she journeyed. Excavated dirt was piled as high as hills, also bleak and brown. Now she grasped what Navarro meant about the processing scarring the earth, maybe forever. She pulled her gaze from the depressing sight.

The twisting road and dense vegetation made concealment from her target easy. Still, she was cautious. On occasion, columns of tall rocks nestled together to create lovely formations. In grassy areas with streams, she smiled in pleasure as she viewed elk, deer, turkey, and squirrel. However, a bear ambling through the woods made her nervous. Her tension mounted when a rocky section exposed a mountain lion sunning itself. The tawny cat glanced her way but didn't appear interested in pursuing her as his next meal. She realized this picturesque area possessed more than human perils to avoid.

When Jim halted a few minutes to secure a dark-blue bandana around his right forearm, Beth reasoned they must be nearing the rendezvous site and that was his identifying signal to the Apache leader. She halted and dropped Sunshine's reins to the ground, leaving the animal free to escape danger if necessary. "Stay, girl," she commanded, and was obeyed.

Beth used trees, bushes, and rocks for concealment as she slipped forward to locate her unknowing guide. Jim walked his sorrel at a slow pace and glanced from side-to-side. She stopped and remained where she was as a precaution against braves scouting for shadows before showing themselves. As another precaution, her hat was left on her pommel and her hair was masked by Navarro's green-and-brown splotched bandana. Amidst the greenery, she wished her buckskins matched the disguise cloaking her head, and resolved to have a seamstress make her an entire masking outfit for future use.

Beth heightened her alert as several Indians left the trees and joined Jim Tiller. Her gaze scanned the area for companions, in particular guards, and saw none. She listened for telltale signs of a foe's presence or approach. She crept nearer and nearer as the white man and five Indians dismounted and secured their horses' reins to bushes.

"Ink-tah," the leader said, motioning for Jim to sit down on a grassy spot. "-Ch' uuné' and Eagle Eye talk."

By the time the men were settled, Beth was as close as she dared to sneak, but close enough to overhear the conversation. Since the men appeared to be strangers, she didn't know why the Indian called him the Apache word for "friend" her partner had taught her.

"Cordell was happy you stayed free long enough for him to get your weapons made and bring them to you."

"Eagle Eye cunning; he wait for sun be strong to fight enemy. On sun Eagle Eye have big magic, Chiricahua, others, leave reservation, follow, fight with Eagle Eye. Whites run like coyote; brave Chiricahua take back land. Eagle Eye not coward, not hide; Eagle Eye wait, grow, like magic flower for many moons. Ysun—The Power, Giver of Life—send you to Eagle Eye to bring magic. When *tasinaaghai . . .* wagons, come?"

"In seven suns, Eagle Eye, to Bear Mountain where you camp."

The Apache leader turned to his followers and repeated the number of days, *"Guusts'iidi duuna'."* He focused on Jim again. "Camp at *Keen-teeli Dzil:* Bear Mountain. -Ch' uuné' bring sticks with magic fire arrows, Eagle Creek, seven suns. No, Bear Mountain; trade, Eagle Creek."

"Where's Eagle Creek? It should be close to your camp because it's dangerous for you and your band to drive the wagons very far. Indian scouts or soldiers could see you. We can move across the land without trouble, but you can't do it without taking big risks."

The Indian nodded and pointed northwest, then drew a map in a dirt spot on the ground between the speakers. Beth peered through foliage and used the fieldglasses but couldn't distinguish anything from her position. Jim studied the crude drawing and nodded understanding.

"You have a good trade for white friend, Cordell. Don't forget and don't break our bargain. No trade from Eagle Eye, no guns and bullets."

"Thunder Gods and Earth Woman guard *bilaahda -ch' uuné'* Cordell want for magic sticks. Eagle Eye not forget, not trick. You trust Eagle Eye. Word good, true. Eagle Eye no want *bilaahda.* You want, you take."

Beth wondered what the Apache word meant and committed it to memory to tell Navarro later, as it supplied their target's motive for such heinous crimes. It was obvious the Indian knew a sufficient amount of English to communicate but had difficulty with some words. The warrior's appearance was more intimidating than the tall and lanky blond's, even with Jim's icy gray eyes and nefarious demeanor. She didn't want to study either man closer or longer as both caused her to tremble from a tangible evil that seemed to exude their pores. As Jim struggled with the language in an attempt to explain what types of weapons were en route, the nervous redhead reasoned she had vital facts that shouldn't be endangered by possible capture so she sneaked from the risky location.

When she reached Sunshine, Beth decided to make certain those clues reached her partner in the event something happened to her. She pulled a short fringe from her waistband and placed it on the ground. With deft fingers, she shaped it like the pad of a bear paw, then cut four short pieces to add as claws. Beside it, she made a triangle; together, he should read *Bear Mountain,* if she recalled the symbols right. She cut more small strips to make out the letters *E E* in line with her previous message to imply it was the Indian's campsite. She used her knife to scratch a line below those patterns as if it were a period at the end of a pictorial sentence, then designed a circle with a long fringe and placed seven stones inside of it to stand for *Seven Suns.* If Navarro thought she meant moons, it mattered little. Next to it, she stretched out a length like a stream. Atop that, she tried to create the shape of an eagle. Since he was familiar with the area, hopefully he would grasp she meant *Eagle Creek.* She couldn't resist knifing another period line before forming *B B* as her signature. With care not to shift the revealing symbols, she covered the markings with a flat rock, and scattered broken grass blades to seize her lover's keen eye. Now, she would sneak ahead to wait for Jim to ride for Morenci and expose Ben to her.

After she led Sunshine to a safe distance, she backtracked to brush away their prints, knowing Navarro wouldn't be duped if he arrived later and searched the location. During their past journey, he had amazed her several times by reading a trail that wasn't visible to most eyes. She walked her horse until she deduced it was safe to mount to retreat a mile or so. But trouble struck without warning when suddenly the Indian party engulfed her.

Alarmed but quick-witted Beth pretended not to recognize them as she asked, "What are you doing? Why are you stopping me?"

Eagle Eye maneuvered his roan closer to her. His jet eyes seemed to bore through her flesh as if seeking bone to crush. A midnight mane hung loose around his broad shoulders of bronzed skin. An open vest exposed scars on a muscled torso. But it was the healed slashes around his cold eyes that caught her attention: as if a compass with them as the center, a line traveled for an inch in all four directions. His hand snaked out and yanked off her bandana. As fiery hair tumbled free, he gaped at her.

Eagle Eye murmured, *"Indaa 'ent'iin . . ."*

Beth was worried by his reaction to her coppery tresses: first, shock and fear, then, fury. The word *scalping* came quickly to mind. "I don't understand. Do you speak English?"

"White witch. You bad sign. You have evil magic. You come."

Startled and dismayed, she asked, "Come where? Who are you? What do you want with me?"

"You *Indaa 'ent'iin:* white witch! No talk! Come!"

Beth recalled in chilling clarity what Navarro had told her about the Indians' belief in and fear of witches. Such unfortunate victims fared the same tortures and executions as those whites in the past accused of being witches or warlocks! *Try to frighten or outwit him.* "If you kidnap me, my family and the soldiers will come after you and attack. Surely you don't want your family and friends to be harmed by your mistake. I have to hurry home before dark or they'll worry and come looking for me. I was only taking a ride and traveled too far into the hills. Move and let me pass."

"You Eagle Eye prisoner. Soldiers and whites not find you. *Indaa 'ent'iin* must die, not do evil, not hurt Eagle Eye victory."

It was Beth's turn to gape in astonishment. "Kill me? Is that what—"

"You die in Eagle Eye camp. You talk, cut out evil tongue."

Shut up, Beth; he's crazy and dangerous. Just watch and listen.

Her rifle, pistol, and derringer were taken by his followers. None of them thought to check her high-top moccasin for the hidden knife. She shuddered as they bound her hands and led her in the opposite direction from Morenci. She wondered if they'd seen her spying and if they'd destroyed her signals to Navarro—that is, if he had followed her. But perhaps her lover had decided he trusted her skills and wits enough to wait for her in Mexico.

The trek across rugged terrain went on for hours; every chance she got, Beth pulled a fringe from under her shirt and released it to drop to the ground. She comprehended her peril, but the mission was safe: all Navarro had to do was shadow Charles and get a message to Dan to set a trap. But if he told the Army to meet him and Zack in the Gila Mountains, they would be at the wrong location. Yet, if he reached this area in advance of the caravan and soldiers, he might find her signals, if nothing and no one disturbed them. She recalled that one of the Indians had left the party after her capture and was perhaps lying in wait to see who came after her. If it was her partner, he could be ambushed and slain like her father and husband. If no one came, they'd know she lied and was a bigger threat than first imagined. *Stay strong, alert, brave, and hopeful, Beth.*

At dusk, Navarro found the rendezvous spot where Jim Tiller had met with the Indians. The evidence told him the talk had occurred this morning and everyone was long gone. What worried him was he found only one set of tracks returning to Morenci. He knew that print pattern belonged to Charles Cordell's best friend. Since Beth wasn't shadowing him now, he worried, why not and where was she?

Alarmed, he examined the area and its surroundings with sharp eyes and wits. He found where she had spied on their targets, and followed her retreat to an enlightening location. There, he tested the edges of the grass blades to determine when they had been broken; the results confirmed his prior calculation of time. He hunkered down, lifted the rock, and sighed in relief when he saw the pictorial message. Since she had left her writing paper and Waterman fountain pen in Mexico, she had used signs he'd taught her to communicate with him. Impressed by Beth's precautions and skills, he warmed with pride and love, then chilled in rising trepidation.

He read the symbols with an ever narrowing gaze and increased heart thudding. He knew where Eagle Creek ran; it was a well-chosen exchange point that offered easy approach for wagons, needed privacy, and many escape paths if danger threatened. The criminal trade would take place in seven suns, if she recalled the difference in the sun/moon symbols. Even if she didn't, a few hours spread on that dark day wouldn't matter when laying a trap for them. He grasped she was reporting the place where Eagle Eye was staying for the next week because of a Tepee symbol beside the bear's paw. His fingers traced the initials she left as a signature, and he smiled.

He collected those two fringes, stuffed them in his pocket, and destroyed the remaining message. There was nothing said about where she was going and why, but she'd clearly halted trailing Jim for some unmentioned reason. Either she left by another route or she was surprised by peril. She also had confidence in his talents because she'd brushed out hers and Sunshine's tracks; this time, with more care and skill than she had used in Mexico. It was getting dark fast in the dense forest; that meant he had to decide her whereabouts in a hurry or be forced to wait until morning to search for clues. He didn't want to waste time because he sensed she was in jeopardy.

If she'd been taken prisoner by the renegades, what his beautiful and clever *-tsíné* didn't realize was she'd left an unclear signal in the animal paw line: Bear Canyon, Bear Wallow, and Bear Mountain were all within a day or less riding distance from Grey Peak and Eagle Creek; and all were cunning campsites for the escaped Apaches. One was north, one was northwest, and one was northeast. If he chose the wrong one . . .

Navarro examined the ground and identified her departure route. When he reached the spot where five horses left the concealing forest and joined her, his heart froze in panic. The hooves that had surrounded Beth were shod, but so were the ones back at the rendezvous point, no doubt belonging to horses stolen by the renegades from whites. It was evident from markings on the ground that a talk had ensued and several captors had gotten very close to her, probably to remove her weapons. Six sets of tracks moved into the woods where, within a few feet, one of the Apaches had done a superior job of obscuring the direction they had taken.

Navarro recalled the saying: "Only an Apache can track an Apache." He studied the ground for clues and errors. The lawman was worried: he was only half Indian with a few years' training in his mother's camp, but the man concealing the rendezvous party's tracks was a highly trained and skilled full-blooded Apache warrior with a lifetime of experience. With that undeniable disadvantage and with night closing in on him, was there any hope of finding Beth before something terrible happened to her? Was his first duty to the woman he loved or to the crucial mission that involved saving so many lives? If he spent time trying to track and rescue his partner or if he was ambushed and killed or snared by the same party, he couldn't get a message to Dan and the Army about what his brave and cunning heroine had learned. Yet, if he went to the nearest town to telegraph new information to them, he could lose Beth forever— if she was still alive. If he didn't locate and save her and if he didn't get word to Dan and if the worst happened because he made the wrong decision, Beth's deed and death would be for naught. The loyal and dedicated female agent wouldn't want it to go that way.

Navarro looked skyward and took a deep breath. *It's your choice, hombre: Beth's survival or the lives of thousands of people.*

His heart drummed with indecision and worry. *What should I do? God and Ysun, help me; for once, I don't know which trail to ride first. I can see the one to Morenci in the night but not covered tracks in the forest, not even with a full moon rising. I love you, Beth Breed. Am I going to lose you, too?*

Damn you, evil spirits, if you take her away from me! Losing Jessie won't even compare to losing Beth! Is it Morenci and duty and peace, or pick a choice of three locations where she might still be alive and I might rescue her?

Night Cloud sensed his master's anguish, approached, and nuzzled the lawman's shoulder. Navarro stroked the animal's forehead in affection and gratitude. He mounted the ebony stallion and murmured, "We have no other choice, my friend. Let's go do what we must and pray for the best."

Chapter Twenty-two

For what must be the hundredth time since yesterday, Beth tested the rope that bound her to a tree in a sitting position. If a tough strip of rawhide didn't secure her chafed wrists at backward angles on each side, perhaps she could reach the knife in her moccasin, cut her bonds, and escape. Despite the large pine's support, her back, shoulders, and neck ached from the unrelenting position and length of confinement. Her buttocks and legs grumbled with near numbness. Her tailbone screamed at the exposed root that was gnawing at it like a famished dog. Her hair was caught and pulled by rough bark if she shifted her head too fast when something seized her attention. Pieces had fallen into her lap this morning as squirrels played or foraged on limbs above her.

The region's mountainous air had been chilly, almost cold, last night with only her garments for cover. But the sun warmed the area with speed. A rotation of braves watched her and several more guarded the encampment, which stayed prepared to flee at first notice of an impending attack. Possessions in "burden baskets" outside their shelters were ready to grab before leaving. Of course, she reasoned as a diversion from her woes, wickiups and brush arbors would be abandoned without a second thought. She grasped how those *ramadas* were built in such a clever way as to disperse smoke from cooking before it could rise above the woods in a noticeable pattern and amount. For water, a river and stream were nearby. Lush grass provided grazing for their stock, a herd Sunshine had joined by coercion. The loyal palomino was hobbled to keep her from seeking out her mistress among human and animal strangers.

Beth was given nothing to drink or eat during the ride to this site or last night after her arrival. But she had received bread and water at dawn.

Otherwise, she was avoided as a rattler, and her attempts to speak with anyone were ignored as if she hadn't spoken or wasn't present. In a way, she understood their ill-feelings. Having lived in Arizona for months, she had heard many things about the Indians who had ruled the territory before the whites came. Their domain was so vast long ago that it was called Gran Apacheria, and encompassed all or parts of six states and a section of Mexico. Now, they couldn't ride or walk or hunt anywhere in freedom, and were forbidden to raid ancestral foes across the Mexican border. Their chiefs had shouted that Mexico couldn't sell this territory to America in the Gadsden Purchase because they didn't own it or even rule it by conquest.

She had been told Apaches were cunning, fierce, skilled fighters who showed no mercy and felt no pity to enemies; to do so marked them as weaklings or men who could be duped. There was no doubt in her mind that she was being treated as an enemy. It didn't matter if she was innocent of hatred and hostility or that she was a woman, as the Apaches were one of the few Indian nations that had female warriors. All that counted was her "white blood," and it went against her.

Despite her mishandling by the leader, Beth remained sympathetic for now, fearful but discerning and compassionate. She assumed there must be no reason in the Indians' eyes as to why they should trust or befriend her when *her* people scorned, taunted, and humbled them. According to allegations those Indians on most reservations were cheated of promised supplies, delivered skinny or sickly cattle, infected with diseases, and forced to stand in long columns under a blazing sun for hours to collect meager or rotting rations that ran out before the line was half gone. Those at San Carlos were said to be humiliated, reduced to begging, deprived, and imprisoned on what this area's Apaches called Hell's Forty Acres, exiled to a section of near wasteland. She had heard charges about appointed reservation lands being given, sold, and loaned to miners and farmers and ranchers by corrupt politicians or deceitful agency officials. The shocking list of alleged physical and emotional abuses went on and on in Arizona and elsewhere, according to Navarro and numerous other sources who were working to get those wrongs righted for the sake of peace and honor.

Beth's eyes scanned her surroundings once more. There was an old man who continued to observe her with an intriguing interest. On many occasions since her arrival, he seemed to reason, then immediately argue with Eagle Eye over an important matter. She noticed that the renegades treated the elder with respect and affection, even those who seemed to disagree with him. Some appeared to believe his words, some seemed on the edge of being persuaded to lean in either direction, and others were visibly unconvinced. The latter group included their scar-faced leader, the only person who used a scowl and belligerent tone with the one who must be their shaman or past chief.

She had overheard part of a talk between them so many times since her arrival that she had committed it to memory, though she couldn't translate the meaning. The older man would say the same things as he pointed at her: *"Kuu -tsiighaa'. -Tsiighaa' ye' aku'i."*

The angry and stubborn warrior would shake his dark head and grit out, *"Todah. Tl'ee' -jet. Indaa 'ent'iin. Chéek'e."*

The white-haired, wrinkled-skinned man would refute, *" 'Andi."*

"Todah."

With resolve in those gentle brown eyes, he would refute again, *" 'Andi."*

"Todah. Chéek'e."

After a repetitive series where neither altered his opposing opinion, the elder would shake his head in concern and murmur, *"Duu 'akada."*

Following one of those curious encounters, Eagle Eye stalked to her location and towered over her until she lifted her gaze to his face. A look so truculent was stamped on it that she almost flinched from its potency.

"Why do you hate me so much? What harm have I done to you?"

"You like coyote; you bring evil, death, bad things."

"I'm not evil just because I'm white. I don't hate and mistreat Indians. I have Indian friends. I speak against the bad things on the reservations. I am not a coyote or witch. I can be your friend and helper."

"You be friend? You help?" he scoffed, and spat on the ground.

"I'm not your enemy, *Ea*—" She halted her tongue before it spoke his name, preventing a perilous mistake. "Eliminate me and you provoke war."

"What is e-lim-men-nate?"

"To murder me, to kill me, to slay an innocent woman."

"You not in-no-cent. No whiteskin in-no-cent. You coyote, enemy."

As he spoke those words between clenched teeth, Beth watched him drizzle fringes over her head, chest, and lap which she had dropped along the way. A malicious sneer curled one corner of his wide, full mouth. His jet eyes gleamed with victory and his parting tone was filled with taunting.

"You not smart as Eagle Eye. You not Flamehair in shaman's vision."

Beth saw his long ebony hair swing outward from powerful shoulders as he whirled and walked away, creating a trail of chilling laughter with each step. In horror, she realized he considered her a threat. To herself and her mission, she was a failure.

She yelled at the retreating warrior, "I left those signals so my family could track me and rescue me! I didn't leave them for soldiers to use to find and attack your camp! Release me, Eagle Eye, or you will find yourself in big trouble!"

Eagle Eye spun to face her with a narrowed gaze that fired imaginary bullets at her. He exposed a violent loss of temper and burning rage that stiffened his body as he screamed at her, "Silence or I will cut out your insulting tongue and wicked heart! No rescue will come; no trail to follow. Soon, you and your people will die."

Beth comprehended his cunning deceit to Jim, and probably to all whites: he could speak very good English! *Don't underestimate him again.* She wondered if the fringes were only those from the trail or if the scout had found her message under the rock and destroyed it. She prayed for Navarro to stay on the crucial mission in order to defeat Charles Cordell and Eagle Eye. She also prayed her partner wouldn't risk his life and steal valuable time to seek and rescue her.

As time passed, the sun moved westward of the secluded camp. Beth couldn't dismiss from her mind what the pugnacious leader had said: "You not Flamehair in shaman's vision." She presumed the older Apache was the shaman he mentioned, and she knew all Indians believed in visions. She concluded that a prophecy about a redhead was at the crux of the two men's conversations. The keen-witted Beth wondered if there was a way she could use their superstitions and beliefs to save her life and win her freedom. But how could she play off of a dream without knowing its contents? How—

Beth's gaze widened and her mouth fell ajar as Navarro Breed walked into the clearing as if he were taking a Sunday stroll in a secure area! His bold approach and physical appearance astonished her. From weeks on the trail and for disguise, his sable hair was longer than its usual shoulder-grazing length; a narrow red sash was secured around his head in Apache fashion. His clean-shaven jawline and upper lip caused prominent Indian features to be noticeable. He wore high-top moccasins and fringed buckskin pants that clung to his splendid physique. A longer and wider red sash was tied around his waist, with ends dangling to his knees. A vest allowed the hard and rippling muscles in his hairless chest and arms and the firmness of his midriff to be exposed. An Indian amulet was suspended around his neck, unlike the one given to Lane. Thongs of a leather-and-beaded armband tied around his left upper arm swayed from a confident stride. The only weapon he wore was a knife in a sheath at his waist!

Heavens, my love, what are you doing here? They'll kill you! Eagle Eye isn't a man to be trusted or challenged. You aren't crazy or reckless, so what daring ruse do you have in mind? You shouldn't have come; the mission is too important to abandon. You said no partner can be rescued if the risks and odds are too great. These are!

Not once did Navarro glance her way or slow his pace as he headed straight for Eagle Eye. As Beth observed the shocking and frightening scene, her heart pounded and she trembled. She felt weak from dread, and from so little food and water for two days. *God, protect him, please.*

During his advance to the renegade leader, Navarro made the sign for *Peace.* He wasn't surprised to be encircled by the band, but he was stunned to see who was standing near the glaring leader. Navarro's expression and behavior did not expose his recognition of Sees-Through-Clouds, the elderly shaman he had captured and taken to San Carlos three years ago, the Wise One who had related to him a vision about Beth—not Jessie. How strange their paths should cross again when a "woman with hair burning as flaming rocks" was trapped between them . . . As he made signs for *Truce, Friend,* and *Apache,* the baffled Special Agent noted that the white-haired man also didn't reveal they knew each other.

Eagle Eye sneered, "You white, not Chiricahua."

"*Shi-ma,* Chiricahua. *Shi-Tsúyé,* Chiricahua. *Shi-Chu,* Chiricahua. *Shi 'ik l'idá beedaajindánde,* Chiricahua. *Tl'ee' K'us,* Chiricahua." Navarro watched how his knowledge and command of their language affected the hostile leader as the hazel-eyed man revealed that his mother, maternal grandfather and grandmother, and maternal ancestors were Chiricahua. He witnessed anger in the warrior's gaze when he related an Apache name.

"*Duu nliida,* Half-breed."

Navarro refused to be provoked by Eagle Eye's insult. "I carry the blood of two sides; *'Andi.'*"

"It is true, you half-breed," Eagle Eye translated the stranger's words to prove he, too, could speak an enemy's language with ease.

"Which tongue do you choose to speak, Eagle Eye?"

"You chose white world. Do not dirty Chiricahua with your tongue."

"My mother's people would not accept me because my father was white, a man she chose to love. That is the reason I entered the white world. I'm bound to *both* worlds, Eagle Eye, and want peace between them."

Navarro witnessed the warrior's command of English during a subsequent tirade.

The rebuttal was so loud and vehement that Beth caught every word. "There can be no peace! We will not live as captives on reservations! We will not cut our hair, wear white man's garments, speak only their tongue! We will not give up our weapons and forget the hunt! We will not be farmers and slaves! We will not honor their special days and forget our rituals and be halted from our dances! We will not put their god in Ysun's place, for the whites have many gods they call the Giver of Life; we have one Great Being with many helpers! We will not go to their schools to learn and do white ways! They can not civilize us when they are not civilized! We will not let their diseases kill our bodies! We will not cower, beg, be shamed! We are Chiricahua; we can not become whites!"

As if noticing how his tirade shocked onlookers, Beth and Navarro watched Eagle Eye force himself to calm down; but his tone remained loud and clear to be heard by his followers.

"Child of Water and Killer of Enemies, children of Ysun and White Painted Woman, wait to help us take back our land and pride. The Thunder Beings will roar with happiness when we reclaim their home. We have done the *Gahan* dance to call mountain spirits to guide us; we will slay the white Evil; the Mountain People will sing and dance soon in victory. The Power is with us, Halfbreed. The Magic Plant grows many and large; soon, Sacred Pollen will be cast upon the face of Earth Mother. In six suns, we will have great magic. Before the next full moon, only Chiricahuas will ride this land."

For those who knew English from years on the reservation, Navarro spoke in a measured pace so his words could be translated for those who didn't. "Your great magic is weapons from a devil called Charles Cordell. He breaks the white law to bring them to you. He'll be captured and punished. If you accept his guns, you and your people will be attacked and killed. The white men coming to trade are evil and greedy; don't trust them."

"Their greed changes nothing. They supply what we need for victory."

Navarro slowed his delivery even more and spoke in a confident manner, and was astonished he wasn't interrupted by the infuriated leader. "There can be no victory for your band, Eagle Eye. General Miles has many soldiers and scouts; he has many weapons, powerful weapons. He rides this very sun to capture or slay the Chiricahua who fled the reservation and returned to warring on the whites. He has more soldiers than trees in these mountains. Friends and allies and enemies of the

Chiricahua have joined the Great White Soldier to help him find you and defeat you; his scouts are Apaches who know this territory and the Apache ways. How long can you hide from them? When the bullets are gone from your trade, the guns you buy will be useless. When that dark day comes, how will you and your braves battle the whites you have challenged? How will you protect your camp and people? The children, the women, the old ones? You give your people false hope and lead them toward destruction. How many of your family and friends must die because you refuse to see the truth and yield to it?"

"The one to die is the white witch who brings bad medicine."

Navarro's heart skipped a beat. "She's not a witch, Eagle Eye. She's not your enemy. Her heart is good and her words are true. She's here to help your people survive, to find peace."

"Let her prove she is not bad medicine."

Sees-Through-Clouds stepped between the two speakers. "She not witch. She Flamehair, Vision Woman. She come to protect and lead us."

"Lead us where, old shaman? To captivity? To dishonor?"

"To peace. To life. To our people's survival. If we to live past days of white man's coming and evil reservations, we must do her words. It what sacred vision command; we must obey."

"It was a dream, Old One, not a vision. The Power would not send a white woman to be our leader. She is evil. She tricks you. She must die."

"If disobey sacred vision, Eagle Eye, Ysun punish with death."

Navarro and Beth observed the favorable effect on the renegades after the shaman's words. But the cunning Eagle Eye was quick to reason against them.

"Do you forget the words of Goyathlay: 'This is my home. Here I stay. Kill me if you wish, for every living thing has to die sometime. How can a man die better than fighting for his own?' His words are true; it is better to die in honor and freedom than to live in shame as the white man's prisoner."

The lawman knew how revered Geronimo was but he had to speak against his teachings. "It's easy to die, Chiricahuas. It takes more courage, wits, and strength to steal peace and life from your enemy. Raid his heart and mind for acceptance and understanding, not his lands for goods he will recover in battle. Be cunning; take the land he offers on this sun; later take more and more by little bits. Become stronger by learning all he can teach you. How can you win victory over an enemy you do not know? You must not be provoked to recklessness by his cruel words and laughter; they cannot pierce the skin and bone of powerful warriors. When insults do not work, they will grow tired of trying and stop speaking them. You will earn their respect for being strong and smart. It is not the Apache way to lose hope, to forget your wits, to be reckless, to make a challenge you cannot win."

"You are blind, Halfbreed, a fool. You are the whiteman's dog."

Practice what you just told them to do; turn the other cheek and stay calm. "Does 'the white man's dog,' an enemy, come in truce to save your people from certain death? No. I am a friend. I am one of the white law."

"You are crazy to enter my camp and to speak with two tongues."

"I do not lie. I earned the right to parlay in truce." Navarro lifted his hands and unballed them to reveal the items he held, the amulets of every scout around the camp. "They are bound to trees at their posts. I did not harm them. By defeating them, I earned the right to enter and speak."

"What do you want from Eagle Eye?"

"Help against the evil whites and peace with good ones, and my woman. Her," he added, and motioned to Beth. Navarro saw the leader's gaze widen in surprise, then glitter with spiteful mischief.

"The Power told me to open my eyes to see better in all directions. With my knife and hand, I obeyed and made these magic marks. She must fight to prove she is Flamehair; she must prove she is no witch."

Navarro controlled his panic with difficulty. "You said she wasn't the sacred vision woman. I will battle you with hands and knives for her possession, as is the Apache way to settle a claim."

"This matter is not between us, Halfbreed. Sees-Through-Clouds says she is Flamehair. She must prove he is right or wrong. If she passes the test, we will become allies. If she fails, both will die a death slow and painful. If you know the Apache customs as you say, you know how a witch must die: we will hang her on a post by her hands with ropes and torture the truth from her tongue. We will make a great fire around her and burn the evil from her body and our land. We will bury her ashes in Earth Mother's belly."

Beth had never experienced such sheer terror. She feared her pounding heart would burst from her chest. She feared she would strangle on her dry tongue and throat. She felt as if every inch of her was quaking. She could be put to a horrible death soon. Navarro could be tortured and slain. The mission could be lost.

"She's a woman, Eagle Eye; she can't fight a warrior in battle. Your heart is black; you use this trick to defeat good, to destroy a sacred vision."

"She will take the test; it is our way. If she fails, both will die."

"Do you fear us and hate peace so much, Eagle Eye, you would have us slain and a sacred vision dishonored by using deceit?"

"I fear no white man, no white woman." He yanked off his vest. "Their long knives cut my flesh; I did not die. Their whips beat me; I did not die. Their bullets entered my body; I did not die. They gave me bad or no rations, and I did not die. They can not kill me. Ysun and his helpers protect me and guide me. I will lead the Chiricahua to victory."

Navarro removed his vest. "I did not die, either; I made peace because peace lets me live to do what I must on new suns and moons."

Eagle Eye stared at the lash marks, and Navarro's implied strength. "I make no peace like a coward! We are Chiricahua; these are our lands! I will not live on a useless reservation like a beaten animal."

"You'll remain there only until you prove you'll keep the truce. Prove you want peace by helping me trap the evil whites." Again, Navarro saw that gleam of malicious mischief in those black eyes, and dreaded its meaning.

"If your woman proves she is Flamehair, we will obey your words. Bring the woman," Eagle Eye ordered two of his followers.

Beth wondered if she could delude them into believing she was this "Flamehair" who had come to give them sacred advice. If so, many lives would be saved, including hers and Navarro's. If she couldn't be convincing, all was lost, and the renegades would go on the warpath. Worse, arms from Charles would entice more disgruntled Apaches to leave the reservation and join a band that appeared powerful enough to fight injustice. Her bonds were cut so she could join the group. Her body was so stiff she could hardly walk or stand straight, and neither Indian assisted her. She was relieved most of the talk had taken place in English, as that let Beth know what was required for success and safety.

The apprehensive redhead did not even glance at Navarro; to do so would be far too distracting and unsettling. She looked first into the gentle eyes of the shaman and smiled. "As you saw in your vision, Wise One, I have come as a messenger from Ysun to help save His children." She drew her partner's knife, severed a fiery lock of brightest copper, and gave it to the older man as a keepsake. She watched him accept the token in gratitude and reverence as if it were a holy gift from an Indian goddess.

Sees-Through-Clouds lifted his treasure skyward and watched the sun enhance its radiant color; the thick curl appeared to blaze with inner fire as if it possessed a captive soul that was aflame. *" 'Ixée, Kuu -tsiighaa'."*

As Navarro replaced his knife, he translated, "Thank you, Flamehair."

Beth smiled and nodded, then focused a stern gaze on the belligerent leader. She paced her imperative speech for easy translation. "You are the evil one, Eagle Eye, not Flamehair. You seek personal honor and revenge at the cost of your own people's lives. A good and wise chief does not think of himself, his glory, his hatred, his hungers; he does what is best for his people. For your people to survive to wait for good days to return is what is best for them. You must help us trap the gunrunners who seek to destroy you with their greed and evil. They are not friends; they do not care about Indians; they only hunger for the trade you offered them. You must surrender to the soldiers, and they will not harm you. You must return to San Carlos to live; in seasons to come, things will get better. The Apaches have many whites with good and honest hearts working to help them get justice. Tl'ee' K'us is one of those men. Flamehair is one of those helpers. We are *-ch' uuné'.*"

She watched a sneer lift one corner of his mouth. "We know of bad things on the reservation and we hate them. We work to expose the evil ones to blame. We work to put good men in charge. If you do not obey the vision, all is lost in land and lives. If you kill us, we cannot help your people, those who ride with you and those who stayed at San Carlos. Make peace with honor by surrender. Do not bring on humiliation and suffering by forcing the soldiers to conquer you. I wish you could live, ride, and hunt in freedom, but it cannot be for many seasons to come. After you earn the white man's trust and friendship, you will be free again." Beth observed favorable responses to her words and alleged identity. She also saw that Eagle Eye was quick to put a halt to her attempts for peace.

"We will not listen to more words until you earn the right to speak."

"How do I earn the right, Eagle Eye?" Beth prayed her expression and reaction didn't give away her trepidation at his shocking reply.

The shaman said, "If your words are true, so shall the arrow from your bow be true. Flamehair come with me to prepare for test."

"Take her, Sees-Through-Clouds; prepare her to die if she fails."

"She not fail; sacred vision true. *Ysun* help her prove words."

As Navarro started to leave with his partner and the shaman, Eagle Eye halted him. "No, you stay. No tricks. Bind his hands and feet. Take his knife. If he tries to escape, slay him, slay the woman."

In the shaman's wickiup, Beth was given food and water to strengthen her. The old man sat on a mat, shook a rattle, and chanted for many minutes. He handed Beth buckskin garments, a medallion, and a hair ornament.

"You wear for ritual. Yellow as sacred Pollen: breath of Ysun, Giver of Life. Moon, sun, stars, lightning give you power to win victory. Fringes, rays of sacred sun and moon; they light path to victory. Moccasins guide steps. Must purify body with water from yucca. It there. I knew you come; I wait long time. I speak with Night Cloud. You prepare for test."

No matter what happens, "Thank you, Sees-Through-Clouds."

"Words not needed; it will of Great Being for Chiricahua to live."

Beth looked at the celestial symbols painted on the sunny garment and footwear. She prayed for the power to save their lives and to help bring about peace. If this band could be persuaded to surrender, she reasoned, perhaps Geronimo's would. Assured of privacy, the agent removed her clothes and bathed in refreshing yucca suds. She donned a simple breechcloth, then the ceremonial dress and moccasins; to her amazement, everything fit. The sunburst medallion was put around her neck. The ornament was secured in braided hair. She was ready to face her destiny.

No, her troubled mind refuted, she wasn't. Her heart pounded and her body trembled. What if, Beth fretted, she couldn't strike the center of a target with an arrow? No doubt Eagle Eye assumed she had never handled a bow and would fail the first test. In the past, she had hit the bull's-eye a few times when calm and after practice; but today, she was shaky and scared, rusty. And how could she perform a feat of great magic? *Heaven help me. If this is my destiny, make my training and experience assist me. If you want peace, dear Lord, help me to achieve it. If we must die, give our loss some special meaning, and Thy will be done.*

Outside, the shaman spoke with Navarro. "Many seasons past, I not tell you all of vision; your heart and head not ready to hear and believe my words. Do not fear, Night Cloud; Flamehair not be defeated by evil."

Navarro sometimes believed in visions, as there were many mysteries in life. But was this one of those powerful wonders? Part of it had come true, but . . . "She's tired and weak, Old One; she's frightened and confused. This is a heavy burden on her shoulders. Are you sure she is the vision woman?"

He nodded a head surrounded with long white hair and smiled. " *'Au,* old friend. Ysun send her, give her strength. Killer of Enemies guide her aim. Child of Water give her courage. White Painted Woman give hope. *Gan,* Mountain People, save her life. She save Chiricahuas from soldiers and evil whites."

Navarro had seen Beth use a bow and arrow, and he wasn't convinced she could pass that test. As to a magic feat, he was even more doubtful. In his bound state, there was nothing he could do to rescue her. If not for the alleged vision, he could have dueled for her innocence of the witch charges and her return to him. With luck, they could have been gone by now. They could be riding to set the mission trap for Charles. He could be leaving her some place she would be safe until he completed their assignment alone. He could be holding her in his arms, kissing her, confessing his love, urging her to take a second chance at love and happiness with him. From the way things looked, he might never get to touch her again or tell her—

"She not fail, Night Cloud. She vision woman. When peace made, Flamehair be your woman. She fill all holes in life, in heart."

It was as if the old man had read and responded to his troubled thoughts. "I hope so, Wise One; I love her and need her."

Beth was summoned to the center of the clearing. She knew she needed time to calm down and to stop trembling. She used the only excuse to come to mind. "I must pray and call the spirits to join us. I need a mat, Wise One, and a ceremonial rattle. May I use yours?"

The redhead drew a circle in the dirt while the shaman fetched the requested items. She placed the mat inside it and took a position on her knees with buttocks resting on moccasin soles, facing eastward as Navarro had told her Indians did to pray. So far, the celestial body she needed later had not appeared, and the other one was sinking fast in the west. She closed her eyes and lifted the painted gord. She hummed and murmured unintelligible French words as she shook it, as if calling the spirits or communing with the Great Being. She drew on facts Navarro had told her to play the crucial role thrust upon her.

Eagle Eye stepped forward and gripped her head with spread fingers, burying them in hair that blazed like a roaring fire beneath the setting sun. He pushed it backward until he could look into her upturned face. Green eyes opened and stared at him. "If you fail or trick us, I will slay you."

Beth had to call his bluff. "You dare to break a sacred circle and interrupt the ceremony with bad medicine from your hatred and mistrust! Do not interfere with things you do not understand and doubt. When I hide the moon in the night sky, you and others must believe and obey. If you do not, Ysun and Killer of Enemies will punish you with death and will destroy your band. Gan will order the Water Monsters from the rivers and lakes to punish you and your followers. If you wish to survive these dark days to live in bright ones ahead, give me time to prove myself."

"If your arrow is not true, your words are not true. If the moon rides its trail as always, you will die when the sun returns. The half-breed who calls you his woman will die first. I will wipe his mixed bloods on your skin and yours will run with his into the mouth of Earth Mother."

Don't let him provoke and unnerve you. "Leave the circle so I can purify it again. The good Spirits will not listen and answer while it is stained with evil from one whose heart is black. Soon, moonlight will not touch the faces of your people or the land of your fathers until I order its return. Then, you will know I speak the truth and the vision is sacred." If the almanac was wrong about a lunar eclipse on Tuesday, May eleventh . . .

Beth was relieved when the truculent man returned to his place. She closed her eyes, prayed, and concentrated on letting go of her tension. She took deep breaths, held each for a time, then released it. She tried to relax every muscle in her body. She called to mind the tips given to her by Steven and Navarro as she visualized her one shot with the Indian weapon.

Navarro couldn't surmise what tricks his lover was planning. It was futile for Beth to stall, if that was what she was doing; no rescue was forthcoming because no one knew either they or the Indians were here, and, his wrists bound together; he was impotent to assist. Navarro knew his partner was clever, brave, and skilled; but would those things help in this predicament? If only he had been given a few minutes to talk with her, give her suggestions and comfort . . .

At dusk, Beth knew she couldn't stall the inevitable any longer. She stood and glanced at the bow and arrow the guileful leader had placed nearby. She shook her head and addressed her words to the shaman: "Night Cloud will string a bow and choose an arrow for me."

Eagle Eye sneered, "You must not use those with evil magic, witch."

"Mine are purified; yours are the evil ones, for they have been touched by one with a black heart. The test does not say I must use yours."

" *'Andi,'* " Sees-Through-Clouds announced before Eagle Eye argued.

The Indian circle was too close and tight for words with her lover, so Beth said, "I must have space and fresh air to do my task."

The shaman told everyone to move backward and was obeyed. For once, Eagle Eye didn't protest, as he was eager to end the matter. Navarro was freed to fetch the sapling and string from his saddle, but under armed guard. He examined the arrows he had made and selected the best one. He was touched by her faith in his talents and glad she asked for weapons she could trust more than an enemy's. He joined Beth. She didn't look at him, perhaps to prevent distraction, as she held his life in her hands. He wanted to tell her of his love, but that would be a worse distraction.

Beth closed her eyes, shook the rattle, and pretended to bless the bow. In a whisper, she asked, "What is *bilaahda?*"

As he strung the bow with a lowered head, he replied, "Silver metal."

"What is the magic flower?"

"Agave, the Century Plant, the tall one I told you about in Mexico."

Beth laid aside the rattle and lifted the arrow. She fingered the shaft to ascertain its feel and weight as he'd taught many days ago. "I remember."

"There's no wind to concern you. Three inches higher for this range." He passed her the weapon. "Don't rush the shot. Get loose first. Plan it with your eyes and fingers. You can do it, partner, or you're fired."

Beth smiled at his humorous attempt to relax her. "Be ready to escape if I miss. You can come back for me later."

Navarro went to stand beside Sees-Through-Clouds. *Do it, my love, because I won't leave without you . . .*

Beth nocked the arrow, took a steadying breath, and drew back the string. She eyed the target, adjusted her aim, and released the arrow. She closed her eyes and listened to it swish through the eerie silence. She heard the thud and lowered the bow to her side. Everyone remained quiet; no shouts neither of victory nor defeat came forth to enlighten her. She opened her eyes and looked at the target. She could hardly believe her good luck: dead center. She did it! Her prayers were answered! Maybe her capture wasn't a mistake or her arrival a coincidence after all. Her triumphant gaze went to Eagle Eye's face, which was a mask of hatred and disbelief. He prevented Navarro from joining her and had the lawman bound once more, claiming her test wasn't over and her identity confirmed until after her magic feat.

The scar-faced leader came forward. His obsidian gaze glanced at the eastern sky, then made a contemptuous sweep over Beth's copper hair and sun-pinkened pale face. He taunted in a tone others could not overhear, "There is no moon to hide. When the sun returns and proves you false, you are dead; the half-breed is dead. After my braves take your body many times on their mats, I will cut out your evil tongue and heart and eyes before you burn. I will feed them to the bear and coyote. You will not win this battle. Sit and speak not. Soon, your body is theirs but your blood is mine."

Beth obeyed, and tried to come up with a backup plan or ruse if nature failed her tonight. So far, the sky wasn't looking cooperative . . .

Eagle Eye was doing his own plotting, in case she succeeded . . .

Chapter Twenty-three

Darkness came, and so did Eagle Eye to where Beth sat alone on the shaman's mat before his wickiup. He pointed to a sluggish full moon on the horizon and asked in a skeptical tone when she was going to do her magic.

"I will begin to steal its light when it is there." She pointed eastward. "It will have none when it is above me and this sacred moment. When it is there," she said, pointing westward, "I will return its full shine." Most of the band had gathered around her as if she were ready to start. Beth used the encounter to her advantage. "As it is with nature on this night, so it is now with the Chiricahua. In time past, they were shiny and full as the moon; whites came as they glowed over the land, and their light vanished for a time; if they travel a road of peace and acceptance as the moon follows its rightful path across the sky, they will be full and shiny again, as will the moon when it returns. Watch and learn, Chiricahuas. Open your hearts and minds to the truth. Obey the will of Ysun, Giver of Life."

"Do not trick us with clever words. Let your deed speak for you."

"It will, Eagle Eye. Eat and rest, Chiricahuas; the ceremony is long and comes late at night as a cunning and victorious thief."

"If you raid the sky and steal the moon's light, I will listen and obey."

Even as he spoke those words before his followers, Beth did not believe him. She warned herself to be on alert for dangerous deceptions.

It wasn't long before the shaman came to sit beside her and bring her food: antelope meat, wild potatoes, dried fruit, fry bread, and wild tea. He pointed to each in turn and said their names as if to teach them to her: *"Ch' ilaé bitsi, 'izee béduusi, 'itsá' ích'i'i, bánxéi, tl' ugaxee'."*

" 'Ixée," she thanked him as she'd heard earlier, and he smiled.

"Flamehair learn swift like antelope run. Do not fear; moon help."

"I hope so, Sees-Through-Clouds, or we all will be in trouble."

They were silent for a time as they ate and drank and reflected.

Beth thought on what she had read about a total lunar eclipse: the moon must be full; it must be at an exact opposite location of the sun; it could be seen from any place in the world; it occurred two to three times a year. If the almanac was accurate, one event was tonight. If not . . .

She put doubts aside to concentrate on other matters. She went over the talk between Jim Tiller and Eagle Eye and the clue she had gathered from Navarro this evening. She planned the impending talk to the renegade band, if the moon didn't fail her.

"Night Cloud good man. He Flamehair man?"

Beth didn't know how to answer. She didn't want to lie to the gentle and kind Indian. She feared if she did so it would show on her face and she would lose his trust and respect, but Navarro had said she was his woman. Her gaze softened and glowed as it fused with the lawman's and they exchanged smiles. "I hope so."

The perceptive old man chuckled. "It so. That good. Be much happy. Ysun reward helpers. Have land, horses, cattle, children. Dress have sacred Pollen. Night Cloud, Flamehair grow many things."

Not a child in my infertile womb; no magic is that real or powerful. "You're a good man, too. I'm honored you believe in me and became my friend."

He had seen which word stole the smile in her cactus-green eyes. "Tell Night Cloud long ago you come to him one day, be his woman."

"I don't understand."

"Three summers past, he take Sees-Through-Clouds to reservation. He not want old shaman hunted, killed. I go. Must be at San Carlos to escape with Eagle Eye; must be at Bear Mountain for Ysun magic this moon."

"You and Navarro are old friends?"

"It true. Long ago, he sad; not want to take Sees-Through-Clouds to bad place. He not happy; have no woman. Tell him Flamehair vision, not all; long ago he not ready to listen, believe. Tell him woman with fire in hair come to him, be his woman. I tell him much trouble come for him, come for Flamehair. Tell him it blow away if ride as one, if he chase the wind. Bad time come; trouble come; Flamehair come to Night Cloud, come to Chiricahua. You wind, blow away evil; Chiricahua safe; you happy."

She was astounded by those revelations. Were they coincidences or something more, one of life's mysteries? "How could you know such things about us and the future, Wise One?"

"Ysun see, know all; tell Sees-Through-Clouds in vision long ago."

"Did Navarro tell you my white name is Beth Wind?" The old man's reaction answered that question: her lover had not and she wondered why.

He straightened his shoulders, stared at her, then smiled. "It good vision, strong vision."

Several points flooded Beth's mind: Navarro had believed for years the shaman's vision was about the eventual return of his lost love, the auburn-haired Jessica Lane Cordell. That mistaken assumption had to be part of the reason he had clung to false hope for so long. No wonder he had exposed such strong and odd reactions to her hair color and name! If he had told Daniel Withers about the shaman's words, that would explain why Navarro briefly suspected Dan of having an ulterior motive for choosing her as his partner.

So, she mused, her "husband" had another secret he hadn't shared with her. Since he was part Apache and had been partly reared by them, maybe he believed in visions. Should she use the vision and this episode to convince her love they must "ride as one" for longer than this assignment? Could she convince him "if he chased the wind" his anguish would "blow away"? Or perhaps the vision and belief in them were the only reasons he'd allowed her to get this close to him. But she wanted him to love her for herself. She wanted—

The shaman nudged her arm. "Flamehair pray, do magic."

Beth pushed aside worries as she checked the moon's position. If the almanac was correct, an eclipse would begin soon. She stood and lifted her hands into the air. "It is time, Chiricahuas. Behold the power of Ysun as he proves my words are true and must be obeyed."

Following the arrow test, people sat on mats and on the ground as they waited, watched, and chatted in muffled tones; the few children with the band were asleep in their mother's laps or in the family's hut. Beth saw Eagle Eye with his closest friends, and he glanced at her often, a mixture of hatred and spite in his gaze. The hour was late, but she knew he remained ready to pounce on her the instant she failed, even if that required staying up all night.

Beth's gaze focused on the celestial target. Soon, there was a black mark on the edge of its illuminating surface. She breathed a sigh of relief, then prayed it wouldn't be a partial eclipse, as she'd promised a total one. While her heart pounded in suspense, the dark shadow grew larger and larger at a steady pace. When the moon seemed to vanish, murmurings of awe were audible, and fingers pointing upward were visible in light cast by campfire. She glanced at Eagle Eye, who was gaping at her in disbelief again.

"Do not fear, Chiricahuas, Ysun and Flamehair will return its light." She chanted unintelligible words as she shook the rattle.

Minutes later, the shadow seemed to creep away as a cunning and skilled thief in the night. The episode continued until a yellowish orb recovered its full radiance and journeyed along its regular path.

"It is done, Chiricahuas. The message from Ysun is to seek peace, not a return to war with the whites. The men who bring you weapons are evil; they will trick you into destroying yourselves. To defeat their evil and to prove to the Great White Leader and his soldiers you want and have earned peace, you must help Night Cloud and Flamehair trap those who come soon to make evil trade. This is the help and guidance Ysun sent me to give to you. Prove to the soldiers and whites you had the power to war against them but chose peace, chose to defeat those who provoke it."

Beth pointed her forefinger at Eagle Eye and scolded, "It is wrong to give the evil whites the *bilaahda* that Gan, the Thunder Beings, and Earth Mother guard for you to use one day. The silver metal is worth much to whites and it can buy much for the Chiricahuas after peace and friendship are in your hands. The evil whites must not invade and plunder the face of Earth Mother and the homes of the Mountain People and Thunder Beings to take *bilaahda* from their secret places. Eagle Eye says the silver metal means nothing to him and would tell the evil whites where to find it, but Flamehair and Ysun say it can buy a glorious future for the Chiricahua."

Careful, woman, but destroy his influence over this band. "Eagle Eye says it is a sign that many agave grow this season, and he is right. But he is wrong about what the sign means. The agave tells of strength and patience. Its seed lies hidden in the body of Earth Mother for many winters. When its time is right, it comes to life and reaches for the sky. It blooms, scatters seeds and sacred Pollen for new life before it returns to the body of Earth Mother, its task done. As with the agave, the Chiricahua must be strong and patient; their seeds of freedom and glory must remain inactive for many seasons. The time will come when Chiricahuas will spring to new life before you return to the body of Earth Mother to join the spirit world. If you disobey Ysun, your life stems will be cut down by soldiers before they can bloom and shatter seeds for future Chiricahuas. As when the dark shadow stood before the moon and hid its light and glory, so the soldiers stand before the Apache and halt theirs. One day, the whites' shadow will move aside and the Chiricahuas' moon will reappear. If you challenge the soldiers and slay innocent whites, their bodies will remain as blackness between the Apache and their moon of survival and renewal. You must teach the whites to accept you by ceasing wars against them, for only friends help friends."

Eagle Eye stalked forward and took a challenging stance before her. He shouted, "We cannot become friends with the whites and their soldiers!"

"You must. The day when the Apache owned and ruled this land is gone. You must learn a new way of life and must accept what has come to be, or all will die and no Apache will walk the face of Earth Mother. There is no shame and dishonor in peace and friendship, Eagle Eye, only in letting your people be slain and your land bloodied with futile battles. There is great honor and pride and glory in stealing hatred and acceptance from past foes, in raiding their hearts to grab life and happiness. You were once a great thief who robbed with cunning and courage; is this task too large and hard for you to do? Now, you are their chief; the survival of your people must come before your desires if you are to be a great leader."

"Your evil magic is powerful, White Witch; you use it to trick us. If you have good magic and a good heart, put out the flames we light around you in a sacred fire. If you are not a witch, you can not burn and die."

Navarro struggled with the thongs securing his wrists together. He couldn't let her be coerced into a stake burning test, one she'd fail for certain. Somehow and some way, she had won a great victory and it mustn't be destroyed. He cursed his helplessness as the bonds refused to yield.

Beth glared at the wicked villain. *Oh, no, you don't.* "I have done the tests you demanded and passed them. I will do no more. I see what trickery is in your black heart; for every test I pass, you will demand another and another as you seek to prove me false, which I am not."

"If you are not a sly witch, do this last test and magic."

"No. I have done as you, the vision, and Ysun commanded."

The leader scoffed, "You are afraid because you are false."

"I fear only the fierce hatred burning in your heart and head, for you seek to use it to destroy your people. That is wrong, evil. It is late. People are tired. We must sleep and rest. We will talk and plan on the new sun. Free Night Cloud; I have earned his life; it is mine."

Before Eagle Eye could protest, the shaman nodded at one of the warriors, who cut Navarro's bonds. Navarro stepped to Beth's side. He readied himself to do battle in case the angry and unpredictable warrior attacked her. "It is done, Eagle Eye. Do not dishonor yourself with defiance against Life Giver. She has proven herself."

"Go, rest, Chiricahuas; Flamehair is vision woman, *Ysun* helper. Flamehair, Night Cloud use Sees-Through-Clouds wickiup. Rest. Talk on new sun. Sees-Through-Clouds sleep under magic moon."

The band dissipated and entered their dwellings. Eagle Eye stalked to his in a stormy mood. The shaman guided Beth and Navarro to his wickiup and nudged them inside. He lowered the cloth door and left them alone. A small fire joined moonlight filtering through a brush roof to cast a soft glow in the secluded and cozy shelter. The hide of a large bear was spread on the ground for a bed, creating a romantic and seductive setting.

"You're an amazing woman, Bethany Wind."

She turned to face him. "You're amazing yourself, Navarro Breed."

He lifted his fingers to stroke her cheek. "We make a good team."

Beth smiled as she nuzzled her face against his hand. "Yes, we do. If our good luck holds out, we have a wonderful success in our grasp. Perhaps we can work together again. Investigating the Indians' charges about abuses on the reservation would be an interesting and challenging case, certainly a worthwhile one."

"Sounds like a good idea."

"To me, too."

"I'm not scared often, woman, but when Eagle Eye demanded that next test by fire, my gut knotted with it. I'm sorry I couldn't help you. I planned to ride in, make a challenge for you, win it, and get us out of here. Might have worked if not for that vision."

Beth toyed with the dangling ends of his red headband as she said, "I have no doubt you would have won me in battle." She noticed he slipped into deep thought for a few moments while she studied his amulet.

Navarro's tender gaze roamed her face as he decided this wasn't the time and place to tell her that he fully intended to pursue and win her when this mission was completed. Soon, he vowed, he would tell her everything; but not here, not now; later, when their duty was done, in a special place and where they wouldn't be disturbed for a long time. Besides, he wanted to prove his feelings with actions. Then, when he revealed his love, it would be easy for her to believe him.

Beth came to a matching decision. Until the assignment was over, she shouldn't bring personal feelings to light and risk breaking his concentration. But at that time she would find a private location, confess, and see how he reacted. If the response she wanted wasn't forthcoming, he wouldn't be put on a tight spot. For a while, let the reality of *her* being the woman in the vision work on him. Now that she had him away from his lost love, she could show him they were perfect for each other. Perfect, she fretted, except for her major flaw. She mustn't deceive him when she confessed her love; she had to tell him she could never bear children so he could take that information into his decision. Maybe it wouldn't—

Navarro tugged on her plait. "How did you know about the eclipse?"

She meshed her gaze with his as she explained about the almanac. "If it had been wrong, we'd be in deep trouble about now."

"But you weren't wrong, partner. It was smart to use the moon; it's one of their special symbols."

"To say I could steal its light was taking a big risk with our lives."

"You had no choice. We have to play the hand destiny deals us."

"You believe strongly in fate, don't you?"

"Yep. Good or bad, we all have one. This deed is part of yours."

"And yours. Maybe this is why we've been forced to live and work as we have, to prepare us for this critical challenge. Maybe this is why you and I were thrust together as partners."

"I think we were thrown together for many reasons."

"Such as?" *Darn you, loose tongue; keep silent.*

Navarro used the opening to begin his task. "We both needed a friend. We needed help in special ways. We needed warmth and light in our cold and dark lives. I've enjoyed your sunshine and company, Mrs. Breed."

Beth laughed in pleasure. "I've enjoyed yours, Mr. Breed."

"You make a beautiful and tempting Indian woman dressed like this."

"You make a handsome and tempting warrior dressed like this. It's good to see your handsome face again," she murmured as she stroked his jawline. "Where did you get this amulet, armband, and other Indian items?"

"They belonged to my grandfather; I kept 'em hidden for years in a cave and collected 'em after prison. I use 'em only when necessary."

"They certainly came in handy today. I almost fainted when you strolled into camp as if you were a member of this band. So whatever possessed you to break the partnership rule, that survival and the mission come first?"

"*You* did; I had to save my partner since she'd done the same for me."

"That was under different conditions. You could have gotten yourself killed. The mission is more important than my life."

He shook his head. "You're a critical part of the mission, Flamehair." *And vital part of my life.* "Your message under that rock was cunning."

"I was sure you would find it if that scout covering our tracks didn't find it first and destroy it. He did find the fringes I was dropping on the trail for you to follow. Eagle Eye was overjoyed to throw them in my face as a taunt."

"So, you knew I'd come chasing after you," he teased.

"I wasn't sure and didn't mean for you to come, but I'm glad you did."

"I had only one problem getting here: You made a tepee instead of a mountain symbol. There's at least three places in these parts with bear in their name, all in different directions."

"But you guessed the right one or you wouldn't be standing here now."

"Because I realized you set up that message in a way to mean mountain. Otherwise, you'd have placed the symbol by his name instead of the bear's. You look bone tired, partner, and tomorrow's gonna be a busy day. Let's turn in."

Beth removed the hair ornament. "What should I say to them?"

"You're doing fine on your own; in fact, perfect. Like it or not, you told them what you had to say."

"True, boss."

"No more 'boss.' We're equal partners now."

No matter how well she had done in the past, Steven had stayed the couple's leader. He had never raised her to the rank of peer. For sure, Navarro was being sincere and honest. She smiled. "You can't imagine how good that makes me feel; but if you don't mind, promote me later. You know these people and the situation better than I do, so keep making the decisions until it's over. The only reason I've handled myself this well is because of everything you taught me. You stay in command and keep giving the orders." *And maybe you'll give the best one of all: Love me, Beth, as I love you.*

"If you mean that, my next order is *rest,* woman; you need some badly. Let's get you outta these clothes and bedded down in comfort."

A surprised but joyful Beth remained still as Navarro unlaced the neckline of the colorful dress. She lifted her arms for him to pull it over her head. She watched him fold the yellow garment and place it on a burden basket. He removed the beaded medallion and put it aside. He knelt, untied her moccasins, and eased them off her feet. After unbraiding her hair, he wiggled fingers into the long strands and loosened them.

As he spread the released coppery mane around her shoulders, Navarro smiled and said, "I like it running free as a sparkling red river." He scooped her into his arms and carried her to the bearskin. With strength and agility as if holding a feather, he knelt and set her on its furry surface. "Get to sleep, woman; you've earned it."

Before he could rise, Beth clasped his head between her hands and gave him a short kiss. "Thanks for teaching me and having faith in me. Most of all, thanks for coming after me and saving my life."

Navarro stayed on his knees and gazed into her lovely face. Her large and expressive eyes seemed to engulf him as tranquil green water. Though she was wearing only a breechcloth, she didn't appear to be embarrassed by her exposed body, as if their familiarity and a trust in him prevented it. To keep his eager hands from seizing the fatigued beauty and caressing her from head to foot, he propped them on his thighs and pressed them into submission. "I believe you're the one who saved my hide again, woman. That makes me twice indebted to you. It's the Apache way: if you fight over a captive and win, she belongs to you, sorta like a slave."

Beth's heart raced with excitement and her body flamed with desire. Her entire being was aroused by his stimulating proximity, playful mood, and fiery gaze. She jested, "So, if a word battle counts and since you were a prisoner, I won you fair and square as my property?"

Navarro chuckled in amusement, and almost squirmed as the flames licking at his body increased their intensity. "If we were Apache."

"We've become skilled at ruses, so why not pretend we're Apache for a little while? Sounds like a perfect way to work out our tensions before we try to get to sleep. I could return the favor if you'd like to join me on this cozy bed. Even if you're not in the mood, I've gotten used to having you close at night so I'll rest better if you lie beside me."

"I stay in the mood for you, Beth," he admitted.

She smiled and peeled off his vest. Her fingers trekked over a smooth, broad chest; an iron hardness lay beneath its tanned flesh. Her hands drifted down the shallow depression from his throat to his navel. She played in the hollows between his neck and collarbones. He was magnificent, totally masculine.

Beth lifted adventurous hands to his face. They roamed cheeks with a smidgen of dark stubble. They traced chiseled features, pausing a moment on high and prominent cheekbones. Several times her forefinger rode a tiny canyon between his mouth and nose while others wandered over his full lips. "You're a splendid specimen, Navarro Breed. It should be a crime for you to be so tempting and wit-stealing. Perhaps I should investigate you thoroughly, obtain evidence to prove those charges, and incarcerate you."

As she made her playful threat, his hands covered her breasts and rubbed their protruding points with his palms. His action made her last few words come out in a near breathless murmur, after the air caught briefly in her throat. He shifted his hands so the sides of his thumbs could stroke the buds and cause them to tauten even more. "If I didn't resist arrest, Agent Wind, would you be a kind and lenient jailer?"

Before she could answer, his arms banded her upper body and leaned her backward so his tongue could travel circles around the tingling peaks. As he kissed and teethed the tips, Beth said in a ragged voice, "The most generous, indulgent, tolerant you could find anywhere if you surrender."

Navarro's mouth took a tasty path up her neck and to her lips. He put all of the love and desire he felt for her into the kisses and caresses that ensued. He guided her downward to the bearskin and lay half atop her, giving his hands free reign to travel in any direction, which they did for several minutes. It had been over a week since their last union in Mexico. His love was so overwhelming and his hunger so enormous, he didn't know if he could control himself very long.

Never before had Navarro come to her with such a blend of tenderness and urgency. It was as if he wanted to possess her fully, stake a claim on her. Was he surrendering to her? Did he care for her more than he realized or more than he could admit so soon after a final break with Jessica? Was he letting go of all restraint, if only for tonight, or perhaps to test that possibility? "Love me, my captive warrior, love me," she urged.

"I will, my beautiful mistress, I will," he murmured in her ear. He used every talent and skill he possessed to make her writhe in need of him.

Beth savored every intoxicating kiss, every titillating touch. Each was so potent and stirring, so passionate. He was the only thought in her mind, the only reality in the world. He was the man she loved and wanted, wanted tonight and forever. Her hands roved his virile body and took delight in that journey. But she craved full contact with him, with nothing and no ghosts between them. Her fingers struggled with the ties to his buckskin pants and loosened the knot with determination. She gripped them on both sides at his waist and tugged downward.

Navarro lifted his hips for her to wriggle the snug garment over them. He rolled away only a few moments to finish their removal, along with that of the wide leather strip that confined his eager manhood. As he did so, Beth cast off her breechcloth. When he pulled her into his arms, their mouths fastened together in a hungry kiss. Their hands reached unclad regions and conquered them in fervent splendor. For as long as they could endure the blissful torment, they gave and took.

"My tolerance has vanished, slave," Beth gasped in his ear, "indulge me. I need you now."

"Mine's been gone for long," he murmured against her lips. He wished for light to view her expressions as he took her, but the fire had died and the full moon had passed. The brush hut was cloaked by obliterating darkness, so Navarro used lips and hands for eyes, and relished the scene.

Both groaned in rapture as their bodies united. Locked as one, their kisses were long, deep, and feverish. They continued a search for ecstasy until that goal was obtained, cherished, and allowed to drift into serenity. They fell asleep snuggled in each other's arms, sated as never before.

Beth stirred, stretched, and yawned. She felt relaxed and happy. She opened her eyes and found herself alone, naked beneath a blanket her lover had placed over her to ward off the morning chill. She realized what had awakened her—voices and noises outside the shelter. She abandoned the makeshift bed, folded the covering, and laid it on the skin. Using yucca soap and water in a leather pouch, she bathed, then donned her trail garments. Before she could leave to join the others, Beth saw her possessions in a pile at the entrance and was pleased to have them returned. She located a brush and groomed her hair. Recalling Navarro's words last night about those wavy tresses, she left them hanging free for his notice.

Last night, her mind echoed and she sighed dreamily. She had enjoyed his kisses and caresses on other occasions, but those he'd given to her after the eclipse touched and thrilled her soul deep. They gave wings to fantasies about a shared future. *You've bewitched me, Navarro Breed. Whatever shall I do if I can't win you?*

"Good morning, partner," a husky voice said from behind her, after Navarro peeked inside to be certain she was up and clothed.

Beth turned, smiled, and almost stumbled as she stopped in mid-stride with unsteadying abruptness. The shaman was with Navarro so, with difficulty, she banked overflowing emotions. She laughed and made a funny face as if the sudden pivot was to blame. "Good morning, Sees-Through-Clouds. Good morning yourself, partner. Am I late in arising?"

Navarro noticed the glow in her verdant eyes and on her rosy cheeks.

If he wasn't mistaken, she had been about to race into his arms if he but gave a slight hint. Her recent responses to him caused joy to flood his heart and hope to run in his veins. "After what you've endured in the last few weeks, you needed and deserved rest. Did you . . . sleep well?"

Beth observed a roguish grin and tone and a possessive gaze. "Never better. Maybe I should order you to hunt me a bear for a skin to go on my bed. I'd like to . . . sleep that well again."

"So would I, lots of times. 'Course, naps aren't bad backups."

Beth halted the double entendres before she became too stimulated to think with clarity or to talk without babbling. She focused her attention on the patient shaman. She noticed perceptive and amused gleams in his age-clouded brown eyes. "Thank you for loaning us your shelter and possessions, Sees-Through-Clouds, and for helping us with this task to save many lives, Chiricahua and white."

"Flamehair, Night Cloud, good friends. Come, eat."

After a meal of ash-baked bread with dried fruits and nuts that was served with wild tea, they went outside to meet with the band.

Sees-Through-Clouds pointed to Navarro's weapons and asked about the twelve-foot rawhide "rope." The Special Agent lifted the whip and explained its purpose to the older man. As a gesture of friendship, neither he nor Beth wore weapons in camp.

Beth noticed Navarro's possessions had been put near the shelter, along with his black stallion. She glanced toward the stream and saw her palomino tethered there to graze and drink. "While you get everyone together, I'm going to visit Sunshine; she must be lonely and confused by now. I'll return in a few minutes. And I'll stay in full sight, partner."

Navarro chuckled as she responded to a caution before he could voice it. "That's fine, just be alert for wild animals and rattlers." He was sure Beth would grasp he was referring to the human kind, one in particular.

Before she could head in that direction, the culprit approached them. Again he demanded she endure a final test, the one by fire.

"No," she said, and offered no explanation or excuse. She looked at her lover and said she would return soon. She walked away to escape the leader's seething rage.

"Give up; she isn't going to take your bait."

Eagle Eye scowled at Navarro's words, whirled, and left the men in a hurry.

In moments, Navarro realized the warrior was stalking the redhead and drawing a knife. "Beth! Watch out!" With lightning speed and agility, the lawman snaked his six-plait whip through the air. The lash hissed and curled around the Indian's uplifted and armed hand. Navarro yanked the handle with all his might and pulled the man off balance. As the foe fumbled with the leather entanglement to free himself to strike again, Navarro bolted toward the location to defend his woman with bare fists.

The weaponless Beth had spun around at the warning and gaped at her attacker, too startled for a moment to react before her partner had done so. As Eagle Eye heard help coming, he gave up trying to remove his bond and lunged toward her. Beth retreated and dodged his grasping hands. To gain time, she made a dash toward the water, with Eagle Eye in quick pursuit.

With the astonished shaman and many braves following, Navarro overtook the assailant and leapt on his back. His strong arms banded the Apache's chest and pinned his also strong arms to his side. The imprisoned and thwarted Indian tried to shake off his burden. The men twisted and grunted as they staggered in soft earth near the stream. Eagle Eye jerked backward and slammed Navarro's body into a tree, loosening his grip enough to escape. The Indian turned and glared at the white man.

"If Flamehair is too scared to prove herself, I will prove my words are true. Fight me in the circle, Half-breed. If I die, I am false. If you die, she is false. If you refuse, I will not join your side for the trap. If my band betrays me, I will find another. If you stop my wagons, I will find more guns and steal them. I will fight all whites and soldiers I find and kill them."

"No!" Beth shouted. "He will not fight you to the death. Why do you resist the sacred vision when I have proven myself? Your heart and plans are evil, Eagle Eye. You must be stopped and punished by these brave and honest men you misguided with your cunning, not by Ysun's helper. We have come to save Chiricahua blood, not spill it." As the Indian foe gaped at her in fierce hatred, Beth heard her words being translated to the band.

"Night Cloud is a coward with a split tongue. He hides behind a witch woman who lies and tricks us. I am Apache; if he carries Apache blood, he must accept my challenge." The warrior smirked at Navarro and muttered, "If you do not, I will come as a thief and slay her in the night. I will track—"

Beth squealed and jumped as three arrows thudded into Eagle Eye's back and cut off the remainder of his threat. She watched him fall face forward to the ground, dead. Her gaze lifted to search for the shooters. Three braves stood with the shaman, their bows now lowered, their faces expressionless. She listened as the older man explained that they had followed *her* orders and removed the leader's evil influence and resistance.

"Come, Night Cloud, talk, plan trap. Warriors help."

Navarro clasped Beth's hand and guided her from the bloody scene. He took her to the shaman's dwelling and told her to relax while he handled the meeting, which would go quicker and easier if he spoke Apache.

Beth nodded agreement. "Thanks for being so fast and skilled."

"If the shaman hadn't asked to see my whip and I hadn't still been holding it, I couldn't have gotten to that snake in time to stop him from reaching you. There surely wasn't time to grab my rifle or pistol. It's as if that wise man sees and knows what's gonna happen around the bend. I'd best join the men. You'll be all right?"

"Fine, partner, just a little shaken. I thought I was a goner. I've met plenty of menacing criminals during my assignments, but none with such formidable hatred and evil. Unless you object, I think I'll conceal my derringer and knife. Being weaponless I feel exposed to everything. And what I said back there, I didn't mean it to sound as if I were commanding them to slay Eagle Eye."

"I know. They were destroying his evil and protecting us. They knew he wouldn't give up trying to kill us. Without realizing it, Beth, you spoke the tribal law, one they knew they had to obey even if you'd said nothing. But every time you speak or act, you convince them you're Flamehair."

"I don't know if that part of the vision is true, but it's helped us."

"If it weren't true, woman, you'd still have black or sunny hair."

"It's eerie being part of a prophecy."

"Sometimes it's lucky in more ways than you know. See you later."

Beth watched him leave and went to rest on the bearskin. *I hope you meant it was lucky because it also said we'd meet. But it didn't say how long I would "stand at your side." For this mission or forever, my love?*

"You're leaving me behind?" Beth asked in dismay.

Navarro cupped her face and locked their gazes. "I have to ride hard and fast to reach Fort Thomas in time to convince the officer in charge to join forces with us. After I tell him my story, he'll have to telegraph the Agency to confirm my identity before he agrees to help trap Charles and his hirelings. I can do this quicker and easier alone." He grinned. "Besides, you'd be a big distraction to lonely soldiers. Stay here where you'll be safe and comfortable. I'll return in a few days; I promise."

"What if something happens to make them doubt I'm Flamehair?"

"With Eagle Eye gone, it won't. The shaman told me he was the only one who knew where the silver is hidden in the Superstition Mountains; the secret was passed father to son each generation. It died with him. That's good, because it won't tempt another warrior to make a similar deal with another gunrunner. When it's over, maybe we can have peace between my peoples."

"I hope so, Navarro. Go ahead. I'll stay here as ordered. I'll be fine."

"Be careful."

"Always."

"You have plenty of supplies and water and ammunition?"

He knew they were both stalling their separation. "Yep."

"You need anything else?"

"Just this." He gave her a short but passionate kiss. "So long."

"So long," she echoed as he walked toward the entry. She followed, watched him mount, send her a smile and wink, and depart. *God, protect you and guide you, my love, and bring you back to me.*

Long days and lonely nights passed as Beth awaited his return. He was overdue by now. The rendezvous was scheduled for noon tomorrow—Monday, May Seventeenth, but no partner or soldiers had arrived or sent a message. To reach the meeting on time, she and the Indians had to leave this afternoon and cover half the distance.

Beth worried that an accident might had befallen Navarro or his horse. Or the Army might not have believed him, and might even have jailed him on some false charge without checking out his story. Or the commanding officer at Fort Thomas might be a part of this wicked plot and . . .

Beth didn't relate those fears to the shaman or the band. But she did tell them it was time to go and said something must have delayed Navarro. She speculated aloud that he and the soldiers could be joining them at the rendezvous point, as it required time for them to muster their supplies and travel in a large group. She told herself that if all else failed, she and these Chiricahuas would carry out the critical trap. If the hour of confrontation approached and no help appeared in advance, she would make that suggestion to the Apaches who trusted her and followed her lead.

When they were packed and mounted, Beth turned to the Indians and said, "Let's ride."

Chapter Twenty-four

Beth and the Chiricahuas broke camp at first light the following morning and rode toward their destination. The shaman stayed at her side and led the entire way from Bear Mountain, across the Blue River, beyond the lofty and cool Coronado Trail, into picturesque hill country with verdant valleys, and to the northern end of Eagle Creek. They journeyed along its edge through a region of grassland with an abundance of mesquites, cacti, and scrubs that was situated between forested mountains. They saw deer, elk, turkey, and other wildlife. Southwestward were the Gila Mountains and Nantac Rim, both in view on the horizon on the clear day.

As they entered one clearing between dense vegetation patches, Beth's gaze widened in astonishment as she saw Navarro sitting on his stallion's back, his right leg out of the stirrup and resting across his left thigh. She watched him tip back his hat and grin.

When the group reached him, he said, "Knew you wouldn't let me down, Flamehair. Glad you made it on time." He spoke to the shaman in Apache. He had told the man to leave at noon yesterday if he wasn't back and had informed him which trail to take. Yet, he'd known Beth would do as she had and arrive.

When the men stopped speaking, she asked, "Where have you been? I was worried. I hoped I was doing the right thing by coming here."

Navarro repeated what he'd just told the shaman and braves in their language. "Most of the troops were on patrol. Had to wait for their return, then given 'em time to resupply and rest before leaving again. No trouble after Captain Blake checked out me and my orders. The soldiers are hiding at the rendezvous point, in case Charles is early. So far, he isn't in sight. I rode ahead to meet you and get the band ready for our tricks. Let's go. We'll talk after we're in position."

They rode to a wooded spot in the hills eastward of the designated clearing. Navarro used his mirror to flash a signal to the soldiers to enter the valley as soon as they had prepared themselves for their daring scheme. Excitement and suspense ran high in the group.

Beth observed as Navarro smeared one of nature's pigments mixed with bear grease on his face and lips to paint them yellow. Afterward, he used black to make thunderclouds on his cheeks and raindrops on his forehead. He finished with an ebony zigzag line of lightning that began at his hairline, traveled down his nose, over his lips, and under his chin. He moved behind a bush for privacy to put on his Indian garments and accessories, then arranged his long sable hair around his shoulders. As he changed clothes, Beth watched the other men as they painted and ornamented themselves; only the shaman did nothing more than witness the stimulating episode.

Navarro returned and said, "If I stay back in the crowd, those culprits won't notice my giveaway eye color. I should pass for Apache."

"Without a doubt, *Tl'ee' K'us,*" Beth murmured praise for his cunning and talents. As her admiring gaze roamed him from head to foot, she decided he looked like a primitive and enchanting god. Her heart raced with love and pride. Her body burned with desire. The look in his eyes exposed confidence, intelligence, and anticipation. He was sheer magic, and he had cast a powerful and unbreakable spell over her.

Navarro tried to ignore the way she was studying him and flushing. She possessed such radiance that he could almost feel the heat from it, and it set his heart and body and soul aflame. Surely such potent desire and respect for him would help him win her later. For now, his thoughts and feelings belonged elsewhere, if he could master them . . . *"Biishe, nzhu,"* he congratulated Nighthawk on the Indian's accurate disguise.

The renegade who would play Eagle Eye's role during the meeting had painted his face in the dead leader's pattern and colors: a blue surface with black slashes over the four alleged cuts around each eye and red triangles on his cheeks, forehead, and an inverted one on his chin. Biishe wore the betrayer's garments and adornments, and had his past friend's horse. Those things in addition to a heavy resemblance to the lost leader should fool even Jim Tiller, who had met the real Eagle Eye. The other Indians were adorned in their chosen designs, a precaution to keep Nighthawk and Navarro's concealed faces from looking suspicious.

When Navarro kept glancing toward the hill opposite their location, Beth asked, "Are you expecting trouble?"

"We have men positioned on several peaks between here and the trail Charles has to use; they'll signal with mirrors when the wagons come into view. We need to be camped in the clearing and looking innocent in case Charles sends scouts to check out the area. We've made certain nothing will expose our trap. The Army's horses are hidden a mile away so they won't make any noise. Those soldiers are tucked in or behind trees, bushes, and rocks so snug not even fieldglasses will detect their presence."

"I'm impressed. You continue to amaze and teach me. Being your partner is one of the best things that's ever happened to me."

Navarro looked at Beth and said, "Sorry you have to stay here and miss the heart of the action. You deserve to be in on their defeat, but it's too risky with you being a woman and a fiery redhead to boot. We don't wanna bust your cover for future assignments; you're far too memorable, Beth Breed. 'Course, if you hide that red hair, dirty your white skin, put on your Indian garments, and paint your face, you could hide behind the others. It's no secret that some of the Apache tribes had female warriors."

"You mean I can go and help? See everything up close?"

"If you promise to keep outta sight and avoid stray bullets."

"I promise. Let me go change; then, you can decorate. Wait, I only have my buckskins with me. Will they be all right for a disguise?"

"Nope." He saw her exuberance fade as disappointment filled her. "Put on those things Sees-Through-Clouds is holding. He says they're yours to keep."

Beth rushed into the woods and donned the ceremonial garments. She tied a buckskin cloth over her hair and tossed a colorful blanket similar to a Mexican rebozo over it. She hurried back to Navarro. "Ready."

The lawman painted her face and neck yellow, then decorated her cheeks and forehead with blue and red designs. He did the same with her pale hands. He didn't tell her to remove the wedding band, as it shouldn't be noticeable at a distance. If it were, the white men would think it was stolen from their kind during a raid. It wasn't necessary to color her legs, as they didn't show with the long dress and high-topped moccasins.

Navarro eyed his completed task and grinned. "Perfect."

One of the braves said, *"Nkeedéndla,"* and pointed to the other hill.

"What is it?" Beth asked.

"He said they flashed the signal; Charles is in sight. Let's ride."

Everyone mounted except the shaman.

"Aren't you coming with us, Sees-Through-Clouds?" she asked.

The elderly man spoke in Chiricahua to Navarro, who translated for

Beth. "He says he'll watch the great deed from here. His task is done in this sacred mission. When the battle is over, he'll return to the hills to live out his days in peace. He says they're short but he will die in freedom. No, Beth, don't argue," he advised to halt her protest. "He's right; it's his way."

Her gaze roamed the deep lines in the old man's face and drifted over his white hair. She noticed how slumped his shoulders were and how tired he appeared after the long journey to this site. She looked into eyes that were clouded by age and troubled vision. This was the last time she would see him, a man who had foretold her destiny and helped it come true. "Goodbye, Sees-Through-Clouds, my friend. I shall never forget you."

Navarro translated for the smiling and misty-eyed shaman again, "Wise One says he will remember Flamehair for all his days left on Earth Mother and for all the days he lives in the spirit world. He says Ysun will guide you and protect you, and White Painted Woman will bless you with treasures. We must go and face our last challenge of this mission, partner."

Beth smiled and waved at the shaman as they left him standing there alone. *God bless you, too, Sees-Through-Clouds: stay safe and happy.*

As they waited in the clearing for the arms rendezvous, Navarro fingered the amulet the shaman had given to him this morning; he had claimed it held great magic. He knew the old man's days were numbered short and he hoped his friend stayed safe until they passed. He had promised to contact President Cleveland, Secretary of War Endicott, and Secretary of Interior Lamar to persuade them to get the Bureau of Indian Affairs to investigate and halt the many injustices against the Apaches. He also promised he would try to get assigned to probe the Chiricahuas' charges of corruption and abuses at San Carlos Reservation. With luck, Beth could work as his partner again. But before a new case was taken on, he wanted to settle personal matters with her. Not much longer, he told himself, until he could do so, as this mission should be completed today.

As suspected, Charles sent two scouts to check the area's security from a distance with fieldglasses. Duped by what they saw, they returned to their boss and reported everything was fine. A coded signal was flashed to Navarro that they and the scene had passed inspection.

In an hour, the noisy caravan of seven freighters, one schooner, and twenty-two men entered the valley. Some of the white men rode on horseback on all sides of the wagons. Others were aboard them, their mounts' reins tied to tailgates. At a steady pace, the miscreants approached their buyers.

Navarro noticed the unfamiliar white man sitting on a wagon seat and assumed it was Ben from Morenci. He also assumed Charles Cordell and Jim Tiller were hidden in the covered schooner since they weren't in sight. As that wagon held a Gatling gun, he warned himself to be alert for trouble.

When the party halted over fifty feet away, Nighthawk and a chosen few other Indians stood and went forward to speak with the seller. The stranger alighted from the wagon and looked at the man he thought was Eagle Eye. The imposter asked if they had the guns and bullets for trade.

"Yes, we have everything we promised. What about you?"

Nighthawk handed him a fake map. "That is my trade."

Blue eyes studied drawings on an old leather skin. He recognized many landmarks. "You're sure this is where we can find the silver metal?"

"I speak true." He took back the skin. "Show me guns for map."

Ben called out orders, and a box was unloaded and pried open. He lifted a lever-action rifle and handed it to the Indian, who accepted and examined the repeating model.

Nighthawk passed other guns to his friends nearby for them to pretend to study. "How many you bring?"

"Many rifles, Eagle Eye, more than you'll need. The wagons are full."

"We look. See all boxes have guns and fire balls."

"Suit yourself. Stand back, boys, and let them have their way."

White hirelings moved back from the wagons so the copper-skinned group could climb aboard and break open crate after crate as if to be sure they weren't being duped with empty or rock-filled ones. When Nighthawk came to boxes of ammunition, he tossed cartridges to his helpers and told them to load the weapons and make sure they worked. A tense Ben protested.

"Make sure rifles good before trade silver metal for bad ones."

"You can do the testing yourself, but your friends don't get rifles until our deal is settled. Choose any rifle you wish and try it out, but only you."

Navarro and Beth remained to the rear of those who hung back at a campfire with the horses. He wondered why Charles and Jim didn't show themselves and why their ill-fated partner was handling this crucial aspect of the sale. "Something's wrong," he whispered to his partner.

"What do you mean?"

"Just a gut feeling." *Go look in that covered wagon;* he tried to send a mental message to Nighthawk. "Stay here. I'm going to nose around."

"What if they recognize you?"

"You think they might, dressed and painted like this?"

"No," she admitted. "But be careful. You've got me nervous now."

Navarro worked his way to the schooner, pulled aside the flap, and was stunned by what he viewed. A culprit was standing at one of two awesome weapons, as if ready to fire it if given the word. The disguised agent kept his expression passive as the man eyed him with a scowl. He saw how the weapons were mounted on wooden stands instead of wheel bases and were facing opposite sides to thwart attacks from either direction. He knew what just one rapid-firing Gatling gun could do to the soldiers and Indians, a reaction he must prevent. He lowered the flap of the wagon and walked to the front as if checking out the team which was part of the deal. In truth, he was searching for a way to get inside and disable the villain before he gave the Army an attack signal. Without exposing his intention, it was impossible.

Navarro went to Nighthawk and told him in Chiricahua to ask to see the big guns in the covered wagon, to demand they be unloaded so he could examine them. Nighthawk obeyed, but Ben refused.

"They're bolted down for travel so they wouldn't get damaged. They're heavy and awkward. It'll take too much time and work to unload them. You'd just have to put them back to haul them to your camp."

Navarro whispered added instructions to Nighthawk.

"Bring big gun from wagon. Teach how to shoot."

"All you do is aim it at your enemies and turn the handle; it's easy."

"Show Eagle Eye how to shoot, how to put in metal bullets. Guns no good if no can shoot. You teach, or trade no good: I take map and go; you take wagons and go."

"We had a deal, Eagle Eye: weapons for silver, and supplies until they arrived so you could stay hidden from soldiers. We've kept our end of the bargain. Nothing was said about teaching you to fire and load them."

"Weapons no good to Chiricahua if not know how to use."

"There's no time for lessons; we need to get back home before dark. Besides, it isn't necessary; as I said, all you do is turn the handle to fire. The ammo crates have picture lessons on how to load them for people who can't read. Just look at the papers and you can figure out that procedure."

Nighthawk consulted in whispers with Navarro again before he scoffed, "You trick Eagle Eye? Big guns no good? You scared I see?"

"You can play with the weapons all you want after we leave. Give me the map and our business is finished. If not, we're leaving with the guns."

Navarro realized the stranger and his culprits were getting anxious;

they were glancing around as they moved toward their horses. Since the lawbreakers had incriminated themselves and the trappers' advantage might be stolen soon, he had no choice but to give the signal. In Chiricahua, he warned the Indians about the lethal power of the big guns and told them to pull back and take cover when he let out a prearranged yell for the soldiers to respond with an attack.

It was too late. The hirelings sensed treachery, pulled their weapons, and began firing at the buyers. On alert, the renegades avoided the rain of bullets. Their shots were returned by the Indians with bows and arrows. Troops with rifles and pistols made their presence and threat known from behind rocks, trees, and bushes.

As ordered by her partner, at the first sign of danger, Beth had taken cover behind a large boulder, carrying his bow and quiver along. She saw mounted outlaws panic and gallop toward a retreat. Soldiers who had closed the gap during the meeting opened fire; that surprised and caused the villains to rein up and turn to escape in the other direction, to receive the same kind of reception. It was clear they were surrounded, so they dismounted and used their horses for protection as they returned gunfire. She watched in horror as the schooner's canvas covering separated at the top and fell to both sides, exposing the enormous threat. Within moments, its deadly blasts drowned those of pistol and rifle noise and people's voices.

Navarro weaved a path toward that target, but was jumped by a culprit before he could reach it. They battled with wits and fists, preventing him from reaching the man with the Gatling gun. That beast was careful where he aimed since his friends and cohorts were mingled with Indians; it seemed as if he was sending out intimidation shots for now. The soldiers didn't want to kill the peaceful party by error either. That precaution compelled them to surge forward to assist.

For defense, the man on the wagon raised the barrel's level to point his powerful gun in the direction of the blue-clad advance. Before he could crank the handle and spit forth injury and death, Beth locked her aim and released an arrow. She prayed it would strike its target or many people would die in this clearing.

It did, at the same time Navarro's knife entered the man's chest. As the villain staggered a moment, he recognized his own arrow and his gaze scanned for his partner to see if she was imperiling herself. She wasn't, and he was relieved. He focused on the battle at hand. He fought his way to the wagon and leapt upon it; he opened fire on villains who were at a safe distance from friends and allies, evoking their surrender.

As soldiers and Indians closed in on the others, those remaining alive also yielded. Within minutes, all Cordell's men were either dead or captured.

Navarro went to the spot where a wounded and bloody Ben writhed in agony. "Who are you? Where's Cordell and Tiller?"

The tormented stranger murmured, "Ben Murphy. From Morenci. Tell my family and friends I tried to avenge and protect them and failed."

Navarro repeated his second question and the man said he didn't know. "Where's the fourth Gatling gun? Does Cordell have it with him?"

"No, he sent an extra one to Diaz as a gift to make him happy."

"Why did you try to provoke war? We're near peace."

The dying man said, "Those savages raped my wife and daughter years ago. My dear Mary killed herself out of shame. My sweet Anne lives in a silent dream world. I wanted those bastards to use these guns to provoke the Army and all whites against them. I wanted them hunted down like the animals they are and destroyed. I wanted those vipers cleared out of their nests in Arizona. With them dead or gone, they'd never harm another white woman again, never attack my copper mine again. I wanted them ki—" The suffering man died before he could reveal more.

Navarro shook his head and muttered, "He hated the wrong people and hunger for revenge made him loco. If the attackers had been Apache, they would have slain everyone or taken the women captive as slaves or to sell. It was probably white men disguised as Indians; I've seen that happen many times before."

Navarro questioned other men about their boss's whereabouts, but none would tell, if anyone knew. He resolved that their evil leader wouldn't escape justice or become a threat to innocents.

Zachariah Abernathy reached the scene. The black man told Navarro how he was contacted by mirror messages that the trap was in progress and to join the signalers. "You must have told them to be on the watch for me."

"I did. What happened to Cordell and Tiller?"

"Don't know. Just got here. Soldiers told me to look for a man with a yellow face marked with black symbols. That's a clever disguise, my friend. Appears everything went as planned; that's good."

"Not everything, Zack; they aren't here; they didn't come."

"Cordell and Tiller?"

"Yep, we missed 'em."

"Don't make sense. They were with the wagons when I was flashed. Must have dropped off someplace after I stopped trailing them miles back. Maybe they were hiding and watching to make sure they wasn't tricked. If that's it, probably long gone by now."

Navarro grabbed fieldglasses and scanned the location on all sides: Nothing. He told Captain Blake that he and Zack would have to pursue the two criminals, while Blake and his troops took charge of the prisoners and wagons and guided the renegades back to the reservation. He asked the officer to let three soldiers take Beth to the train station in Clifton.

"What?" she asked in astonishment.

Navarro excused them from the men and took her to a private spot. "Cordell and Tiller already have a big jump on us and they're probably riding as fast as the wind to get away; that gap will get wider while we supply and search for their tracks. Me and Zack can ride faster without you, Beth. Besides, there's two of us and only two of them. No need for you to ride a hard trail with us. I want you to go to Clifton and take a train to Tucson to wait for me there. Please, obey this final order."

"How will I explain my return, and without my husband?"

"Tell everybody the ranch sites in Texas didn't suit us. Tell 'em I'm looking at one more in northern New Mexico, then, we're going to check out Arizona. Tell 'em that New Mexico area sounded too rugged and far so I asked you to wait for me in Tucson where you'd be safe and comfortable. Ask Harrison to help us locate a ranch. That story should fool everybody until I join you."

"Wait for me there" . . . "You sure you won't need me to come along?"

"I'm sure. Besides, I don't need any distractions. You can wash that mess off your face and hands with those yucca suds the shaman gave you, but wait until you're away from here. No need to bust your cover to more men than necessary. If you leave now, you can make town by dark."

He handed her money to rent a room for the night and to buy a train ticket. "Get packed and moving, woman. I'll see you in Tucson soon."

Beth eyed him a final time, smiled, and said, "Be careful, partner, Charles and Jim are dangerous and tricky."

He wished he could give her a farewell embrace and kiss. "I promise nothing will happen to me and Zack. Now move out while you've got plenty of daylight. I'll finish up here and start backtracking their trail."

"What about the shaman?"

"I'm sure he's on his way home by now. He'll be fine, so don't worry. Captain Blake said he's gonna speak to the government about rewarding the Chiricahuas with their ancestral grounds; that's what they were promised in the treaty. Until then, they've agreed to return to the reservation.

When Geronimo hears about this daring deed, maybe he'll surrender, too."

"I hope so, for the sake of peace and his people's survival. Goodbye."

Navarro watched Beth leave with an escort to Clifton to catch the train to Tucson, via Lordsburg. She was gone only minutes before he missed her. He gathered supplies, joined Zack, and they departed.

In less than two hours, he found the wooded peak where the sly culprits had waited and watched the trap unfold. Signs said they were long gone. He flashed mirror signals to Captain Blake, who was prepared to begin his own trek to glory.

By Tuesday evening, Beth was in a cozy room in a Tucson boarding-house. She had chosen it over a hotel because of the possible length of time she might be required to wait in town for Navarro.

Since she had told her family in her April letter that she'd come to visit within the next few months, she wouldn't be postponing that trip by staying here for a week or so. Besides, she dared not wire or write them from Tucson, which might expose her true identity to an overly curious person in either office. Yet, she couldn't leave until she knew Navarro was safe and they had a serious talk. She prayed that impending conversation went as hoped and, if it did, he could make that journey with her to meet her family. *Come soon, dear heart, and love me as I love you.*

On Wednesday, Beth enjoyed visits with the owner of the land office and with the Carters. They were all surprised and delighted to see her again. She told them the story Navarro had made up for her to use. She did the same with any acquaintance or friend she encountered during walks around town. To ensure the tale's credence, she met with Melvin Harrison about assistance. Her ex-boss promised to check out several ranches he had heard about and wired for information within an hour of their conversation. Kate and Henry had her trunks delivered and insisted she eat supper with them. During that meal, the redhead played her role as Beth Breed with skill, and with nibblings of guilt and with hopes it would be true one day.

As she lay in bed after returning to her room, Beth's fingers stroked the ebony carving from Zack and daydreamed about Navarro. She reflected on the hasty message Dan had passed to her. While en route to the Carters for dinner, they had met on the sidewalk and halted a few minutes as if they were only exchanging brief and cordial greetings. Luck was on her side, and no one had been within hearing range of their words. The news was that Navarro had defeated Jim Tiller near Lordsburg, her train stop after Clifton, and the agents were in pursuit of Charles, who was galloping across New Mexico. The assumption was the villains had split up to increase their chances of escape and probably planned to rendezvous somewhere later. But Jim's horse had gone lame, slowed his pace, and finally halted it. In less than an hour after the culprit bought a replacement in Lordsburg, he was overtaken.

Beth wondered if Charles dared to go to Texas and try to entice his brother to conceal him from the law, or to exact misguided revenge on Matt before he was arrested. She had asked Dan if they should wire the Cordells a warning, but her superior had said no.

One beaten and one to go. Surely that task won't take long.

Friday morning, Melvin came to speak with his ex-employee. "I can hardly believe our luck, Beth," he said in an exuberant mood. "I've found a ranch that sounds perfect for you two. It's located southwest of Flagstaff. That's not as large and busy a place as Tucson but it's made steady progress since the railroad arrived five years ago. You'll be less than eighty miles from the capital in Prescott, unless it gets moved back to Tucson or over to Phoenix; that's always been a big rivalry. No Indian troubles or feuds in that area, but Fort Verde is about fifty miles south if any fracas start. Timber and cattle lured in plenty of people and businesses of all sizes and kinds. What meat and food isn't raised nearby and sold in town comes in by train. There shouldn't be a problem filling your needs."

If the facts weren't so interesting and enlightening and Melvin so sincere and kind, Beth might be amused by his zealous persuasion. "Why are the owners selling?"

"Because of advanced age and infirmities; they have a lawyer friend searching for a family to take over the place, a couple who'll love and respect the property like they did. I can guarantee there are no water and grazing problems and there's been no trouble with rustlers. I'm familiar with the area, so I'll tell you a little about it, but I'd rather you judge most of it for yourself without bias in either direction."

Beth listened as he painted a glorious word picture of lush grasslands mingled with several forests for firewood and dotted with lovely meadows. He spoke of an ample water supply, miles of fencing, a lovely house with five rooms, and sturdy outbuildings. "She sits in the shadows of beautiful rolling hills that lead into splendid mountains; they'll be good for providing breezes in summer and protection from any blowing snow in winter. You should be able to see the San Francisco Mountains from your porch or the range. It's a thousand prime acres. The foreman and wranglers are running and guarding the property until it's sold; they'll go to work for the buyer if that's agreeable to both parties. Naturally the owners have only the highest praise for their cowboys. If you want to go see it tomorrow and, if it suits you, we can show it to Navarro after his arrival. For the right couple, Beth, the price is excellent, almost a steal: thirty dollars per acre, and that includes the stock, structures, and equipment. You see, more than make a big profit, they want to find the best people to take over."

"You sound as if they've already moved out."

"They have, a week ago. Their children and grandchildren live back East; they're going to move in with the oldest son. Family got split up when the three children went east to fancy schools, and stayed. It seems that neither of the boys wanted to be ranchers; the girl met and married a Boston lad. There's one more enticement: they've included most of the furnishings with the house. They took only family keepsakes and sentimental pieces. You'd have to buy little. That will save you and Navarro plenty of money. It's the perfect find. This is why those Texas ranches didn't work out; fate wanted you to have this one."

Beth was consumed by eagerness and elation. "If it matches your description, it *is* perfect. What time do we catch the train for Flagstaff?"

They discussed their schedule and other details before Melvin left. The redhead almost danced around the room as golden dreams formed inside her spinning head. If she purchased the ranch, she and Navarro could use it as a home base between missions as partners or single agents. It would give them a fine place to rest, have fun, build something special, get closer, and wait for their next assignment. They could prepare it for future retirement when age, injury, or desire evoked their resignations.

Her mind argued that it was wrong to live and sleep with a man to whom she wasn't wed; that's how she had been reared and taught at home and at church. Yet, her heart reasoned, she felt married to Navarro because the vows they spoke were in church before God, a minister, and witnesses; and they were from her heart and soul. The relationship between them didn't feel wicked and wrong. She felt like his wife.

They possessed a marriage certificate and people believed they were wed. Could Navarro be persuaded to continue their marital ruse? Could it become legal one day?

At four o'clock, Beth responded to her superior's summons. In his office, she smiled and said, "That was clever, Dan, to send a messenger to tell me we have banking business to discuss about a possible ranch loan. Have you heard from Navarro? Is that why you wanted to see me?"

"Yes. Zack arrived by train earlier today and gave me a report."

"Only Zack?"

Dan nodded, and observed her for enlightening signs.

"Has something happened to Navarro? Is he hurt or . . ."

"No, he's fine. He's heading on to Texas to visit with the Cordells. He wanted to speak with them in person about the brother. Chances are some newspaper will pick up the story and the Cordells might see it. Navarro thought it best if the news came from him, and he'd be there to answer any questions they had. He should take a week or two to reach Tucson. Why don't you take the two weeks off owed you and go visit your family in Denver now? I can send you word there about your next assignment."

"Does that mean they caught up with Charles?"

"Near Deming in New Mexico. He's dead; Zack was forced to shoot him. Frankly, I'm relieved it wasn't Navarro's finger on the lethal trigger. That should make his talk with old friends easier."

"I'm sure it will, and I'm sure Jessica and Matt will be grateful he took the time and effort to bring the bad news in person." She knew Tucson was a lot closer to Deming than the ranch was. She was waiting here for him, but Jessica and Lane were there, bonds to his past. Yet, word could spread fast these days with newspapers, telegraph, train, and, even in some places, the telephone; so an immediate trip to the ranch was necessary, in his heart and mind. *At least a week, probably two or more.*

Dan attempted to test her feelings for Navarro again, because she hadn't exposed them so far, at least not the ones he hoped she would. "By the time Navarro completes his business there and you finish your family visit, you'll both be ready for reassignment. Do you have any objection to being teamed up with him again in the future, if the right case comes along? Did you two work all right together? Any problems or conflicts?"

Beth wondered if Navarro asked him to pass along that message to get her out of Tucson before his return so a serious talk could be avoided. Maybe now that the partnership was over, he believed their relationship was, too, and he wanted to prevent an uncomfortable situation. If he had wanted her to continue waiting for him, he would have told his best friend, and asked Dan to tell her. Wouldn't he? She was still playing his wife, but he hadn't even sent her a telegram since her arrival. He could have done so from Deming before leaving for Texas and . . .

"What's that long silence about, Beth? Were there problems?"

"No, I was considering what you said about Denver. I suppose you're right. The mission is over now so there's no reason to hang around Tucson, right?" Dan shrugged and smiled. Beth decided that Navarro would know where and how to find her if their relationship wasn't over. She smiled and said, "When you see Navarro, tell him how good it was to work with him. He's the best, Dan, just like you said, a bonafide living legend. He taught me plenty. As to being partners again, I'm willing if he is. Of course, he might have gotten his fill with a female tagalong. If not, you know how to reach me. I'll be ready to return to duty on June seventh, if that's all right with you."

"It is. Goodbye, Beth. Have a safe trip and enjoyable visit. I'll let you know about your new assignment."

"Thank you, Dan. Goodbye." She departed with head held high, shoulders straight, and a feigned pleasant expression on her face.

After she entered her room, Beth realized Daniel Withers hadn't asked for a verbal or written mission account from her. She surmised he was waiting for Navarro to give it, and there were telegram updates along the trail and Zack's report earlier today.

Zack! her mind shouted. Navarro's other good friend and recent partner was in town, if he hadn't talked with Dan and left. Should she locate him and ask . . . No, she decided, she shouldn't probe his friends for clues or facts they might not want—or think it was their place—to give.

What should you do, Beth? Wait and hope or leave and hope? When he returns, will he expect to find you here as he asked or gone as his silence implies? Do you go visit Caroline and Robert or do you keep your appointment with Melvin Harrison? You have to retire someday and make a home someplace, and you don't want to live in Denver.

Beth reflected on the week she had spent on the Cordell spread and all she had learned about ranching. Even if she purchased the Flagstaff ranch and lived there alone between assignments, it sounded wonderful. Why couldn't her original plan work, she reasoned, even without Navarro? She could use her time off to inspect the land and structures, then make a decision. If it was everything Melvin had said, she could buy it and settle in before June seventh. She could do as the previous owner was doing now: let the foreman and hands run and guard it during her absences. A home, her home . . . a retreat between episodes of battling evil and consorting with villains and risking her life . . . a place where she could have something beautiful and good in an existence where she often viewed so much ugliness and bad. She could have her belongings in Denver sent to the ranch, things from her parents' home; she could hang pictures and put out keepsakes. She could cook and eat at her own table instead of in restaurants and boardinghouses. She could have friend and family visits . . . parties . . . neighbors . . . a real life and her own identity.

Why not? You're strong, smart, and brave: you can do it.

Beth took out pen and paper to do a little arithmetic. A thousand acres at thirty dollars per acre was thirty thousand dollars; she multiplied that inside her head and jotted it down. She added up the inheritances from her father and husband, savings from her salary, and money earned on jobs as assignment covers. The Agency had funded all her artifices so she hadn't been required to pay subterfuge expenses out of her pocket. Nor had the Agency ever asked her to turn in the money she earned while employed in places like the Red Palace or Harrison's land office.

Beth smiled as she read the large figure. She could easily afford to pay the entire amount in cash. Yet, she recalled the Cordells' warning about being prepared for emergencies, like the ones that almost destroyed their livelihood and took their home. She deduced, if she paid half of the asking price and the bank financed the other, that would leave her plenty of savings to ward off any future disaster. Since Dan was a friend, her superior, and a banker, surely he would loan her the balance, especially if she backed up the arrangement with cash savings. If anything forced her to retire early, she'd have money in the bank for support and for mortgage payments, and she'd have earnings from cattle sales.

It sounds enticing, Beth, but see the place first.

Monday evening, Beth strolled through her new home to admire it. The kitchen was large and efficient. There were two windows for air and light, and a back door for bringing in water from a well near the porch and wood for the stove. As there was no dining room, all eating would be done there on a heavy wooden table with artistically carved legs and six chairs. A fine craftsman had attached many cabinets to the walls and floor for storage. The lower ones had wide counters for doing chores. A pantry was built between the kitchen and a bedroom; it still held many staples, dried and canned vegetables and fruits, and cured meats hanging from cords on ceiling nails. The remaining space between those two rooms held a water closet for bathing and privacy needs, with a door opening onto the porch, one of two that spanned the full length of the house, front and rear.

She entered the parlor, another large room that was airy and bright with many windows. There were two couches, several chairs, tables, lamps, and a shelf where, according to the dust lines, books and family treasures had been. She walked to the oversize fireplace and could imagine the enormous amount of heat it would send forth during winter. On a raised hearth rested tools with which to tend it and in a far corner was a desk where the owner no doubt did the bookwork for his ranch and perhaps where the couple wrote letters to their children. All the windows had lacy curtains for beauty and shades for privacy. Three floral area rugs remained in their places and appeared in good condition. The painting above the mantel must have been a special one, as it was gone, leaving the wood lighter in that square. Beth had placed her ebony wolf and saguaro cactus on the table by the couch she favored.

Two of the bedrooms were regular size and had small fireplaces for heat. They were furnished sparsely, with only beds, chests, and sidetables holding lamps. The owner's room was different. The bed had four tall posters and was wider than normal. There was a chest, armoire, and vanity. A stuffed chair with a table and lamp beside it would allow for quiet reading before a cozy fireplace. As Melvin had said, the elderly woman left behind linens for the bedrooms and bath, and everything she needed in the kitchen. It was true as well that the woman had taken only her personal belongings and treasures.

Beth walked to the front porch and sat in one of the rockers. Since the house faced east, the setting was shaded this time of day. Except for the singing of birds, chirping of crickets, croaking of frogs in a nearby stream, and noises from her stock, it was quiet and serene. The air was fresh and invigorating; she took deep breaths and savored it. The sky was blue and clear, with reflections of an impending sunset altering its color every so often. She looked at snowcapped mountains in the distance, hills and peaks with forests of mostly ponderosa pine and juniper, and grasses and wildflowers swaying in the gentle breeze. She rocked for a while, then walked around the house in a yard enclosed by white pickets.

Beth let her proud gaze roam corrals, wood and barbwire fences, barns and sheds, a smithy, two outhouses—one for the hired hands and one for the owner—a woodpile with chopping block, chicken coop with hens and two roosters, and an empty pen for pigs. The oblong bunkhouse had an attached kitchen, and the men did their own cooking by rotation. There were three wells—one for the home, one for the chuckhouse, and the third for easy watering of a garden that was sprouting. Those green heads told Beth the owners had decided to move after planting time. With one in the ground, all she had to do was tend it, harvest it, and put up the vegetables for winter that she and the men didn't use in season. She hoped she remembered the procedure.

She had kept on the four wranglers and a foreman, and would begin paying their salaries next month. Her herd—cattle and bulls—consisted of Galloways, Durhams, and Herefords, and she had a nice string of fine horseflesh. She grinned as she recalled how Sunshine already had taken to a prancing sorrel who had caught her eye the first day. It seemed the cherished mare liked this location as much as her mistress did. *Mine,* Beth thought as she returned to the kitchen to make hot tea. *All mine.*

Daniel Withers and Melvin Harrison had left earlier after she signed two sets of papers they brought with them for the purchase of the ranch and the mortgage. Melvin had been delighted with her decision to buy, for more reasons than the money he would make as a finder's fee. He was overjoyed to help out a friend and for that person to be so appreciative. He had taken Dan a sealed letter with her instructions for the transfer of funds from Denver and a loan request, and her superior had promptly honored them.

Dan had asked the owner of the Tucson boardinghouse to pack Beth's possessions so he could bring them to her, and had waited and observed while the woman did so to make sure she wasn't too nosy. Dan had arrived, carried out his financial task, and departed in what appeared to be a mixture of astonishment and curiosity. They hadn't been given a moment of privacy for him to ask why she had made the startling decision, but she did manage to slip him a note of explanation and thanks before he rode off with Melvin. She had related the genuine reasons, minus any mention of hopes that Navarro would join her there, preferably as her husband. She had written she would get settled in and be ready for an assignment by June seventh.

Beth took her hot tea and entered her bedroom to unpack the trunks. As she did so, she came across the wedding gifts from her Tucson friends. She thought of the gifts hidden at the Mexican border and wondered if Navarro would ever retrieve them. *Just work, don't think and worry.*

That week drifted into another as Beth learned her way around the property and got acquainted with her hired hands. Still, no word or visit came from the man she loved. The long time without his appearance or a message did not look promising to her.

On Wednesday morning, Beth felt nauseous and was retching again, as she had been for several days. She realized she was too weary and sleepy for the condition to be normal. Perhaps her illness was because her menses hadn't come since . . . the end of March and this was June. From past work with her brother in his medical practice, if she didn't know any better, those symptoms implied she was . . . pregnant. She couldn't be! She was infertile, even if she had worn that sacred Pollen dress and the shaman had told her she would have children. She added up the symptoms once more. Her conclusion seemed accurate, but how? Her agent's mind investigated the contradictory matter.

Was it possible that girl had lied to Steven about being pregnant with his child, and that was why she vanished before he could wed her? Had the problem been Steven's and not hers?

Beth paced and pondered the unexpected dilemma. If she told Navarro, would he think she was only trying to trap him? Would he be angry, and resistant to marriage? Or would he be happy to have another child, a child with his name, because, as far as the world was concerned, she was still Beth Breed. Would he marry her to make certain his second child wasn't born a bastard as Matt had ensured for Lane? Would he want to become a family with her and the child? Even if he didn't love and want her, he was an honorable man who would do what was necessary to protect his child. Beth hated to tell him the news, as she feared it would prevent her from ever knowing how he truly felt about her. Yet, she must. He could share as much of their lives as he desired, and he would make a good father for certain. But there was another matter to handle first; she would do that tomorrow.

After tending her morning sickness, Beth wrote out a coded telegram to her superior to tell Dan she had mailed a written resignation to the Agency. She couldn't return to duty on Monday. She would retire and rear her child on this tranquil and safe ranch. She didn't know if it was wicked of her to do so in an unwed state but joy flooded her heart at this change in her destiny. Navarro's baby . . . Their baby . . . As far as she was concerned, this little one was conceived in sacred love.

After that crucial letter was penned and sealed, she summoned one of the wranglers and sent him into Flagstaff to mail the letter of resignation and wire a telegram.

She would take care of notifying Navarro in a week or so. After her shock wore off, she'd request information on his whereabouts, write or wire him, and tell him she needed to see him as soon as possible.

Chapter Twenty-five

"Mr. Withers, Mr. Breed is here to discuss a loan with you, sir."

"Show him in, Evans," the banker told his employee.

"Mr. Breed, Mr. Withers will see you, sir."

Dan stood as Navarro entered his office and approached his desk. The two friends shook hands as the door was closed.

"Hope you don't mind me dropping in during daylight but I wanted to get our talking done as fast as possible. Seemed like a good excuse I used."

"It was. Glad to see you back and safe."

"Took longer than I figured. Ran into bad weather and a robbery I had to stop on the way back. Me and Night Cloud grabbed a train in El Paso so we could hurry."

"You spoke with the Cordells?"

"Yep, and it was hard on all of us." He related what he had told Matt and Jessie, then said he left the ranch the same day. "I figured I best get back here pronto. My partner's probably chewing her nails off with worry. I doubt that telegram on Thursday settled her down much. Where is she staying? I'll go see her and let her know I'm finished and back."

"The assignment's been over, Navarro. She's gone."

The agent was confused. "To visit her family in Denver?"

"No."

"You already put her on another case?"

"No."

Navarro became edgy and worried. "Stop dancing around that jittery horse; get on him, and tell me where she is."

"Beth won't be taking any more assignments; she resigned today."

"What are you jawing about? Beth wouldn't resign. She wouldn't leave Tucson before I arrived. My telegram said I was on the way."

"She left the twenty-second of last month. She didn't get your wire, unless Melvin or the boardinghouse owner told the clerk where to forward it. She purchased a ranch in Flagstaff on the twenty-fourth of May. She's living there. She isn't coming back to work for the Agency."

"Why?"

"All I know is what this note says. She passed it to me when I took the loan papers there for her to sign. Melvin was with me, so we couldn't talk." Dan stayed silent while Navarro read the list of reasons she had given.

"But this says she'll be ready to return to duty on Monday."

Dan passed him the coded telegram to decipher and read. "She sent me that wire today. I don't know why."

"This doesn't make any sense. What changed her mind so fast?"

"Maybe the ranch and her recent perils did. Maybe that dose of trail medicine was too much for her to take. I know the ranch is a beauty. She paid Melvin half of the purchase price and borrowed the rest from me."

"But she quit her job. How can she repay the loan?"

"I shouldn't discuss her personal finances with you, but I will reveal, she has no money problems. When she came here she played her role with perfection, as always. Melvin found this ranch and wanted her to inspect it. After I repeated Zack's report to her, I thought she was heading to visit her family. Instead, she took off to Flagstaff with Melvin and never returned. He came back and told me she was buying the spread. We went up a few days later for her to sign our papers. After she passed me that note, I thought it made sense. Then, that wire came from nowhere this morning. As it said, she's mailed a written letter to the Agency. I was planning to go up this weekend to speak with her and see what's really going on. I even asked her if she'd work with you again if a case came up, and she agreed."

"Are you hinting maybe she changed her mind 'cause she didn't want to risk having to work with me again?"

"Certainly not. Why would I think such a crazy thing? Far as I can tell, you two became good friends and splendid partners. Isn't that correct?"

"Damn right, it is! I couldn't have had a better partner." He related all Beth had done and learned on the trail and her actions in the renegade camp and at the trap. "She's amazing, old friend. Has real spunk and grit. Long on courage and smarts. She's gentle and caring. Easy talker. Trustworthy and dependable, full of concern and feeling for others. Speaks her mind on most things but doesn't rub your nerves raw. Top caliber agent, don't come any better. And best company I've had."

"You don't have many good things to say about her, do you?" Dan teased. "I was certain Beth wouldn't disappoint you or me or the Agency. Or herself. When she came here with John and Steven, I was impressed by her from the start. She's never let me down. When this assignment came up, I realized she was the perfect match for you, professionally and personally. I'm delighted to hear I was right. Are those feelings why you're upset she's gone?"

"Partly."

"What's the rest of the picture? Or is that being too nosy?"

"I love her and want to marry her. She said she'd wait here for me."

"Do these old ears deceive me? Did you say what I thought you said?"

"You heard right. Your little trick worked on me and I was hoping it had worked on her. If that was true, she would have waited for me."

"Maybe she didn't wait because I told her to visit her family while you were seeing the Cordells, then be ready for reassignment on Monday. I told her your trip would take a few weeks. I didn't think about you hopping a train to rush back to her. Maybe you scared her with that confession of love and marriage proposal. Maybe she needed thinking time, privacy."

"Haven't told her yet. Planned to do it soon as I left you."

"She doesn't know the truth?" After Navarro shook his head, Dan suggested, "Why don't you get yourself up to Flagstaff and get your answer?"

"Since she left without a message, maybe that isn't a good idea."

"It's an excellent idea. She's still playing her mission role; she purchased that ranch under the name of Beth Breed. Remember?"

"Your note said that was to protect her cover with Melvin because he was her previous assignment."

"I think there's more to it. Besides, she didn't hear from you, so what was she supposed to think except you didn't care about her? Could be she thought I was implying she should leave because you didn't want her here."

"After we finish our talk, I'll check with the telegraph office. Let's tie up this case so I can do some thinking."

"Not much to discuss. Zack reported on Cordell and Tiller's deaths and that clever trap you pulled on them. Captain Blake sent in his report and I received a copy of it. The weapons have been turned over to the Army for their use. Miles is still in hot pursuit of Geronimo. Word is that sly fox is working his way toward Mexico; he's probably planning to take refuge in his Sierra Madre stronghold again. It appears Miles and his troops are taking the heart out of their fighting spirit. One of the scouts said it's because the old chief doesn't want to battle and slay his own people, and Miles has plenty of them in his units. He's past sixty and he's been running for months; it has to be wearing him down. Miles has been sending those Indians on the reservation to Florida, even Crook's Apache scouts. He doesn't want any more of them to be tempted to escape from San Carlos and join Geronimo for one last grab at glory and freedom. Blake's put in good words for the Chiricahuas who helped with that trap, but I don't know how much good it's going to do them. All of them may have to spend a few years in Florida until the Army's assured of peace. I know that isn't fair or right, but our hands are tied at this point. I promise to keep putting pressure on the government to correct that wrong."

"Thanks, Dan, I'd be much obliged."

"As for Ben Murphy, that's a tragedy. Poor man was filled with so much hatred and bitterness he couldn't think clearly, and Cordell took advantage of his madness. Ben's daughter is being sent to an institution back East where she'll receive excellent care. Murphy was a wealthy man, so there's plenty of money for her support. Who knows, maybe those doctors can cure her of her own kind of madness? At least Murphy's at peace now, or I hope he is."

"So do I. But there's one point Zack didn't tell you because he wasn't around when I jumped Tiller. He was circling the clearing to flank him. After I got the drop on Tiller, he tried to bargain for his life and freedom by telling me where he and Charles hid those gold coins they got from Diaz. They buried them in case of trouble and planned to retrieve them later."

"How did they know about the trap?"

"Tiller saw one of the soldiers change positions and knew they'd been betrayed by the Indians, so they hightailed it before the action started. They split up before Lordsburg and were to reconnect at the Texas border near Guadalupes. Back to the coins—they're from a legal sale, so Cordell's share should rightly go to his brother. The other half should go to the Indians for improvements on the reservations, supplies, maybe healthy cattle. After I settle my situation with Beth, I'll take a couple of men, collect the bags, and turn them over to you because I know you'll do what's right with them."

"I agree with your suggestion, but I'll have to get it approved by the Agency and BIA first. Was it difficult seeing Jessie and Lane again?"

Navarro was caught by surprise at the change of topic. "Nope, but that was because of Beth; she'd already worked her magic on me. Jessie and Matt are happy; they're good for each other. And it was good for me to learn that for myself in person. Jessie and those days we shared will always be special to me, but I love Beth and want to spend my life with her."

Dan beamed with affection and pleasure. "Love must be contagious; as soon as Zack filed his report, he took off to Sante Fe fast as lightning to visit that little lady who caught his eye last year. He decided if he kept her waiting too much longer, some other fellow would steal her away. Who knows, maybe I'll find me a good woman to court and snare. If I can make such a splendid match for you and Beth, surely I can do the same for myself. You, Zack, and other agents have been my family, and the bank and Agency have been my existence since I lost my dear wife years ago. The Lord didn't see it in His way to give us children, but we had each other and that was plenty. You're lucky Bethany Wind came along for you; love is precious. I suggest you get to Flagstaff and fight for her. With a little effort, I believe you can persuade her to stay married to you."

"Trouble is, that was a trick, old friend. I wish she was really my wife."

Dan withdrew a certificate from his drawer and passed it to the sable-haired man. "Read that; it's legal and binding; it's the real one. What you carried with you on the trail was a fake. This isn't."

"But it says . . ."

Beth stood at the kitchen window and gazed over the scene beyond the lovely house. She knew she was going to enjoy living and working on this land, but she would be happier if she could share it with—

"It's a beautiful ranch, like its owner."

The redhead jumped and whirled to find Navarro leaning against the doorjamb and smiling. "You startled me; I didn't hear you come in."

Her nearness almost stole his breath and wits. "Sorry, guess it's a habit of mine to move quietly. You looked almost too peaceful to disturb."

Beth tried to relax but it was difficult. "It's good to see you safe and sound, Navarro. Dan told me you and Zack took care of Charles and Jim. How did Jessica and Matt handle the bad news?"

"About as expected; it was hardest on Matt."

"I imagine so. Having a brother use and betray you must be awful. It was kind of you to go there and tell them in person rather than letting them read about it in a letter or a newspaper account they couldn't question."

"I was hoping you'd understand and agree with that decision. I didn't tell them about Charles's hatred and bitterness or about that diseased cattle. Wouldn't have served any good purpose; just cause them anguish and shame. I told them Charles was selling illegal guns to renegades, and he was killed during a shoot-out with the law. He'd told Matt the weapons were for Diaz and would help halt *bandidos* from crossing the border and raiding, including his brother's ranch. Like you figured, Jessie was suspicious of him and she'd already told Matt her feelings. Matt was planning to contact Charles for answers. That was one of the reasons why I had to go there. I figured Matt might try to track down his brother later and learn plenty of bad stuff the wrong way. Besides, I owed it to them to handle it myself."

"What did you say about us and our ruse? Were they hurt and angry?"

"At first, but after we talked, they understood and forgave us. I said we were married, both agents, and worked as a team. I apologized for us having to trick them, but said we did it to protect them from danger and repercussions and possible incrimination. I said we couldn't confide in them because we didn't know if they'd believe the black truth about Charles, and we needed them to act normal so he wouldn't get suspicious. After I explained the case to them, they realized how important it was."

"How are they doing since Charles gave them that money?"

"They've bought new stock and paid off their debts. They asked me to say hello and to tell you not to worry about what we did. In fact, Jessie asked for you to write her after we got settled. I'll let you decide how to handle her request." Navarro glanced around and said, "You look good in this homey setting."

Beth smiled. "To my surprise and pleasure, it feels good; in fact, wonderful. That's why I bought it. Melvin located the property through a friend; I've already signed the papers. Dan took care of the transfer of my money from the Denver bank and handled the financial angle."

Navarro chuckled as he teased, "I thought you were a permanent trail woman and diehard agent. Thought you weren't gonna settle down soon."

"I suppose that stay at the Cordell ranch spoiled me, changed me more than I realized until I saw this place." Beth told Navarro her original plan to use it as a home base between assignments. "But after a few days, I got used to it here, decided to retire and stay. Besides, that last case provided me with enough adventure and perils to last a lifetime. I'm ready for a new kind of challenge."

"Like ranching and homelife?"

"Don't you agree that's a big challenge for an ex-agent? For a woman?"

"Yep, especially after the way we've lived for the last few years."

"Do you think I can learn to be a rancher and make a success of things here?"

"You'd stand a better chance with good help at your side."

"The ranch hands agreed to work for me; the foreman, too."

"I mean, somebody closer to you. A husband, Beth," he clarified.

"That isn't a position I can hire a man to fill."

Navarro withdrew a piece of paper from inside his shirt. He walked to the table and unfolded it there. "According to this marriage certificate from Tucson, Beth Breed, that position is already filled."

"That document is an imitation, only a part of our ruse. It's between Navarro Breed and Elizabeth Lawrence; even if it were legal, that isn't me."

"The one the preacher gave us to use was a fake. The one he gave Dan to hold for us is legal, has our real names on it: Navarro Breed and Bethany Wind. If you remember, the preacher never called you Elizabeth Lawrence a single time during the ceremony, just Beth, your real name."

"What do you mean?"

"It seems our superior and friend didn't lie to the preacher; he told him our real identities, what we needed, and why. He didn't make that preacher lie in his church and while holding his Bible. He really married us, woman."

Beth lifted the paper and read it: the date, location, and names were accurate! "You mean . . . we really are husband and wife? It's legal?"

"That's about the size of it. We're bound to each other."

"I swear I didn't know. I wasn't a party to tricking you. So, you came to see me because I have to sign something before you and Dan can dissolve it? You need my help to get a release from the marriage?"

He shook his head. "I came to ask you not to get out of it."

"I don't understand."

"I like you being Beth Breed and want you to stay Beth Breed."

"Didn't Dan tell you I've retired? Besides, for the kinds of missions you accept, you don't require a counterfeit spouse for a partner."

Move slow and easy, hombre; don't spook her into bolting. "I want you to stay my wife for selfish, not work, reasons."

"So you can have a home to use between assignments, like I was planning to do originally? You want your good friend to stay around for companionship? Keep your pleasing lover for other needs?"

"Those aren't my motives. I admit they sound wonderful and so does becoming a rancher, but the reason is, I love you and I need you."

Beth stared at him and wondered if she'd heard him right or if she was only suffering from a cruel delusion. "What did you say?"

"I love you and need you, Beth Breed, only you, with all my heart."

"You love . . . *me?*"

"Only you, woman. I've never loved or wanted or needed anybody as I do you, not even Jess. With her, it was different. We were young, hurting, and in need. Jess and I had a long talk while you and I were at the ranch, and we got our heads cleared about the past and present; I guess we finally had a chance to say a real goodbye. You're the one who made me realize it was over, had been over for years. I knew before we reached the ranch, I wanted you. I have to confess, I kept denying the truth like it was a snake about to bite me."

Beth remained silent, as he didn't appear to be finished, and wasn't.

"I've been trying to show you how I feel before I told you so you'd have no doubt it's true. Guess I didn't do a very good convincing job." He walked to where she was leaning against the cabinet. He cupped her face and gazed into her eyes. "Best I can figure, I fell in love with you in Tucson; 'course I didn't know it. Dan was clever to force us to fake a romance. Somehow and somewhere during our ruse, it stopped being a pretense. The more I got to know you, the more I got ensnared by you. But I was scared of being hurt again and scared you could never love and accept a man like me, so I fought it like an enemy. Then, the truth hit me on the head one day: you were perfect for me and I'd be loco to let you get away without a chase. If you'll stay my wife, I'll try my best to make you happy. We can have a good life together. Maybe in time, you'll learn to love me, too."

"I can't learn to love you, Navarro, I—"

In panic, he interrupted, "Just give it, me, a chance to prove you're wrong. I know I've had a sorry birth and life until a few years ago, but I—"

Beth pressed her fingers to his lips to silence him and halt his pain. "Let me finish what I was about to say. I can't learn to love you, Navarro Breed, because I *already* love you. It was just as you described; I fell in love with you in Tucson before we married. The more I came to know you, the more I came to love and want you. Steven and I were like you and Jessica: we were young and adventurous and in need. I'm over Steven, but I feared you weren't over Jessica. As with you, I didn't want to risk rejection and anguish. I wanted and needed you so much, I was going to offer you a home between assignments, a friend, and a lover. I hoped that relationship would blossom into much more in time. Ever since the day we married, even though I believed it wasn't for real, I've longed to stay Beth Breed."

Navarro pulled her into his arms to embrace her. They hugged, kissed, laughed, and snuggled for several minutes.

He parted them to tell her, "I sent you a telegram after I saw Matt and Jessie and told you I was on the way to Tucson. You'd already left. The clerk didn't know what to do when he couldn't locate a Mrs. Navarro Breed or Beth Breed registered at any of the hotels. I didn't give any instructions about forwarding or returning it to me if it couldn't be undelivered, so he had it under the counter when I spoke with him. I didn't think to tell him to check with boardinghouses or to contact Dan or Harrison if he couldn't find you. Since he's new in town, he didn't know who any of you are. I can guess how not hearing from me gave you wrong thoughts."

"I admit, I was hurt and worried. But things worked out perfectly."

"Yep; they did. I have two gifts for you."

He removed Steven's gold wedding band, placed it on the cabinet, and slid the one he had purchased for her on her finger. "I bought this in El Paso while I was waiting for the train to bring me to you in Tucson. And had this one made by a photographer taking the same trip." He opened the antique locket to reveal a picture of himself. "I hoped it would keep me near your heart and on your mind so much you'd have to give in and take a chance with me."

"They're wonderful presents, the best you could bring. No, Navarro Breed is the best surprise you could bring to me. My husband . . . The words send tingles all over me. I love you so much. I hope you like the ranch; if I'd known about your feelings, I would have let you inspect it first and been in on the decision."

"It's a perfect choice, Beth, just as you are. Come with me, wife." He grasped her hand and guided her to the hitching post outside the picket fence. He withdrew the sign Big John had made for them. "I took time to retrieve this while I was in Texas. Let's hang it on the front gate." He saw her smile and nod. He removed the past owner's sign and suspended theirs on the curved nails. "Navarro and Beth Breed, that's much better. If the circle B brand isn't taken, we'll register it as ours."

"Sounds marvelous, our initial inside a ring like a wedding band."

"We're locked together for life, woman, and I'll never let you go."

"I'll make certain you don't. I think you'll love it here. You can meet the men later; they're working the range. I'm sure you'll like them. They reminded me of the hands Jessica and Matt have; that's why I asked them to stay on with me. I hope I judged their character as well as I did yours."

"I've no doubt you did, love. We'll be happy together and living here."

"I'll miss you terribly when you're away on missions."

He chuckled and murmured, "No, you won't, my love; I'm resigning, too. Gonna be a full-time husband and rancher." He left off *father* on purpose because of what she'd told him in the past, and what Dan had said about being content without children if necessary. *And she may change her mind.*

"You're retiring, too?"

"I told Dan I would if this meeting worked out as I hoped and prayed. All I have to do is write and mail an official letter. Dan's losing two of his best agents, but he has only himself to blame for throwing us together. Somehow that sly fox knew it would work out between us. He's a good man and a good friend. He put love for us above risking our losses."

"Yes, he did, and I'm glad. You're full of surprises, dear heart." *Shall I give you one?* "What do you want to name our first son or daughter? I thought Daniel Trask Breed would be nice for a boy; it would link our names with the man who got us together. Sierra Breed sounds wonderful for a girl, since Mexico played such a large role in opening our eyes and hearts. What do you think? Do you have any special names for our first child?"

"I thought you didn't want any children."

"I've always wanted them, and would like to have several, but I believed I couldn't have any. A girl supposedly became pregnant by Steven years before we met and wed, but she ran out on him before he could marry her. After six years without children and thinking he'd fathered a child, I assumed the problem was mine; so did he. I now suspect she lied to Steven and that's why she vanished, fear of exposure. Those times I slept with you, I didn't think I was risking getting pregnant, but I was wrong. It must have happened on our first or second time; that would put our baby due the end of January."

Beth watched him as her words struck home. "I was willing and ready to fight Jessica for your love; then, I found out about Lane, and your hunger for another child when I thought I couldn't give you one. I was being selfish, Navarro; I was going to have you for as long as our mission lasted; then let you leave to find a woman who could give you a child. I decided in Eagle Eye's camp to tell you about my love and problem as soon as our assignment ended and we had privacy to talk about personal things. When I came to the ranch, I intended to purchase it, settle in, and return to work, hopefully as your partner for as many times as Dan could arrange it and you were willing. A few days ago, I realized in shock that I was pregnant. The baby is why I resigned. I was planning to contact you next week and tell you everything. I was hoping you wouldn't object to me and the baby keeping your name. I was going to let you be as much a part of our lives as you wanted. But since I seduced you in the desert, it wasn't right to coerce you into marriage."

Navarro's left hand flattened over her lower abdomen. "A baby?" He saw her nod and look a little insecure. His hazel gaze and heart filled with joy and wonder. "Thank you, Beth. I can hardly believe my good luck."

"Then you aren't upset? Aren't angry with me?"

As he hugged her and spread kisses over her face, he said, "Of course not. I love you and I want our child. This baby will have my name. We'll raise him here, love him, protect him, guide him. Of course I want him."

"I know Lane can't be replaced, and I won't ever try to do that."

"Lane has a good father and home. I love him and want what's best for him, and I believe he has that where he is and without me in his life. If he ever needs my help, I'll give it, and I know that's what you'd expect and want me to do. But from now on, *we're* a family, my only family. I love you, woman, more than ever. How lucky can a man get? A wife, a home, a ranch, a child—all in the same day. We have each other and a fresh start. Our future couldn't look brighter than these locks, Flamehair."

"The shaman told me we'd have land, horses, cattle, and children. He said that dress I was wearing was dusted with sacred Pollen, so you and I would grow many things. He said Ysun would reward us for what we did. I wonder how he could make such accurate prophecies?"

"I don't understand those things, but I know they happen. Years ago, he told me about meeting you. That's one vision I'm glad came true."

"So am I."

Navarro glanced at the waxing moon that was rising early. "It seems like a long time since we were under that full moon in Eagle Eye's camp and you passed your tests as Flamehair."

"Almost four weeks ago, and so much has happened since that night. So much has happened since we met months ago, wonderful things. Neither of us imagined we'd ever be standing here together today and with so many blessings to count."

For a few moments, each did as she said. They reflected on the past, the family and friends who had been or still were parts of their lives, loved ones they had lost to death or sacrifice or change, their careers as agents, their daring and glorious adventure together, and the love and future they now shared.

Beth knew she would have lost herself in Steven Wind, as Navarro knew he would have lost himself in Jessica Lane. Those first loves would always be special episodes in their lives. But it was as if they had been waiting for each other to come along, to be awakened from dark dreams to a golden reality.

Beth broke their reveries. "I have a lot of things from my parents' home stored in Denver; they'll be lovely in ours. After we get settled, we should go fetch them. Then, you can meet my family and relatives. I'm sure you'll like Robert and Caroline. I know they'll love and accept you as quickly and easily as I did. They'll be delighted by the news of our marriage and retirement. My family is yours now, my love."

"I'm gonna enjoy having kin and being a rancher. Most of all, I'm gonna love being your husband and the father of our children."

"We're blessed to have each other and so many wonderful things."

He related the romantic news about Zack and about Dan's romantic inclinations. "I'll sit my littie fox beside that black wolf of yours; I saw them when I strolled through the house; they'll make a nice pair, like we do. Zack carved mine out of cedar, so it's red like your beautiful hair. Seems that trail-duster was giving us hints with those carvings. If we go to Tucson for business or to visit Dan, we won't have to worry about exposing our identities or have to trick our friends again."

"You'll have to wire Dan tomorrow to let him know the news, but I doubt he's worried about you failing this mission, my matchless agent."

The ex-desperado-turned-lawman murmured, "I've chased wild winds in two different worlds ever since I was born, and I finally captured the best Wind of all. You blew on me in Tucson and swept me away, woman. *Shu,* how I love you, Beth Breed."

Navarro sealed their lips to stress his vow. Beth snuggled into his embrace and returned it with almost feverish desire. His fingers played in her radiant locks as her hands drifted over his back. Soon, they wanted total possession of each other, an exquisite union of bodies to match the glorious one which bound their hearts. They had been married for months, but this seemed like their wedding day, a time of commitment.

"Now that we're officially wed, Mr. Breed, why don't we go inside our new home and . . . consummate our marriage, since we didn't realize we were doing it that night in the desert?" She patted her lower abdomen and joked, "Once the baby is born, it'll demand lots of attention, time, and energy, according to Jessica and Matt. We'll have to write them soon and tell them our good news; I know they'll be as happy for us as we are for them. For now, we'd better take advantage of the seven months of privacy we have left before he or she begins to flourish."

"My thoughts exactly, Mrs. Breed," he murmured in a husky tone.

Navarro lifted his cherished wife in strong arms and carried her to the four-poster bed. He lay her there and gazed at her for a minute as love and pride surged through him. As predestined and as foretold by the wise old shaman years ago, Tl'ee' K'us would not walk alone forever; Kuu 'tsiighaa', "Flamehair," was at his side and without ghosts or obstacles between them.

She coaxed, "Lie down, Agent Breed, and carry out your assignment. The best mission in life is ahead for us."

Navarro's hazel eyes gleamed with love and desire as Beth removed her clothes and tossed them to the floor. He did the same and joined her, this time to chase and capture a wild and wonderful wind of passion.

Author's Note

Geronimo and his renegade band continued to raid in Arizona and Mexico and to elude General Miles's troops for months. Then, the Indians took refuge in the mountains near Sonora until late August. On September 3, 1886, Geronimo and his followers surrendered to General Miles at Skeleton Canyon in Arizona. The Indians were promised they could return to their homeland after an exile in Florida to prove the hostilities were over and peace would reign. As usual, that promise was broken.

En route to Florida, the train was halted in Texas and a decision was made against hanging Geronimo for his crimes. General Crook was the white officer who intervened and prevented the legendary leader from being executed. Geronimo and the Chiricahuas were heralded as the last warrior and tribe to be conquered by the white man. Geronimo was separated from his family for months. Finally, he and others were transferred to Fort Sill in Oklahoma Territory in 1894. He became a public sensation for years until his death on February 17, 1908, without returning to his native Arizona.

While researching this book, my husband, Michael, videotaped an interview with Geronimo III, the legend's grandson, who lives near Tucson and is a fascinating man with keen wits and sharp eyes at 112 years old. One of my treasures is a photograph he signed for me, one that is shown in countless history books. To my -ch' uuné', 'Ixée.